ARCHER'S VOICE

MIA SHERIDAN

FOREVER

New York   Boston

Copyright © 2016, 2018 by Mia Sheridan
Cover design by Elizabeth Stokes
Cover copyright © 2018 by Hachette Book Group, Inc.

Forever
Hachette Book Group
1290 Avenue of the Americas
New York, NY 10104
forever-romance.com
twitter.com/foreverromance

First published as an ebook in 2016
First trade paperback edition: February 2018

Forever is an imprint of Grand Central Publishing. The Forever name and logo are trademarks of Hachette Book Group, Inc.

The publisher is not responsible for websites (or their content) that are not owned by the publisher.

The Hachette Speakers Bureau provides a wide range of authors for speaking events. To find out more, go to www.hachettespeakersbureau.com or call (866) 376-6591.

Library of Congress Control Number: 2017961168

ISBN 978-1-5387-2735-5 (trade paperback edition)
ISBN 978-1-5387-2736-2 (ebook edition)

Printed in the United States of America

LSC-C

Printing 26, 2023

This book is dedicated to my boys, Jack, Cade, and Tyler. The world needs as many good men as possible. I'm proud to be putting three of them out there. Brothers 'til the end.

The Legend of Chiron the Centaur

The centaurs, as a group, were known to be rabble-rousers, given to drunkenness and rowdy, lusty behavior. But Chiron wasn't like the rest—he was called the Good Centaur, and the Wounded Healer, wiser, gentler, and more just than those of his kind.

Sadly, he was shot by his friend Hercules with a poison arrow when Hercules was fighting the other centaurs. Because Chiron was immortal, he was unable to find relief from this incurable wound, and lived his life in agonizing pain.

Eventually, Chiron came upon Prometheus, who was suffering an agony as well. Prometheus had been sentenced to eternal torment by the gods and was tied to a rock, where, every morning, an eagle was sent to eat Prometheus's liver, and every evening, it grew back.

Chiron offered to willingly give up his life for Prometheus, therefore setting them both free from their eternal torment. Chiron dropped dead at Prometheus's feet. But because of his goodness and service, Zeus made Chiron a part of the stars, the constellation Sagittarius, where his beauty could be gazed upon for all time.

Chiron's wound symbolizes the transformative power of suffering—how personal pain, both physical and emotional, can become the source of great moral and spiritual strength.

ARCHER'S VOICE

CHAPTER ONE

Archer—Seven Years Old; April

Grab my hand! I got you," I said real soft, the helicopter lifting off the ground as Duke grabbed Snake Eyes's hand. I was trying to play as quiet as I could—my mama was banged up again and I didn't want to wake her where she was sleeping up in her room. She'd told me to watch cartoons up in bed with her, and I had for a while, but when I saw she was asleep, I'd come downstairs to play with my G.I. Joe toys.

The helicopter landed, and my guys jumped out and ran under the chair I had put a towel over to make into part of an underground bunker. I picked up the helicopter and lifted it off the ground again with a *whop, whop, whop* sound. I wished I could snap my fingers and make this a real helicopter. Then I'd pull my mama onto it and we'd fly away from here—away from *him*, away from the black eyes and my mama's tears. I didn't care where we'd end up as long as it was far, far away.

I crawled back into my bunker, and a few minutes later, I heard the front door open and close, and then heavy footsteps walking through our foyer and down the hall toward where I was playing. I peeked out and saw a pair of shiny black shoes and the cuffs of what I knew were uniform pants.

I crawled out as fast as I could, saying, "Uncle Connor!" as he kneeled down and I threw myself into his arms, making sure to stay clear of the side where he kept his gun and police flashlight.

"Hey, little man," he said, hugging me to him. "How's my rescue hero?"

"Good. See the underground fortress I built?" I said, leaning away and proudly pointing back over my shoulder at the fort I had made under the table using blankets and towels. It was pretty cool.

Uncle Connor smiled and glanced behind me. "I sure do. You did a good job there, Archer. I've never seen a fortress quite as impenetrable looking as that one." He winked and smiled bigger.

I grinned. "Wanna play with me?"

He messed my hair, smiling. "Not right now, buddy. Later, okay? Where's your mama?"

I felt my own face fall. "Um, she's not feeling real good. She's laying down." I looked into Uncle Connor's face and golden-brown eyes. The picture that popped into my head right away was the sky before a storm—dark and sort of scary. I moved back slightly, but as quick as that, Uncle Connor's eyes cleared and he pulled me into him again, squeezing me.

"Okay, Archer, okay," he said. He set me back from him and held on to my arms as his eyes moved over my face. I smiled at him and he smiled back.

"You have your mama's smile, you know that?"

I smiled bigger. I loved my mama's smile—it was warm and beautiful and it made me feel loved.

"But I look like my daddy," I said, looking down. Everyone said I had the Hale look about me.

He just stared at me for a minute, looking like maybe he wanted to say something, but then changed his mind. "Well, that's a good thing, buddy. Your daddy's a handsome devil." He smiled at me, but it didn't move up into his eyes. I looked at him, wishing I looked like Uncle Connor. My mama told me once that he was the most handsome man she'd seen in her whole life. But then she'd looked guilty like she shouldn't have said that. Probably because he wasn't my daddy, I guessed. Also, Uncle Connor was a police officer—a hero. When I grew up, I was gonna be just like him.

Uncle Connor stood up. "I'm gonna go see if your mama's awake. You play with your action figures and I'll be down in a minute, okay, buddy?"

"Okay." I nodded. He messed my hair again and then walked toward the steps. I waited a couple of minutes, and then I followed him up silently. I stepped around every squeak, holding on to the banister to move me forward. I knew how to be quiet in this house. It was important that I knew how to be quiet in this house.

When I got to the top of the stairs, I stood just outside the door to my mama's room, listening. The door was open only a crack, but it was enough.

"I'm okay, Connor, really," my mama said, her voice soft and still sleepy.

"You're not okay, Alyssa," he hissed, his voice breaking at the end in a way that scared me. "Jesus. I want to kill him. I'm done with this, Lys. I'm done with the martyr routine. You might think you deserve this, but Archer. Does. Not," he said, spitting out the last three words in a way that let me know his jaw was tight like I'd seen it before. Usually, when my daddy was around.

I heard nothing but my mama's soft crying for a few minutes before Uncle Connor spoke again. This time his voice sounded strange, no expression in it.

"You wanna know where he is right now? He left the bar and went home with Patty Nelson. He's screwing her three ways from Sunday in her trailer. I drove by and could hear it from inside my car."

"God, Connor," my mama's voice choked out. "Are you trying to make this worse—"

"No!" his voice roared and I jumped slightly. "No," he said more quietly now. "I'm trying to make you see that it's enough. *It's enough*. If you think you needed to pay a penance, it's paid. Don't you see that? You were never right in that belief, but for the sake of argument, let's say you were—it's paid up, Lys. It's long since paid up. Now we're all paying. Christ, do you wanna know what I felt when I heard the sounds coming out of that trailer? I wanted to bust in there and beat the shit out of him for humiliating you, disrespecting you that way. And the fuck of it all is that I should be happy he's with someone other than you, *anyone* other than the woman that is so fucking deep under my skin, I couldn't dig you out with a jackhammer. But instead, I felt sick about it. Sick, Lys. Sick that he wasn't treating you right, even though him treating you right might mean I could never have you again."

It was quiet from inside the room for a couple of minutes, and I wanted to peek inside, but I didn't. All I heard was my mama's soft crying and some slight rustling.

Finally, Uncle Connor went on, his voice quiet now, gentle, "Let me take you away from here, baby, please, Lys. Let me protect you and Archer. Please." His voice was filled with something I didn't know the name for. I sucked in a quiet breath. He wanted to take us away from here?

"What about Tori?" my mama asked quietly.

It was a couple of seconds before Uncle Connor answered, "I'd tell Tori I was leaving. She'd have to know. We haven't had any kind of real marriage for years anyway. She'd have to understand."

"She won't, Connor," my mama said, sounding scared. "She won't understand. She'll do something to get even with us. She's always hated me."

"Alyssa, we're not kids anymore. This isn't about some stupid competition shit. This is about real life. This is about me loving you. This is about us deserving to have a life together. This is about me, you, and Archer."

"And Travis?" she asked quietly.

There was a pause. "I'll work something out with Tori," he said. "You don't need to worry about that."

There was more silence, and then my mama said, "Your job, the town..."

"Alyssa," Uncle Connor said, his voice gentle, "I don't care about any of that. If there's no you, nothing else matters. Don't you know that by now? I'll resign from my job, sell the land. We'll live a life, baby. We'll find some happiness. Away from here—away from this place. Somewhere we can call our own. Baby, don't you want that? Tell me you do."

There was more silence, only I heard soft sounds like maybe they were kissing. I had seen them kissing before when my mama didn't know I was spying, like I was doing now. I knew it was wrong—mamas weren't supposed to kiss men who weren't their husbands. But I also knew daddies weren't supposed to come home drunk all the time and slap their wives in the face, and mamas weren't supposed to look at uncles with the soft look my mama always got on her face when Uncle Connor came around. It was all mixed up and confused, and I wasn't sure how to sort it all. That's why I spied on them, trying to understand.

Finally, after what seemed like a long time, my mama whispered, so I could barely hear, "Yes, Connor, take us away from here. Take us far, far away. Me and you and Archer. Let's find some happiness. I want that. I want you. You're the only one I've ever wanted."

"Lys...Lys...my Lys...," I heard Uncle Connor saying between heavy breaths.

I snuck away, making my way back down the stairs, in between the noisy spots, not making a sound, moving in silence.

CHAPTER TWO

BREE

I slung my backpack over my shoulder, picked up the small dog carrier on my passenger-side seat, and closed the car door behind me. I stood still for a minute, just listening to the morning cricket songs echoing all around, almost, but not quite, drowning out the soft swish of the trees rustling in the wind. The sky above me was a vivid blue, and I could just make out a sliver of glistening lake water through the cottages in front of me. I squinted at the white one, the one that still had the small sign in the front window declaring that it was for rent. It was clearly older and slightly run-down, but it had a charm about it that immediately appealed to me. I could picture sitting on the porch in the evenings, watching the trees surrounding it sway in the breeze as the moon came up over the lake behind me, the smell of pine and fresh water in the air. I smiled to myself. I hoped the inside offered a little charm, too, or at the very least, some *clean*.

"What do you think, Phoebs?" I asked softly. Phoebe chuffed agreeably from her carrier.

"Yeah, I think so, too," I said.

An older sedan pulled up next to my small VW Bug, and an older, balding man got out, walking toward me.

"Bree Prescott?"

"That's me." I smiled and took a few steps, shaking his hand. "Thanks for meeting me on short notice, Mr. Connick."

"Please, call me George," he said, smiling back at me and moving toward the cottage, both of us kicking up dust and dead pine needles with each step. "Not a problem meetin' you. I'm retired now, so I don't really have a schedule to keep to. This worked just fine." We walked up the three wooden steps to the small porch, and he pulled a ring of keys out of his pocket and began searching for one.

"Here we go," he said, putting the key in the lock and pushing the front door open. The smell of dust and faint mildew greeted me as we stepped inside and I looked around.

"The wife comes out here as often as possible and does some dusting and basic cleaning, but as you can see, it could use a good once-over. Norma doesn't get around quite as well as she used to with her hip arthritis and all. The place has been empty all summer."

"It's fine." I smiled at him, putting Phoebe's dog carrier down by the door and moving toward what I could see was the kitchen. The inside needed more than a basic cleaning—more like a complete scrub down. But I immediately loved it. It was quaint and full of charm. When I lifted a couple of covers, I saw that the furnishings were older but tasteful. The wood floors were wide-planked and beautifully rustic, and the paint colors were all subtle and calming.

The kitchen appliances were older, but I didn't need much as far as a kitchen went anyway. I wasn't sure I'd ever want to cook again.

"The bedroom and bathroom are in the back—" Mr. Connick started to say.

"I'll take it," I cut in, then laughed and shook my head slightly. "I mean, if it's still available, and okay with you, I'll take it."

He chuckled. "Well, yes, that's great. Let me get the rental agreement out of my car, and we can get that all taken care of. I listed the security deposit as first and last, but I can work with you if that's a problem."

I shook my head. "No, that's not a problem. That sounds fine."

"Okay then. I'll be right back," he said, moving toward the door.

While he was outside, I took a minute to walk down the hall and peek into the bedroom and bathroom. Both were small, but they would do, just as I'd figured they would. The thing that caught my attention was the large window in the bedroom that faced the lake. I couldn't help smiling as I took in the view of the wooden dock leading to the calm, glassy water, a stunning blue in the bright morning light.

There were two boats far out, not much more than dots on the horizon.

Suddenly, looking out at that water, I had the strangest sensation that I wanted to cry—but not with sadness, with *happiness*. Just as soon as I felt it, it started to fade, leaving me with an odd nostalgia I couldn't begin to explain.

"Here we go," Mr. Connick called, and I heard the door shut behind him. I left the room to sign the papers for the place I would call home—at least for the next little while—hoping against hope this was where I'd finally find some peace.

* * *

Norma Connick had left all her cleaning products at the cottage, and so after I had lugged my suitcase out of my car and put it in the bedroom, I got to work. Three hours later I pushed a damp piece of hair out of my eyes and stood back to admire my work. The wood floors were clean and dust-free, all the furniture was uncovered, and the entire place was thoroughly dusted. I had found the bed linens and towels in the hall closet and washed and dried them in the small stacked washer and dryer next to the kitchen, and then made up the bed. The kitchen and bathroom were scrubbed and bleached, and I had opened all the windows to let in the warm summer breeze that came off the lake. I wouldn't get too used to this place, but for now, I was content.

I unpacked the few toiletries I'd thrown into my suitcase, placed them in the medicine cabinet, and then took a long, cool shower, washing the hours of cleaning and more hours of travel off my body. I had broken up the sixteen-hour drive from my hometown of Cincinnati, Ohio, into two eight-hour hauls, staying overnight in a roadside motel one night and driving through the next to arrive this morning. I had stopped at an Internet café in New York the day before and looked online for rental properties in the town where I was headed. The town in Maine I had chosen as my destination was a popular tourist attraction, and so after more than an hour of searching, the closest I could get was across the lake, in this small town named Pelion.

After drying off, I put on a pair of clean shorts and a T-shirt, and picked up my phone to call my best friend, Natalie. She'd called me several times since I'd first texted her and told her I was leaving, and I'd only texted her back. I owed her an actual phone call.

"Bree?" Nat answered, the sounds of loud chatter in the background.

"Hey, Nat, is this a bad time?"

"Hold on, I'm going outside." She put her hand over the

mouthpiece, said something to someone, and then came back on the line. "No, it's not a bad time! I've been dying to talk to you! I'm at lunch with my mom and my aunt. They can wait a few minutes. I've been worried," she said, her tone slightly accusing.

I sighed. "I know, I'm sorry. I'm in Maine." I had told her it was where I was heading.

"Bree, you just took off. Geez. Did you even pack anything?"

"A few things. Enough."

She huffed out a breath. "Okay. Well, when are you coming home?"

"I don't know. I thought I might stay here for a little while. Anyway, Nat, I didn't mention this, but I'm running low on money—I just spent a big chunk on a security deposit for my rental. I need to get a job, at least for a couple of months, and make enough to fund my trip home and a few months of living expenses once I get back."

Nat paused. "I didn't realize it was that bad. But, Bree, honey, you have a college degree. Come home and put it to use. You don't need to live like some kind of vagabond in a town where you don't know a single person. I already miss you. Avery and Jordan miss you. Let your friends help you get back to life—we love you. I can send you some money if it means getting you home more quickly."

"No, no, Natalie. Really. I…need this time, okay? I know you love me. I do," I said quietly. "I love you, too. This is just something that I need to do."

She paused again. "Was it because of Jordan?"

I chewed on my lip for a couple of seconds. "No, not entirely. I mean, maybe that was the straw, but no, I'm not running away from Jordan. It was just kind of the last thing I needed, you know? Everything just got to be…too much."

"Oh, honey, a person can only *take* so much." When I was quiet, she sighed and said, "So the semi-strange, impromptu road trip is already helping?" I heard the smile in her voice.

I laughed a quiet laugh. "In some ways, maybe. In other ways, not just yet."

"So they haven't gone away?" Natalie asked quietly.

"No, Nat, not yet. But I feel good about this place. I really do." I tried to sound chipper.

Nat paused again. "Honey, I don't think it's about the place."

"That's not what I mean. I just mean, this feels like a good place to get away to for a little bit…oh gosh, you've gotta go. Your mom and aunt are waiting for you. We can talk about this another time."

"Okay," she said hesitantly. "So you're safe?"

I paused. I never felt entirely safe. Would I again? "Yes, and it's beautiful here. I found a cottage right on the lake." I glanced out the window behind me, taking in the beautiful water view again.

"Can I come visit?"

I smiled. "Let me get settled in. Maybe before I turn back around?"

"Okay, deal. I really miss you."

"I miss you, too. I'll call again soon, okay?"

"Okay. Bye, honey."

"Bye, Nat."

I hung up the phone, went to the big window and drew the shades in my new bedroom, and climbed into my freshly made bed. Phoebe settled in at my feet. I fell asleep the minute my head hit the pillow.

* * *

I woke up to the sounds of birdcalls and the distant lap of water hitting the shore. I rolled over and looked at the clock. It was just

past six in the evening now. I stretched and sat up, orienting myself.

I got up, Phoebe trotting along behind me, and brushed my
teeth in the small bathroom. After I rinsed, I studied myself in the
medicine cabinet mirror. The dark circles under my eyes were still
there, although less pronounced after the five hours of sleep I had
just gotten. I pinched my cheeks to bring some color into them,
gave myself a big, cheesy, fake grin in the mirror, and then shook
my head at myself. "You are going to be okay, Bree. You are strong,
and you are going to be happy again. Do you hear me? There's
something good about this place. Do you feel it?" I tilted my head
and stared at myself in the mirror for a minute longer. Lots of
people gave their own reflection pep talks in the bathroom, right?
Totally normal. I snorted softly and shook my head slightly again.
I rinsed my face and then quickly pulled my long, light brown hair
back into a messy twist at the nape of my neck.

I went out to the kitchen and opened the freezer, where I had
put the frozen meals that were in a cooler on ice in my car. I hadn't
had a lot of food to bring with me—just the few things that were in
my refrigerator at home: a few microwavable meals, milk, peanut
butter and bread, and some fruit. And half a bag of dog food for
Phoebs. But it would do for a couple of days before I had to find
the local grocery store.

I popped a pasta meal into the microwave sitting on the counter
and then stood there eating it with a plastic fork. I watched out
the kitchen window as I ate, and noticed an old woman in a blue
dress and short white hair come out of the cottage next to mine and
walk toward my porch with a basket in her hands. When I heard
her light knock, I tossed the now-empty cardboard meal box in the
trash and went to answer.

I pulled the door open, and the old lady smiled warmly at me.

"Hi, dear, I'm Anne Cabbott. Looks like you're my new neighbor. Welcome to the neighborhood."

I smiled back at her and took the basket she offered me. "Bree Prescott. Thank you. How nice." I lifted a corner of the towel on top of the basket, and the sweet smell of blueberry muffins wafted up to me. "Oh gosh, these smell delicious," I said. "Would you like to come in?"

"Actually, I was going to ask if you'd like to come have some iced tea with me on my porch. I just made some fresh."

"Oh." I hesitated. "Okay, sure. Just give me a second to put on some shoes."

I stepped back inside and set the muffins on my kitchen counter and then went back to my bedroom, where I had kicked off my flip-flops.

When I returned, Anne was standing at the edge of my porch waiting for me. "Such a lovely night. I try to sit out in the evenings and enjoy it. Pretty soon I'll be complaining about how cold it is."

We started walking toward her cottage. "So you live here all year-round?" I asked, glancing over at her.

She nodded. "Most of us on this side of the lake are year-round residents. Tourists aren't interested in this town as it is. Over there"—she nodded her head toward the far side of the lake, barely visible from this distance—"is where all the tourist attractions are. Most in this town don't mind that, like it even. Course all that's going to change. The woman who owns the town, Victoria Hale, has plans for a bunch of new development that will bring the tourists here as well." She sighed as we climbed the steps to her porch, and she sat down in one of the wicker chairs. I sat on the two-person porch swing and leaned back on the cushion.

Her porch was beautiful and homey, full of comfortable white wicker and bright blue and yellow cushions. There were pots of flowers everywhere: wave petunias and potato vine cascading over the sides.

"What do you think about bringing tourists here?"

She frowned slightly. "Oh, well, I like our quiet little town. I say let them stay over there. We still get the passers-through, which are enough for my taste. Plus, I like our small-town feel. Supposedly condos are going up here, so there won't be any more lakeside cottages."

I frowned. "Oh, I'm sorry," I said, realizing she meant she'd have to move.

She waved her hand dismissively. "I'll be okay. It's the businesses in town that will be closed down because of the expansion that I worry more for."

I nodded, still frowning. We were quiet for a second before I said, "I vacationed on the other side of the lake with my family when I was a little girl."

She picked up the pitcher of tea on the small table next to her, poured us each a glass, and handed me one. "Did you? What brings you back here now?"

I took a sip of my tea, purposefully stalling for a couple of seconds. Finally I said, "I'm on a short road trip. I was happy there that summer." I shrugged. I tried to smile, but talking about my family still brought a tightness to my chest. I settled on what I hoped was a pleasant expression.

She studied me for a second, taking a sip of her own tea. Then she nodded. "Well, dear, I think that sounds like a good plan. And I think if this place brought you happiness before, it can bring happiness again. Some places just agree with people, I think." She smiled warmly, and I smiled back. I didn't tell her that the other reason I was here was that it was the last place my family had been truly happy and carefree. My mother was diagnosed with breast cancer when we got home from that trip. She died six months later. From then on, it had just been my dad and me.

"How long are you planning on staying?" Anne asked, pulling me out of my reverie.

"I'm not sure. I don't really have a specific itinerary. I will need to get a job, though. Do you know anyone who's hiring?"

She set her glass down. "Actually, I do. The diner in town needs a morning waitress. They're open for breakfast and lunch. I was in the other day and there was a sign up. The girl who worked there before had a baby and decided to stay at home with him. It's right on the main street in town—Norm's. Always nice and busy. You tell them Anne sent you." She winked at me.

"Thank you." I smiled. "I will."

We sat quietly for a minute, both sipping our tea, the sound of crickets singing in the background, and the occasional mosquito buzzing past my ear. I could hear distant shouts from boaters on the lake, probably about to head in and call it a night, and the soft sound of the lake lapping on the shore.

"It's peaceful here."

"Well, I hope you don't find this forward, dear, but it seems like you could use a good dose of peaceful."

I let out a breath and laughed softly. "You must read people well," I said. "You're not wrong there."

She laughed softly, too. "Always have been good at peggin' people. My Bill used to say he couldn't hide anything from me if he tried. Course, love and time will do that, too. You get so the other person is practically another part of you—and you can't hide from yourself. Although some are good at tryin', I suppose."

I tilted my head. "I'm sorry. How long has your husband been gone?"

"Oh, it's been ten years now. I still miss him, though." Melancholy skated briefly across her features before she pulled her shoulders up and nodded her head at my glass. "He used to like a little bourbon in his sweet tea. Made him frisky. Course I didn't mind. Kept him smiling and only took a minute or two of my time."

I had just taken a sip of tea, and I put my hand over my mouth to not spit it out. After I had swallowed it down, I laughed and Anne grinned at me.

I nodded after a minute. "I guess men are pretty simple that way."

"Us women learn that young, don't we? Is there a boy waiting back home for you?"

I shook my head. "No. I have a few good friends, but no one else is waiting back home for me." As the words spilled from my lips, the true nature of my aloneness in the world felt like a sucker punch to my gut. It wasn't news to me and yet, somehow, saying the words brought it home in a way that the knowledge itself didn't. I drained my glass of tea, attempting to swallow down the emotion that had suddenly overcome me.

"I should get going," I said. "Thank you so much for the tea and the company." I smiled at Anne and she smiled back, beginning to stand as I did.

"Anytime, Bree. You need anything at all, you know right where I am."

"Thank you, Anne. That's very kind. Oh! I do need to make a trip to a drugstore. Is there one in town?"

"Yes. Haskell's. Just drive back through town, the way you came in, and you'll see it on your left. It's right before the one stoplight. You can't miss it."

"Okay, great. Thanks again," I said, stepping down the steps and giving her a small wave.

Anne nodded, smiling, and waved back.

As I walked back through my own yard to get my purse out of the house, I spotted a lone dandelion full of fluff. I bent and plucked it out of the ground and held it up to my lips, closing my eyes and recalling Anne's words. After a minute, I whispered, "Peace," before I blew and watched the fluff float out of sight, hoping that somehow one of those seeds carrying my whisper would reach that something or someone who had the power to make wishes come true.

CHAPTER THREE

BREE

The sky was just beginning to dim when I drove into Pelion, a quiet, almost old-fashioned, little downtown area. Most of the businesses looked to be family or individually owned, and large trees lined the wide sidewalks where people still strolled in the cooler late-summer twilight. I loved this time of day. There was something magical about it, something *hopeful*, something that said, *You didn't know if you could, but you made it another day, didn't you?*

I spotted Haskell's and pulled into the parking lot to the right of it and into a spot.

I didn't need groceries just yet, but I *was* in need of a few basic necessities. It was the only reason I'd run out at all. Even though I had slept five hours or so today, I was tired again and ready to settle into bed with a book.

I was in and out of Haskell's in ten minutes and walking back to my car in the deepening twilight. The streetlights had blinked on in the time I had been in the store, and were casting a dreamy glow over the parking lot. I pulled my purse up on my shoulder and switched the plastic bag from one hand to the other, when the bottom of the plastic tore open and my purchases fell to the concrete, several items rolling away, out of my immediate reach. "Crap!" I swore, bending down to pick up my stuff. I opened my large purse and started tossing in the shampoo and conditioner I'd picked up, when I saw someone stopped in my peripheral vision, and I startled. I looked up just as a guy bent down with one knee on the asphalt and handed me the bottle of Advil that had rolled away, apparently directly into his path. I stared at him. He was young and had shaggy, long, slightly wavy brown hair that was in desperate need of a cut, and facial hair that looked more neglected than purposefully rugged. He might be handsome, but it was hard to make out exactly what his face looked like under the overly long beard and hair that fell over his forehead and down around his jaw. He was wearing jeans and a blue T-shirt that was stretched across his broad chest. The T-shirt had had a message on it at some point, but now was so faded and worn away that it was anyone's guess what it once said.

I noticed all of this in the few brief seconds it took me to reach for his extended hand holding the bottle of pain medication, at which point our eyes met and seemed to tangle. His were deep and whiskey-colored, framed by long, dark lashes. *Beautiful.*

As I stared at him, it felt like something moved between us, almost as if I should reach out and try to grab the air surrounding our bodies—like perhaps my hand would come back holding something tangible, something soft and warm. I frowned, confused, but was unable to look away as his eyes quickly darted from mine. Who was this strange-looking guy, and why was I sitting here frozen in front of him? I shook my head slightly and snapped myself back to reality. "Thanks," I said, taking the bottle from his still-outstretched hand. He said nothing, not looking at me again.

"Crap," I quietly swore once more, returning my attention to the items strewn on the ground. My eyes widened when I saw that my box of tampons had opened and several of them were lying on the ground. *Kill me now.* He picked up a few and handed them to me, and I quickly stuffed them in my purse, glancing up at him at the same time he glanced at me, but there was no reaction on his face. Again, his eyes darted away. I felt color rising in my cheeks and tried to make small talk as he handed me a few more tampons, and I snatched them and threw them in my purse, suppressing a hysterical giggle.

"Darn plastic bags," I breathed out, fast-talking, then taking a deep breath before continuing, a little slower this time. "Not only bad for the environment, but unreliable, really." The guy handed me an Almond Joy candy bar and a tampon, and I took them from him and dropped them into my open purse, groaning inwardly. "I tried to be good about using my own reusable shopping bags. I even bought really cute ones in fun patterns…paisley, polka dot"—I shook my head, stuffing the last tampon on the ground in my purse—"but I was always leaving them in my car, or at home." I shook my head again as the man handed me two more candy bars.

"Thanks," I said. "I think I've got the rest of this." I waved my hand over the four remaining Almond Joys lying on the ground.

I looked up at him, my cheeks heating again. "They were on sale," I explained. "I wasn't planning on eating these all at once or anything." He didn't look at me as he picked them up himself, but I swore I saw a minuscule lip twitch. I blinked and it was gone. I squinted at him, taking the candy bars from his hand. "I just like to keep chocolate around the house, you know, for a treat once in a while. This here should last me a couple of months." I was lying. What I had bought would last me a couple of days, *if that*. I might even eat several of them on the car ride home.

The guy stood and so did I as I lifted my purse over my shoulder.

"Okay, well, thanks for the help, for rescuing me…and my… personal items…my chocolate, and coconut…and almonds…"I laughed a small, embarrassed sound, but then grimaced slightly. "You know, it would really help me out if you would speak and put me out of my misery here." I grinned at him, but immediately went serious as his face fell, his eyes shuttering and a blank look replacing the warmer one I had sworn was there moments before.

He turned and started walking away.

"Hey, wait!" I called, starting to step after him. I stopped myself, though, frowning as the distance grew between us, his body moving with grace as he started to jog slowly toward the street. The strangest feeling of loss washed over me as he crossed and walked out of sight.

I got in my car and sat there unmoving for a couple of minutes, wondering at the odd encounter. When I finally started the engine, I noticed there was something on my windshield. I went to turn on the spray, when I stopped and leaned forward, looking more closely. Dandelion seeds were scattered across the glass, and as a light breeze blew, the fluffy ends were caught in the moving air and danced delicately off my windshield as they took flight, moving away from me, in the direction the man had gone.

* * *

I woke up early the next morning, got out of bed, pulled up the shades in my bedroom, and stared out at the lake, the morning sun reflecting on it, making it a warm, golden color. A large bird took flight, and I could just make out one singular boat in the water, close to the distant shore. Yeah, I could get used to this.

Phoebe jumped off the bed and came to sit by my feet. "What do you think, girl?" I whispered. She yawned.

I took a deep breath, trying to center myself. "Not this morning. This morning you're okay." I walked slowly toward the shower, relaxing minimally, hope blooming in my chest with each step. But as I turned on the spray, the world around me blinked out and the shower became the sound of rain beating on the roof. Dread seized me, and I froze as a loud clap of thunder pounded in my ears and the feel of cold metal moved across my bare breast. I flinched at the jerkiness of the gun tracing my nipple, the cold making it pebble as the tears flowed faster down my cheeks. Inside my head sounded like the high-pitched shriek of a train screeching to a stop on metal rails. *Oh God, Oh God*. I held my breath, just waiting for the gun to go off, ice-cold terror flowing through my veins. I tried to think of my dad lying in his own blood in the room beyond, but my own fear was so all-consuming that I couldn't focus on anything else. I began to shake uncontrollably, the rain continuing to beat against the—

A car door slammed outside, snapping me back to the here and now. I was standing in front of the running shower, water puddling on the floor where the curtain was open. Vomit rushed up my throat, and I turned just in time to make it to the bowl, where I heaved up bile. I sat there gasping and shaking for several minutes, trying to get hold of my body. The tears threatened to come, but I wouldn't let them. I squeezed my eyes shut and counted backward from one hundred. When I made it to one, I took another deep breath and stumbled to my feet, grabbing a towel to mop up the growing puddle in front of the open shower.

I stripped off my clothes and stepped under the warm spray, leaning my head back and closing my eyes, trying to relax and come back to the present, trying to get the shaking under control.

"You're okay, you're okay, you're okay," I chanted, swallowing down the emotion, the guilt, my body still trembling slightly. I *would* be okay. I knew that, but it always took a little while to shake the feeling of being back *there*, in that place, in that moment of utter grief and terror, and then sometimes several hours before the sadness left me, but never completely.

Every morning the flashback came, and every evening I felt stronger again. Each dawn I had hope that *this* new day would be the one that would set me free, and that I would make it through without having to endure the pain of being chained in grief to the night that would forever separate *now* from *then*.

I stepped out of the shower and dried off. Looking at myself in the mirror, I thought I looked better than I did most mornings. Despite the fact that the flashbacks hadn't ended here, I had slept well, which I hadn't done much of over the past six months, and felt a sense of contentment that I attributed to the lake outside my window. What was more peaceful than the sound of water lapping gently on a sandy shore? Surely some of that would seep into my soul, or at the very least, help me get some much-needed sleep.

I went back to my bedroom and dressed in a pair of khaki shorts and a black button-down shirt with cap sleeves. I was planning on going into the diner in town that Anne had mentioned, and wanted to look presentable since I'd be asking about the— hopefully still available—job. I needed one as quickly as possible.

I blew my hair dry and left it down and then put on a minimum of makeup. I slipped on my black sandals and was out the door, the warm morning air caressing my skin as I stepped outside and locked up.

Ten minutes later, I was pulling up to the curb outside of Norm's. It looked like a classic small-town diner. I looked in the big glass window and saw that it was already half-full on a Monday morning at eight a.m. The HELP WANTED sign was still in the window. *Yes!*

I opened the door, and the smell of coffee and bacon greeted me, the sounds of chatter and soft laughter coming from the booths and tables.

I walked toward the front and took a seat at the counter, next to two young women in cutoff jean shorts and tank tops—obviously not part of those stopping in for breakfast on their way to the office.

As I took a seat on the rotating, red-vinyl-covered stool, the woman now sitting next to me looked at me and smiled.

"Good morning," I said, and smiled back.

"Good morning!" she said.

I picked up the menu in front of me, and a waitress, an older woman with short gray hair, standing at the kitchen window, looked over her shoulder at me and said, "I'll be right with you, honey." She looked harried as she flipped through her order pad. The place was only half-full, but she was obviously alone and having trouble keeping up. Morning crowds were always looking for quick service so they could make it to work on time.

"No rush," I said.

A few minutes later when she had delivered a couple of meals and came up to me, she said distractedly, "Coffee?"

"Please. And you look slammed—I'll make it easy on you and have the number three, just as it comes."

"Bless you, honey." She laughed. "You must have experience waitressing."

"Actually"—I smiled and handed her the menu—"I do, and I know this isn't a good time, but I saw the HELP WANTED sign in the window."

"Seriously?" she said, "When can you start?"

I laughed. "As soon as possible. I can come back later to fill out an application or—"

"No need. You have waitressing experience, you need a job, you're hired. Come back later to fill out the necessary paperwork, but Norm's my husband. I have the authority to hire another waitress, and I just hired you." She held out her hand. "Maggie Jansen, by the way."

I grinned at her. "Bree Prescott. Thank you so much!"

"You're the one who just made my morning better," she called as she went down the counter to refill the other coffee cups.

Well, that was the easiest interview I'd ever had.

"New in town?" the young woman next to me asked.

I turned to her, smiling. "Yes, just moved here yesterday, actually."

"Well, welcome to Pelion. I'm Melanie Scholl, and this is my sister, Liza." The girl to her right leaned forward and extended her hand.

I shook it, saying, "Really nice to meet you."

I noticed the bathing suit ties sticking out of the backs of their tank tops and said, "Are you vacationing here?"

"Oh no," Melanie laughed, "we work on the other shore. We're lifeguards for the next couple of weeks while the tourists are here, and then we go back to work at our family's pizza parlor during the winter."

I nodded, sipping my coffee. I thought they looked about my age, Liza most likely the younger one. They looked similar with their reddish-brown hair and the same large blue eyes.

"If you have any questions about this town, you just ask us," Liza said. "We make it our business to know all the dirt." She winked. "We can tell you who to date, too, and who to avoid. We've pretty much run through them all in both towns—we're a wealth of information."

I laughed. "Okay, I'll keep that in mind. I'm really glad I met you girls." I started to turn forward, when something occurred to me. "Hey, actually, I have a question about someone. I dropped some stuff in the pharmacy parking lot last night and a guy stopped to help me. Tall, lean, good build, but...I don't know, he didn't say a word...and he had this long beard—"

"Archer Hale," Melanie broke in. "I'm shocked he stopped to help you, though. He doesn't usually pay anyone any attention." She paused. "And no one usually pays him any attention, either, I guess."

"Well, I don't know if he had too much of a choice," I said. "My stuff literally rolled right in front of his feet."

Melanie shrugged. "Still unusual. Trust me. Anyway, I think he's deaf. That's why he doesn't speak. He was in some kind of accident when he was a kid. We were just five and six when it happened, right outside town, on the highway. His parents were killed, and the town police chief, his uncle. That's when he lost his hearing, I guess. He lives at the end of Briar Road—he used to live with his other uncle who homeschooled him, but that uncle died a couple of years back, and now he lives by himself out there. He never even used to come into town until his uncle died. Now we see him every once in a while. He's a total loner, though."

"Wow," I said, frowning, "that's so sad."

"Yeah," Liza chimed in, "because, have you seen the body on him? Of course, runs in the genes. If he wasn't so antisocial, I'd do him."

Melanie rolled her eyes, and I put my hand up to my lips so coffee wouldn't spew out of my mouth.

"Please, you hooker," Melanie said, "you'd do him anyway, if he'd look your way once."

Liza considered that for a second and then shook her head. "I doubt he'd even know what to do with that body of his. A true shame." Melanie rolled her eyes again and then glanced up at the clock above the order window.

"Oh darn, we gotta go or we're gonna be late." She took out her wallet and called to Maggie, "I'm leaving the bill on the counter, Mags."

"Thanks, hon," Maggie called back as she walked quickly by, holding two plates.

Melanie scribbled something down on a napkin and handed it to me. "Here's our number," she said. "We're planning a girls' night on the other side of the lake soon. Maybe you'd like to come with us?"

I took the napkin. "Oh, okay, well, maybe." I smiled. I scribbled my number down on a napkin and handed her mine as well. "Thanks so much. That's really nice of you." I was surprised how much my mood was boosted after talking to two girls my age. Maybe that's what I need, I thought, to remember that I was a person with friends and a life before tragedy struck. It was so easy to feel like my whole existence began and ended that terrible day. But that wasn't true. I needed to remind myself of that as much as possible.

Of course, my friends back home had tried to get me to go out a few times in the months following my dad's death, but I just hadn't been up for it. Maybe going out with people who weren't so acquainted with my tragedy would be better—after all, wasn't that what this road trip was about? A temporary escape? The hope that a new place would bring new healing? And then I would have the strength to face my life again.

Liza and Melanie walked quickly out the door, calling and waving to a few other people sitting in the restaurant. After a minute, Maggie set my plate down in front of me.

As I ate, I considered what they had said about the guy named

Archer Hale. It made sense now—he was deaf. I wondered why that hadn't already occurred to me. That's why he hadn't spoken. Obviously, he could read lips. And I had completely insulted him when I made the comment about him saying something. That's why his face had fallen and he walked away like that. I cringed inwardly. "Nice one, Bree," I said quietly as I bit off a piece of toast.

I'd make it a point to apologize next time I saw him. I wondered if he knew sign language. I'd let him know I could speak it if he wanted to talk to me. I knew it well. My dad had been deaf.

Something about Archer Hale intrigued me—something I couldn't put my finger on. Something that went beyond the fact that he couldn't hear or speak and that I was intimately acquainted with that particular disability. I pondered it for a minute, but couldn't come up with an answer.

I finished my meal, and Maggie waved me off when I asked for my check. "Employees eat for free," she called, refilling coffee down the counter from me. "Come back in any time after two to fill out the paperwork."

I grinned at her. "Okay," I said. "See you this afternoon." I left a tip on the counter and headed out the door. *Not bad*, I thought. Only in town one day and I've got a home, a job, and a sort-of friend in my neighbor, Anne, and maybe in Melanie and Liza, too. There was an extra spring in my step as I walked to my car.

CHAPTER FOUR

BREE

I started work at Norm's Diner early the next morning. Norm himself worked the kitchen and was mostly grumpy and grumbly, and he didn't talk to me much, but I saw him shoot Maggie looks that could only be described as adoring. I suspected he was really just a big softie; he didn't scare me. I also knew I was a good waitress and that Maggie's stress level had dropped significantly an hour after I started, and so I figured I had an in with Norm right off the bat.

The diner was bustling, the work straightforward, and the locals who ate there pleasant. I couldn't complain, and the first couple of days went by quickly and smoothly.

On Wednesday after I got off work, I drove home, showered, changed, and pulled on my swimsuit and a pair of jean shorts and a white tank top, intending to go down to the lake and do a little exploring. I put Phoebe's leash on her and locked up behind me.

As I was leaving my house, Anne called to me from her yard, where she was watering the rosebushes. I walked over to her, smiling.

"How are you settling in?" she asked me, setting her watering can down and walking over to her fence where I was standing.

"Good! I've been meaning to come over and thank you for letting me know about the position at the diner. I got it, and I'm waitressing there."

"Oh, that's great! Maggie's a gem. Don't let Norm scare you off—he's all bark and no bite."

I laughed. "I figured that out pretty quickly." I winked. "No, it's been good. I was just going to drive down the road and check out the lake a little bit."

"Oh, good. The docks don't make for a very good walk right here—of course, you probably figured that out. If you go down to Briar Road, you can follow the signs to the small beach." She gave me brief directions and then added, "If you want it, I have a bike that I don't use anymore. With my arthritis, I just can't grip the handlebars so that I feel safe. But it's practically new and it even has a basket for your dog." She looked down at the little dog in question. "Hi there. What's your name?" She smiled down at Phoebe, who chuffed happily, dancing around a bit.

"Say hi, Phoebe."

"What a cute girl you are," Anne said, bending down slightly to let Phoebe lick her hand.

She stood up and said, "The bike is in my spare bedroom. Would you like to see it?"

I paused. "Are you sure? I mean, I would love to ride a bike down to the lake rather than take my car."

"Yes, yes." She waved me toward her as she started to walk to her house. "I would love to see it put to use. I used to pick blueberries up that way. They grow wild. Bring a couple of bags and you can put them in the bike basket when you're done. Do you bake?"

"Um," I said, following her into her cottage, "I used to. I haven't in a while."

She glanced back at me. "Well, maybe the blueberries will inspire you to pick up an apron again." She smiled as she opened a door right off the main room.

Her cottage was casually decorated with well-used, slipcovered furniture and lots of knickknacks and framed photos. The smell of dried eucalyptus hung in the air. It immediately felt comforting and happy.

"Here we go," Anne said, wheeling a bike out of the room she had entered seconds before. I couldn't help grinning. It was one of those old-fashioned bikes with a big basket on the front.

"Oh my goodness! It's fabulous. Are you sure you want me using this?"

"Nothing would make me happier, dear. In fact, if it works for you, you keep it."

I smiled at her, wheeling it out onto her porch. "Thank you so much. This is so kind of you. I really…thank you."

She came out behind me and helped me lift it down the steps. "My pleasure. It makes me happy to know it's being used and enjoyed."

I smiled again, admiring it, when something occurred to me. "Oh! Can I ask you a question? I ran into someone in town, and someone else I met mentioned that he lives at the end of Briar Road. Archer Hale? Do you know him?"

Anne frowned, looking thoughtful at the same time. "Yes, I know *of* him anyway. You'll actually be passing right by his land on your way to the small beach. You'll see it—it's really the only property on that stretch of road." She paused for a second. "Yes, Archer Hale…I remember him as a sweet little boy. Doesn't talk now, though. Suppose it's because he doesn't hear."

I tilted my head. "Do you know what happened to him exactly?"

She pressed her lips together and hummed softly. "There was

a big car crash outside of town right about the time my Bill got his diagnosis. Suppose I didn't pay quite as much attention to the details as the rest of the town did—just grieved along with them. But what I do know is that Archer's parents and his uncle, Connor Hale, the owner of the town and the chief of police, died that day, and that whatever afflicts Archer happened in that accident. Hmm, now let me think…" She paused. "He went to live with his other uncle, Nathan Hale. But he died three or four years ago, some kind of cancer, from what I recall." She looked past me, staring into space for a couple of seconds. "Some in town say he isn't right in the head. Archer, I mean. But I don't know about that. Might just be them passing off his uncle's personality onto him. My younger sister went to school with Nathan Hale and he never was quite right. Wicked smart, but always slightly strange. And when he came home from the army, he was even more…different."

I frowned up at her. "And they still sent a little boy to live with him?"

"Oh, well, I suppose he presented okay to the county. And anyway, far as I know, he was the only family that boy had left." She went quiet again for a minute. "Haven't talked about the original Hale boys in years now. But they sure did always cause a stir. Hmm." She was quiet again for a few beats. "Now that I think about it, it really is a sad situation with the younger Hale boy. Sometimes in small towns, people who have been around forever sort of…become part of the backdrop, I guess. In the town's attempt to move past the tragedy, Archer might have just gotten lost in the mix. Such a shame."

Anne lapsed into silence again, seeming to be distracted by her memories, and I thought I'd better be off.

"Hmm, well"—I smiled—"thanks again for the directions. I'll stop by later."

Anne brightened and seemed to snap back to the present. "Yes, that would be nice. Have a lovely day." She smiled, turned back around, and grabbed the watering can she had set down on her porch, as I wheeled the bike through her front gate.

I put Phoebe in the basket, and as I got on the bike and pedaled slowly toward the entrance of Briar Road, I thought about what Anne had told me about the Hale brothers, and about Archer Hale. It didn't seem like anyone knew the exact story of what had happened to Archer—or had they forgotten the details? I knew what it was like to lose both your parents, not in one fell swoop, though. How would you even begin to deal with something like that? Did your mind allow you to process one loss at a time? Wouldn't you go crazy with grief if that much of it inundated your heart at once? Some days I felt like I was barely holding on to my emotions from moment to moment. I supposed we all coped in our different ways—pain and healing as individual as the people who experienced them.

The sight of what must be his property snapped me out of my own thoughts. There was a high fence surrounding it, the tops of trees too numerous and too thick to see anything beyond the high structure. I craned my neck to see how far the fence went, but it was hard to tell from the road, and there were woods on either side. My eyes returned to the front of the fence where I could see a latch, but it was closed.

I wasn't sure why I stood there, just looking at it and listening to the mosquitos buzz. But after a few minutes Phoebe barked softly, and I continued to head down the road to the beach access where Anne had directed me.

I spent a few hours down at the lakeshore, swimming and sunning myself. Phoebe lay on a corner of my towel in the shade, sleeping contentedly. It was a hot August day, but the breeze off the lake and the shade of the trees behind the shore made it comfortable. There were a few people farther down the small beach area, but it was mostly deserted. I figured that was because this side of the lake was only used by locals. I lay back on the towel I had brought and looked up at the tips of the swaying trees and the patches of bright blue sky, listening to the lapping water. After a few minutes, I closed my eyes, just intending to rest, but instead fell asleep.

I dreamed of my dad. Only this time, he hadn't died right away. He crawled into the kitchen just in time to see the man dart out the back door.

"You're alive!" I said, beginning to sit up off the floor where the man had left me.

He nodded, a gentle smile on his face.

"You're okay?" I asked haltingly, fearful.

"Yes," he said, and I startled, for my dad had never used his voice, only his hands.

"You can speak," I whispered.

"Yes," he said again, laughing slightly. "Of course." But it was then I noticed his lips weren't moving.

"I want you back, Dad," I said, my eyes tearing up. "I miss you so much."

His face went serious, and it looked like the distance between us was increasing even though neither of us had moved. "I'm so sorry you can't have us both, Little Bee," he said, using my nickname.

"Both?" I whispered, confused, watching the distance between us grow even more.

Suddenly, he was gone, and I was alone. I was crying, and my eyes were closed, but I could feel a presence standing over me.

I startled awake, warm tears coursing down my cheeks, the very edges of the dream fading into mist. As I lay there trying to gather my emotions, I swore I heard the sound of someone moving away, through the woods behind me.

* * *

I got into the diner early the next morning. Despite sleeping well, I had had a particularly bad flashback that morning, and I was having trouble shaking the melancholy that still clung to me.

I dove into the morning rush, keeping my head down and my mind occupied with the business of taking orders, delivering food, and refilling coffee. By nine when the diner started to empty out, I was feeling better, lighter.

I was restocking the condiments at the counter when the door to the diner opened and a young man in a police uniform walked in. He removed his hat and ran his hand through his short, wavy brown hair before he nodded over at Maggie, who smiled back at him and called out, "Trav."

His gaze moved to me as he walked toward the counter, and our eyes locked for a second. His face lit up with a smile, his straight, white teeth flashing as he took a seat in front of me. "Well, you must be the reason that Maggie's got a smile on her face this morning," he said, extending his hand. "I'm Travis Hale."

Oh, another Hale. I smiled back, taking his hand. "Hi, Travis. Bree Prescott."

He sat down, bringing his long legs under the counter. "Good to meet you, Bree. What brings you to Pelion?"

I chose my words carefully, not wanting to come off as some kind of weird nomad. Although, I supposed that was sort of what I was at the moment, if I had decided to be completely truthful. "Well, Travis, I recently graduated college and decided to take sort of a freedom road trip." I smiled. "Ended up here in your pretty little town."

He grinned. "Exploring while you can," he said. "I like it. Wish I had done more of that myself."

I smiled back, handing him a menu just as Maggie came up behind me. She grabbed the menu and tossed it under the counter. "Travis Hale must have that thing memorized by now," she said, winking at me. "Been coming in here since his mother had to sit him in a booster seat to reach the table. Speaking of your mother, how is she?"

He smiled. "Oh, she's fine. You know, she keeps busy, never lacking for a social circle. Plus, she's extra busy with all the town expansion plans."

Maggie's lips pursed, but she said, "Well, you tell her I said hi," and smiled kindly.

"Will do," Travis said, turning back to me.

"So your last name is Hale," I said. "You must be related to Archer Hale."

Travis's brow furrowed slightly and he looked confused for a moment. "Archer? Yeah, he's my cousin. You know him?"

"Oh, no," I said, shaking my head. "I ran into him in town a few days ago and I asked about him...he was a little..."

"Weird?" Travis finished.

"Different," I corrected, considering. I waved my hand. "I've only met a few people and he was one of them so...I mean, not that I actually met him per se, but..." I grabbed the coffeepot off the machine and held it up to him questioningly. He nodded and I started to pour him a cup.

"Hard to meet someone who doesn't speak," Travis said. He looked thoughtful for a second. "I've tried with him over the years, but he just doesn't respond to niceties. He's in a world of his own.

Sorry he was part of your welcome wagon. Anyway, good to have you here." He smiled, taking a sip of his coffee.

"Thanks," I said. "So you're a Pelion police officer?" I asked, stating the obvious, but just making conversation.

"Yup," he said.

"On track to become the *chief* of police," Maggie interrupted, "just like his daddy before him." She winked, walking by on her way back to the table next to the counter we used for breaks.

Travis raised his eyebrows and smiled. "We'll see," he said, but he didn't look doubtful.

I just smiled at him, and he smiled up at me. I didn't mention that Anne had told me about his father, whom I assumed was Connor Hale. I thought it might sound weird if he knew I had already asked about his family. Or at least, about the gist of the tragedy that had happened to them.

"Where are you staying?" he asked.

"Oh, right on the lake," I answered. "Rockwell Lane."

"In one of George Connick's rentals?"

I nodded.

"Well, Bree, I'd love to show you around sometime if you're available." His whiskey-colored eyes moved over me.

I smiled, studying him. He was handsome; there was no doubt about that. I was pretty sure he was asking me out, not only being friendly. Dating just wasn't the most brilliant idea for me at the moment, though. "I'm sorry, Travis, things are kind of… complicated with me right now."

He studied me for a couple of seconds, and I flushed under his stare. "I'm a pretty simple kind of guy, Bree." He winked.

I laughed, thankful that he broke the tension. We chatted easily enough while he finished his coffee and I continued to fill the condiments at the counter and tidy up.

Norm came out of the kitchen just as Travis was getting up to leave. "You flirting with my new waitress?" Norm grumped.

"I have to," Travis answered. "For some unknown reason, Maggie still won't leave your sour ass for me." Travis winked at Maggie, who was wiping down a table next to the counter. "She'll come around one of these days, though. I hold out hope."

Norm snorted, wiping his hands down the grease-stained apron covering his potbelly. "She comes home to this at night," he said. "What would she want with you?"

Travis chuckled, turning to leave, but calling to Maggie, "You come find me when you get tired of this ill-tempered lug."

Maggie laughed, patting her short salt-and-pepper curls, and Norm grumbled his way back into the kitchen. At the door, Travis turned back around to me, saying, "My offer stands, Bree."

I smiled as he closed the door behind him.

"You watch out," Maggie said to me. "That boy will charm the pants right off of you." But she smiled as she said it.

I laughed, shaking my head and watching out the window as Travis Hale got in his police cruiser and pulled away from the curb.

* * *

That evening, I took my bike down Briar Road again and picked blueberries along the side of the road. When my bag was half-full and my fingertips were stained dark purple, I started for home. On my way back, I sat on my bike on the side of the dusty road in front of Archer's property and looked at the fence in front of me for no particular reason—at least not one that I could explain to myself. After a few minutes, I started pedaling home.

That night I dreamed that I was lying on the shore of the lake.

I could feel sand beneath my bare skin, the granules biting into my flesh as I rocked against it, a man's welcome weight above me. There was no fear, no distress; I wanted him there. The water came up over my legs like smooth, cool silk caressing my skin and soothing the sting of the abrasive sand.

I woke up gasping, my nipples pebbled painfully against my T-shirt and my pulse beating rhythmically between my legs. I tossed and turned until I finally fell asleep, somewhere close to dawn.

CHAPTER FIVE

BREE

I was off from the diner the next day. When I woke up and looked at the clock, it was 8:17. I startled slightly. I hadn't slept that late in months and months, but I supposed it was to be expected being that I'd hardly slept the night before. I sat up slowly, the room coming into focus. I felt heavy and groggy as I swung my legs over the side of the bed. My sleep-filled head had barely started to clear when a sound came from outside, just a branch dropping, or a boat engine backfiring in the distance, but my brain grabbed it and catapulted me straight into my waking nightmare—I froze, terror seizing up my muscles, my brain screaming. I watched through the small window in the door separating my dad and me. He saw me in his peripheral vision, and started signing *Hide*, over and over, as the man screamed at him to put his hands down. My dad couldn't hear him, and his hands continued to move only for me. My body jolted as the gun exploded. I cried out and my hand flew up to my mouth to stifle the sound as I stumbled backward, instantly filled with shock and horror. I tripped on the edge of a box and fell down backward, drawing my legs up under me, trying to make myself as small as possible. I didn't have a phone back here. My eyes flew around the room looking for something I could hide behind, somewhere I could crawl. And that's when the doors swung open...

Reality rushed back in as the world around me cleared, and I felt the bedspread gripped in my fists. I let out a gasping breath and stood shakily, rushing to the toilet just in time. *God, I can't do this forever.* This had to stop. *Do not cry, do not cry.* Phoebe sat on the floor at my feet, moaning softly.

After several minutes, I got hold of myself. "It's okay, girl," I said, petting Phoebe's head reassuringly, for her, but also for me.

I stumbled to the shower, and twenty minutes later as I dressed in my swimsuit, shorts, and a blue tank, I felt a little better. I took a deep breath, closed my eyes, and grounded myself. I was okay.

After finishing a quick breakfast, I slipped into my sandals, grabbed my book and my towel, called to Phoebe, and stepped outside into the warm, slightly muggy air, the mosquitos already buzzing around me, a frog croaking somewhere close by.

I took a deep inhale of the fresh air, the smell of pine and lake water filling my lungs. As I climbed on my bike, Phoebe in the basket in front, I was able to exhale.

I rode down to Briar Road again, returning to the small beach area I had sat on a couple of days before. I immersed myself in my novel, and before I knew it, I was finished and two hours had flown by. I stood up and stretched, looking out at the still lake, squinting to see the other side where boats and Jet Skis moved through the water.

As I folded up my towel, I thought it was a stroke of luck that I had ended up on this side of the lake. The peace and quiet was just what I needed.

I put Phoebe back in the basket, pushed my bike up the slight incline to the road, and pedaled slowly toward Archer Hale's fence.

I pulled to the side as a mail truck drove past me, the driver holding up his hand in greeting. The tires kicked up dust so that I coughed, waving aside the gritty air in front of me as I pulled back onto the road.

I rode the short distance to the fence and then stopped. Today, because of the way the sun slanted in the sky, I could see several rectangles on the wood that were just a little bit lighter, as if signs had hung there once but had been removed.

Just as I began to start moving again, I noticed the gate was very slightly ajar. I paused and stared at it for a few seconds. The mail-man must have been delivering something here and left it open.

I pulled my bike forward and leaned it against the fence as I pulled the gate open a bit farther and peeked my head inside.

I sucked in a breath as I took in the beautiful stone driveway leading to the small white house about a hundred feet from where I was now standing. I didn't know what I had been expecting ex-actly, but this wasn't it. Everything was neat and tidy and well cared for, a small span of recently mowed emerald-green grass between some trees, to one side of the driveway, and a garden con-tained in wood pallets directly to the left.

I leaned back out, starting to close the gate when Phoebe jumped out of the bike's basket and squeezed herself through the narrow opening.

"*Shit!*" I sputtered. "*Phoebe!*"

I pulled the gate back open just a bit and peered inside again. Phoebe was standing just down the driveway, looking back at me, panting.

"Bad dog," I whispered. "Get back here!"

Phoebe looked at me, turned tail, and trotted farther away. I groaned. *Well, shit!* I walked through the gate, leaving it open slightly behind me, and continued to call to Phoebe, who apparently thought I could kiss her little doggie ass as much as she was listening to me.

As I moved closer, I could see a large stone patio and walkway in front of the house, built up on either side and adorned with large planters full of greenery.

As my eyes moved around the yard, it suddenly registered that there was a loud banging noise ringing out every few seconds. Was someone cutting wood? Is that what that sound was?

Phoebe trotted around the house and out of sight.

I tilted my head, listening, and adjusting my weight between one foot and then the other. What should I do? I couldn't leave Phoebe here. I couldn't go back to the gate and yell loudly for Archer to answer—he couldn't hear.

I had to go in after her. Archer was in there. I was not a girl who was willing to put herself in dangerous situations. Not that I had before—and yet, danger had found me anyway. But still. Walking into unknown territory wasn't something I was thrilled to be doing. *Damn little misbehaving dog.* But as I stood there considering, working up my nerve to go in after Phoebe, I thought about Archer. My instincts told me he was safe. That had to count for something. Was I going to let that evil man make me doubt my own instincts for the rest of my life?

I thought about how my hair stood up on my arms the minute I heard the bell ring at our front door that night. Something inside me had known, and standing here now, something inside me felt like I wasn't in danger. My feet moved forward.

I walked down the driveway slowly, inhaling the pungent smell of sap and freshly mowed grass, continuing to call softly to Phoebe.

I took the stone path around the house, trailing my hands along the painted wood. I peeked around the back of the house and there he was, his bare back to me as he raised an ax over his head, his muscles flexing as he swung downward, cracking an upright log straight down the middle so that three pieces all fell outward and landed on the dirt.

He bent down and picked them up and placed them in a stack of neatly piled pieces sitting under a tree, a large tarp off to one side.

As he turned back around to the stump where he was chopping the smaller pieces, he caught sight of me, startled, and then froze. We both stood there staring at one another, my mouth slightly open and his eyes wide. A bird trilled somewhere nearby and an answering call echoed through the trees.

I closed my mouth and smiled, but Archer remained staring for several beats before his eyes did one quick sweep of me and returned to my face before narrowing.

My eyes moved over him, too, his well-defined naked chest, all smooth-skinned muscles and rippling abs. I had never actually seen an eight-pack, but there it was, right in front of me. I guessed that even slightly strange, silent hermits weren't exempt from exceptional physiques. *Good for him.*

He was wearing what looked like a pair of khakis, cut off at the knees and tied at his waist with a...was that a *rope?* Interesting. My eyes moved downward to the work boots on his feet and back up to his face. He had tilted his head to one side as we studied each other, but his expression remained the same: wary.

His beard was just as scraggly as the first time I had seen him. Apparently, his knack for lawn trimming didn't extend to his own facial hair. That could use some major edging. As long as it was, he must have been growing it for some time now—years probably.

I cleared my throat. "Hi." I smiled, moving closer so he could clearly read my lips. "Sorry, to uh, bother you. My dog ran in here. I called her, but she didn't listen." I looked around, no Phoebe in sight.

Archer brushed his overly long hair out of his eyes, and his brow furrowed at my words. He turned his body, lifted the ax and buried it in the tree stump, and then turned back around to me. I swallowed heavily.

Suddenly, a little white fur ball shot out of the woods and trotted toward Archer, sitting down at his feet and panting.

Archer looked down at her and then bent and petted her head. Phoebe licked his hand exuberantly, whining for more when he withdrew and stood up. *Little traitor.*

"That's her," I said, stating the obvious. He continued to stare.

"Uh, so, your place," I went on, waving my hand around, indicating his property, "is really nice." He continued to stare at me. Finally, I tilted my head. "Do you remember me? From town? The candy bars?" I smiled.

He continued to stare.

God, I needed to leave. This was awkward. I cleared my throat. "Phoebe," I called. "Come here, girl." Phoebe stared at me, still sitting at Archer's feet.

I moved my eyes between Archer and Phoebe. They were both completely still, two pairs of eyes trained on me.

Well.

My eyes settled on Archer. "Do you understand me? What I'm saying?" I asked.

My words seemed to get his attention just a little. He stared at me for a beat and then his lips pursed and he let out a breath, seeming to make a decision. He walked around me and toward his house, Phoebe following close behind. I turned to watch him, confused, when he turned, looked at me, and signaled me with his hand to follow him.

I assumed he was walking me back to the gate. I hurried behind him, speed-walking to keep up with his long strides, the little traitor known as Phoebe staying with Archer the whole time, but turning to watch me follow, yapping excitedly.

When I made it up to where he was standing waiting for me, I said, "You're not, like, an ax murderer or something, are you?" I was joking, but it did occur to me again that if I screamed, there wasn't anyone who would hear me. *Trust your instincts, Bree*, I reminded myself.

Archer Hale raised his eyebrows and pointed down the slight incline to where he had left his ax, stuck in the stump. I looked down at it and back at him.

"Right," I whispered. "The whole ax-murderer thing doesn't really work if you don't have your ax."

That same minuscule lip quirk I had seen in the parking lot of the drugstore made the decision for me. I followed him the rest of the way to the front of his house.

He opened his front door, and I gasped when I looked inside and saw a big brick fireplace flanked by two floor-to-ceiling bookcases full of hardbacks and paperbacks. I started moving toward them like a mind-numb, book-loving robot, but I felt Archer's hand on my arm and halted. He held up his finger to indicate he'd just be a minute and walked inside. When he came back out a couple of seconds later, he had a pad in his hands and he was writing something on it. I waited, and when he turned it to me it said in very neat, all uppercase letters:

YES, I UNDERSTAND YOU.
IS THERE ANYTHING ELSE YOU NEED?

My eyes darted up to his, and my mouth opened slightly to respond, but I snapped it shut before answering his question. Kind of a *rude* question, by the way. But really, did I want anything else?

I chewed on my lip for a minute, switching my weight between legs again as he watched me, waiting for my answer. The look on his face was wary and watchful, as if he had no idea if I was going to answer him or bite him, and he was prepared for either.

"Uh, I just, I felt bad about the other day. I didn't know you didn't…speak, and I just wanted to let you know that it wasn't intentional, what I said…I just…I'm new in town and…" Well, this was going really well. Jesus. "Do you want to get a pizza or something?" I blurted out, my eyes widening. I hadn't exactly decided to go there, I just had. I looked at him hopefully.

He stared back like I was an advanced math problem he couldn't interpret.

He frowned at me and then brought his pen to the pad, never breaking eye contact. Finally, he looked down as he wrote and then raised the pad to me:

NO.

I couldn't help the laugh that erupted. He didn't smile, just kept looking at me suspiciously. My laughter died. I whispered, "No?"

A brief look of confusion passed over his face as he watched me, and he picked up his pad and wrote something else. When he held it up, he had added a word under his first one. It now said:

NO,
THANKS.

I let my breath out, feeling my cheeks heat. "Okay. I understand. Well, again, sorry for the misunderstanding in the parking lot. And…sorry for barging in on you today…that my dog…" I scooped Phoebe up in my arms. "Well, it was nice to meet you.

Oh! By the way, I didn't really meet you. I know your name, but I'm Bree. Bree Prescott. And I'll just let myself out." I hitched my thumb over my shoulder, walked backward, and then turned hurriedly and walked briskly back up the driveway toward the gate. I heard his footsteps behind me, walking in the opposite direction, back to his woodpile, I assumed.

I let myself out the gate, but didn't close it all the way. Instead, I stood on the other side, with my hand still on the warm wood. *Well, that was weird.* And embarrassing. What had I been thinking, asking him to have pizza with me? I looked up at the sky, putting my hand to my forehead and grimacing.

As I stood there thinking about it, something occurred to me. I had meant to ask Archer if he knew sign, but in my awkwardness, I had forgotten. And then he brought out that stupid pad of paper. But it was now that I realized Archer Hale had never once watched my lips as I talked. He had watched my eyes.

I turned around and walked back through his gate, marching back down to the woodpile behind his house, Phoebe still in my arms.

He was standing there, holding the ax in his hands, a piece of wood standing upright on the stump, but he wasn't swinging. He was just staring at it, a small frown on his face, looking deep in thought. And when he spotted me, a look of surprise flashed over his face before his eyes settled into that same narrow wariness.

When Phoebe saw him, she started yapping and panting again.

"You're not deaf," I said. "You can hear just fine."

He remained still for a minute, but then he stuck his ax in the stump, walked past me, and looked back in the same way he did the first time, gesturing for me to follow him. I did.

He walked through the door of his house and again emerged with the same pad and pen in his hands.

After a minute, he held up the pad.

I DIDN'T TELL YOU I WAS DEAF.

I paused. "No, you didn't," I said softly. "But you can't speak?"

He looked at me, brought the pad up, wrote for half a minute, and then turned it toward me.

I CAN SPEAK. I JUST LIKE TO SHOW OFF MY NICE PENMAN-SHIP.

I stared at the words, digesting them, furrowing my brow, and then looked up at his face. "Is that you being funny?" I asked, still frowning.

He raised his brows.

"Right," I said, tilting my head. "Well, you might want to work on that."

We stood there staring at each other for a few seconds, when he sighed heavily, brought the pad of paper up again, and wrote:

IS THERE SOMETHING ELSE YOU WANT?

I looked up at him. "I know sign language," I said. "I could teach you. I mean, you wouldn't get to show off your penmanship, ha-ha, but it's a quicker way to communicate." I smiled, hopeful, trying to make him smile, too. *Did* he smile? Was he even capable?

He stared at me for several beats before he placed the pad and pen down gently on the ground next to him, straightened up, brought his hands up, and signed, *I already know sign language.*

I startled slightly, and a lump came to my throat. No one had signed to me for over six months and it brought my dad, the feel of my dad's presence, front and center.

"Oh," I breathed out, using my voice because Phoebe was in my arms. "Right. You must have talked to your uncle that way."

He frowned, probably wondering how I knew about his uncle at all, but he didn't ask. Finally, he signed, *No*.

I blinked at him, and after a minute cleared my throat. "No?" I asked.

No, he repeated.

Silence again.

I exhaled. "Well, I know it sounds kind of stupid, but I thought maybe we could be…friends." I shrugged, letting out an uncomfortable laugh.

Archer narrowed his eyes again but just looked at me, not even writing anything down.

I looked between him and the pad, but when it became clear he wasn't going to "say" anything, I whispered, "Everyone needs friends." *Everyone needs friends? Really, Bree? Good grief, you sound pathetic.*

He kept looking at me.

I sighed, feeling embarrassed again, but also disappointed. "Okay, well suit yourself, I guess. I'll just go now." Truly, why was I disappointed? Travis had been right—this guy just didn't respond to niceties.

He stared at me, unmoving, his deep, whiskey-colored eyes flaring as I began to back away. I wanted to move all that shaggy hair out of his face and get rid of the facial hair so I could really see what he looked like. He did seem to have a nice face under all the shaggy scruff.

I sighed heavily. "Okay. Well, then, I guess I'll be on my

way..." *Just shut up already, Bree and GO. Clearly this person wants nothing to do with you.*

I felt his eyes following me as I turned and walked up the driveway and out his gate, this time shutting it firmly behind me. I leaned against it for a minute, scratching absently under Phoebe's chin, wondering what was wrong with me. What had been the point of all that? Why hadn't I just gotten my damn dog and left?

"Damn dog," I said to Phoebe, scratching her more. She licked at my face, woofing softly. I laughed and kissed her back.

As I got on my bike and started riding away, I heard the chopping begin again.

CHAPTER SIX

Archer—Seven Years Old; May

Where was I?

I felt like I was swimming upward in the pool at the YMCA, the top of the water miles and miles away. Noises started up in my ears and there was a pain in my neck, almost like a really bad sore throat that was both on the inside and the outside. I tried to remember how I'd gotten hurt, but only shadows moved around my head. I pushed them away.

Where was I?

Mama? I want my mama.

I felt the tears, hot and heavy, leak out of my closed eyes, down my cheeks. I tried not to cry. Strong men shouldn't cry. Strong men should protect others, like my uncle Connor. Only he had cried. He had cried so hard, yelling up at the sky and falling to his knees right there on the pavement.

Oh no. Oh no. Don't think about that.

I tried to move my body, but it felt like someone had tied weights to my arms and legs, even my fingers and toes. I thought I might be moving just a little, but I wasn't sure.

I heard a woman's voice say, "Shhh, he's waking up. Let him do it slowly. Let him do it himself."

Mama, mama. Please be here, too. Please be okay. Please don't be lying on the side of the road.

More warm tears slipped out of my eyes.

My entire body suddenly felt like hot pins and needles were being stuck in my skin. I tried to yell for help but I didn't even think I parted my lips. Oh God, the pain seemed to be waking up everywhere, like a monster coming alive in the dark under my bed.

After a few minutes of just breathing, just coming closer and closer to what I could feel was the surface, I opened my eyelids, squinting because there was a bright light right above me.

"Turn down the light, Meredith," I heard to my left.

I opened my eyes again, letting them get used to the light, and saw an older nurse with short blond hair looking down at me.

I opened my lips. "Mama," I tried to say, but nothing came out.

"Shhh," the nurse said, "don't try to talk, honey. You were in an accident. You're in the hospital, Archer, and we're taking real good care of you, okay? My name is Jenny and that's Meredith." She smiled sadly and pointed to a younger nurse behind her who was checking something on the machine next to my bed.

I nodded. Where was my mama? More tears fell down my cheeks.

"Okay, good boy," Jenny said. "Your uncle Nathan is right outside. Let me go get him. He'll be real happy you're awake."

I lay there, staring up at the ceiling for a few minutes before the door opened and shut and Uncle Nate was looking down into my face.

"Welcome back, little soldier," he said. His eyes had red all around them and he looked like he hadn't showered in a while. But Uncle Nate always looked a little weird in some way or another. Some days he had his shirt inside out, others he was wearing two different shoes. I thought it was funny. He told me it was because his brain was so busy working on more important stuff, he didn't have time to think about whether his clothes were put on right. I thought that was a good answer. Plus, he slipped me good stuff like candy and ten-dollar bills. He told me to start a stash somewhere no one could find my money. He said I'd thank him later and gave me a wink like I'd know what "later" was when it came.

I opened my mouth again, but Jenny and Uncle Nate both shook their heads, and Jenny reached for something on the table next to her. She turned around with a pad and a pencil and handed it to me.

I took it from her and brought it up, writing one word:

MAMA?

Jenny's eyes moved away from that word, and Uncle Nate looked down at his feet. Right in that moment, the whole accident came screaming back into my brain—pictures and words pounding through my mind so that I slammed my head back on the pillow and clamped my teeth together.

I opened my mouth and screamed and screamed and screamed, but the room remained silent.

CHAPTER SEVEN

BREE

On Saturday as I was clocking out at the diner, a number came up on my phone that I didn't recognize.

"Hello," I answered.

"Hey, Bree? This is Melanie. We met in the diner last week?"

"Oh, hi!" I said, waving bye to Maggie as I walked toward the door. "Yes, of course, I remember you."

Maggie smiled and waved back.

"Oh, good!" she said. "Well, I hope I didn't catch you at a bad time, but me and Liza are going out tonight, and we wanted to see if you'd like to join us."

I stepped outside into the muggy afternoon sunshine and started walking toward my car. I remembered my thoughts about trying to be a normal girl again, do normal girl stuff. "Um, well, yeah, okay, that sounds good. Sure, I'd love to."

"Okay, great! We'll pick you up. Nine okay?"

"Yeah, that's good. I'll be ready." I gave her my address and she knew right where it was, and so we said goodbye and hung up.

Just as I was putting my key in the lock, I noticed a group of boys about ten or twelve years old on the other side of the street, laughing uproariously. The bigger of the boys was pushing a smaller kid who was wearing glasses and had an armful of books. As the big kid gave the smaller boy a particularly hard shove, the boy lurched forward, his books scattering on the sidewalk. The other boys laughed some more and walked off, one of them calling behind him, "Nice one, freak!" Even from across the street, I could see the embarrassment that washed over the small boy's face right before he squatted down to pick up his books.

Little jerks. God, I hated bullies.

I headed across the street to help the boy.

When I got there, he looked up at me cautiously, his chin quivering slightly. I noticed he had a light scar where he must have had surgery to fix a cleft palate. "Hey," I said, smiling a small smile at him and bending down to help him pick up the books. "You okay?"

"Yeah," he said quietly, his eyes darting to me and then away as his cheeks colored.

"You're a reader, huh?" I asked, tilting my head toward the books.

He nodded, still looking shy.

I looked at the title in my hand. "Harry Potter...hmm. This is a good one. Do you know why I like this one so much?"

His eyes found mine and he shook his head no, but didn't look away.

"Because it's about an underdog who no one at all believed in—this funny-looking kid in glasses who lived under his aunt and uncle's stairs. But guess what? He ends up doing some pretty cool stuff despite everything he has going against him. There's nothing better than watching someone no one expects to win come out ahead, don't you think?"

The little boy's eyes grew wide, and he nodded his head.

I stood up and so did he. As I handed him the books I had collected, I said, "Keep up the reading. Girls love it." I winked at him and his face broke into a huge grin, beaming at me. I smiled back and turned to walk away, when I noticed Archer Hale standing in a doorway just a few stores down, watching us, an intense, unreadable expression on his face. I smiled at him, tilting my head, and something seemed to pass between us again. I blinked and Archer looked away, turning to walk down the street. He looked back at me once as he moved away, but when I caught his eye, he immediately turned again and kept walking.

I stood there for a couple of seconds, watching Archer walk in one direction, and then turned my head to see the little boy walking in the opposite direction. I huffed out a breath and turned around and walked back across the street to my car.

I stopped at the local nursery on the way out of downtown and picked up some flowers and soil and a couple of plastic planters.

When I got home, I changed into shorts and a T-shirt and spent a couple of hours repotting the flowers, placing them on my porch, and doing a general yard cleanup, including weeding, and sweeping off the front steps. One of them was loose and getting looser, but I was a disaster when it came to home improvement projects. I'd have to call George Connick.

When I stood back to admire all my work, I couldn't help smiling at my little cottage. It was adorable.

I went inside and took a long shower, scrubbing the dirt from under my nails and shaving everywhere. Then I turned on the small radio that was in the cottage, and listened to a local music station while I took some extra time doing my hair, drying it, and curling it with a curling iron so that it was long and wavy. I put on my makeup carefully and then lotioned up my legs so that they would look nice in my stretch knit, dark silver dress with the scoop

back. It was casual yet sexy, and I hoped it would work for where
we were going tonight. I made it even slightly more casual with
my slip-on black sandals.

The last time I had worn this dress was a graduation party my
dorm threw. I had drunk my fair share of keg beer, laughed with
the other girls on my floor, and made out with a guy I had always
thought was cute but hadn't spoken to until that night. He wasn't
a very good kisser, but I was just drunk enough not to care.

As I stood there remembering, thinking about the girl I was,
I *missed* her. I missed my old self. I hadn't been a girl unmarked
by tragedy. I wasn't naïve to the ways of the world. I knew you
weren't guaranteed anything and that life wasn't always fair. But
my father and I had survived the tragedy of my mother's illness together, and we were strong. I had never once considered that he
would be snatched from me in an instant, in a senseless moment
that left me alone and reeling. And that I wouldn't get to say goodbye.

Perhaps this road trip I was on wasn't the answer I had hoped it
was. It hadn't really been a conscious choice, though.

Everything in Ohio had reminded me of my dad, my grief, my
fear, and my loneliness. Several numb months after that night, I
had packed a small suitcase, put Phoebe in her dog carrier, got in
my car, and drove off. It felt like the only option. The sadness was
suffocating, claustrophobic. I needed to escape.

I forced myself to snap out of it before I sunk too far down into
fear and melancholy. It was Saturday night, the weekend. And on
the weekend, normal girls went out with their girlfriends and had
some fun. I deserved a little bit of that, didn't I...didn't I?

Melanie and Liza pulled up in front of my cottage a few minutes after nine, and when I saw their headlights, I went outside,
locking up behind me.

The door to the small Honda swung open and Justin Timberlake blared out, breaking the silence of the night.

I grinned as I pulled the back door open and got in to Melanie and Liza saying warmly, "Hey!"

"You look hot!" Liza offered, looking back over her shoulder as Melanie pulled away.

"Thanks." I smiled. "You, too!" They were both wearing skirts and tank tops, and I felt relieved that I had chosen a similar outfit.

As we drove the thirty minutes to the other side of the lake, we chatted casually about my job at the diner and how I liked Pelion so far, and Melanie and Liza told me a little bit about their summer lifeguarding.

We pulled up in front of a bar called the Bitter End Lakeside Saloon, a small wooden structure by the side of the road with a parking lot out front. As we got out of Melanie's car, I could see that the front was decorated with fishing poles, oars, boating signs, tackle boxes, and other things lake related.

We walked inside to the smell of beer and popcorn, the sounds of laughter, loud talk, and pool balls hitting each other. The bar looked a lot bigger on the inside than the outside had indicated. It felt simultaneously dive-like and trendy, with more fishing items and signs adorning the walls.

We showed our IDs to the bouncer and took a seat at a table by the bar. By the time we got our first round of drinks, there was already a line forming at the door.

We spent the first twenty minutes or so laughing and chatting. Melanie and Liza were scoping out the guys they thought were cute and trying not to make it obvious. Melanie noticed someone almost immediately and went about the business of catching his eye. It worked and, after a few minutes, he came over and asked her to dance.

She followed him away from our table, looking back and winking as Liza and I shook our heads, laughing. We signaled the waitress for another round. I was already having fun.

As I tipped back my beer, a man just walking in caught my eye. His head was turned, but I could see his broad shoulders and long, muscular legs encased in a pair of well-worn jeans. *Oh, wow.* Just the sheer size of him, his build, and his wavy brown hair made me blink and train my eyes his way as he began to turn. He turned toward me, laughing at something the guy next to him said, and our eyes met. Travis Hale. His eyes flared slightly, and his smile grew larger as he made a beeline for our table.

Two girls trailing along behind him stopped and looked dejected when they saw where he was headed. They turned to the group behind them.

"Bree Prescott," he said, his eyes lowering to my breasts for a flash before returning to my face.

"Travis Hale," I answered, smiling and taking another pull on my beer.

He grinned at me. "I didn't know you'd be here tonight." He glanced over at Liza and said simply, "Liza." She took a sip of her drink and said, "Hey, Trav."

Liza stood up and said, "I'm gonna go to the ladies' room. I'll be back."

"Oh, okay, do you want me to go with you?" I asked, starting to stand.

Travis put his hand on my arm. "I'm sure she can manage."

"I'm good," Liza said, her eyes lingering on Travis's hand on my arm. "I'll be back in a few." And with that, she turned and walked off.

Travis looked back at me. "So I thought *I* was the one who was supposed to give you the welcome tour."

I laughed and then shrugged, looking up at him through my lashes.

He grinned again. He had a really nice grin. Somewhat predatory, I supposed, but was that a bad thing? I guess it depended. But I had two drinks in me, and so, for right then, it felt good.

Travis leaned in. "So, Bree, this road trip you're on…when's it going to end?"

I considered his question. "I don't really have a specific plan, Travis. I suppose I'll turn around and go home eventually." I took a drink of my beer.

He nodded. "Think you'll stick around here for a while?"

"Depends," I said, frowning slightly.

"On what?"

"On if I keep feeling safe here," I blurted out. I didn't necessarily mean to say it, but the beer was hitting my empty stomach and my bloodstream like a truth serum.

I sighed and peeled up the edge of the label on my beer bottle, suddenly feeling exposed.

Travis studied me for a couple of beats and then smiled a slow grin. "Well, that's good then, because as it turns out, safety is my specialty."

I raised my eyes to his face and couldn't help laughing at his cocky expression. "Oh, I have a feeling that you're anything but safe, Officer Hale."

He faked hurt and slid his body into the seat that Liza had vacated a few minutes before. "Well, that hurts me deeply, Bree. Why would you say that?"

I laughed. "Well, for one"—I leaned forward—"if those blondes who came in with you could shoot poison arrows with their eyes, I would have been dead about fifteen minutes ago. And the redhead to my left, she hasn't taken her eyes off you for one second since you got here. I even think I saw her wipe a little drool off her lip. I have a feeling they all have plans for you tonight." I raised one eyebrow.

He kept his eyes trained on me, not glancing at any of them. He leaned back, cocking his head and bringing one arm over the back of his chair. "I can't help the ideas other people get in their heads. And anyway, what if my plans are different? What if my plans involve you?" He smiled lazily.

God, this guy was good. All cool charm and self-confidence. But it felt good to harmlessly flirt with someone—I was glad I hadn't completely forgotten how.

I smiled back at him and took a sip of my beer, keeping my eyes on him.

His eyes narrowed in on my lips around the neck of the bottle and flared slightly.

"Do you play pool?" I asked after a minute, changing the subject.

"I do anything you want me to do," he said easily.

I laughed. "Okay then, impress me with your geometry skills," I said, starting to stand up.

"Absolutely," he replied, taking my hand.

We moved over to the pool tables, and Travis ordered us another round as we waited for our turn. After a little while, Melanie and Liza and the guys Melanie had met all came over, too, and we spent the rest of the night laughing and playing pool. Travis was way too good at pool and won every game easily, clearly taking pleasure in showing off his skills.

Liza had switched to water early on so she could drive us home, and I did as well close to midnight. I didn't want the next day, which was my day off, to be spent recovering in bed.

When the lights flashed, indicating the bar would be closing,

Travis pulled me into his body and said, "God, Bree, you're the most beautiful girl I've ever seen." His voice was like silk. "Let me take you out to dinner this week."

The drinks I had had earlier were wearing off, and I suddenly felt slightly uncomfortable by Travis's smooth moves and forward flirting. "Um…," I hedged.

Liza interrupted us suddenly saying, "Ready, Bree?" and Travis gave her an annoyed look.

"Everyone has to eat," Travis offered, looking back at me and smiling charmingly. I laughed and hesitantly wrote my number down on a napkin for Travis, making a mental note to buy more minutes. I had forgotten my cell phone back in Cincinnati when I left and had picked up one of those toss-away cell phones. It worked for me, but I just kept forgetting to keep it stocked with minutes.

I said good night to everyone, and Liza, Melanie, and I left, laughing all the way to the car.

Once we got on the road, Melanie said, "Travis Hale, Bree? Geez, you went straight to the Pelion dating big leagues, didn't you? Hell, the state of Maine big leagues."

I laughed. "Is that what Travis Hale is considered?"

"Well, yeah. I mean, he gets around, but I don't blame him. Girls usually throw themselves at him, trying to pin him down. Maybe you'll be the one that finally does it." She winked back at me, and Liza laughed.

"Have you girls…?"

"Oh, no, no," they both said simultaneously. Then Liza continued. "Too many of our friends hooked up with him and then thought they were in love. We've seen the destruction he leaves in his wake. Just be careful."

I smiled, but didn't say anything. Careful was my middle name these days. However, despite the fact that Travis's flirting had made me feel slightly uncomfortable at the end of the night, I was proud of myself for taking a few steps in that direction at all. And I'd had a fun time.

We chatted a little more about the other guys they had met, and before I knew it, we were pulling up in front of my cottage.

I climbed out, whispering, "Bye! Thank you so much!" not wanting to wake any of the neighbors.

"We'll call you!" they said in unison, waving back and then driving away.

I washed my face and brushed my teeth and that night, I went to bed smiling, thinking, *hoping*, maybe I'd *wake* up smiling, too.

CHAPTER EIGHT

BREE

I woke up gasping. Before I could even sit up, I was catapulted straight into the mother of all flashbacks. It had the strength and vividness of the ones I had had directly following my father's murder—complete with my dad lying in a pool of blood, his lifeless eyes staring up at the ceiling. I gripped the bedsheets and rode it out, that same loud screeching sound filling my brain until reality finally took hold and the world around me cleared.

A few minutes later, I leaned over the toilet, tears swimming in my eyes. "Why?" I moaned, full of self-pity, full of the pain and grief the memories brought.

I pulled myself up and shakily got into the shower, refusing to spend the rest of the day in bed like I wanted to now, like I had done for months after that night.

The flashback sure had killed the happy buzz I had going on last night.

I took a quick shower and pulled on my suit, shorts, and tank. For some reason, spending time down at the little lake beach out on Briar Road filled me with a particular sense of contentment. Yes, I had had that dream about my dad there, but despite the sadness of missing him, and the dream bringing that up, I had woken from it with a feeling of hope. I liked it there.

I set out on my bike, Phoebe riding in the basket in front. The morning was bright and already getting hot. It was the end of August; I had no idea when the weather started to turn in Maine, but for now, it still felt like summer.

I turned onto Briar Road, letting my bike coast as I brought both legs out to the side. I took my hands off of the handlebars for a few seconds and let my bike steer itself, bumping over the small stones on the dirt road and laughing out loud. Phoebe barked several times as if to say, *Be careful, daredevil.*

"I know, precious cargo. I won't wreck us, Phoebs."

When I got to the lake, I laid my towel and cooler down in my usual spot and waded into the cool water, Phoebe watching me from the shore. The water felt delicious, lapping gently against my thighs as I waded farther out. Finally, I immersed myself completely and began swimming, the water flowing against my body like a cool caress.

As I turned around and headed back, I heard an animal, a large dog most likely, I thought, howling as if it was in great distress. Phoebe started yapping excitedly, running back and forth along the beach. I pulled my body out of the water completely and stopped to listen, the howling continuing to my left, in the direction of Archer Hale's property.

I wondered if his acreage possibly extended all the way to this small beach? I guessed it very well could. I walked over to the edge of the woods, and when I pushed some brambles aside and squinted in through the trees, I couldn't make anything out other than more trees. But about a hundred feet in, I saw a whole bunch of blackberry bushes. I sucked in a breath, excitement filling me. My dad had made this insanely good blackberry cobbler. If only he could see this bounty right in front of me. I started toward the crop of bushes, but when a branch caught my bare tummy, I hissed in a breath and retreated. I wasn't dressed for blackberry picking. That would have to be for another day.

I returned to my towel, dried off, and then sat back down. I spent several hours there, reading and lying in the sun, before Phoebe and I headed for home. As usual, I paused briefly in front of Archer's gate, wondering again at what those faded spots on his fence had once said.

"Stalker much, Bree?" I whispered to myself. As I was pedaling away, I heard the same distressed dog howling. I hoped whatever that was, Archer had a handle on it.

* * *

I went home and changed and then drove downtown to stop in at the Pelion Public Library. I spent an hour there picking out several new books. Unfortunately, I had left my e-reader back in Cincinnati and so I was back to paperbacks. I didn't realize how much I had missed the smell and feel of an old-fashioned book in my hands. Also, no downloading, no account. I hadn't been on Facebook for over six months, and I didn't miss it.

I dropped the pile of books in my passenger seat and then headed to the grocery store to stock up for the week.

I spent a good amount of time going down every aisle, reading labels and filling up my cart. By the time I was ready to check out, the big windows in front of the register told me it was dusk outside.

"Hi." I smiled at the woman behind the register.

"Hey," she said, snapping her gum. "Any coupons?"

"Oh, no," I said, shaking my head. "Never could get the hang of that. Whenever I tried, I always ended up with twelve boxes of something I didn't even eat and laundry soap that left big clumps of…" I trailed off when I realized the girl in front of me was ringing my order up with one hand and texting on her phone lying on the cash register with the other. She wasn't listening to a word I was saying. Okay, fine.

"Sixty-two eighty-seven," she said, popping her gum again.

I pulled the money out of my wallet. Sixty dollars even. *Shit.*

"Oh gosh," I said, my cheeks heating, "I'm so sorry, I thought I was paying attention. I only have sixty. I have to put something back."

She sighed heavily and rolled her eyes. "What do you want to put back?"

"Uh"—I started digging through my already-packed bags— "how about this? I don't really need this." I handed her the new sponge I had bought, just to replace the old one at my cottage.

"That's only sixty-four cents," she said.

I blinked and someone in line behind me grumbled. "Oh, um, well, let's see…" I dug around a little more. "Oh! How about these? I don't really need these." I handed her the new package of razors I had gotten. She reached for them and I pulled them back. "Wait, actually, I kind of do need these. Half-Polish and all." I laughed nervously. Clerk girl did not laugh. "Um…" I stuck my head back in my bags, noting more grumbling behind me.

"Uh, thanks," I heard the clerk say, and when I looked up at her confused face, she said slowly, "He's got you," indicating her head to her right. Confused, I leaned forward and looked past the bitter-faced old man standing right next to me to see Archer Hale standing behind him, his eyes homed in on me. He was wearing a sweatshirt with the hood up even though it was hardly chilly.

I smiled, tilting my head slightly. The clerk cleared her throat, getting my attention. I took my receipt out of her hand and moved forward to stand at the end of the counter.

"Thank you so much, Archer," I said.

Archer kept his eyes focused on me. The clerk and the old man looked from me back to Archer, twin expressions of confusion on their faces.

"I'll pay you back, of course." I smiled again, but he didn't. I shook my head slightly, looking around, noting that people at the registers to my right and left were watching us now.

The old man paid for his couple items and moved past me after a minute, and Archer set a large bag of dog food down on the conveyor belt.

"Oh!" I said. "I was down at the lake today and I thought I heard a dog howling from your property. It sounded like one was in pain." He glanced at me, handing some bills over to the clerk. I looked around again, noting all the eyes still on us. Archer Hale didn't appear to be aware of them at all.

I huffed out a breath and signed to Archer, *These people sure are nosy, aren't they?*

Lip quirk. Blink. Gone.

He took his purchases and walked past me. I turned and wheeled my cart behind him, feeling dumb and self-conscious again. I shook my head to myself and headed toward my car. I took one last glance in Archer's direction and saw that he was looking back at me as well.

My mouth fell open when he raised his hand and signed, *Good night, Bree.* He turned back around, and seconds later he was gone. I leaned back against my car and grinned like a fool.

CHAPTER NINE

Archer—Fourteen Years Old

I walked through the woods, stepping over the spots I knew would twist my ankle, around the particular branches that would seemingly reach out and grab me if I got too close. I knew this land by heart. I hadn't left it in seven years now.

Irena meandered to the right of me, keeping my pace, but exploring the things a dog's nose found interesting. I snapped my fingers or clapped my hands together if I needed to call her to catch up to me. She was an old dog, though, and responded to me only half the time—whether it was because she was hard of hearing, or just stubborn, I wasn't sure.

I found the net trap I had helped Uncle Nate install a couple of days before and began working to take it down. I could appreciate that this kind of thing helped quiet whatever voices Uncle Nate seemed to hear in his head, and I could even appreciate the fact that these types of projects kept me busy, but what I couldn't stand was hearing small animals get caught in them in the middle of the night. And so I went around the property disassembling what we had assembled only days before, and looking for the ones Nate had done on his own.

Just as I was finishing up, I heard voices, laughter, and splashing water coming from the lake. I set down the things I had gathered up in my arms and tentatively walked toward the sounds of the people I heard playing on the shore.

As soon as I came to the edge of the trees, I spotted her. Amber Dalton. It felt like I groaned, but of course, no sound came out. She was in a black bikini, and she was coming out of the lake, soaking wet. I felt myself stiffen in my pants. Great. That seemed to happen all the damn time now, but somehow, it happening in response to Amber made me feel weird, ashamed.

Despite being mortified about the whole issue, I had tried to ask Uncle Nate about it last year when I turned thirteen, but he just threw some magazines at me that had naked women in them, and went off into the woods to set up more traps. The magazines didn't exactly explain a whole lot, but I liked looking at them. I probably spent too much time looking at them. And then I'd slide my hand into my pants and stroke myself until I sighed out in release. I didn't know if it was right or wrong, but it felt too good to stop.

I was staring so hard at Amber, watching her laugh and wring out her wet hair, that I didn't see *him* arrive. Suddenly, a loud, male voice said, "Look at *that*! There's some kind of freaky Peeping Tom in the woods! Why don't you say something, Peeping Tom? Have anything to *say*?" And then he muttered under his breath, but just loud enough for me to hear, "Fucking freak."

Travis. My cousin. The last time I'd seen him was right after I'd lost my voice. I had still been bedridden at Uncle Nate's when Travis and his mom, Aunt Tori, came to visit me. I knew she was there to see if I would say anything about what I'd found out that day. I wouldn't. It didn't matter anyway.

Travis had cheated at a Go Fish game and then whined to his mom that I was the one who was dishonest. I was too tired and was hurting too much, in every way, to care. I had turned my head to the wall and pretended to sleep until they left.

And now, there he was on the beach with Amber Dalton. Hot shame filled my face at his mocking words. All eyes turned to me as I stood there, exposed and humiliated. I brought my hand up to my scar, covering it. I wasn't sure why, I just did. I didn't want them to see it—the proof that I was guilty and damaged—*ugly*.

Amber looked down at the ground, seeming embarrassed herself, but then glanced up a second later at Travis and said, "Come on, Trav, don't be *mean*. He's disabled. He can't even *talk*." The last sentence was practically whispered, as if what she was saying was some kind of secret. A few eyes looked at me with pity, skittering away when my own met theirs, and others glittered with excitement, watching to see what was going to happen next.

My entire face throbbed with humiliation as everyone continued to stare at me. I felt frozen to the spot. Blood was making a whooshing sound in my ears, and I felt light-headed.

Finally, Travis moved over to Amber and wrapped his hands around her waist, pulling her into him and kissing her wetly on the mouth. She seemed stiff, uncomfortable as he ground his face into hers, his eyes open, trained on me, standing behind her.

That was the catalyst that finally got my feet moving. I spun around, tripping over a small rock right behind me and sprawling on the ground. Pebbles under the pine needles dug into my hands, and a branch scraped my cheek as I went down. Loud laughter exploded behind me and I scurried up, practically running back to the safety of my house. I was shaking with shame and anger and something that felt like grief. Although what I was grieving for in that moment, I wasn't exactly sure.

I *was* a freak. I was out here alone and isolated for a reason—I was to blame for so much tragedy, so much pain.

I was worthless.

I stomped through the woods, and when tears sprang to my eyes, I let out a silent yell and picked up a rock and threw it at Irena, who had never left my side since the people on the beach started making fun of me.

Irena yelped and hopped to the side as the small rock struck her hind flank, and then immediately moved back next to me.

For some reason, that dumb dog returning to my side after I'd been cruel to her was the thing that made the tears start flowing relentlessly down my cheeks. My chest heaved, and I swiped at the wetness falling from my eyes.

I fell to the ground and brought Irena into my arms, hugging her to me, petting her fur and saying, *I'm sorry, I'm sorry, I'm sorry*, over and over in my head, hoping dogs had mind-reading power. It was all I had to offer her. I rested my cheek on her fur and hoped she'd forgive me.

After a little while, my breathing started slowing and my tears dried up. Irena continued to nuzzle my face, letting out small whines when I hesitated between pets.

I heard pine needles crunching behind me under the weight of someone's feet and knew it was Uncle Nate. I kept looking straight ahead as he sat down next to me, bringing his knees up, like mine.

For several long minutes, we both sat like that, not saying anything, just staring ahead, Irena's panting and occasional soft whines the only sounds among us.

Finally, Uncle Nate reached over and took my hand in his, squeezing it. His hand felt rough, dry, but it was warm and I needed the contact.

"They don't know who you are, Archer. They have no idea. And they don't deserve to know. Don't let their judgment hurt you."

I took in his words, turning them over in my mind. I had to guess he'd seen that exchange somehow. His words didn't make complete sense to me—Uncle Nate's words usually didn't—but somehow they comforted me anyway. He always seemed to be right on the border of something profound, but just falling short of anyone else but him understanding the depth of his own thought. I nodded to him without turning my head.

We sat there for a while longer, and then we got up and went inside for dinner and to bandage up my cut cheek.

The laughter and splashing in the distance grew fainter and fainter until it finally faded completely away.

CHAPTER TEN

BREE

A few days after Archer Hale waved to me in the grocery store parking lot, I worked the early shift at the diner, and when I got home that afternoon, I saw Anne sitting on her front porch. I walked over and greeted her and she smiled, saying, "Iced tea, dear?"

I unlatched her gate and walked through it and up her steps. "That sounds great. If you can stand the smell of me—eau de griddle and bacon fat."

She laughed. "I think I can manage. How was your shift?"

I collapsed on her porch swing, leaning back and shifting my body toward the small fan she had running next to her. I sighed with comfort.

"Good," I answered. "I like the job."

"Oh, that's wonderful," she said, handing me the glass of tea she had just poured. I took a grateful sip and then leaned back again.

"I saw you being picked up by the Scholl girls the other night, and I was so happy to see you've met some friends. I hope you don't mind having such a nosy neighbor." She smiled kindly and I smiled back at her.

"No, not at all. Yes, I went over to the other side of the lake with them. We ran into Travis Hale and hung out with him at the Bitter End."

"Oh, you've been meeting all the Hale boys."

I laughed. "Yes, are there more?"

She smiled. "No, just Archer and Travis among the younger generation. Suppose Travis is really the only chance of another Hale generation now."

"Why do you say that?"

"Well, I don't see Archer Hale coming off his property to date, much less marry someone, but again, I don't know a lot about him other than that he doesn't speak."

"He does speak," I said. "I've talked to him."

Anne looked surprised and tilted her head slightly. "Well, I had no idea. I've never heard him say a word."

I shook my head. "He signs," I said. "And so do I. My dad was deaf."

"Oh, I see. Well, I never even thought of that. I guess he presents himself as someone who doesn't want much to do with anyone else, at least the few times I've seen him in town." She frowned slightly.

"I don't think anyone has ever really tried," I said, shrugging. "There's nothing wrong with him, though, except maybe his people skills, and that he can't speak out loud," I said, looking over her shoulder, picturing Archer. "And a few fashion issues." I grinned.

She smiled back. "Yes, he does have an interesting look to him, doesn't he? Of course, I imagine if you cleaned him up, he'd look more than presentable. He comes from a long line of lookers. Actually, all the Hale boys were so good-looking, they were practically inhuman." She laughed girlishly and I grinned at her again.

I took a long drink of tea and tilted my head to the side. "You don't remember exactly what happened with the other two brothers the day of Archer's accident?"

She shook her head. "No, only what I heard in town. I don't know what happened between them to cause all that tragedy. I try to remember them as they were—how every girl in a hundred-mile radius swooned over them. Course those boys took advantage of that, even Connor, who was the least rowdy of the three. But as far as I remember, the only girl any of them ever took a real interest in was Alyssa McRae."

"All *three* of them?" I asked, my eyes widening. *This* sounded like a story.

"Hmm," she said, looking off into the distance. "It was a right soap opera around here with them, mostly between Connor and Marcus Hale. Those two boys were always competing over something. If it wasn't sports, it was girls, and when Alyssa came to town, there was only one girl they competed over. Nathan Hale didn't make any bones about the fact that he was interested, too, but the other two didn't pay too much mind to him, I suppose. Like I said before, he was always a little different."

"Who finally won her?" I whispered.

Anne blinked and looked at me, smiling. "Marcus Hale. She married him—shotgun wedding we called it back then. She was in the family way. But she lost that baby and it wasn't until years later that she got pregnant again, with Archer." She shook her head. "After she married Marcus, that girl always looked sad, and so did Connor Hale. I suspected they both felt she made the wrong choice. Of course, with all the drinking and womanizing Marcus Hale still did, even after he and Alyssa got married, the whole town pretty much knew she made the wrong choice."

"And then Connor Hale became the chief of police?"

"Yes, yes he did. Got married, too, trying to move on as well, I suppose. And he had Travis."

"Wow. And then it all ended in so much tragedy."

"Yes, yes...very sad." She looked at me. "But, dear, you being able to speak to Archer, well, I think that's wonderful." She shook her head slightly. "Makes me realize how little we all did for that boy." She looked sorrowful and lost in thought.

We both sat quietly for a couple of minutes, sipping our tea before I said, "I better go shower and change. I'm going to bike down to the lake again today."

"Oh good. I'm so glad the bike is working out for you. Get as much lake time in as you can. The weather will be turning soon."

I smiled, standing. "I will. Thank you, Anne. And thank you for the chat."

"Thank you, dear. You bring a smile to an old woman's face."

I grinned at her and waved as I walked down her steps and through her gate.

* * *

An hour later, I was biking down Briar Road, my basket holding a water bottle, my towel, and my sweet, naughty little dog.

As I rode past Archer's house, I slowed my bike, dragging my feet in the dust. His gate was open slightly. I stared at it, stopping completely. I hadn't seen a mail truck driving back down the road. Had Archer left it open himself? I tilted my head, considering the situation. I brought one finger up and tapped my lips, thinking. Would it be totally uncool to go onto his property uninvited again? Or had he left the gate open slightly *as* an invitation? Was that completely ludicrous for me to even think? Probably.

I wheeled my bike forward and leaned it against the high fence, picking Phoebe up and peeking my head inside the open gate, intending to have just a quick look. Archer was walking away, toward his house, but when he heard the squeak of his gate, he turned, his eyes on me, no surprise in them.

I stepped inside. *Hi*, I said, putting Phoebe down and signing. *I'm really hoping that your open gate meant you were okay with me coming in, and that I didn't just trespass again. That would be embarrassing.* I grimaced, bringing my hands to my cheeks and holding my breath for his answer.

His deep, amber eyes watched me for a few seconds as color moved up my face, and something gentled in his expression.

He was wearing a pair of jeans that looked like they were about to disintegrate, they had so many holes in them, a fitted white T-shirt—*too fitted*—and bare feet.

I wanted to show you something, he said.

I let out my breath and couldn't help the smile that spread over my face. But then I cocked my head to the side, confused. *You knew I was coming?*

He shook his head slowly. *I thought you might. I see the bike tracks.*

My face flushed again. "Oh," I breathed out, not signing. "Um…"

Do you want to see, or not?

I just looked at him for a second and then nodded. *Okay. Wait, where's your ax?*

He raised one eyebrow, studying me for a couple of beats. *Is that you being funny?*

I laughed, feeling delight in the fact that he had brought up our last conversation. *Touché.* I grinned. *What do you want to show me?*

They're right over here.

They? I asked, walking forward with him, down the driveway, through the trees.

He nodded, but didn't expound.

Phoebe saw a bird take flight across the lawn and went running after it as fast as her short legs could carry her.

We reached his little house and took a few steps down the tiny front porch, only big enough for the white rocker and small storage box it held.

He moved the rocker aside and I gasped.

Oh my God! I said, sucking in a breath and moving forward.

That sound you said you heard a few days ago? That was Kitty here, giving birth.

I grinned as I looked down at the sleeping mama dog, three tiny brown puppies rooting lazily at her belly, clearly having just eaten and falling into a milk coma. But then my brows furrowed when I processed what he had just said and I looked over at him. *Your dog is named Kitty?*

He moved his hair out of his face slightly, looking at me. *Long story. My uncle confided in me that the animals on our property are spies who worked for him, and he named them accordingly. Her full name is Kitty Storms. She was trained by the Russian foreign intelligence agency. She works for me now.*

Uh-oh, this wasn't good. *I see,* I said. *And you believe this?* I eyed him cautiously.

Well, her operations are mostly kept to squirrel tracking and apparently—he gestured to where she slept with the puppies—*covert meetings with fertile male subjects.* Something that looked like it might be amusement danced in his eyes.

I breathed out a laugh and then shook my head. *So, your uncle was a little…*

Paranoid, he said. *But harmless. He was a good guy.* I thought I saw a brief flash of pain wash over his features before he turned his head to the puppies again.

I touched Archer's arm and he jolted and turned to me. *I heard your uncle passed away a few years ago. I'm sorry.*

He looked down at me, his eyes sweeping over my face. He nodded, barely perceptibly, and turned back to the puppies once again.

I studied his profile for a few seconds, noting how nice it was, at least what I could see of it. Then I bent down to get a closer look at the puppies.

I grinned back up at Archer, who squatted down next to me. *Can I hold one?* I asked.

He nodded.

Are they boys or girls?

Two boys, one girl.

I scooped up one little warm, soft body and brought it to my chest, cradling its sleeping weight and nuzzling my nose into the soft fur. The puppy mewled and started rooting at my cheek, its wet nose making me giggle.

I looked at Archer, who was watching me closely, a small smile on his lips. It was the first one I had gotten, and it startled me slightly. I stared at him, our eyes meeting and tangling just like the first time we had met. I felt confused as everything inside me sped up. I stared at him, rubbing my cheek absently against the velvety softness of the puppy's fat belly.

After a minute, I put the puppy down so I could sign, *Thank you for showing them to—*

He reached out and stopped my hands, looking into my eyes. I looked at him questioningly and then moved my eyes down to his large hand resting on mine. He had beautiful hands, powerful, but elegant at the same time. I looked back up at him.

He brought both hands up and said, *You can speak the old-fashioned way. I can hear you, remember?*

I blinked at him and after a few seconds brought my hands up. *If it's okay with you, I'd like to speak your language.* I smiled a small smile.

He stared at me, an unreadable expression in his eyes before he stood up.

I have to get back to work, he said.

Work? I asked.

He nodded at me, but chose not to elaborate. Well, okay then. *Then I guess I should go?*

He just looked at me.

Can I come back? I asked. *To see the puppies?*

He frowned at me for a second, but then nodded yes.

I breathed out. *Okay. If your gate is open, I'll know it's okay to come in.*

He nodded again, a smaller nod this time, barely noticeable.

We stared at each other for a few more seconds before I smiled and turned around and walked back up his driveway. I called to Phoebe, who came running this time, and scooped her up. I turned around at his gate, and he was still standing in the same place, watching me. I waved a small wave and closed his gate behind me.

CHAPTER ELEVEN

BREE

The next day, I walked down Archer's driveway hesitantly, biting my lip. I heard what sounded like rock hitting rock somewhere on the back side of his house. As I rounded the corner, I spied Archer, shirtless, on his hands and knees laying stones for what looked like the beginning of a side patio.

"Hi," I said softly, and his head snapped up. He looked slightly surprised, but...pleased? Maybe? He certainly wasn't the easiest person to read, especially since I couldn't see all of his features clearly under his beard and the hair that fell over his forehead and around his jaw.

He nodded and raised his hand, indicating a big rock that was sitting to the right of his project, and went back to his work.

I had left the diner at two and then had gone home and taken a quick shower, gotten on my bike, and ridden out to Archer's. I had left Phoebe with Anne because I wasn't sure if other dogs should be around the puppies yet or not.

When I had arrived at Archer's gate, I wasn't able to help the smile that overtook my face when I saw that it was very slightly open.

I made my way over to the rock he had just indicated and sat on the edge of it, watching him quietly for a minute.

Apparently he was a stonemason in his free time? It must have been him who had laid the long driveway and patio in front of his house. The guy was full of surprises, one after the other. I couldn't help but notice the way his biceps flexed and strained as he lifted each stone and set it in its place. No wonder the guy was so cut. All he did was work.

"Okay, so I made a list," I said, eyeing him and scooting my butt higher on the large rock, making myself more comfortable.

Archer looked up at me, raising his eyebrows.

I was using my voice to speak so that he could continue working without having to watch me.

But he sat up on his knees, putting his gloved hands on his muscular thighs, and looked at me. He was wearing a pair of faded workout shorts, kneepads, and work boots. His naked chest was tan and had a light sheen of sweat on it.

A list? he asked.

I nodded, leaving the small piece of paper on my lap. *Names. For the puppies.*

He cocked his head to the side. *Okay.*

So, I said, *feel free to veto, I mean, them being your dogs and all, but I thought Ivan Granite, Hawk Stravinski, and Oksana Hammer were top choices.*

He stared at me. And then his face did something miraculous. It broke out into a grin.

My breath hitched in my throat and I gaped at him. *You like them?* I finally asked.

Yeah, I like them, he said.

I nodded, a slow grin taking over my face. Well, okay then.

I sat there for just a little while longer, enjoying the summer sunshine and his presence while I watched him work—his strong body moving the stones around, placing them where he wanted them to go.

He glanced up at me a few times and gave me a small, shy smile. We didn't exchange many words after that, but the silence between us was comfortable, companionable.

Finally, I stood up and said, "I have to get going, Archer. My neighbor, Anne, has an appointment and I need to pick up Phoebe."

Archer stood, too, wiping his hands on his thighs and nodding. *Thank you*, he signed.

I smiled and nodded and walked toward his gate. I rode home with a small, happy smile on my face.

* * *

Two days later I drove past Archer's house on my way back from lying on the small lake beach, and his gate was slightly open again. A thrill shot down my spine as I got off my bike. I let myself in and walked down his driveway, carrying Phoebe in my arms.

I knocked on his door, but there was no answer, so I followed the sounds of the dog barks I heard coming from the direction of the lake. When I stepped through the trees, I spotted Archer and Kitty a little ways down the shore. I walked to meet him and when he spotted me, he gave me a small, shy smile and said, *Hi.*

I smiled, squinting at him in the bright sunshine. I placed Phoebe down and said, *Hey.*

We walked along the shore for a little bit in easy silence. The more time we spent together, even not speaking, the more comfortable I felt with him. I could sense he was growing more comfortable with me, too.

Archer picked up a rock off the beach and chucked it at the lake. It skipped across the lake again and again and again, barely eliciting any spray from the still water. I laughed loudly in delighted surprise.

Show me how you just did that!

Archer watched my hands and then looked down at the sandy shore, searching for a stone.

He found one he was happy with and handed it to me. *The flatter, the better*, he said. *Now throw it sort of like a Frisbee, so the flat side of it glances off the surface of the water.*

I nodded and lined up my shot. I threw it and watched as it skated over the surface once and then came up and hit the water again. I whooped and Archer smiled.

He picked up another small stone and chucked it at the lake. It hit the surface and skipped...and skipped...and skipped about twenty times. "Show-off," I muttered.

I looked over at his amused face. *You're good at everything you do, aren't you?* I asked, cocking my head to the side and squinting at him.

He looked thoughtful for a few seconds before signing, *Yes.*

I laughed. He shrugged.

After a minute I asked, *Your uncle homeschooled you?*

He glanced at me. *Yes.*

He must have been smart.

He thought about that for a second. *He was. Mostly with math and anything science related. His mind would wander, but he taught me what I needed to know.*

I nodded, remembering Anne telling me that Nathan Hale was always smart in school. *Before I came out here, I asked about you in town*, I said, feeling slightly shy.

Archer looked over at me and frowned slightly. *Why?*

I tilted my head and considered that. *After the first time we met...something drew me to you.* I bit my lip. *I wanted to know you.* My cheeks heated.

Archer stared at me for a second as if he was trying to figure something out. Then he picked up another flat stone and threw it at the water, making it skip so many times that my eyes lost it before it ever stopped.

I shook my head slowly. *If they only knew.*

He turned fully toward me. *If who only knew what?*

Everyone in town. Some of them think you're not right in the head, you know. I laughed softly. *It's laughable, really.*

He shrugged again and picked up a stick and threw it to Kitty, who was coming toward us on the shore.

Why do you let them think that?

He let out a breath and stared at the lake for a few seconds before turning to me. *Just easier that way.*

I studied him and then sighed. *I don't like it.*

It's been this way for a long time, Bree; it's fine. It works for everyone involved.

I didn't understand it exactly, but I could see the tense lines of his body as we talked about the town, so I backed off, wanting him to feel comfortable with me again.

So, what else can you teach me? I asked teasingly, changing the subject.

He raised an eyebrow and looked into my eyes. My stomach clenched, and a strange swarm of butterflies fluttered underneath my ribs. *What can you teach me?* he asked.

I shook my head slightly, tapping my pointer finger on my lips. *I could probably teach you a thing or two.*

Oh yeah? What? His eyes flared very slightly, but then he looked away.

I swallowed. "Um," I whispered, but then continued in sign so that he would have to look back at me. *I used to be a really good cook.* I wasn't sure why I said it. I didn't really have any intention of cooking for anyone, or teaching anyone to cook. But in that moment, it was the first thing that came to my mind, and I wanted to fill the strange awkwardness that had lapsed between us.

You want to teach me how to cook?

I nodded very slowly. *I mean, if that's not one of the many things you've already mastered.*

He smiled. I still wasn't used to getting them, and this one made my heart speed up just a little bit. They were like a rare gift that he gave out. I snatched it up and stored it somewhere inside of me.

I'd like that, he said after a minute.

I nodded, smiling, and he gifted me with another smile back.

We walked along the lakeshore for another hour, finding rocks and skipping them in the water until I could get mine to skip three times.

When I got home later, I realized I hadn't had such a good day for a really long time.

* * *

The next day, I packed up some sandwiches at the diner, drove home, showered and changed, put Phoebe in the bike basket, and rode out to Archer's again. Despite the fact that I was the one showing up at his house and initiating our time together, I felt like he was putting in effort as well, just by allowing me to visit him.

So, Archer, I said, *if your uncle didn't know sign language, how did you speak to him?*

We were on his lawn, Kitty and the pups lying on a blanket with us, the puppies' fat little bodies waddling around, getting lost in their blindness before their mama nuzzled them back to her.

Phoebe was lying nearby, too. She was mildly curious about the puppies, but didn't pay them much attention.

Archer looked up at me from where he was lying, his head propped up on his hand. He sat up slowly so that he could use his hands.

I didn't do much speaking. He shrugged. *I wrote it down if it was important. Otherwise, I just listened.*

I regarded him silently for a minute, wishing I could see his expression better—but it was hidden under all the ungroomed hair. *How did you learn sign language?* I finally asked quietly.

I taught myself.

I tilted my head, taking a bite of the pastrami sandwich in my hand. Archer had polished off his sandwich in about thirty seconds flat, eating most of it, but sharing pieces of pastrami with Kitty. I put the sandwich down. *How? From a book?*

He nodded. *Yeah.*

Do you have a computer?

He looked up at me, frowning slightly. *No.*

Do you have electricity?

He looked at me with amusement. *Yes, I have electricity, Bree. Doesn't everyone?*

I chose not to enlighten him to the fact that he kind of came off as someone who didn't necessarily have *any* modern conveniences. I tilted my head. *Do you have a television?* I asked after a minute.

He shook his head. *No, I have books.*

I nodded, considering the man in front of me. *And all these projects that you do—stonework, gardening—you just teach them to yourself?*

He shrugged. *Anyone can learn to do anything if they have the time. I have the time.*

I nodded, picking a piece of meat out of the side of my sandwich and chewing it for a second before asking, *How did you get all the stones for the driveway and the patio?*

Some I collected around the lake, some I bought in town at the garden shop.

And how did you get them back here?

I carried them, he said, looking at me like it was a crazy question.

So you don't drive? I asked. *You walk everywhere?*

Yes, he answered, shrugging.

Okay, enough with the twenty questions, he said. *What about you? What are you doing in Pelion?*

I studied him for a second before answering, his golden-brown eyes trained on me, waiting for what I was going to say. *I'm sort of on a road trip*—I started, but then I stopped. *No, you know what? I ran away*, I said. *My dad…passed away and…some other stuff happened that I had a hard time handling, and I freaked out and ran away.* I sighed. *I'm not sure why I just told you that, but that's the truth of it.*

He studied me for a little longer than I was comfortable with, feeling exposed, so I looked away. When I saw his hands move in my peripheral vision, I looked back at him. *Is it working?* he asked.

"Is what working?" I whispered.

Running away, he said. *Is it helping?*

I stared at him. *Mostly, no*, I finally answered.

He nodded, regarding me thoughtfully before looking away.

I was glad he didn't try to come up with something encouraging to say. Sometimes an understanding silence was better than a bunch of meaningless words.

I looked around the immaculate yard, to the small house, compact but well kept. I wanted to ask him how he had the money to live out here, but I didn't think that was polite. He probably lived off of some insurance policy his uncle had left him...or maybe his parents. God, he had had so many losses.

So, Archer, I finally said, moving the conversation in another direction, *that cooking lesson I mentioned...Are you free this Saturday? Your place. Five o'clock?* I raised an eyebrow.

He smiled slightly. *I don't know. I'll have to check with my social secretary.*

I snorted. *You being funny?*

He raised an eyebrow.

Better, I said.

He smiled bigger. *Thank you, I've been working on it.*

I laughed. His eyes twinkled and moved to my mouth. Those butterflies took flight again and we both looked away.

After a little bit, I gathered up my stuff and my little dog, said goodbye to Archer, and started walking up the driveway.

When I got to the gate, I paused, looking back at the small house behind me. It suddenly occurred to me that Archer Hale had taught himself an entire language, but hadn't had a single person to talk to.

Until me.

* * *

The next day, as I was carrying a Reuben with a side of fries to Cal Tremblay and a BLT with a side of potato salad to Stuart Purcell at table three, the bell rang over the door and I looked up to see Travis walking in, wearing his uniform. He smiled big at me and gestured to the counter, asking if I was working it. I smiled and nodded, saying quietly, "Be right there."

I delivered the food in my hands, refilled their waters, and then walked back behind the counter where Travis was now sitting.

"Hey," I greeted him, smiling. "How are you?" I held up the coffeepot and raised my brows questioningly.

"Please," he said to the coffee, and I started pouring. "I've been trying to call you," he said. "Are you avoiding me?"

"Avoiding—oh crap! I ran out of minutes. Damn." I put my palm to my forehead. "Sorry, I have one of those pay-as-you-go phones, and I rarely use it."

He raised his eyebrows. "Isn't there any family back home that you keep in touch with?"

I shook my head. "A few friends, but my dad passed away six months ago and...no, there's really not."

"Jesus, I'm sorry, Bree," he said, concern filling his expression.

I waved it away. I refused to get emotional at work. "It's okay. I'm okay." I was mostly okay, sometimes okay. Better these days.

He studied me for a second. "Well, the reason I was calling you was to see if you'd like to do that dinner we talked about?"

I leaned my hip against the counter and smiled at him. "So you tracked me down when I didn't answer my phone?"

He grinned. "Well, I wouldn't exactly call it a high-level, spy-caliber track-down operation."

I laughed, but his wording reminded me of Archer, and for some strange reason, something like guilt quivered in my gut. What was that about? I had no idea. Our friendship was blossoming, but he was still closed off in many respects. I understood it, I guessed, and it made me so mad that the whole dang town ignored him, when in fact, he was this incredibly smart, gentle man who as far as I could tell had never done anything wrong to anyone. It wasn't fair.

"Hello, earth to Bree," Travis said, snapping me out of my reverie. I had been staring out the window.

I shook my head slightly. "I'm sorry, Travis. I just got caught up in my own thoughts there for a minute. My brain can seriously be a black hole sometimes." I laughed softly, embarrassed. "Anyway, uh, sure, I'll go to dinner with you."

He raised his eyebrows. "Well, try not to sound too excited about it."

I laughed, shaking my head. "No, sorry, I just...just dinner, right?"

He grinned. "I mean, maybe an appetizer...maybe even some dessert..."

I laughed. "Okay."

"Friday night?"

"Yes, okay." I held my finger up to a couple that had just sat down in my section, and they smiled. "I gotta get back to work, but see you Friday?" I scribbled my address down on a piece of paper from my order pad and handed it to him.

"Yeah, how about I pick you up at seven?"

"Perfect." I smiled. "See you then." As I walked around the counter to the table, I could see him leaning back on his stool to check out my ass as I walked away.

CHAPTER TWELVE

BREE

I worked early on Friday and drove home to get ready for my date with Travis.

I took a long, hot shower and spent extra time with my hair and makeup, trying to work up some excitement at just being a girl who was about to be picked up for a date.

What if he kissed me? Nervous flutters started in my belly. Strangely, again, Archer came to my mind, and so did a vague sense of guilt. That was silly—Archer was only my friend. I thought maybe there was a little something between us, though, only what it was, I had no real clue. It was confusing and strange, unknown territory. He had a nice face, from what I could see of it anyway, but was I attracted to him? I furrowed my brow at myself in the mirror, pausing in my eyeliner application. He definitely had a nice body—no, scratch that, an *amazing* body, totally drool-worthy—and I admired it constantly, but attracted? How could you be attracted to someone who was so different from anyone you'd ever been attracted to before? Still, I couldn't deny his charm. When I thought of him, pictured his shy smile and the way his eyes constantly took in every little thing about me, my tummy fluttered. Yes, there was something there—*what*, I couldn't be completely sure.

Travis, on the other hand, was seemingly easy to be attracted to. He had it all—smooth moves and the kind of good looks any girl in her right mind would find appealing. Apparently, I wasn't exactly in my right mind. But maybe giving myself a little push was a good thing, a necessary thing. It'd been over six months now…

I finished up my makeup. I didn't need to overcomplicate this. It was just a date. With a cute guy, a nice guy.

And I didn't need to be so nervous. I wasn't inexperienced—and I wasn't a virgin. I had had three semi-serious boyfriends in college, and I had even thought I might be in love with one of them. It had turned out he was in love with every girl on my dorm floor—or at least in love with getting into their pants behind my back, and that had ended badly. But the point was, I had no need to be nervous about Travis Hale. This was just a date, and only a first date at that. And if I didn't want to see him again, I wouldn't. Simple.

Travis knocked on my door at seven o'clock sharp, gorgeous in a pair of dress pants and a button-down shirt. I had chosen a black wrap dress that hugged the few curves I had and my silver heels. I had left my hair down and curled it very loosely with a curling iron. He looked me over appreciatively and handed me the bouquet of red roses he had in his hand, already in a glass vase.

"You look gorgeous, Bree."

I brought the flowers to my nose, smiling. "Thank you," I said, setting the vase down on the table next to the door and taking his arm as we walked to his large dark silver truck.

He helped me into it and we chatted about how I was settling in to Pelion on the drive to the restaurant.

He brought me to a place called Cassell's Grill on the other side of the lake, which I had already heard was the nicest restaurant around. What I had heard seemed likely enough—it was dim and romantic with a beautiful view of the shoreline out the huge windows that surrounded it.

When we sat down at our table and I remarked how beautiful the restaurant was, Travis said, "Pretty soon we won't have to come across the lake for places like this. We'll have plenty to choose from in Pelion."

I looked up from my menu. "So you like the proposed changes, I take it?"

He nodded. "I do. Not only will it modernize the town, but it will bring in more income for everyone, my family included. I think most people will be happy in the end."

I nodded, wondering at that. From the talk I'd heard here and there in the diner, most people in town weren't thrilled about turning Pelion into another big, modern tourist retreat.

"Plus," he continued, "I'll be taking over the land the town is on soon, so I've been working with my mother on some of the planning."

I looked up at him, surprised. "Oh, I didn't realize."

He had a slightly smug expression on his face. He took a sip of water and said, "The land this town is on has been in my family since the first people of Pelion made it their home. It's always been passed down from firstborn son to firstborn son, once that son is twenty-five. Not this February, but next, I'll be running things."

I nodded. Before I had moved to Pelion, I hadn't even realized that people *owned* whole towns. "I see. Well, that's great, Travis. And the fact that you also followed in your dad's footsteps and became a cop—I admire that a lot."

Travis looked pleased. He wined and dined me, keeping the conversation light and fun. I was having a good time. When we were in the middle of our meal, and he asked me what I had been doing for fun in town other than my night out with Melanie and Liza, I paused, and then said, "Actually, I've been spending some time with Archer."

He choked on his sip of water, bringing his napkin up to his mouth. "Archer? You're joking, right?"

I shook my head, frowning. "No. Did you know he signed?"

"Uh, no," he said. "He wouldn't even look at me the last time I acknowledged him in town."

I studied him. "Hmm, well, he's not the most trusting person. But I think he has a really good reason for that. Maybe you should try a little harder."

He looked at me over the rim of his wineglass before taking a sip. "Maybe. Okay." He paused. "So what do you two do together exactly?"

"Well," I said, "talk mostly. I sign, too—my dad was deaf."

He looked surprised for a second. "Well, that's a coincidence. What does Archer have to say?"

I shrugged. "We talk about a lot of stuff. He's nice, and smart, and…interesting. I like him."

Travis furrowed his brow. "Okay, well, hey, Bree, be careful of him, okay? He's not exactly…stable. I know that for a fact. Trust me." He looked up at me with concern. "I wouldn't want him to do anything to hurt you."

I nodded at him. "I'm not worried about that," I said softly.

I didn't ask about his dad and Archer's dad, even though I knew a little bit about the supposed rivalry between them. For some strange reason, I wanted to hear about it from Archer, not Travis. I wasn't sure exactly why—perhaps it was the fact that Archer and I had formed more of a friendship than Travis and I had as of yet.

In any case, Travis changed the subject after that and moved us back onto lighter ground. After he had paid the bill and we got in his truck, he took my hand across the seats and held it all the way back to my cottage.

He walked me to the door, those butterflies swarming in my belly again. When we got to my porch and I turned to him, he took my face in his hands and pressed his lips to mine. His tongue pushed into my mouth and I froze up slightly, but he pressed forward, and after a couple of seconds, I relaxed. He kissed me with skill, his hands moving to my shoulders and then down over my back without me even realizing it until he was cupping my ass and bringing me up against him. I felt his arousal through his pants and broke the kiss, both of us breathing hard as I looked up into his lust-filled eyes. Something felt…off. It must just be me. I needed to take things slowly. The last time a man had looked at me with lust in his eyes had been the most traumatic moment of my life. I needed to take baby steps here.

I smiled at Travis. "Thank you for a really nice night," I said. He smiled back and kissed my forehead gently.

"I'll call you. Good night, Bree."

He turned and walked down my steps, and when his truck started up, I went inside and closed my door behind me.

* * *

The next day, I woke up early, had a doozy of a flashback—apparently, date night out with a cute guy wasn't the cure there, either—and then dragged myself to the kitchen for a cup of hot tea.

When I remembered that today was my cooking lesson with Archer, happiness shivered through me, replacing the feeling of dread from the flashback. I needed to figure out what I should show him how to make. A nervous thud pounded in my chest when I considered cooking again. Was this a good idea? I had said baby steps last night when it came to intimacy, and baby steps with cooking felt right, too. I wasn't actually going to be immersing myself in a complicated meal creation. I was going to be showing Archer how to prepare something simple. It was perfect. I felt good about it. And I was looking forward to spending time with him.

I stood at the sink, steeping my tea bag and sipping carefully at the hot liquid, considering all of that and feeling better. The flashback had been a bad one, but once again, I was going to be okay. Until tomorrow, when it would happen again. I leaned heavily against my counter, trying not to let the depression of that thought take over.

Thankfully work was busy at the diner, and the day flew by. I headed home and showered, put on a pair of jean shorts and a tank top, and sat down at my kitchen table and made a list of ingredients. When I was done with that, I grabbed my purse and keys and slipped on my flip-flops.

Ten minutes later, I was pulling into the parking lot of the downtown grocery store. I smiled to myself as I walked toward the front door, recalling the last time I'd been here and how I'd felt when Archer turned around and said good night to me. I'd felt like that person who opens her door and a sweepstakes team is waiting outside. Two words from a silent boy—my unexpected windfall. It had *thrilled* me.

I checked out with enough money this time, thank you very much, and drove the short distance back to my cottage.

Men like steak and potatoes. And Archer lived by himself. I thought I'd show him how to perfectly cook a steak, make a simple potatoes au gratin and a side of roasted Parmesan green beans.

As I had been looking over the fruit selection for a dessert, I had remembered the blackberry bushes right off the beach. I didn't have anything else to do until it was time to be at Archer's, so I thought some blackberry picking for a cobbler sounded like a good plan. I'd pack everything up and head over to the lake at about four thirty to give myself half an hour or so to collect what I needed. Might as well take advantage of summer fruit picking while I could. Plus, it was pleasant, mindless work that resulted in something wonderful. I liked it.

When I got back to my cottage, I got everything ready, packed it up in Tupperware containers, and put it in my larger cooler. All the things I was bringing would have to sit both strapped on the back of my bike and in my basket, but I thought that would be okay.

Phoebe was going to have to sit this trip out, but she'd survive. I'd take her for an extra-long walk on the lakeshore tomorrow.

I stepped outside into the warm, only slightly muggy air and smiled, happiness running through me. Why was I more excited to go show my strange, silent boy how to cook for himself than I had been making out with the town hottie on my porch last night? *Whoa.* I stopped and just stood beside my bike for a minute. *My* strange, silent boy? *Not hardly, Bree. Just get on your bike and go show your friend how to make a decent meal for himself.*

I left my bike leaning against a tree at the beach entrance as usual and walked to the wooded area next to the shore. I moved the branches and bushes aside very carefully as I peered through. There they were—a whole crop of blackberry bushes loaded down with succulent fruit, ripe for the picking. It would be a shame to leave all of that to rot and fall to the ground.

I stepped through the bushes gingerly and slowly, avoiding the sharp branches that poked out. Once I had made it through the initial overgrowth, there was a clearing that I could walk through easily enough straight to the berries.

I made my way to them and plucked one soft, ripe berry off the bush, popping it in my mouth. I closed my eyes as the sweet juice burst across my tongue, and moaned softly. God, that was good. These were going to make a delicious cobbler.

I started picking them carefully and dropping them in the small basket I had brought with me. After a while, I started humming as I picked. It was cooler in here, the woods keeping out the heat of the late afternoon sun, only small patches of sunshine coming through breaks in the trees, the feeling of warmth caressing my skin as I moved through them.

I stepped farther into the woods toward a lone blackberry bush holding an abundance of berries. I reached toward it, my lips curved in a smile, and suddenly, my ankle twisted harshly beneath me and I was grabbed violently from behind, arms everywhere, my head smacking into the ground before my entire body was catapulted up and off the dirt, into the air.

I screamed and screamed and screamed, but he wouldn't let go. He had found me—he had come for me. And this time, he was going to kill me. I struggled and thrashed and screamed, but his grip just got tighter around me.

It was happening again. Oh God, God, God, it was happening again.

CHAPTER THIRTEEN

ARCHER

I laid the last of the stones in its spot and stepped back to survey my work. I was satisfied with what I saw. The circular pattern had proven to be a bit challenging, but in the end, it all came down to math. I had worked out the configuration on paper first, mapping out the diagram and spacing before I had even laid the first stone. Then I had used string and stakes to make sure the sloping was just right so the rain flowed away from my house. It looked good. Tomorrow, I'd collect some sand from the shore and sweep it between the cracks and spray it down.

But right now, I needed to take a shower and get ready for Bree. *Bree.* Warmth filled my chest. I still wasn't a hundred percent sure about her motives, but I had let myself begin to hope that it really was just friendship she sought. Why with me, I didn't know. It had started with the sign language, and maybe for her, that fulfilled something. I wanted to ask her why she wanted to spend time with me, but I wasn't sure about the social rules there. I could figure out advanced masonry diagrams, but when it came to other people, I was lost. It was just easier to pretend they didn't exist at all.

Of course, it had been so long, I wasn't sure what came first, the town acting as if I were invisible, or me sending the message that I *wanted* to be invisible. Either way, I embraced it now. And Uncle Nate had definitely embraced it.

"It's good, Archer," he had said, running his hand over my scar. "There's no one on God's green earth who can torture you for intel. You show 'em your scar and pretend you don't understand, they'll leave you alone." And so I had, but it hadn't been hard. No one wanted to believe any different. No one cared.

And now, so much time had passed I felt like there was no going back. I had been okay with it—until she came waltzing onto my property. And now, I was getting all kinds of crazy, unwelcome ideas in my head. What if I went to see her at the diner she worked at? Just sat right at the counter and had a cup of coffee like I was a regular person?

How would I order a cup of coffee anyway? Just point at everything like a three-year-old while people laughed and shook their heads about the poor mute? No way. Just the thought alone filled me with anxiety.

As I was stepping out of the shower, that's when I heard the distant screaming. I jolted and pulled my jeans on quickly, putting my T-shirt on as I ran for the door. Shoes…shoes…I looked around and the screaming continued. That sounded like Bree. *Forget the shoes.* I ran out of my house and toward the woods.

I followed the sound of her anguished cries through the brush, down toward the lake to the beach at the very edge of my property. When I saw her, tangled in the net, thrashing and flailing, eyes closed tight, crying and screaming out, my heart felt like it burst wide open in my chest. Uncle Nate and his damn traps. If he wasn't already dead, I'd have killed him.

I ran toward Bree and put my hands on her within the tangled rope. She jolted and began whimpering, bringing her hands up

over her head and curling into a ball as much as she could within
the trap. She was like a wounded animal. I wanted to roar with
the anger coursing through me at my inability to reassure her. I
couldn't tell her it was me. I released the top of the trap. I knew
how these things worked. I had constructed enough of them as
Nate and I sat on rocks down by the lake, and he plotted out the
security of his compound.

She was shuddering violently now, little whimpers coming
from her, tensing whenever my hands brushed her. I lowered her
to the ground and removed the ropes from around her body. Then
I picked her up in my arms and started back through the woods to
my house.

Halfway there, her eyes opened and she stared up at me, fat
tears rolling down her cheeks. My heart beat rapidly in my chest,
not from the strain of carrying her up the hill—she felt like a
feather in my arms, I was so filled with adrenaline—but from the
fear and devastation I could see etched into her beautiful features.
There was a big red welt on her forehead where she must have hit
her head before the trap lifted her. No wonder she was all discom-
bobulated. I clenched my jaw, swearing again to knock Nate out
when I got to the afterlife.

As Bree stared up, she seemed to recognize me, her wide eyes
moving over my face. But then her expression crumpled and she
burst into sobs, bringing her arms up around my neck and pressing
her face into my chest. Her cries wracked her body. I held her
more tightly as I stepped onto the grass in front of my house.

I kicked open the door and walked through, sitting down on
my couch when I got inside, Bree still in my arms, crying harshly,
her tears soaking my T-shirt.

I wasn't sure what to do, so I just sat there, holding her as she
cried. After a little while, I realized that I was rocking her and my

lips were on the top of her head. That's what my mom used to do when I got hurt or was sad about something.

Bree cried for a long, long time, but finally her cries grew quieter and her warm breath on my chest came out in gentler exhales.

"I didn't fight," she said softly after a few minutes.

I held her away from me just a bit so she could see my questioning eyes.

"I didn't fight," she repeated, shaking her head slightly. "I wouldn't have fought, either, even if he hadn't run." She closed her eyes, but then opened them a few seconds later, looking at me with heartbreak.

I lifted her slightly and laid her down on my couch, her head propped on the pillow at the end. My arms were sore and cramping from holding her in the same position for so long, but I didn't care. I would have held her for the rest of the night if I thought she needed me to.

I drank her in, still so beautiful even in her pain, her long, golden-brown hair lying in loose waves and her green eyes shimmering with tears. *Didn't fight who, Bree?*

The man who tried to rape me, she signed, and my heart crashed to a stop before resuming a fast, erratic beat in my chest. *The man who murdered my father.*

I didn't know what to think, what to feel. I certainly didn't know what to say.

I didn't fight him, she repeated. *Not when I saw him holding the gun on my dad and not when he came for me. My dad told me to hide and that's what I did. I didn't fight*, she said, her face filling with shame. *Maybe I could have saved him*, she said. *He killed my dad, and then when he came for me, I still didn't fight.*

I studied her, trying to understand. Finally, I said, *You did fight, Bree. You survived. You fought to live. And you did. That's what your dad was telling you to do. Wouldn't you have done the same for some-one you loved?*

She blinked at me, and then something in her expression seemed to relax as her eyes roamed over my face. And something inside of me felt like it released, too—although I wasn't sure exactly what.

Bree's tears started to fall again, but the distant look of agony in her eyes seemed to dim just a little bit. I scooped her back up and held her against me once more as she cried quietly, and more gently this time. After a little bit, I felt her breathing deepening. She was asleep. I laid her back on the couch again and went and got a blanket and covered her up. I sat there with her for a long time, just staring out the window, watching the sun lower in the sky. I thought about how Bree and I were so different...and yet so similar. She carried the guilt of not fighting when she thought she should have, and I carried the scar of what happened when you did. We had each reacted differently in a moment of terror, and yet we both still hurt. Maybe there was no right or wrong, no black or white, only a thousand shades of gray when it came to pain and what we each held ourselves responsible for.

CHAPTER FOURTEEN

BREE

I woke up and pried my eyes open. I could feel that they were swollen. The room was dim, just a single standing lamp on in the corner next to one of the built-in bookcases. I was lying on a worn leather couch, and an older wooden coffee table sat in front of me. The curtains on the window were open, and I could see the sun had set completely.

I moved the blanket that was over me to the side. Archer must have done that. My heart squeezed. *Archer.* He had taken care of me. He had saved me.

I sat up, and despite my sore eyes and the spot on my forehead that was slightly tender to the touch, the rest of me felt pretty good, rested. Surprising since I had turned into a wild animal when that net came down on me. I had realized very distantly what was happening as Archer was removing it from my body. Why there was a trap set on his property, I wasn't sure, but figured it had something to do with his uncle.

God, I had *freaked*. I was embarrassed now. But somehow I felt relieved, too. Somehow I felt…lighter? When I had realized I was being carried and looked up into Archer's concerned eyes, I felt *safe*, and so the tears had finally fallen.

I was interrupted in my thoughts as I heard Archer's footsteps behind me, returning to the room.

I turned around to thank him, an embarrassed smile on my lips, but when he came into sight, I froze. Sweet mother of all that was holy. He had his hair pulled back, and he had shaved his face.

And he was...*beautiful*.

I gaped.

No, not beautiful. He was just masculine enough to take the edge off what otherwise would be full-on male prettiness. His jaw was not hard, slightly square, but not in an exaggerated way. His lips were wider than they were full, a beautiful light, rosy color.

With his hair pulled back and his facial hair gone, I could see how his eyes and nose fit perfectly in the portrait of his face. Why had he ever hidden it? I had known he had a nice face somewhere under all that shag, but not this. I had never imagined *this*.

Just as I was about to speak, he moved closer to me, into the light, and it was then that I saw the scar at the base of his throat— pink and shiny, the skin raised in locations and flat in others. It stood out harshly against the beauty of the features above it.

"Archer," I breathed out, staring.

He paused in his movement, but didn't say anything. He stood there, uncertainty in the expression on his face and in the way he held himself, rigid and unmoving. And I could do nothing but stare, spellbound at his beauty. Something pulled tightly inside me. He had no idea. None.

Come here, I said, indicating the couch next to me. I turned around as he walked around it and sat down at my side.

My eyes moved over his face. *Why did you do it?*

He was silent for a couple of beats, looking down, taking his bottom lip between his teeth before he brought his hands up and said, *I don't know.* His expression turned thoughtful, his eyes meeting mine, and then he continued. *When you were in the trap, I couldn't speak to you to reassure you. You can't hear me...I can't help that.* He looked down for a second and then back up at me. *But I want you to see me.* An expression of vulnerability washed over his face. *Now you can see me.*

I felt a tugging in my chest. I got it. I understood. This was his way of making me feel more comfortable about exposing a part of myself to him—by doing the same for me. I brought my hands up and said, *Yes, now I can see you. Thank you, Archer.* I felt like I could stare at him forever.

After a minute, I breathed out and spoke again. *And thank you for...what you did earlier.* I shook my head slightly. *I'm embarrassed. You rescued me. I was a mess.* I looked up at him. *I'm sor—*

He grabbed my hands in his to stop my words and then pulled his own back. *No, I'm sorry*, he said, his eyes intense. *My uncle set traps all over this land. I've tried to find all of them and take them down, but I missed that one.* He looked away. *That was my fault.*

I shook my head. *No, Archer. It wasn't your fault.* I shook my head again. *No. And anyway, as much as I'm sorry that I flipped my lid—*I laughed, embarrassed, and Archer smiled a small smile at me—*maybe I...needed that. I don't know.*

His brow furrowed. *Do you want to tell me about it?*

I fell back on the sofa and breathed out. I hadn't talked about that night with anyone, except the police detectives on the case. Not a single person. Not even my best friends. They only knew my dad had been shot by a robber and I had witnessed it, but not the rest, not everything. But for some reason, I felt safe talking about it now. I felt safe with Archer. And there was something about telling the story with my hands that was comforting to me.

We were just about to close that night, I started. *The guy who usually worked the front counter at our deli had already left and my dad was there, doing some bookkeeping. I was in the back baking bread for the next day. I heard the door chime and it took me a minute to wash my hands and dry them off. Once I did, and I went to the kitchen door, I could see through the small window that there was a man holding a gun on my dad.* Tears welled up in my eyes, but I continued.

My dad saw me in his peripheral vision and he kept signing, "Hide." The man was screaming at him to give him money. My dad couldn't hear him, though, and so he didn't respond. I took a deep breath as Archer watched me with those eyes that never missed a thing, taking in my words, his silent support giving me the strength to continue.

Before I even had time to process what was happening, the gun went off. I paused again, picturing that moment in my mind and then shaking my head, bringing myself back to the present—back to Archer's compassionate eyes.

I found out later that it hit my dad in his heart. He died instantly. Fat tears fell out of my eyes. How could I have more tears? I took another calming breath.

*I tried to hide in the kitchen, but I was in shock and stumbled and fell, and he must have heard me. He came in after me and—*I shivered at the memory before continuing—*his eyes were bloodshot, dilated, he was shaky…He was obviously on something.* I paused, biting my lip. *But he looked at me in this way and I knew what he was going to do. I knew.* I looked up at Archer and he was sitting so still, his eyes boring into mine. I took another deep breath.

He made me undress and he…started tracing my face with his gun, each feature. Then he moved down to my breasts. He told me he was going to…violate me with the gun. I was so terrified. I closed my eyes briefly and looked to the side, away from Archer. I felt his fingers on my chin and he turned my face back to him, and something about that gesture felt so loving that I breathed out a small, choked sob. It felt like he was telling me that I didn't need to be ashamed, didn't need to turn away from him. My eyes met his again.

He almost raped me, but before he did, we both heard the sirens— and they were getting closer. He ran. He ran out the back door into the storm. I closed my eyes for a second and then opened them again. *I hate storms now—the thunder, the lightning. It brings me right back there.* I took another deep, shaky breath. I had just told all of what happened that night, and I had survived.

Bree, Archer started, but he didn't seem to know how to go on. I didn't need him to, though. Just my name held so lovingly in his hands made my heart feel lighter.

Archer's eyes moved over my face before he asked, *That's why you left? That's why you drove here?*

I shook my head. *After my dad was murdered, I found out that he had let his life insurance policy lapse. He had let a lot of things slide while I was away at college. I wasn't really surprised. My dad, he was the salt of the earth, the kindest man you'd ever want to meet, but he was about as disorganized as they come.* I let out a small laugh on an exhale.

I looked at Archer, and his eyes encouraged me to continue. There was something about the way he was looking at me—an understanding in his eyes that calmed me, strengthened me.

When I found out I would have to sell the deli to pay for all the funeral expenses, and the other bills associated with the business, I just...went numb, I guess. It didn't take long before I got an offer on the business, but it hurt so badly to sign the paperwork, I could hardly breathe. I shook my head again, not wanting to return to that day, even in my mind. *It was like losing another piece of my dad. He had owned that deli all my life—I had practically grown up there.*

Archer took my hand in his for a brief second and then let it go, saying, *I'm sorry*. I had heard those words before, but looking at him in that moment, I knew they had never held as much weight as they did when Archer spoke them.

Did they arrest the man who killed your father?

I shook my head. *No. The police told me that the guy who shot my dad had most likely been a strung-out junkie who didn't even remember his crime the next day*. I paused for a minute, thinking. Something had never felt quite right about that...but the police were the experts. Still, I sometimes found myself looking over my shoulder even when I didn't immediately recognize that I was doing it.

Archer nodded, furrowing his brow. I drank him in, feeling lighter, like I had shed something I didn't realize I had been carrying. I smiled a small smile at him. *Way to ruin your cooking lesson, huh?*

Archer paused and then smiled back at me, his straight teeth flashing. I noticed now that one of his bottom teeth was slightly crooked, and something about that made me love his smile even more. I wasn't even sure why—maybe it was just one of those perfect imperfections. He had a crease in each cheek, not dimples exactly, just the way his cheek muscles moved when he smiled. I stared at those creases as if they were twin unicorns that he'd been hiding from me under his beard. *Magical.* My gaze moved down and lingered on his mouth for a second. When my eyes finally moved to his, his widened slightly before he looked away.

I went and got your bike and your coolers while you were sleeping, he said. *I put everything in my refrigerator. I think it's fine. It was on ice.*

Thank you, I said. *So rain check on the cooking lesson?* I laughed, putting my palm on my forehead and groaning slightly. *I mean, if you'll let me back on your property again?*

He smiled at me, not saying anything for several minutes. Finally, he lifted his hands. *I'd like that. And I promise not to string you up from a tree next time.*

I laughed. *Okay, deal?*

He grinned, the beauty of it knocking me on my ass, and then said, *Yeah, deal.*

I kept grinning at him like a loon. Who the hell knew that this day would turn out with me laughing? Not the girl who had been caught in a trap and strung up in the woods and lost her mind in front of the beautiful (as it turned out), silent man.

I sobered when he swallowed, and my eyes moved to the scar at the base of his throat. I reached out to touch it gingerly and Archer shrunk back, but then stilled. I looked up into his eyes and let my fingertips very gently graze the injured skin.

"What happened to you?" I whispered, my hand still at his throat.

He swallowed again, his eyes moving over my face, looking as if he was trying to decide whether to answer me or not. Finally, he lifted his hands and said, *I was shot. When I was seven. I was shot.*

My eyes widened and I brought one hand up and covered my mouth. After a second, I brought my hand down and croaked out, "Shot? By who, Archer?"

My uncle.

My blood ran cold. *Your uncle?* I asked, confused. *The one who lived here on this land with you?*

No, my other uncle. The day I lost my parents, my uncle shot me.

I don't... I don't understand. Why? I asked, knowing that my expression conveyed the horror I felt. *On purpose? Why would—?*

Archer stood up and let his hair down out of whatever had been holding it away from his face. He walked to a small table behind the couch and picked up a small tube of something. When he walked back over to the couch and sat down next to me again, putting the tube on his lap, he said, *I'm going to put some of this antibiotic ointment on your scratches so they don't get infected.*

I guessed that he was done talking about himself. I wanted to press, but I didn't. I knew better than anyone that if you weren't ready to talk about something, no one should try to force you to.

I looked down at my arms and legs. There were several small scratches and a few larger ones. They stung very slightly, but nothing serious. I nodded okay to Archer.

He opened the ointment and began using one finger to rub a little bit on each abrasion.

As he leaned closer to me, I inhaled his clean soap scent, something masculine and all Archer right beneath it. His hand stilled, and his eyes darted to mine and held my gaze. Time seemed to stop, and my heart sped up right before Archer broke our gaze and looked away, putting the top back on the small tube and setting it down in his lap.

That'll help, he said, standing up again. That's when I noticed his feet and gasped. There were cuts all over them, large and small, and they looked red and slightly swollen. *Oh my God! What happened to your feet?* I asked.

He looked down at them as if he was just noticing that he was injured. *I couldn't find my shoes when I heard you screaming*, he said. *They'll be fine.*

Oh, Archer, I said, looking down. *I'm so sorry. You should bandage them. If you have some, I'll wrap them for—*

No need. I put some ointment on them. They'll be fine in the morning.

I sighed. Surely ointment would help, but it wouldn't heal him overnight. Not with injuries that looked that bad. His feet looked shredded. God, he had run over rocks and sharp branches and thorny ground cover to rescue me.

I stood up. *Can I use your bathroom?*

He nodded, pointing at a door right off the main room.

I walked past him and into the small bathroom. Everything was clean and tidy in here, too—the sink and mirror shiny and a light lemony fragrance in the air. I couldn't fault his housekeeping skills, that was for sure.

Sitting on the vanity was a bar of soap on one side, and on the other side, every form of dental cleaning product available: an electric toothbrush, floss, several different bottles of mouthwash, dental picks, and—I picked up a bottle—fluoride tablets. Okay, so the guy was a little overly serious about dental health. Nothing to fault him for there, either, I guessed.

I used the restroom and then went back out to join Archer. I smiled at him. *So, I see you're pretty serious about your teeth*, I said teasingly.

He smiled back and shook his head slightly, bringing one hand to the back of his neck. His hair hung in his face, and I wanted to pull it back the way he'd had it so I could see his beautiful face better again.

My uncle didn't trust doctors or dentists. He said they'd implant tracking devices if given access to your body. I watched him pull a rotten molar with a pair of pliers once. He grimaced. *The health of my teeth became a big priority after that.*

I cringed. *Oh God! That's awful*, I said, *about your uncle pulling his own tooth, I mean. Being diligent about dental health, though—it's a good habit.* I couldn't help laughing, and he smiled back at me, seeming more relaxed.

After a second, he asked, *Are you hungry?*

Starving.

He nodded. *I don't have a big selection. I could make some soup.*

That sounds great, I said. *Let me do it. I promised you a big meal and instead had a nervous breakdown. Really bad manners.* I bit my lip, but then laughed softly, shrugging my shoulders apologetically.

He looked at me and chuckled, his diaphragm moving under his T-shirt, but no sound coming from his mouth. It was the very first time he'd done something close to laugh in my presence. I drank it in, loving those creases in his cheeks.

We made dinner in his small, not surprisingly clean, kitchen. Chicken noodle soup and rolls. When I looked in his refrigerator, I turned back to him. *Peanut butter, jelly, applesauce? Are you six?* I grinned at him.

He didn't smile back, though, just looked at me for a few beats as if considering my question. *In some ways, yes, Bree. In other ways, no.*

The smile disappeared from my face. *Oh God, Archer, I'm sorry. That was really inconsiderate—* But he grabbed my hands to stop me and we stood that way for a few seconds, both of us just staring at our entwined fingers.

Finally, he let go and said, *Bonus for friends of mine, though—I have twirly straws in that cabinet right there. We can blow bubbles in our chocolate milk.* He tilted his head, indicating a cabinet over my shoulder.

I turned around slowly and then turned back to him to see him grinning. I tilted my head to the side. *You being funny?*

He just kept grinning. I laughed. *Good work*, I said, winking.

Archer showed me where his pots and pans were, and I got busy heating up the soup. The appliances were older, but Archer had installed the most beautiful cement countertops. I'd seen something like it on an HGTV show one time, but they were nowhere near as beautiful as the ones he had done. As the soup heated, I ran my hand along them, marveling at his skill.

We ate at his small kitchen table and then cleaned up, mostly in companionable silence. I couldn't help being aware of him as he moved around the kitchen, his tall, lean body skirting mine. I could see every muscle under his T-shirt, and I watched his arms flex as he washed and dried the dishes we had used, while I pretended to wipe down the already-clean counters.

When he was done, he turned to me, still holding a dishrag. He dried his hands as we looked at each other, something sizzling in the air between us. I swallowed hard, and I saw him swallow, too, my eyes lingering on his scar for a portion of a second.

I looked back up at him and said, *I should go.*

He put the towel down and shook his head saying, *I can't let you ride your bike home in the dark, and I can't walk that distance yet.* He looked down at his feet, indicating his injuries. *I'll be fine in the morning and walk you then.*

I nodded. "Um...," I said, then signed, *Okay. I can sleep on your couch.*

Archer shook his head. *No, you can sleep in my bed.* When my eyes got wide, his face paled, and he closed his eyes for a couple of beats. *I mean, I'll sleep on the couch and you can take my bed*, he clarified. Spots of color stained his cheekbones and I swear I felt my heart flip over once in my chest.

"I couldn't do that," I whispered.

Yes you can, he said, walking past me, out of the kitchen.

I followed him through the door across from the bathroom and looked around at the sparsely furnished room: just a bed and a dresser and a small chair in the corner. There weren't any knick-knacks or photographs or anything.

I just washed the sheets a couple of days ago. They're...clean, he said, looking away from me, those same red spots appearing on his upper cheekbones.

I nodded. *Okay*, I said. *Thank you, Archer. For everything. Thank you.*

He nodded at me, our eyes lingering, and when our shoulders touched as he was walking out of the room, I felt him jerk slightly. He closed the door behind him.

I looked around the room one more time and noticed that there actually was a small photograph lying down on the top of his dresser. I walked over and picked it up delicately. It was a beautiful girl, her long brown hair flowing over her shoulder, laughing at the person behind the camera. She looked carefree and happy. She looked like she was in love. I realized why her smile looked so familiar—it was Archer's smile. This must be his mother, Alyssa McRae, I thought. I turned the photo over and on the back was written,

My beautiful Lys, Love forever, C.

C? Connor. Archer's uncle. The man who had shot him? He was such a town hero, though—they must not know he had shot his nephew. "But how is that possible?" I asked the girl in the photo softly. Her large brown eyes remained smiling, not giving me a clue. I placed the photo back down where it had been.

I undressed quickly, down to my underwear and bra, and pulled back the covers and got in Archer's bed. It smelled like him: soap and clean male.

As I lay there in his bed, I thought of him in the other room, his long body probably hanging over the end of the couch. I inhaled the scent of him on his sheets and pictured him shirtless, the moonlight shining in on his smooth, bare chest, and I shivered slightly. He was just mere feet from me on the other side of the wall.

Thinking about Archer that way felt just a little dangerous—I didn't know if it was a good idea. Considering it now, I realized that there had been a chemistry between us from the very start. It had just been difficult to classify because of all the ways he was so different. And I *still* felt a little confused. But apparently my body did not feel confused at all as my hormones flash-fired through me, my veins filling with heat, my mind unable to let go of the images of him and me tangled together in these very sheets, those beautiful whiskey-colored eyes filled with passion.

I turned over and adjusted the pillow, groaning softly into it and closing my eyes tightly, willing myself to sleep. After a little while, even though I had slept for several hours earlier that evening, I fell into a peaceful sleep and didn't wake up until the sunrise, muted by the trees around the house, was lighting the room.

* * *

I sat up and stretched, looking around at Archer's room in the morning sunlight. I pulled on my shorts and tank and peeked my head out his door. He was nowhere in sight, and so I headed straight across the hall to his bathroom. I did my business and used my finger to brush my teeth and gargled with his mouthwash. I washed my face and looked at myself in the mirror. I looked okay. My eyes were still very slightly swollen, but other than that, I didn't think my freak-out had left me looking too worse for wear this morning. I smoothed my hair back and leaned against the sink.

Thinking of my freak-out had me thinking of the flashback that was sure to come on any second now. It would be better if I had it alone, out of Archer's sight. He probably already thought I was half-nuts. Letting him see my PTSD episode would definitely convince him I was fully there.

I stood against the sink for a few minutes, closing my eyes and willing the flashback to do its worst while I was locked away behind closed doors. Nothing happened.

I turned on the water and imagined it was the rain falling down around me, just like that night. Nothing happened.

I tried to stamp down the hope that blossomed in my chest— I had been hopeful in the recent past that the flashbacks had stopped, right before being cast into an attack.

I closed my eyes and thought about the night before, what Archer had said to me when I told him my deepest shame, that I had done nothing as my father was gunned down, as I was almost raped. He hadn't looked at me with disgust…but rather with *understanding*. Relief washed through my body again at the memory alone.

And I had cried more than I knew I could. I had cried a river of tears…for my dad, for the loss I felt every day at losing my best friend, *my person*…for losing *myself* somewhere along the way, for running away…

I opened my eyes, biting my fingernail and worrying my brow. Is that what I had needed? Was that the purpose of the flashbacks all along? To force me to face what I was running from? That felt right. But it was only part of it. Maybe I needed to feel safe and accepted in my pain before I was set free from this daily misery. I had needed someone who would understand and hold me as I cried.

I had needed Archer.

I swung the bathroom door open and walked quickly through the house, calling to him. He wasn't inside. I ran outside and called his name. After a few minutes, he walked through the trees from the direction of the lake and stood there looking questioningly at me.

I didn't think you'd be up this early, he said.

I ran down the slope and stopped right in front of him, grinning broadly, my excitement bubbling out of me. I laughed, looking at his beautiful face. I still wasn't used to seeing all of it. Or most of it at least. He still desperately needed a haircut.

I didn't have a flashback this morning, I said, my hands moving quickly.

He frowned, looking at me, confused.

I shook my head, laughing a small laugh. *I guess I just can't believe it…I mean, I always have one. Every day. I've had one every single day for six months*, I said, my hands moving quickly, my eyes filling with tears.

Archer kept looking at me, understanding coming into his eyes, a flash of compassion moving over his expression.

I have to go let Phoebe out and feed her, I said, swiping quickly at my tears. I took Archer in again, joy washing through my body. He had given me an incredible gift and I was giddy. I wanted to spend the day with him, and I didn't care that I was always the one doing the asking. *Can I come back later?* I blurted out, looking at him expectantly.

His eyes moved over my face for a couple of seconds, and then he nodded his head.

I grinned. "Okay," I breathed out. I stepped forward and his eyes widened slightly, but he didn't move. I wrapped my arms around him and held him tightly. He didn't wrap his arms around me, but he let me hug him.

After a minute, I stepped back and smiled at him again. *I'll be back.*

Okay.

Okay, I said again, grinning bigger.

A smile tugged at the corner of his mouth, but he just nodded at me.

I turned around and ran up the wooded slope to his house and then up his driveway. My bike was leaning against the inside of his fence. I wheeled it through the gate and started for home. Here and there, I coasted down the dirt road with my head tilted up to the sky, feeling happy, feeling alive, feeling *free*.

CHAPTER FIFTEEN

BREE

When I got home, I let Phoebe outside to do her business. I felt lighter, happier, as if I had shed the chains that had held me tied to the pain and grief of my loss for the last six months. As I stood in the bright sunshine waiting for Phoebe, a feeling of deep peace washed over me. I would never, ever forget my dad. He would be with me in everything I did for the rest of my life. Letting go of the chains of grief and guilt didn't mean letting go of *him*. My dad loved me; he would want me to be happy. The relief that flooded my body almost made me sob. I choked back the emotion and called to Phoebe, walking back inside.

After I'd fed her I sat down and drank a cup of tea. I thought about my dad the whole time I sat there, remembering special moments we'd shared, reminiscing about his little quirks, picturing his face so clearly in my mind. I focused on what I'd had, on what some people never got for even a minute. I'd had him for twenty-one years. I was *lucky*—I had been blessed. When I stood up to put my dishes in the sink, I was smiling.

I went to the bathroom and turned on the shower and stripped off my clothes. My scratches looked a lot better. Apparently, the ointment Archer applied had worked.

Archer…I sighed, so many confusing emotions and feelings swirling through my body. A warm feeling filled my chest whenever I thought of him.

I wanted to know his story. I wanted to know everything about him. But, instinctively, I knew I shouldn't push the issue of what had happened the day his uncle shot him. The chief of police, *his uncle*, shot him. God, how did you wrap your mind around that? And what the *hell* had happened to bring that about?

Half an hour later I was dressed in shorts and a T-shirt, my hair dry and put up in a ponytail.

As I was slipping on my flip-flops, I glanced at my phone sitting on the top of the dresser and picked it up. It had two messages. I listened. They were both from Travis. I threw the phone back down. I'd call him back, just not right now.

I lifted Phoebe and started outside to head back to Archer's house. I considered something as I was about to close my door, and turned back. A few minutes later, I was riding away from my cottage toward Briar Road.

* * *

"Hey." I smiled when Archer opened the door to his house. He had left his gate slightly open so I could enter and bring my bike inside and let Phoebe head off to find Kitty and the pups.

He smiled back and opened the door wider for me to enter.

I went inside and turned back around to him. I took a deep breath. *Thanks for having me back here, Archer.* I bit my lip, considering. *I hope you don't mind…after last night…there was no other place in the world I wanted to be than here with you today.* I tilted my head, studying him. *Thank you.*

He watched my hands as I spoke, looking up into my eyes finally, a pleased expression on his face. He nodded at me and I smiled.

I took him in. He was wearing the same worn jeans that looked like they could disintegrate at any second and a tight, navy-blue T-shirt. His feet were bare…and, as I looked down, I saw that they did look a lot better, mostly because the swelling had gone down. But the cuts and scratches still looked painful. I flinched and looked back up at him.

They're fine, Bree, he said, obviously having noticed my reaction to his injuries.

I was still doubtful, but I nodded anyway. I tilted my head to the side. *So, Archer, I brought something with me, but before I show you, I just want you to know that if you don't like the idea…or…just want to say no to me, I'll completely understand.*

He raised an eyebrow. *This sounds scary.*

I breathed out a small laugh. *No…just…well, let me show you.* I went over to the small bag I had brought and pulled out my scissors.

Archer looked at them warily.

I thought you might want a haircut, I said, and then hurried on, *but if you don't, that's okay, too. I'm not saying you need one, but, well, you need one. But I can also just take off a little—more like a trim.*

He smiled a slightly embarrassed smile and put his hand on the back of his neck, but then took it down and looked up at me. *I'd like that.*

I grinned. *You would? Okay! I mean, I'm not the greatest, but I can make it straight. I trimmed my dad's hair many times.*

He smiled. *Cut as much as you want, Bree.*

Well, what do you want? I'll do whatever you'd like.

He looked at me, something warm coming into his eyes, although he didn't smile. He looked at me seriously, swallowing before he said, *I want you to like it. Do whatever you want.*

I hesitated, not wanting him to feel like he was doing something he didn't want to do. *You sure?*

Very, he said, walking into the kitchen and pulling one of the chairs from his kitchen table into the middle of the floor where the hair could be easily swept up.

I went to his bathroom and got a towel and the comb sitting on his sink, and then joined him in the kitchen, wrapping the towel over his shoulders.

I began cutting his hair, focusing on the work of measuring and evening. He had told me I could do what I wanted and so I was going to go short. I wanted to see his face, and I had a vague notion that he used his hair to hide. Was it my job to strip him of that? No. But he had given me permission, so I was going to take it. It would grow back if he wanted it to.

I sat the comb aside and used my fingers to comb through his dark, silky hair before using the scissors. Running my hands through his thick, very slightly wavy strands felt intimate and sensual, and my heart rate rose as I moved my body around his, cutting the back first and then the front. Each time I ran my hand slowly along his scalp, Archer shivered slightly. I leaned in closely as I worked with his hair, drawing in the scent of his shampoo and the clean smell of his body. I detected soap, but just underneath that was the musky scent of his maleness, and it made my tummy clench with desire.

As I moved in front of him, smoothing the hair back from his forehead, I looked down into his face, and his eyes met mine right before he closed them tightly. It looked almost as if he was in pain, and my heart squeezed. Had anyone since his mother touched him with tenderness?

I continued to work, and when I leaned in close to get the hair above his ear, his breath hitched. My eyes darted to his face again. His pupils were dilated slightly and his lips were parted. My nipples hardened under my T-shirt, and Archer's eyes moved down, widening when he homed in on my chest. His eyes shot to the side, those red patches appearing on his upper cheekbones, and he fisted his hands, which were sitting on his muscular thighs.

I leaned over him to snip more hair, my chest coming in close to his face. I heard his breath hitch and begin to come out faster, little exhalations of air breaking the silence of the kitchen. I glanced down as I leaned back and saw his arousal through his pants, thick and hard.

I quickly moved around behind him, evening his hair some more and trying to get my own breathing under control. My eyes felt glassy, and I hoped I was doing okay—I couldn't concentrate, wetness pooling between my thighs. I was so turned on I could barely stand: at his nearness, the way it felt to touch him, and the knowledge that I was affecting him, too. I'd never gotten aroused this quickly—and from a freaking haircut. But clearly he was right there with me.

As I moved around to stand in front of him again, I could see he was trembling very slightly.

"There," I whispered. "You're done. It looks really good, Archer." I kneeled down in front of him and swallowed hard when I took in the complete look.

I set the scissors down on the counter behind me and turned back around, kneeling up as high as I could go and moving closer to him, my heart beating loudly in my ears and between my legs. I gazed up at him, glancing quickly at his mouth. His eyes darted quickly to my lips as well. God, I wanted him to kiss me so badly I ached.

He stared down at me and swallowed thickly, his Adam's apple moving in his throat, and his scar pulling upward. As we stared at each other, uncertainty moved across his face, and he balled his fists more tightly on his thighs.

Suddenly, he scooted the chair back and stood up and, shocked, so did I.

You need to go now, he said.

Go? I asked. *Why, Archer, I'm sorry, did I—?*

He shook his head. I could see his pulse beating in his neck. *No, nothing, I just…have things to do. You should go.* He was breathing harshly as if he'd just run five miles. In all the times I'd watched Archer do physical labor, I'd never seen him become breathless from it. He looked pleadingly at me.

"Okay," I whispered, color moving up my face. "Okay."

I gathered my scissors and walked to the main room to put them in my purse. I turned to Archer.

Are you sure? I didn't—

Yes, please, yes, he said.

My eyes moved downward and I could see that he was still fully hard. I swallowed again. I didn't know what to think. Was he embarrassed that he was turned on? Or was he upset that he was turned on by me? Had I been too forward? Did he just want to be friends and I had totally misread him? Hurt and confusion clouded my mind.

"Okay," I said again, moving toward his door.

He grabbed my arm gently as I passed him, and I startled slightly. *I'm sorry. I really do appreciate the haircut.*

I stared at him again, noting how beautiful he looked, freshly shaven, the new haircut and the same flush high on his cheeks, his eyes glassy, the golden-brown color even brighter than usual.

I nodded and walked out his door. Phoebe was on the porch, so I scooped her up and hurried out Archer's gate.

CHAPTER SIXTEEN

BREE

I rode home slowly. By the time I was turning onto my street, I realized I didn't remember any of my ride home. I had ridden in a fog, oblivious to anything around me, solely focused on my feelings of confusion and hurt.

As my cottage came into sight, I saw a big truck parked in front and a figure standing on my porch. *What the heck?*

As I rode closer, I saw that it was Travis. I got off my bike and leaned it against my fence, picked Phoebe up, and walked toward him, a confused smile on my face.

"Hey, stranger," he said, coming toward me.

I laughed softly. "I'm sorry, Travis. I'm not trying to be a stranger, and I did get your messages. I've just been really busy." I met him at the base of my steps.

He brought his hand through his hair. "I'm not trying to stalk you." He smiled an embarrassed smile. "It's just, I really enjoyed spending time with you the other night, and the town is holding a police and fire department parade in a few weeks. There's always a dinner afterward to honor my father—it's kind of a big deal for the town…I was really hoping you'd come with me." He smiled.

"Of course, I hope you'll do something with me sooner than that, but I wanted to make sure I asked you in advance about the dinner. It's important to me."

I bit my lip, not knowing what to do. And then it occurred to me—his father was the man who had shot Archer. Honor him? How could I? I didn't want to hurt Travis; I liked him. I just liked Archer more. Oh God. I did. I really, really did. But Archer had thrown me out of his house, whereas Travis was making a concerted effort to track me down to spend time with me. Even if it was for an event I didn't feel comfortable attending. I just wanted to go inside my house and think about things. I wanted to be alone.

I smiled. "Travis, can I think about it? I'm sorry...that whole complicated thing...I just..."

A flash of something that looked like anger or disappointment flashed ever so briefly over his face before he smiled and said, "How about if I call you in a day or two with the details and you can say yes to me then?" He smiled.

I laughed softly and said, "Okay, call me in a couple of days."

He grinned, seeming appeased, and then leaned down to kiss me, and I turned my head slightly so he could kiss my cheek. He frowned as he straightened back up, but didn't say anything.

"Talk to you soon," I said softly.

He nodded once and then walked around me and headed to his truck. I watched him from where I stood, his broad shoulders and muscular backside filling out his jeans nicely. He really was a catch. Why didn't I feel any spark? I sighed and went inside my house with Phoebe.

I went back to my room and lay down on the bed, and before I knew it, I had fallen asleep. When I woke up, the room around me was dark. I looked over at the clock. Ten eighteen. I had slept most of the afternoon and evening away. Probably because I hadn't slept well in Archer's bed...so aware of him in the room right beyond. I groaned at the thought of Archer, wondering what he was doing right now. I hoped I hadn't completely messed things up between us.

I sighed and sat up, and Phoebe came trotting into the room. "Hey, girl," I said softly. "You probably need to go outside, don't you?"

I walked her to the front door and slid my flip-flops on, noting that I needed to throw the rotting roses sitting on the table by my entry into the garbage. When I opened the door, I immediately saw something sitting on the mat on my porch. Confused, I bent down and picked it up. I sucked in a breath and then started grinning. It was a "bouquet" of Almond Joy candy bars held together in the middle with a little piece of string, tied neatly in a bow.

I turned it around in my hands, grinning stupidly, happiness blooming in my chest. I guessed this was an apology? Or...a gesture of friendship? What exactly did it mean? I groaned. This man!

I laughed out loud, hugging the candy bars to me and then standing there, grinning like a fool some more. Awkward boy. Sweet, silent Archer Hale.

* * *

I worked six to two the next day and was practically skipping when I entered the diner. It was my second non-flashback morning. When I had gone to bed the night before, I was slightly scared that that morning had been some kind of weird fluke. But no, it looked like it wasn't. I felt like a whole new person. A lighter person, a person filled with *hope* and freedom.

As the breakfast crowd was thinning out, Norm called from

the kitchen, "Maggie, I gotta take a break in the back. Call me if someone comes in." He removed the plastic gloves on his hands, stepped away from the grill, and headed to the small office behind the kitchen.

Maggie shook her head.

"Is he okay?" I asked.

"Damn stubborn ass is sick, but of course, he won't hire another cook. He's cheap *and* he thinks he's the only one who can do anything." She shook her head again.

I frowned, pausing in my counter wipe down and turning to Maggie. I tilted my head, considering, and then said, "Maggie, if you ever need help in the kitchen, my family owned a deli and I used to cook there. I think I could muddle through here...I mean, you know, if it ever became necessary."

Maggie studied me. "Well, thanks, honey. I'll keep that in mind."

I nodded and turned back to my counter cleaning duties.

Just as I was finishing up, the bell above the door rang and I looked up to see a woman I'd estimate to be in her midforties walk into the diner. She was wearing a light beige, short-sleeved pantsuit that looked like it was designer, and though I didn't know a whole lot about brand names, even I knew that the large double *C* logo on her purse stood for Chanel.

She had glossy blond hair swept up into a chignon, with a few pieces artfully framing her face. Her makeup was impeccable, if a little too heavy, painted on a tight face that had clearly seen a plastic surgeon's scalpel.

"Well, hello, Mrs. Hale," Maggie said, rushing over to her like the queen of England had just walked through her door.

"Maggie," she said, barely glancing sideways at her as she moved toward me at the counter. A waft of expensive-smelling perfume—heavy on the lilies and roses—tickled my nose. I sneezed, bringing my upper arm up to cover my mouth and nose and then bringing it down again. "Excuse me!"

The woman looked at me like I might be contagious. Geez, a *God bless you* wasn't a lot to ask, was it? Wow, I was getting really good vibes here.

"I'll wait while you wash your hands."

"Uh, right, okay, I'll be right back to take your order."

"I'm not ordering."

I paused. *Okay*… But I just nodded and went to the back where I washed and dried my hands and then hurried to the front. As I was walking toward the counter, it suddenly occurred to me to ask myself why I was taking orders from this person anyway.

"How can I help you?" I asked, keeping my distance from the counter, not wanting to go into a sneezing fit again. I was pretty sure I was allergic to her.

"I'm Victoria Hale; I'm sure you've heard of me."

I looked at her blankly. "No, I'm sorry, I haven't," I lied, taking some small measure of satisfaction from the look of anger that briefly flashed over her face. What a bitch.

But then she quickly recovered. "Well, then I'm glad I came in to introduce myself. I'm Travis Hale's mother. I understand you're seeing him socially?"

"Uh, I…" I paused. What the hell was going on here? "I went on one date with him," I said, furrowing my brow and studying this brazen woman. I wouldn't be going out with Travis again, but this woman didn't need to know that.

"Yes, so I've heard," she said. "That's fine, I guess. Travis chooses the women he wants to…see. What I'm not fine with is that you've apparently made a friend of Archer Hale."

My eyes widened and my mouth dropped open. How in the hell

did she know that? I crossed my arms over my chest. "As a matter of fact," I said, "he's more than a friend." I raised my chin, looking down at her. Okay, so that wasn't exactly true—at least as far as Archer was concerned—but I wanted to see the look on her face when I said it. Her disdain for Archer was obvious, for what reason I had no idea. And the best way I could think to defend him in that moment was to tell her I was seeing him.

She looked at me for a couple of seconds and then laughed, making a bolt of anger spear through my body. "Well, isn't that familiar? Another little girl leading the Hale boys around by their male parts?" Then her eyes narrowed. "That boy has a violent side. Has anyone told you?"

My mouth dropped open. "A violent side?" I laughed. "You're wrong about that—"

She waved her hand, silencing me. "You ask him, little girl. I've heard you know sign language and are teaching it to him. Ask him about how he tried to assault me several years ago." She nodded, as if agreeing with herself.

I said nothing, staring at her, not correcting her in her assumption that I was teaching Archer to sign.

"Stay away from him," she continued. "Nothing good can come of it. And for a girl who isn't a stranger to violence, I'd think you'd heed my warning. There's no telling when he's going to crack and do something to hurt you. Mark my word. He's done it before. Have a good day."

And with that, she turned around and headed for the door, nodding very slightly to Maggie, who was now sitting at the break table trying to look like she wasn't eavesdropping.

I was floored. That woman had looked into me—had looked into who I was and what was in my past? *Why?* And of all the bitchy, condescending…bitches! Who were really bitchy!

When the door had closed, Maggie rushed over to me. "What in the heck was that about?" she asked, eyes wide.

I was still standing there frowning. "I literally have no idea. Who does that woman think she is?"

Maggie sighed. "Tori Hale has always been high-and-mighty since the day she strode into town—even more so after she married Connor Hale. She's uppity and a little hard to handle, but what do you say about a woman who owns the whole damn town, including all the businesses, and has more money than God?"

"That she needs to purchase herself a better personality?" I offered.

Maggie chuckled softly. "I won't disagree with you, but..." She shrugged. "She mostly keeps to her various social clubs on the other side of the lake. I have no real reason to interact with her. Of course, she's not making any new fans with what she's planning to do with the town."

I looked at Maggie. "Will that affect you and Norm?"

She shook her head. "We don't know yet. No one's seen the final plans. The only thing anyone knows for sure is that condos are going up on the shore."

I looked back out the window where Victoria Hale had disappeared around the corner a couple of minutes earlier. "Hmm."

"Now what's this about you seeing Archer Hale?" Maggie asked, interrupting my thoughts.

I breathed out, looking over at her and resting my hip against the counter. "That may have been a slight exaggeration, but I've been going out to his property and spending time with him. I like him."

"I always thought he was simpleminded."

I shook my head vigorously. "Not at all. He's intelligent, and funny, and sweet. He's really amazing," I said, blushing slightly and looking down when Maggie looked curiously at me.

"You really do like him," she said, looking shocked. "Well, who would have ever guessed? Hmm."

"I do," I said. "There's a lot to like. Anyway, what was Victoria Hale talking about—Archer being violent?"

Maggie shrugged. "No idea. I never saw anything like that. Like I said, I always thought he was simple. Of course, I wouldn't be too surprised, either. It's in the genes, I guess. His father was a mean drunk. That poor wife of his tried to cover the bruises, but we all knew…"

I leaned my hip against the counter. "Did anyone do anything?" I asked, feeling a heaviness in my heart for Archer's mother.

Maggie nodded. "Connor Hale, his brother, was always out there. It came to blows with those two several times from what I know." She shook her head again.

I bit my lip, wondering again what had really happened between those two brothers so long ago.

"I better go check on Norm," Maggie said. "Gotta make sure he didn't croak back there in the office. Wouldn't be good for business."

I laughed softly and got back to work, my mind full with questions about brothers, secrets, a girl they both loved, and a bitchy widow. I wondered how the whole puzzle went together, and where Archer fit in among it all.

CHAPTER SEVENTEEN

BREE

I left the diner later that afternoon and noticed that it felt markedly cooler—still warm and mostly summerlike, even though it was the beginning of September, but I thought the feel of fall was in the air. The leaves were just beginning to change color here and there, and I saw jeans and sweaters in my near future. I paused at my car. Did that mean I was going to stay here? I'd been in Pelion less than a month, but already I was starting to think of it as home. I'd have to think about it all. For right now, I didn't feel any rush.

I opened the door to my car and suddenly felt a light tap on my shoulder. I startled, inhaling a sharp breath and whirling around. A pair of golden-brown eyes met mine. For the briefest portion of a second, I was confused as my eyes scanned the beautiful face under a head of short, dark, cropped hair. *Archer.* I breathed out, laughing and putting my hand to my chest.

He smiled. *Sorry.*

I laughed again. *It's okay. I just didn't hear you approach.* I furrowed my brow. *What are you doing here?*

I'm here for you, he said, stuffing his hands in his pockets and looking down at his shoes for a second before bringing his hands out of his pockets and back up. *Is that okay?* He kept his head bowed, but looked up at me, squinting slightly. My stomach flipped.

Yeah, that's okay, I said, smiling at him. *I got the bouquet you left for me. I loved it.*

He nodded, his lips tipping up, but then his face took on a worried expression. *I'm sorry about yesterday*, he said, raking his hand through his short hair. *I should explain, I—*

Archer, I said, grabbing his hand to stop him from speaking, *how about that cooking lesson tonight and we can talk then? Would that be okay?*

He studied me for a second and then nodded yes, sticking his hands back in his pockets and glancing around nervously.

I smiled. *Okay, great…good. I'll go home and get cleaned up and bike over.*

He nodded yes again.

Get in, I said, pointing to my car. *I'll drive you home.*

He looked at my car like it was a flying saucer. *No, I'll walk.*

I frowned at him. *Archer, honestly. Why walk when I can drive you?*

He started to back away. *I'll see you in a little while.*

I just looked at him until he turned and started walking away. *Well, suit yourself then*, I thought. It was then that I noticed all the people looking my way curiously, walking by slowly, not even trying to hide their nosiness. Geez, small towns could be seriously annoying. Was there any privacy here at all?

I got in my car and drove home.

* * *

Once I got to my cottage, I took a quick shower and dressed in my pale yellow linen shorts and my favorite white tank top. I dried my hair partway and tied it back loosely, leaving a few strands out to frame my face. I took a few extra minutes in front of the mirror, wanting to look nice for Archer, and feeling excited flutters at the thought of spending time with him.

Twenty minutes later Phoebe and I pulled up to Archer's open gate and wheeled inside, and I closed it behind us.

As usual, Phoebe took off across the yard, in search of Kitty and the puppies that were now following after their mama as she went on covert missions all over the property. I smiled to myself. I think I would have liked to meet Uncle Nate.

Archer came out of his house and smiled at me, and I grinned back, walking toward him. It was going to take me some time to get used to his new look. God, he was gorgeous. Granted, his clothes were still a little odd for a twentysomething guy who…wait, how old *was* Archer anyway?

About twenty feet from him, I signed, *How old are you?*

He looked confused for a second, and then looked off in the distance as if he was calculating and said, *Twenty-three.*

I stopped, frowning. *Why do you look confused?*

He shook his head slightly. *Uncle Nate didn't exactly celebrate birthdays, so I forget the year sometimes. My birthday is December second.*

I didn't know what to say to that. No one had celebrated his birthday? All these years? It seemed like a relatively simple thing and yet, for some reason, it made my heart squeeze painfully.

I'm sorry, Archer, I said when I got right up to him.

He shrugged as if it was neither here nor there. *Come inside?*

I nodded.

"By the way," I said, following behind him into his house, "you don't know anything about my front step, do you?" I noticed that it wasn't loose anymore when I had gotten home from work earlier. There was no way George Connick would know about that. I hadn't called him. The last person who'd been up my steps was Archer.

He looked back at me and turned his body slightly. *It was dangerous*, he said. *I went over and fixed it earlier today. It only took a few minutes.*

I breathed out. "Thank you. That was really thoughtful." God, this man. He was going to kill me with sweetness overload.

He simply nodded as if it were nothing.

When we got inside, he took my hand and led me to the couch, and we both sat down. I looked at him expectantly. Taking in this big, beautiful man, with a body many men spent hours at the gym for, sitting in front of me, so obviously shy and uncertain, was something I could hardly wrap my mind around—and yet it made my heart pick up speed and warmth rush through my veins. He seemed so uncomfortable, but he took a deep breath and signed, *About yesterday...I—*

Archer, I interrupted, *you don't have to explain. I think I understand—*

No, you don't, he interrupted back. He rubbed his hand over his new, short hair. *Bree, I'm not...* He let out a sigh, clenching his jaw slightly. *I'm not experienced with...* His eyes bored into mine, shining with intensity. I felt that intensity between my thighs. I couldn't help it; my body reacted to him whether I asked it to or not.

Can I ask you a question? he asked, those same red spots appearing high on his cheekbones. God, he was beautiful to me.

Anything.

Did you...want me to kiss you yesterday? Did you want me to touch you? His lips parted slightly, and he watched me for my answer like his life depended on it.

Yes, I said without hesitation. I had played games with guys in the past. Games of flirtation and hard-to-get, but with Archer, I didn't give it a second thought. Complete honesty was the only thing I would give him. I would never purposefully hurt this beautiful, sensitive, wounded man more than he had already been hurt.

He let out a loud whoosh of breath. *I wanted to kiss you, to touch you. I just didn't know...if you wanted that, too—*

I smiled, looking up at him through my lashes. *Archer*, I said, taking his hand and bringing it to my heart, which was beating wildly in my chest. "Do you feel that?" I whispered, using my voice since my hands held his against me. "This is how you affect me. My heart is pounding, because I want you to kiss me so badly that I can barely breathe."

His eyes widened, and his pupils dilated so large that his golden-brown eyes looked dark brown. Something almost palpable passed between us. He looked from my eyes to my mouth and back to my eyes again. I didn't move, instinctively knowing that it meant something to him to take the lead here. I sat still, my eyes roaming to his mouth, too. He licked his lips, and that small movement sent a spark of electricity straight between my legs. I squeezed them together lightly, trying to relieve the ache that was building there.

Kiss me, kiss me, I chanted in my mind, the tension building so much that when his head finally started slowly moving toward mine, I almost groaned in relief.

He moved toward me, his lips parting slightly, the look on his face a mix of uncertainty and blatant lust. I'd never forget that look—as long as I lived, I'd never forget the sheer beauty of the expression on Archer's face. Next time it wouldn't be the same.

Once he had kissed me, his first kiss, this I knew, it would never be the same again. I drank it in, memorized it, made it a part of me. And then his lips reached mine and I did groan, a breathless sound that came unbidden up my throat. His eyes opened, and for a second he paused, his eyes growing even darker before he pressed his lips firmly against mine, shutting his lids once more. I closed mine, too, and soaked in the feel of his soft lips tasting mine, experimenting, brushing softly and then pressing again. After several seconds, he moved his body closer to mine, and his tongue swept across the seam of my lips, which I immediately opened, inviting him in without reservation. His tongue entered my mouth tentatively, and I used my own to tangle with his. He pressed his body even closer, and a small exhale released from his mouth to mine, as if he were breathing life into me. And maybe he was. Maybe he had been all along.

He laid me back gently on the couch, his mouth never disconnecting from mine, and leaned over me, tilting his head. The kiss went deeper as his tongue continued to sweep inside my mouth, mine meeting his in a slow, erotic dance.

And nothing had ever felt more right.

The delirious relief that bloomed in my heart at the feeling of how much I wanted this man above me, kissing me, almost made me want to weep with happiness.

After several minutes, he pulled away, breathless, sucking in air and looking into my eyes. I stared back at him and smiled, but instead of smiling back, he pressed his lips back to mine and brought his hands up, raking his fingers through my hair, gripping gentle handfuls. It felt so good that I moaned again, pressing my hips upward into his hard body. I could feel his erection, hard and thick, and I wiggled until it was pressed right where I needed it, the heat of it radiating through the material of his jeans and the thin fabric of my linen shorts. He expelled another small puff of air into my mouth and I drank it down, knowing that it was a moan that didn't have sound.

He pressed his erection down gently and broke his lips from mine to look down questioningly into my face, to see if I was okay with what he was doing. His gentleness and his concern with what I desired made my heart constrict in my chest. "Yes," I breathed out. "Yes."

He resumed kissing me and now added the gentle rolling of his hips so his erection moved over my clit in delicious circles. I wondered if he knew that the movements that were bringing him pleasure were bringing me pleasure, too. I made a point to express what I loved about what he was doing, by panting into his mouth and pressing my hips up into him. He adjusted his movements according to my reactions, and the fact that he was so in tune with my own pleasure sent another bolt of arousal to my core, causing my clit to tingle and swell, the blood pulsing furiously there. I thought dazedly how much of this dance between a man and a woman was pure instinct, pure unspoken communication.

As he moved above me, my stiff nipples rubbed on his chest, causing more sparks to shoot downward.

Another burst of air came out of his mouth and, at the feel of it, my body tightened deliciously and I shuddered in release, breaking free from his mouth and crying out, my back arching slightly off the couch.

I felt him shudder, too, and then go still above me, his breathing ragged. When I opened my eyes, he was staring at me, a look of pure, awestruck wonder. He sat up, still looking at me and signed, *Was that supposed to happen? Just from kissing, I mean?*

I laughed and nodded, bringing my hands up. *Yes*, I said, *I mean, yes, sometimes that happens.*

I leaned up and kissed him lightly on his mouth. When I leaned back, his face broke into a huge grin. Oh God, my heart. My heart couldn't take those grins. They were too much: too beautiful and too overwhelming.

I laughed at the slightly smug look on his face. I wasn't going to tell him that coming in your pants wasn't exactly something to be smug about, because the truth of it was, I didn't think I'd ever been half as turned on as I was on this couch with him a few minutes before. So, he could be smug for now. I laughed again, with happiness, and kissed him quickly again.

I leaned back and said, *I'm not going to give you that cooking lesson right now. I'm going to cook for you. I want to take care of you tonight. Is that okay?*

He studied me, something warm and gentle coming into his beautiful eyes, and he simply nodded yes.

* * *

While Archer washed up, I made myself at home in his small kitchen and got to work preparing a meal for him. It was the first time I had cooked in almost a year, but I felt nothing except happy and satisfied as I chopped and mixed and prepared, humming as I worked. Archer came in and poured potato chips into a bowl and took a container of onion dip out of his refrigerator and set it on the counter. *Appetizer*, he said, smiling.

Fancy. I laughed, and then pushed a few chips aside to get to one that had folded over during the frying process. Those were my favorite. They were slightly crunchier and were perfect to use as a little scoop for the dip. I popped it into my mouth and grinned at him, getting back to work.

We didn't talk much as I cooked, since my hands were busy, but

Archer seemed content just to watch me, standing with one narrow hip propped against the counter. I glanced at him a couple of times, standing there with his arms crossed over his chest and a small, happy smile on his face.

Several times he pulled me to him and kissed me deeply, and looked awestruck again when I didn't stop him. Then I grinned and found another folded chip and popped it into my mouth.

When dinner was done, I set his table and we sat down, and I dished up the food. Archer grabbed my hand and said, *Thank you for this*, looking almost like a little boy who didn't quite know how to express what he truly meant. *Thank you*, he repeated. I understood what that simple thank-you meant, though. No one had taken care of him in a long time.

He took a bite and sat back, and his face took on that same dreamy expression that had been on his face after our first kiss. I grinned. *Good?*

He nodded, still chewing. *You were right; you're a really good cook.*

I smiled. *Thank you. I used to cook at our deli. My dad and I came up with all of the recipes. We used to cook and bake together.*

I stared off behind Archer, picturing my dad flicking flour at my face and then pretending it was an accident. I felt my lips tip up—the memory bringing a warmth to my chest, not the tightness I had experienced over the last six months whenever my dad's memory came to mind.

You okay? Archer asked, looking at me, concerned. My lips curved into a wider smile, and I grabbed Archer's hand, squeezing it.

Yeah, I'm good.

Suddenly rain started falling gently outside the kitchen window, and I looked over, furrowing my brow slightly. I looked back at Archer when I saw his hands moving in my peripheral vision.

It's not supposed to storm tonight, he said, obviously reading my mind.

I breathed out and smiled, relaxing my shoulders.

Archer studied me, grabbing my hand and squeezing it.

I got up and went to his front door, calling to Phoebe, who was already on the porch. I brought her inside, and she settled herself on the rug in the living room.

I returned to the table, and Archer and I got back to our food, neither one of us saying anything for a couple of minutes as we both continued eating.

After we'd eaten, Archer helped me clear the dishes and clean up the kitchen. As I dried a plate he had just washed, I said, "Archer, something happened at the diner today that I wanted to ask you about."

He looked over at me, his hands in the sudsy water, and nodded.

I set the dry plate in the cabinet and signed, *A woman came into the diner today and . . .* I paused, thinking about my wording. *She didn't threaten me exactly—more like a warning, I guess. But she told me to stay away from you.*

Archer was staring intently at my hands, and his eyes darted to my face, his brow furrowing. He cocked his head to the right, but he seemed on guard almost as if he knew what I was about to say.

Victoria Hale? I said, and immediately his jaw hardened and he turned his head, looking down into the sudsy water. He was still for several seconds before he brought the pan he had been scrubbing up out of the water and threw it into the other, empty side of the sink, causing a loud, sudden clattering sound and making me startle.

He brought his wet hands back and raked them through his hair, then stood stock-still, that same tic in his jaw clenching and relaxing again and again.

I touched his arm gently, and he didn't look at me, although his body relaxed slightly.

I drew my hand back and paused for a second, taking in his tense body and strained expression, thinking that I'd never seen Archer Hale angry. I'd seen him wary, and shy, and uncertain, but never angry. I wasn't sure what to do.

He took a deep breath, but said nothing, looking over my shoulder, his mind suddenly somewhere far away.

Will you tell me about her, Archer?

His eyes darted back to me, clearing. He took another deep breath and nodded yes.

We dried our hands and left the last of the dishes in the sink, moving into the main room. I sat down next to him on the couch and waited for him to speak.

After a second, he looked at me and said, *When my uncle was dying, his head seemed to . . . clear a little sometimes.*

He drifted off again for a second, gazing over my shoulder momentarily and then snapping back to the present. His eyes found mine again.

It was almost like that cancer ate up some of whatever it was that made him . . . different mentally. He had these moments of normalcy that I'd never witnessed in him before, or at least not for extended periods of time.

Sometimes during those times, he would confess things to me—about all kinds of stuff. Things that he had done in his life, how he had loved my mother . . . A brief flash of pain crossed his features before he went on.

One day, I came into his room and found him crying, and he pulled me over to him and kept telling me how sorry he was. When I asked him why, he told me that when I was in the hospital right after I was shot—he brought one hand up to his scar unconsciously, rubbing it gently, and then brought his hand back down—*the doctors told him that my voice box could possibly be repaired, but there was a limited time frame in which to do it.* He paused again, his jaw clenching a few more times, bitterness filling his expression.

But then he told me how he'd told Victoria about the scheduled surgery, and she started planting it in his head that it would be better if I couldn't speak. If I couldn't speak, I couldn't be questioned. She exploited his paranoia so he canceled the surgery and missed the opportunity for me to ever talk again.

I sucked in a breath, horrified. *Why?* I asked. *Why would she do that? Why wouldn't she want you to speak?*

He shook his head, looking away for a second. *Because I know things that she doesn't want shared. Or maybe she just hates me. Maybe both. I've never really figured it out.* He shook his head again. *But it doesn't matter.*

I furrowed my brow, confused. *Archer, surely she knows that you can write—that you can communicate if you want to. What is it she doesn't want shared?*

He took a deep breath. *It doesn't matter, Bree*, he repeated. *It's nothing I'd ever talk about anyway. That's the worst part about it. She took my one opportunity to be normal, to be a real person, to live a life like other people do—and all for nothing. I would have never told her damn secret anyway.*

"Archer"—I grabbed his hands, bringing them to my heart as I had done earlier—"you are a real person; you can live a life like other people do. Who told you you can't?" It felt like my heart was cracking. This sweet, smart, gentle man thought so little of himself.

He looked down, shaking his head, unable to respond to me because I held his hands against my chest.

I didn't ask him more about the secret he held against Victoria.

I knew that Archer would confide in me as he felt comfortable. He had lived his life alone and isolated, with no one to talk to for so long. Just like me with the cooking and the intimacy...baby steps. In our own ways, we were both learning to trust.

I did have one final question, though. I let go of his hands and signed, *Why would she tell me you're violent?* It was almost ludicrous. Archer was the gentlest man I had ever met.

She came out here after my uncle died, after she'd seen me in town a couple of times. I have no idea why, and I don't care. I was angry, and hurting. I pushed her out my gate. She fell on her ass. He looked ashamed, although he had no need to, at least not in my book.

I pursed my lips. *I understand, Archer. She deserved it and much more, too. I'm sorry.*

He looked over at me, studying my face. He tilted his head, something seeming to come into focus in his eyes. *You didn't pay her any attention. You asked me about her after we...kissed.*

I nodded. *I know you*, I said simply.

He looked like he was working out a puzzle. *You believed me over her immediately?*

Yes, I said. *Absolutely.*

We stared at each other for a couple of beats, and then his face broke into one of those heart-stopping grins. I almost groaned, heat racing through my veins. That smile was mine—I was going to wager that no one had made Archer Hale smile like that in a long, long time. I felt greedy and possessive of that beautiful smile. I grinned back.

Can we kiss some more? he asked, his eyes shining with desire.

I laughed.

What? he asked.

Nothing, I answered. *Nothing at all. Come here.*

We made out on Archer's couch for a long time. But it was

sweet and gentler this time, our intense need from earlier quenched for the time being. We learned each other's mouths, memorized each other's taste, and just enjoyed the intimacy of kissing, lips to lips, breath to breath.

When we opened our eyes and he stared down at me, smoothing my hair back and tucking a piece behind my ear, his eyes told me everything his voice couldn't. We communicated a thousand words, without a single one being spoken.

Later, after the gentle rain shower had dwindled to nothing, Archer walked me home, wheeling my bike next to him, Phoebe sitting quietly in the basket.

He grabbed my hand, looking at me shyly and smiling as I smiled back, feeling my heart swell in my chest.

Then he kissed me on my front steps, a kiss so sweet and gentle that my heart ached and I could feel his soft lips on my own long after he had walked away and turned the corner, out of sight.

CHAPTER EIGHTEEN

BREE

The next day, my phone jolted me out of a deep sleep. I looked at the clock. Four thirty in the morning? What the hell?

"Hello," I said groggily, pressing the answer button.

"Honey?" It was Maggie.

"Hey, Mags, what's up?" I asked, concerned now.

"Honey, I'm taking you up on your offer to work the kitchen today. Norm was up all night pukin' his guts up—sorry for the TMI—and there's no way he can go into the diner. If you decide you don't wanna do it, that's okay. But, if so, we're gonna have to put a CLOSED sign on the door."

I paused very momentarily, knowing that closing the diner for even one day was going to take money out of their pockets. Their children were grown, but I had heard Maggie mentioning to a friend that she and Norm had been working their butts off the last couple of years to make up for the retirement they hadn't put away while their kids were in college. "Of course I'll do it, Maggie."

She let out a breath. "Okay, great. Thanks so much, hon. I'll see you there shortly?"

"Yeah, and give Norm my best."

"Will do, honey, thanks."

I hung up. I was going to be cooking for people today. I sat there for a couple of minutes, but didn't feel anxious about it—other than the nervousness of being able to keep up with the orders that came in. Maybe it was because I had gotten my feet wet cooking for Archer, or maybe it was just because I was in a better place now, concerning my emotions and fears. In any case, I didn't have time to sit here thinking about it all day. I needed to get to the diner and start getting the kitchen ready.

I took a quick shower, put on my uniform, and dried my hair and pulled it back into a low bun, making sure all my hair was contained. I took Phoebe out and then fed her, and rushed out the door.

Ten minutes later, I was walking into the diner, Maggie obviously having just gotten there minutes before me.

"I'll help you set up," she said. "It's pretty straightforward, though. If you feel comfortable making eggs, a few omelets, bacon, and pancakes, you'll be fine. Nothing we serve is too complicated."

I nodded. "I think I'll be fine, Maggie. Just let the customers know that this is my first day, and hopefully they'll tolerate their meal being a few minutes later than they're used to."

"I'll take care of them," she assured me.

We got busy gathering all the omelet ingredients from the refrigerator and putting them in the containers at the back of the counter behind the grill for easy access. Maggie beat several cartons of eggs and put them in containers in the refrigerator under the counter so they would be ready for me to pour straight into omelet pans as well. Half an hour later, and I felt like all my ingredients were prepared. Maggie started brewing coffee and turned the sign around on the door from CLOSED to OPEN.

The bell began ringing over the door a few minutes later as the first customers started arriving.

I spent the morning making omelets, frying rashers of bacon and hash browns, and pouring Norm's pancake batter onto the griddle. A few times I fell behind just a bit, but overall, for my first time in this particular kitchen, and cooking for large amounts of people in a short time frame, I felt great about the job I'd done. I could tell Maggie was pleased, too, by all the winks and smiles she shot me through the open window. "Doing a bang-up job, honey," she called.

When things started to slow down a bit, I started putting my own twist on a few of the dishes: a little garlic in the eggs I used for the omelets, a splash of cream in the scrambled eggs, buttermilk instead of water in the pancake batter—things my dad had taught me.

As I was cleaning the kitchen in preparation for lunch, I whipped up my special potato salad with bacon, and a roasted pepper pasta salad that had been a favorite in our deli. I smiled as I did it, my heart rejoicing in the fact that this wasn't a sad task, but rather something that kept my dad's memory alive.

Lunch went even better than breakfast as I had a full handle on the kitchen now and how all the appliances worked.

Maggie told everyone about the two salad "specials," and by twelve thirty, both batches were completely gone.

"Rave reviews on those salads, honey," Maggie said, smiling. "Think you'd like to whip up a few more batches for tomorrow?"

I grinned. "Sure thing," I said happily.

By three o'clock, when the diner closed for the day, Maggie and I were exhausted, but high-fived each other, laughing. I was tired, but happy and satisfied.

"Need me again tomorrow?"

"I hope not. Hopefully Norm's on the mend, but I'll let you know." She winked at me. "You did a real fine job back there." She looked thoughtful. "Even when Norm's back, think you'd be interested in making some of those salads as a regular item?"

"I'd love to."

I left the diner, smiling happily, and headed to my car. As I was almost there, a police cruiser pulled into the parking space next to mine, Travis inside.

I stood next to my own car, not getting in, waiting for Travis to turn his cruiser off and get out.

He walked over to me, a smile on his face that looked less than genuine.

"Hey, Bree."

"Hi, Travis." I smiled.

"Is it true?"

The smile disappeared from my face. "Is what true?" I said, figuring I knew exactly what he was asking about.

"That Archer is more than a friend to you?" He leaned his ass against my car and crossed his arms in front of him, his eyes trained on me.

I sighed, looking down for a minute and then back up to Travis. "Yes, Travis, it's true." I put my weight on one hip, feeling slightly uncomfortable in front of this man whom I had kissed. "In fact, I'm, um, seeing him."

He laughed. "Seeing him? How's that?" He looked truly confused.

I was instantly angry, as I stood up straighter. "How's that? Because he's a good man—he's smart and sweet and…why am I explaining this? Look, Travis, the truth is…I like him, and I wasn't trying to lead you on by going out with you. But I wasn't really sure at that point what was going on with Archer and me.

And now I am. And so I hope you understand when I tell you I don't want to see anyone else. Just him. Just Archer."

His eyes narrowed on me, anger flashing across his face. But just as quickly, he schooled his expression and shrugged. "Listen, I'm not happy about this. I'm interested in you, so yeah, this pretty much sucks to hear." He pursed his lips. "But, listen, if you've found a way to communicate with Archer, how can I be angry about that? That kid's had a hard enough time of it. I'm not too selfish to see that he deserves some happiness. So…I wish you two the best, Bree. Really."

I let out a breath, deciding to ignore his "kid" comment about Archer and remind him that Archer was actually a couple of months older than him. I let that go and said, "Thanks, Travis. I appreciate that a lot. Friends?"

He groaned. "Ouch. Friend-zoned." But then he smiled and it looked genuine. "Yeah, friends."

I grinned at him and exhaled. "Okay, good."

We smiled at each other for a second, and then he tilted his head to the side, looking as if he was thinking. "Listen, Bree, this whole situation has kind of made me realize that I've been an asshole not trying harder to be a friend to Archer. Maybe I dismissed him too quickly, thinking his silence meant he wasn't interested in being friends. Maybe it was me who just didn't try hard enough."

I nodded, excited. "Yes, he just wants to be treated like a normal person, Travis. And no one in town seems to do that. They all just ignore him, pretend he doesn't exist." I frowned.

He nodded, studying me. "You're a good person, Bree. I'm going to drive out there later this week and say hi to him."

I grinned. "That would be great, Travis. I think he might like that."

"Okay." He smiled. "Now I'm going to go drown my sorrows in Maggie's cherry pie."

"Diner's closed," I said, giving him a mock sad face and then smiling.

He smiled back. "Yeah, but Maggie's still in there, and when she gets a look at my face, she'll dish me up a piece." He winked. "Have a good day, okay?"

I breathed out a soft laugh. "You, too, Travis." I got in my car and drove home, singing along with the radio the whole way.

* * *

An hour later I was showered and in a pair of dark, fitted jeans and a light blue T-shirt with my hair hanging long and loose. Ten minutes after that, I pulled up in front of Archer's gate with Phoebe in my basket. I opened the gate, which was left open a crack, and set Phoebe down to go find her friends.

I leaned my bike against Archer's fence and started walking down his long driveway, just as he appeared around the side of his house, wearing ripped jeans, work boots, and nothing else. His chest was slightly shiny with perspiration, and he used his arm to wipe the sweat that dotted his forehead as well. Obviously, he had been working on one of his many projects again.

My stomach dipped at the sight of that beautiful body, and I thought about how I wanted to see all of it—every bit. Soon? Hopefully soon.

He grinned at me and started walking faster; a flock of butterflies took flight between my ribs. I started hurrying toward him, too.

When I had almost reached him, I ran the last little ways and flew at him as he caught me and lifted me in his arms, me laughing happily as he spun around and laughed silently up at me.

I brought my face to his and kissed him hard, getting lost in the sweet cinnamon flavor of his mouth, mixed with that singular flavor that was only him. I kissed him all over his face, smiling and loving the slightly salty taste of his skin.

He gazed up at me in that way that made me feel cherished. His expression was simultaneously wondrous and joyful. I realized that I put that expression on this beautiful man's face. My heart melted and my tummy clenched again. I rubbed my thumb over his cheekbone and gazed down at him from where he held me above him. "I missed you today," I said.

He smiled at me, and his eyes told me everything that his hands couldn't as he held me close to him. He brought his lips to mine again and kissed me deeply.

After a few minutes, I came up for air. "You really got hold of the kissing thing quickly, didn't you?" He chuckled silently, his chest vibrating against mine.

He let me down and signed, *You're extra happy today.*

I nodded as we walked toward his house. We went into his kitchen, where he poured both of us glasses of water while I told him all about cooking at the diner.

He drank his water, watching me chatter away, obviously finding pleasure in my happiness. Sweet man. His throat moved with each swallow of his water, his scar stretching as he drank. I stopped talking and leaned forward and kissed it, thinking momentarily about what he had told me yesterday about Victoria Hale, the evil bitch. What kind of horrible demon did you have to be to do what she had done to Archer, ensuring his handicap was one he'd have to live with forever, ultimately isolating him and making him feel damaged and limited. I wasn't a violent person, but when I thought about it, I felt like I could easily inflict physical pain on her and not feel the slightest bit of guilt.

I wrapped my arms around Archer's waist and put my head against his chest, listening to his heartbeat. I turned my face into his warm skin and nuzzled my nose against it, inhaling his musky scent. I darted my tongue out to taste him and felt him harden against my stomach. I pressed into him, squeezing him tighter, and he shivered slightly.

He threaded his fingers through my hair until I moaned, my eyes fluttering closed. I opened them to look up at him, and he was gazing down at me with that same look of awe that made my heart beat out of time in my chest. For several seconds we just looked at each other before he brought his lips to mine and his tongue entered my mouth, warm and wet, sliding deliciously over my own. Sparks shot downward, and I pressed into Archer's erection harder to get relief from the intense throbbing that had started between my legs. But that only made it worse. "Archer...," I breathed out, breaking free from his kiss.

He brought his arms from around me, and his eyes seared into mine, the look on his face somehow both nervous and hungry. *I know you like my hands in your hair. Show me other ways you like to be touched. Teach me what you like*, he said.

As his hands made the words slowly, my breath hitched, and more moisture gathered between my legs. As erotic as his question was, I felt slightly unsure, too. No one had ever asked me anything like that—and I didn't know exactly what to do, where to begin. I swallowed heavily.

Without looking away from my eyes, Archer walked me backward to his couch and laid me down gently. I blinked up at him and bit my lip. Standing above me like that, his erection tenting the front of his jeans, he looked like every fantasy I'd ever had come true. Only my imagination had been lacking, because I had never thought to add the look of awe and lust clouding my fantasy's beautiful features. I had never thought to give him those gorgeous whiskey-colored eyes with the fringe of dark lashes. I couldn't have known that Archer Hale existed somewhere in this crazy, crowded world, and that he had been made just for me.

And in that moment, I knew. I was falling in love with the beautiful, silent man staring down at me. If I hadn't already fallen.

He sat down on the couch next to me and leaned in and kissed me sweetly and then leaned back, running his hands through my hair again until I moaned. I loved that. If Archer simply ran his fingertips over my scalp all night long, that might be enough for me—*might*. Okay, it wouldn't be. But it still felt great. I smiled up at him, and he looked at me questioningly.

"My neck," I whispered. "I like my neck kissed."

He leaned in immediately and ran his soft lips over the skin there. I arched my neck back and sighed, using my own fingers to run through his soft, thick hair.

He experimented with sucking gently on the sensitive skin below my ear and then feathering his lips down my throat, and I told him with my moans what I liked best. And just like Archer, he was good at everything he did—learning quickly and easily how to make me pant and writhe beneath him.

With my arousal, I got bolder, pushing his head lower to my breasts. He understood immediately and leaned back and cupped his hands over them, feeling their weight.

His eyes shot to mine, shining with lust, and then moved back to my body as he lifted my shirt and pulled it over my head. He ran his eyes over me as I lay there in my simple white lace bra, and he inhaled sharply.

I reached up and unhooked it and let it fall to the side. Archer's eyes widened slightly as he stared at my breasts. Under other circumstances I might have felt uncomfortable, but the blatant hunger shining in his eyes and the look of appreciation on his face were so intense that I glowed under his scrutiny.

You're the most beautiful thing I've ever seen, he said.

"You can kiss me there, Archer," I whispered, wanting to feel his warm, wet mouth sucking on my nipples so badly I ached.

His eyes flared, and he leaned in immediately as if it was exactly what he'd wanted to do and had just been waiting for my direction.

I gasped and moaned as he used his tongue to taste and lick one nipple and then the next. My blood was roaring through my veins, and I couldn't help it when my hips thrust upward, seeking relief from the deep throb that was beating between my legs, begging to be filled.

Archer continued to tease and suck my nipples until I was moaning with a combination of ecstasy and agony.

"Archer," I panted out. "It's too much. You have to stop."

He brought his head up and looked at me with a small frown. *Not good?* he asked.

I laughed, a small, tortured sound. "No, too good," I said, biting my lip.

He tilted his head, studying me, and then nodded. *You need relief*, he said. *Show me how to do it with my hand.*

I blinked at him. "Okay," I whispered. I realized I was still using my voice, instead of my hands, even though there was now room between us, and brought them from around his waist to sign, *Take my jeans off?*

He immediately turned to unbutton and unzip my jeans, and then stood to pull them down my legs. His erection still filled his jeans. He must need some relief, too. I desperately wanted him inside of me, but I knew it would be his first time. I thought we should build up to that. There was no rush.

He returned to where he had been sitting next to me and looked at me questioningly again. I took his hand and put it slightly under the waistband of my underwear. I could feel that they were already drenched.

He reached down tentatively, and when his fingers reached my folds and slid into my wetness, I moaned and leaned my head back, one leg falling to the side, against the couch back, to give him better access. His fingers sliding over me and slightly inside felt so good.

After a minute, he moved down my body and slid my underwear off and gently positioned my leg against the couch back again. He moved up and used his finger to trace my lips and now watched as he did it. I was open and exposed to him in the most intimate way possible. But strangely, I didn't feel shy. When his finger hit my swollen bundle of nerves, I gasped and moaned and pressed toward his fingers. His eyes flared, and he circled his finger around it as I moaned and moved my head from side to side on the couch cushion. I felt the blood, now pulsing at a slow simmer, begin to boil. "Faster, please," I begged.

Archer sped up, his finger making tight circles on my pulsing clit as he moved it in response to my cries and moans. He had gotten me so worked up, it only took minutes before my body tightened and then released gloriously in a shower of pleasure so intense that I screamed out Archer's name, arching my back upward and then collapsing on the couch.

When I opened my eyes, Archer was staring at me, his lips parted slightly with that same mixture of adoration and lust on his face.

He moved up the couch and kissed me tenderly, nipping at my lips teasingly. I could feel the smile on his mouth, and I smiled against his lips.

But then when I wiggled slightly, he inhaled suddenly, and I remembered that he was probably in a needy situation now, too.

Without speaking, I pushed him back and nudged him gently with my hands until he was sitting on the couch, leaning against the back. His gaze followed me the whole time, waiting to see what I was doing. I stood up and shimmied my underwear up my legs so I wouldn't trip myself with them down around my ankles.

I kneeled down in front of him and unbuttoned his jeans, glancing up at him. He watched me eagerly. He literally had no idea what I was doing. Oh my God. I knew Archer had been isolated here on this property, but I wondered if his uncle had ever talked to him about sex...I wondered how much he knew about the things men and women did in the bedroom. Or on the living room couch.

I pulled his jeans down, and his cock sprang free. I stared at it for a second, my lips parting. He definitely wasn't lacking in that department. Just like the rest of him, it was large and beautiful. And it looked painfully hard, the head purple and engorged.

I looked up at him and he was watching me, uncertainty now clouding his features. *You're beautiful*, I signed, and he visibly relaxed.

I leaned forward and licked the swollen tip of him lightly, and he jolted and sucked in a breath. I looked up at him with satisfaction, and his eyes were large, his pupils dilated even further.

I leaned forward again and licked up the back of his cock, from the base to the tip, and then circled my tongue around the tip again. His breathing grew ragged, and I could hear him drawing in big gulps of air.

I put my mouth over the head and used my fist to hold the base of his arousal as I sucked him as far back into my throat as I could. I brought my mouth up and down on him for a couple of strokes, and when I leaned back to see if he liked what I was doing, he pressed himself toward me, begging me with his eyes to keep going. I smiled slightly and then put my mouth back on him.

He brought his hands up to my head and started threading his fingers through my hair again as I moved up and down on his hard length.

After less than a minute, I felt him grow even bigger and harder in my mouth, and his panting got louder as he began to thrust toward my face. Just a few strokes and he froze, his thick, salty essence bursting into my mouth. I swallowed it and then swirled my tongue over the head of his cock one final time before raising my head to look at him.

His hand was in his own hair now, gripping the strands right above his forehead, and he was looking down at me like he had just discovered the Holy Grail. I smiled up at him smugly. *Good?* I signed.

He just nodded his head, that same awe-filled expression on his face. I leaned up and planted myself on his lap, kissing his mouth. He kissed me deeply for several minutes and then leaned back.

Will you do that again?

I let out a small laugh. *Yes. Not, like, now*—I grinned—*but yes. I will.*

I kissed him again and then got up off his lap, pulling my clothes back on as Archer hiked his jeans up over his narrow hips. I had seen most of him now, but not completely. I couldn't wait to see him bare all over. I couldn't wait to feel him skin to skin as he moved inside of me. I shivered. Even though I had had an orgasm less than fifteen minutes before, I felt warmth spreading through my veins.

I moved back onto his lap and kissed his neck, darting my tongue out to taste the saltiness there. He had been working in the yard earlier, sweating lightly, but everything about him was delicious to me. I inhaled deeply as his arms came around me, holding me tightly to him. I felt safe and protected, and I was bursting with happiness.

After a minute, I brought my head up and asked, *Archer, your uncle, did he teach you about…sex?* I flushed slightly, not wanting to embarrass him. What a strange situation it was to be sitting on the lap of the sexiest guy I had ever known, a beautiful twenty-three-year-old man, and asking him if he knew what sex was. Not that I was overly worried about him in that department—evidently he was a quick study and an A-plus pupil. I figured he knew the reproductive aspects of sex; I assumed he took biology. But did he know anything about the variety of things men and women did together?

Archer shrugged. *No. His mind didn't really work that way. He always seemed to be working out some problem in his head—or protecting our property. I asked him about it once when I was thirteen or so, and he gave me a couple of magazines.* He looked away, looking slightly uncomfortable. *There were some articles in them…and I got the gist of it.* He frowned, studying me for a minute. *Does it bother you that I've never…*

Before he could finish, I was shaking my head. *No, Archer. You're the sexiest man I've ever known. Even that day you stopped in the parking lot to help me, I was drawn to you then. Even with the crazy beard and the long hair.* I grinned and he smiled back.

I think we're pretty good together, don't you? I teased, kissing his neck.

He smiled a genuine smile this time and nodded back, kissing me on my lips.

We stayed that way for a few minutes, just kissing lightly and holding each other, me nuzzling his delicious-smelling neck. I could have stayed there all day.

I lifted my head when I remembered the conversation I'd had with Travis. *Hey, I saw Travis in town today, and he asked me about coming out here to see you.* Archer furrowed his brow but didn't say anything. I didn't mention the fact that I'd gone on one date with Travis. It hadn't meant anything anyway, and I'd never had feelings for him, so why bring it up now?

Anyway, I went on, *he said he felt bad that he didn't have more of a relationship with you.* Archer raised one eyebrow. *He said he was gonna come out here this week to visit.*

Archer looked dubious. *What?* I asked. *You don't like him?*

I moved off his lap, next to him on the couch so we could use our hands to talk more easily. In the short time I'd known him, we had gotten really good at speaking sign language together, using a type of shorthand for words we both understood, only spelling out portions of words, things like that. It now took us about half the time to make a statement as it would have a couple of weeks earlier.

Archer was significantly better on his own than he had been when I first signed with him, picking up things from me as we went along. After all, I had spoken it all my life. It was my second language. He had only learned it from a book, and this was the first time he was putting it to actual use. Just a couple of weeks before, he had spelled out things he didn't have the sign for—that wasn't the case anymore.

No, not really, he said. *He messes with people, Bree.* His jaw tensed with some memory or another as he stared off into space. *I haven't even seen him in a couple of years—except driving around town in his police car.*

I studied him. *Well, I think he's changed. He's a really nice guy, actually. Maybe you could give him a chance when he comes here? Wouldn't it be nice to have some family in town that you actually have a relationship with?* I thought how I'd do anything to have even one person to call family—how I'd do whatever I could to foster a relationship if I had the opportunity. And I wanted that for Archer. I hated the thought of him out here all alone all the time, except for me. I wanted friends for him, family...I wanted him to be happy, to be a part of the community.

Archer still looked skeptical, but he took in what I'm sure was a hopeful expression on my face and asked, *You want me to give him a chance?*

I slowly nodded yes.

He kept looking at me for a minute. *Okay then, I will*, he said simply.

I cupped my hand on his cheek, leaning in and kissing his soft lips. "I know that isn't easy for you. Thank you," I said, speaking with my voice right against his lips.

He nodded, pulling me into him again and holding me against him tightly.

CHAPTER NINETEEN

ARCHER

I'd never been happier in my life. Every day, I worked around the property as the puppies chased at my heels, getting into trouble wherever they could, knocking stuff over and causing general puppy mayhem.

And every afternoon, my heart lurched happily when I heard the squeak of my gate, telling me Bree had arrived.

We would talk, her telling me about her day. Her eyes shined as she told me about all the new recipes she was coming up with at the diner now that Norm and Maggie had given her the job of re-vamping some parts of the menu. She looked so proud and happy when she laughed and told me how even Norm had admitted, al-beit begrudgingly, that her side-dish recipes were better than his. She said she had plans to move onto some of the main dishes next, and then winked after she said it, making my chest squeeze tightly at how beautiful she was.

Sometimes I felt like I stared at her too much, and tried to look away when she caught me. I wanted to gaze at her all day long, though—to me, she was the most beautiful woman in the world.

I loved the way her brown hair had little streaks of gold in it when the sun hit it. I loved how her eyes slanted up ever so slightly and how her lips were full and pink, like a rosebud. I loved kissing them. I could kiss them forever. They tasted like peaches.

I loved the shape of her face—like a heart. And I loved her smile, the way her whole face lit up and her happiness shined right out of her eyes. It was beautiful and genuine, and it made my heart skip a beat each time she turned it in my direction.

I loved her slim body and the way her skin was white where her bathing suit covered it. I adjusted myself in my pants and moved the thought of Bree's body out of my mind. I was working right now, and I needed to focus.

I smeared a little more mortar between the stones I was positioning on the sides of the cement back steps. They were just stones I had gathered down by the lake, but I thought they made the plain steps blend in more nicely with the new stone patio.

I was just finishing up when I heard my gate open and then close. I frowned. Who in the hell could that be? Bree was working at the diner until two today. It was only noon.

I stood up and walked around my house to look up the driveway and saw Travis, in his uniform, walking down slowly, looking around as if he'd never been here before. Although, the last time he'd seen the place I was a kid, and it had looked a lot different.

Travis spotted me and looked surprised. We walked the couple of feet between us to meet each other in front of the house.

"Hey, Archer."

I wiped my hands on the rag I was holding and regarded him, waiting for him to tell me why he was there.

"The place looks nice."

I nodded, acknowledging his compliment. I knew it looked good.

"You've been working hard."

I nodded again.

He sighed. "Listen, man, Bree told me how you two have been spending time together, and I…" He ran his hand through his hair, seeming to consider. "Well, I guess I wanted to come here and say hi. And that I'm sorry I haven't been out before this."

I kept studying him. Travis had never been easy for me to read. I had fallen into his traps before when he tried to pretend he was my friend and then metaphorically shot me in the back. Even when we were both kids, even before my accident. I didn't necessarily trust him now, but I supposed maybe people could change—it'd been a long time. I was going to give it a try. For Bree. Only for Bree. Because I thought that would make her happy. And I'd do anything to make Bree happy.

I nodded at him, giving him a very small curve of my lips, and gestured to the house, asking if he'd like to come inside.

"Yeah, yeah, sure," he said.

We walked to the front door and I let him in before me, walking behind him and pointing to the kitchen. I went straight to a cabinet and got a glass and filled it with water from the tap and took a long drink.

When I was done, I pointed to the glass and to him and raised my eyebrows.

"No, thanks," he said. "I'm on my lunch hour right now, so I can't stay long. What I actually wanted to know was whether you'd like to go out with me and some of the guys tonight? Nothing big—just a simple guys' night out, a few beers, some laughs."

My brows furrowed and I stared at him. I pointed to my scar and made a fake laughing movement.

Travis breathed out. "You can't laugh?" And he actually looked embarrassed. I'd never seen that look on Travis's face. Maybe he had changed a little. "Wait…" He seemed to reconsider. "You can laugh. A soundless laugh is still a laugh. Come on, the point is, wouldn't you like to have some fun? Get away from this little house for a night? Be a normal guy?"

I wanted to be a normal guy. Or at least, I wanted Bree to see me as a man who was at least a little bit like other men. I had never wanted that before. In fact, I had wanted the opposite—to look as abnormal as possible so no one looked at me. But now, now there was Bree. And I longed to give her what she deserved, not a sad hermit who never left his property. I was sure that she had gone on dates with men before me. They had probably taken her to restaurants and coffee shops. I didn't know how to do any of that. I needed to learn.

I nodded at Travis and mouthed, *Okay.*

He looked a little bit shocked, but grinned—his big white teeth flashing. "All right, then!" he said. "I'll be back to pick you up later tonight. Nine o'clock okay?"

I shrugged. That seemed kind of late, but what did I know about what time guys' night out should start.

Travis extended his hand and I reached forward, clasping it. "Okay, see you then." He smiled. "I'll let myself out." And with that, he walked out of my kitchen and closed my front door behind him.

I leaned against the counter and crossed my arms over my chest, thinking. For some reason, I didn't have a good feeling about this. But I wrote it off to nerves and went to get in the shower.

* * *

At ten minutes past nine Travis opened my gate, and I stood up from the chair on the porch where I had been waiting. I walked up the driveway and locked my gate behind me. Travis had a big dark silver truck, and it was idling in the road. I took a deep breath. The last time I'd been in a car—that I remembered anyway, I didn't think the ambulance counted—was the day I lost my voice.

I gritted my teeth and climbed up into it, forcing thoughts of that day out of my mind.

Travis revved the engine and started driving.

"So, man," he said, looking at me, "you clean up pretty well. You might even be better looking than me." He laughed, but it didn't reach his eyes.

Bree had practically jumped up and down when I told her I was going out with Travis and his friends, whoever they were. Then she had helped me pick out a decent outfit, not that I had much to choose from.

"Archer," she had asked me, holding up a shirt, "when was the last time you went clothes shopping?"

I had shrugged. *My uncle did that. He bought me some stuff when I was eighteen.*

She had regarded me quietly for a minute and then said, "And let me guess, you weren't quite as…" She waved her hand toward me, indicating my muscles, I guessed. "Developed."

I nodded and shrugged.

She sighed as if this was a problem and started digging through my raggedy clothes. Finally she came up with a pair of jeans that were decent and she said could pass for purposefully worn, and a button-down shirt I'd forgotten about that had been a little big on me when my uncle initially bought it.

Bree seemed satisfied and so I was, too. Maybe I'd even go into town and pick up a few new things if it made Bree happy that I looked nicer.

Travis turned to a music station on the radio, and we drove along just listening to the music for a little while. When I noticed that we were heading out of town, I tapped Travis and pointed at the road and raised my shoulders questioningly.

"We're going to a club on the other side of the lake. It's called Teasers." He looked over at me, raising his eyebrows, and then looked back at the road.

After a minute, he looked over at me again. "Can we talk? Man-to-man?"

I raised my eyebrows, not knowing exactly where this was going and feeling slightly uncomfortable.

"You get physical with Bree yet?"

I glanced quickly over at Travis and back at the road. I didn't especially want to talk to him about this, although if I had fully trusted him, I might have wanted to ask him a question or two. But I didn't. Until he proved otherwise to me, I was going to assume that he was mostly *un*trustworthy.

"Okay, I get it, you don't want to say anything about Bree." He was silent for a minute. "Can I at least assume you haven't gone all the way?"

I shrugged my shoulders and nodded. I guessed it was okay to tell him what we *hadn't* done.

He smiled, and in the dim lighting of his truck, his teeth flashed and a shadow crossed his face, and for a second, he looked like one of those evil clowns I saw in the stores at Halloween. I blinked and it was just Travis again.

"I'm assuming you want to, though, right?"

I looked over at him and narrowed my eyes, but nodded. Of course I did. Who wouldn't? Bree was sweet and beautiful.

He smiled again. "Okay. Well, I'm gonna tell you how it is, Archer, when you're…seeing a girl as beautiful as Bree. She most likely has some experience, and she's going to want you to know what you're doing when you take that big step. That's why I'm taking you to this club. There are women who will let you… practice with them. Get it?"

My heart started pounding. *Not really*, I wanted to say. Instead I just stared at him, narrowing my eyes again to let him know he'd need to explain this further. So far, I didn't like it. Not one single bit. But most of all, I didn't like thinking about the experience Bree might have, the men she might have been with in the past. In fact, it made my blood run cold and made me feel like I wanted to punch something. I'd rather not think about that at all.

Plus, Bree had told me it didn't bother her that I didn't have any experience in that area. Had she been telling the truth? Doubts started to settle in my chest, making it difficult to swallow.

Travis seemed to read my thoughts. "Girls will tell you they don't mind if you're inexperienced, but trust me, she's going to appreciate you knowing what you're doing when you get her in bed. You don't want to fumble around like a damn fool with her, do you? Embarrass yourself?"

I looked out the window, wishing I could tell him to turn his damn truck around and take me home. This was not my vision of what tonight was about.

"Hey, don't look so pissed, man. All men do it, trust me. Single, married—my friend Jason has been married for almost ten years now, and he still takes advantage of the girls in the back rooms. His wife looks the other way because she benefits from it, too. Get it?"

I continued staring out the window, thinking about Uncle Nate and how he had gone out sometimes and come back smelling like women's perfume and had lipstick all over his shirt collar. He didn't have a girlfriend or a wife, so he must have been seeing women like the ones Travis said worked at this club we were going to. And Nate was a good man. I wished he were still alive so I could ask him about this.

I knew I wasn't stupid, but I also knew I had a lot to learn. I read all these books constantly, but when it came to the real world, to the way people related to each other, to the way they acted and reacted, I felt like I was constantly playing catch-up—I didn't like the way it felt.

We pulled up in front of a building with dark windows and a big parking lot out front. There was a huge pink-and-black-neon sign that read TEASERS, in flashing letters.

We pulled into a parking spot, and Travis turned to me. "Listen, don't feel like you have to do anything you're uncomfortable with. But trust me when I say, if you do see someone you like, go for it. Bree will appreciate it. It's what men do, Archer."

I sighed and pulled the door open. I'd go inside with Travis. If nothing else, Bree would be happy that I had the guys' night out she was so enthusiastic about.

We walked up to the door, and a big guy with a shaved head and a T-shirt that read EMPLOYEE asked for our IDs. Well, there went that. I didn't have an ID. I started to turn around, but Travis grabbed my arm and leaned in and flashed his badge and said something to the big guy. He nodded and waved us in.

Inside the club, the music was blaring—something about sex and candy—and I squinted in the dim lighting as I took in the room. There were small tables placed around a big runway in the center, and my eyes widened as a half-naked woman slid down a gold pole. For a few seconds, I simply stood there and stared at her before Travis grabbed my arm again and pulled me forward to a table where two other guys sat with half-empty drinks in front of them.

"Hey, assholes," Travis said, swinging one of the chairs around backward and sitting down on it, looking at me, and pointing to the chair next to him. I took a seat.

"Jason, Brad, this is my cousin, Archer."

"Hey, man," Jason said, holding out his hand. "Glad you could join us." I shook it and noticed that Travis had been telling the truth. He wore a wedding ring.

"Nice to meet you," Brad said, and I shook his hand as well.

A waitress came over in what looked to be a swimsuit with a small skirt and asked if we'd like to order drinks.

Travis turned to the girl and glanced at her name tag and said, "Hi, Brenda," and smiled. She giggled and looked around our table.

"Well, you're a fine-looking group of boys," she said, grinning at us. I smiled politely when we made eye contact.

"What can I get you?"

Travis leaned forward. "A round of shots—Cuervo Gold, and a round of Yuengling."

The waitress smiled and went off to get our drinks. Travis chatted with Brad and Jason while I watched the show onstage. As the girl opened her legs and slid slowly down the pole, I felt myself harden slightly in my jeans and scooted into the table so the other guys couldn't see. Travis looked over at me and smiled knowingly.

The waitress placed our drinks down on the table, and Travis handed her some cash. She leaned over and stuck it down between her large breasts. I swallowed heavily. I didn't know what to think of all this.

Travis turned around and held up his shot glass and said, "To Archer! And an unforgettable night!" The other guys raised their glasses, laughing and calling, "Hear! Hear!" I watched them as they downed the liquid in one quick gulp and then stuck limes in their mouths. I did the same, forcing myself not to spit it out when it burned its way down my throat. My eyes watered, and I stuck the lime in my mouth and sucked out the sour liquid. It helped.

Travis smacked me on the shoulder and said, "That's it!" and raised his beer to me. I picked mine up and raised it to him and took a swallow, grimacing slightly at the taste of that, too.

Uncle Nate had been a drinker. He kept it around our house, and I had tried it once when I was fifteen or so. He seemed to like it so well. It had tasted like rubbing alcohol to me, and I had spit out the first sip I'd taken. Why he liked it so much, I wasn't sure.

I stayed away from it after that. Plus, my dad had been a rip-roaring drunk, and I still remembered him coming home barely able to walk but still with enough strength to smack my mom around.

I moved those thoughts aside and looked back up to the stage. There was a new girl up there now—petite, with long light brown hair. She reminded me a little bit of Bree. I watched as she started gyrating to the music, sliding up and down the pole with one leg wrapped around it. She leaned backward, her hair falling back as she arched all the way over. I brought the beer bottle to my lips and took a huge swallow.

This was all too much—the loud music pumping through the speakers, all the whoops and hollers and loud talk around me, the sights and the sounds overwhelming me, and my body responding to things I wasn't quite sure I was okay with. But the beer seemed to be helping now, making things just foggy enough that all the input was bearable, and some of my confusion seemed unimportant.

When the girl's dance was done, all the guys at the front of the stage leaned forward and started putting dollar bills in her underwear. One waved what looked like a twenty at her, and when she crawled over to him, he reached between her legs and stuck it under the material of her crotch. I looked away.

I'd had enough. I didn't have a frame of reference for everything going on, and it made me feel less than, like everyone here had one up on me. I didn't like it. It was the reason I stayed on my own plot of land and didn't attempt to interact with anyone. The last thing I needed was another reason to feel like everyone except me knew what the hell was going on.

I turned to Travis, starting to stand up, pointing to the door. Travis pushed my shoulder roughly, and I sat back down on the chair hard, my jaw clenching.

He leaned toward me, pursing his lips and taking one shoulder between his fingers and thumb as I narrowed my eyes at him. If he thought he was going to keep me here against my will, he had another think coming. I'd hitchhike home if I had to.

"Listen, bro," he said quietly so the other guys couldn't hear, I guessed, although they were busy whooping and hollering at the girl on the stage. "You think Bree doesn't enjoy a little something on the side right now? In fact, I should know." He looked at me knowingly and leaned in closer. "I love how her lips taste like peaches."

My eyes flared and my gut clenched. He had kissed Bree?

Travis sighed. "I'm just trying to help you out, Archer. Bree doesn't think you can satisfy her, and so she comes where she knows she's gonna get what she needs." He raised his eyebrows, obviously indicating himself. "And as it is, you probably can't give that to her. That's why I brought you here, man."

I sat back in my chair, frowning up at the stage, where a brunette was bent over a chair. Bree was kissing other men? Bree was kissing Travis? Anger raged through my bloodstream. But maybe I couldn't blame her. Maybe I was reading her all wrong— I thought she liked what we did together, but how the hell did I really know? How could I *not* be coming across as a complete and utter novice? She probably *was* bored.

Another round of beers showed up at our table, and I took a big drink of the full beer in front of me.

I was unhappy and angry about the thought of Bree with Travis, but the alcohol and the girls onstage were making the blood flowing through my veins feel hot—and I was turned on. I wanted nothing more than to go home to Bree. I wanted to kiss her and taste her everywhere. I wanted her to take me in her mouth again...but I wanted to know that I was doing it right. I didn't want to feel like the virgin I was.

The girl up onstage ran her hands up her own breasts and then grabbed the pole and mimicked the sex act on it. I was fully hard under the table. Getting up and leaving wasn't an option just then.

The other guys were still splitting their attention between the stage and among each other, chatting and laughing loudly. I wasn't listening to them anymore. I continued drinking—the taste of it had grown on me.

A blonde that had been up onstage a little earlier came up to our table and leaned down to whisper in Jason's ear. He laughed and got up, following her through a door next to the stage. I glanced at Travis, and he raised his eyebrows at me, grinning broadly. He leaned toward me. "I have a surprise for you," he said loudly over the music. "I think you'll like it."

He looked behind him and signaled to someone, and a minute later a girl walked over to our table. She smiled at me and I stared at her; she looked so familiar.

Travis leaned forward. "Archer, you remember Amber Dalton? She works here now."

Amber Dalton: the girl I had had a crush on when I was fourteen. The one Travis humiliated me in front of. The liquor coursing through my system must have been the reason I felt no embarrassment in front of her. I just continued to look at her, taking in her shoulder-length black hair, and those same large brown eyes I had loved all those years ago. She was still as pretty as I remembered her.

"Archer Hale?" she whispered, her eyes widening. "My God, I had no idea." Her gaze moved over me. "Well, you grew up just fine, didn't you?" She smiled, and I couldn't help the pleasure that swept through me. It felt like what happened all those years ago had been made okay by the appreciation of my physical appearance shining in her eyes.

"Amber," Travis cut in, "I do believe Archer is ready for that private time I discussed with you." He winked at her.

My head seemed to clear a little and I shook it no, and held out my hand to shake hers—my *nice to see you again* gesture.

Instead, she ignored my outstretched hand and planted herself on my lap, the overwhelming scent of sweet vanilla wafting off her. I stiffened slightly, not knowing what I should do with my hands other than keep them hanging by my sides.

"Sounds great!" she crooned, leaning closer and wiggling down on my still-semihard erection. I sucked in a breath. This felt weird, but good. I wasn't sure what to do.

As the music pumped steadily in the background, Amber leaned into me and whispered in my ear, "Damn, you're gorgeous, Archer. And your body..." She trailed a finger down my chest. "You know I liked you all those years ago, right? I saw how you watched me down by the lake. I wanted you to come out...but you never did..."

I watched her finger as it moved steadily down my chest to end at the waistband of my jeans, where she dipped it just a little bit inside and then started moving back up my chest. Now I was fully hard again.

"Go on, you two." Travis laughed. "Have fun."

Amber jumped off my lap, stood up, and yanked me up, too. I walked a little bit behind her to hide my condition, swaying slightly. Damn, I was drunker than I thought.

Amber led me to the same door Jason had disappeared through, down a long, dim hallway, and then pulled me in through a door on the left, shutting it behind her.

There was a chair in the middle of the room, and she walked me to it and then pushed me down gently.

She walked over to a table and fiddled around with something, and a minute later, music started wafting through the speakers on the wall. The music was nice this time, though—not overly loud and overwhelming. I felt better in here.

Amber walked toward me, and I forced my eyes not to droop. It felt like the blood in my veins was buzzing, but I felt numb at the same time.

She straddled my lap, and her perfume wafted up at me again, tickling my nose. She swayed to the music for a few minutes, closing her eyes and leaning back so I could study her. She was pretty, but not like Bree. Now that I was looking at her up close under lights that were a little brighter than out by the stage, I didn't like all the makeup on Amber's face, and I thought there was something a little harsh about the way she looked—something different than when she was a teenager.

She swayed back up until she was completely upright and brought the front of her tank top down. Her breasts popped out, and she grabbed my hands herself and planted them on her. My dick throbbed in my jeans. I rubbed her nipples the way Bree liked, and Amber tossed her head back, moaning. I squeezed her lightly. Her breasts were bigger than Bree's, but they felt different—not soft, but almost overly firm, and the skin stretched and shiny.

Amber opened her eyes and brought her head up and then studied me, her eyes dropping as she licked her lips. "You know," she
said, unbuttoning the top two buttons on my shirt, "we're just supposed to give lap dances in here, but Travis tipped me extra to give
you anything you want." She reached her hand down and rubbed
me through my jeans. My eyes fell closed, and I panted out harshly.

"God, you're big, honey," she breathed, running her lips down
the side of my neck now. She sucked the skin there, making me
jump slightly when I felt her teeth nip me. "Mmm," she moaned,
rubbing herself against me. "I can't wait to ride that big, thick cock
of yours, gorgeous. Do you like it fast and wild or slow and deep?
Hmm?" she crooned. "We're gonna find out, aren't we, baby?"

My body reacted to her words, but inside, something about this
felt wrong. I didn't even know this girl. Was I really supposed to
use her for sex and then go home to Bree, the girl I actually cared
about? Is that really what Jason did with his wife? I wanted Bree
to see me like she saw other men—I didn't want her to want to
kiss Travis—but this, this seemed…God, I couldn't think through
the alcohol and the way Amber was rubbing me through my jeans.
All my thoughts were jumbled together, my emotions all over the
place. I needed to get out of this room. I'd just get this over with
and go home. And then first thing in the morning, I'd go to Bree.

* * *

I stumbled out of the room ten minutes later and went to find
Travis. He was still at the table where we had been sitting, a redhead on his lap. I tapped him on his shoulder. He looked back over
at me, and a huge smile came over his face. He nudged the redhead off his lap and said, "Ready to go home, buddy?"

I nodded, frowning. That's all I wanted, just to get out of here and go to Bree. I wanted to hold her. Depression swept through me when I thought about what I'd done with Amber. I tried to move that aside, though—I didn't do anything the other men hadn't done, apparently. And I'd seen plenty of wedding rings here. Evidently, wives accepted that kind of thing. I guessed I really was a freak, though, because I wouldn't do it again. I felt empty and unhappy...and ashamed.

We drove across the bridge to Pelion. Travis was silent the entire trip, a small smile curving his mouth up. I didn't care what the hell he was smiling about—the alcohol was making me sleepy, and I rested my head against the window and closed my eyes, thinking of Bree.

Travis shook me what seemed like a few seconds later, and I blearily opened his door and stepped out. Right before I closed it, Travis winked at me and said, "Let's do this again, bro." I didn't acknowledge his words, just turned my back on his truck. It was then I noticed we were in front of Bree's cottage. I turned around to get back in Travis's truck, but he revved the engine, and I stumbled back as he peeled off noisily.

CHAPTER TWENTY

BREE

I turned over in bed, smiling out the window at the dark lake beyond. I had called Melanie and Liza when I found out Archer was going out with Travis, and we had had a girls' night of our own.

We'd gone down to the local pool hall in town and drank a few beers and laughed and talked, mostly about small-town gossip. Apparently, there was a girl in town who was having affairs with at least three married men. The wives of Pelion were in an uproar. Of course, I didn't think the girl was as much to blame as the men who had made the vows and broken them. But I guessed it was less painful to believe that their men had been lured away by some kind of magic temptress than that they were just lying, cheating assholes.

We also talked a lot about Archer, and I told them all about him. They listened to me with shocked but excited looks on their faces. "My God, we had no idea, Bree," Melanie said. Then she was thoughtful for a minute while I took a drink of my beer.

"You know, though," she continued, "you're really the only one who could have figured that out. You knowing sign...and ending up here...and him being alone, with no one to talk to—it's like the most beautiful kind of fate." I had smiled dreamily at that, letting her words wash over me. It was. That's what it felt like. *The most beautiful kind of fate.*

We made a pretty early night of it and got home by eleven, since I had to work in the morning, and I had showered and then read for a while. I turned off my light and was thinking about Archer and wondering how his night was going. I was so proud of him for agreeing to go out with Travis. He had looked so leery and unsure, and I knew that most of the reason he'd gone was because I'd encouraged it. But it was still such a big step. He had barely been off his own property, except for the occasional trip into town to get groceries or supplies for his projects, since he was seven years old. Going out to a bar or a restaurant was a big deal. I hoped he had had at least a little bit of fun.

I turned over again, when I heard a car door shut loudly and what sounded like a big truck go roaring off. *What the heck?* Phoebe perked her head up at the end of my bed and let out a soft bark.

My heart sped up, fear sweeping through me. I steadied my breathing, though—if this were someone intending me harm, if it was *him*, he definitely wouldn't announce himself with a bunch of avoidable noise.

"Stop being paranoid, Bree," I murmured. But I tiptoed to the front room anyway, Phoebe at my heels.

I pulled the edge of the curtain back and peeked out the window. I saw a large form walking unsteadily away from my cottage. Was that... Archer? Yes, yes it was.

I hurried to my door and flung it open, calling softly, "Archer?"

He turned around in the road and just stood there.

I cocked my head to the side, smiling a small, confused smile. "What are you doing here?" I asked. "Come here, I'm in my pj's."

He stood there for a few beats, swaying very slightly, looking…
I squinted my eyes into the dim light…drunk and upset. Oh geez,
did Travis get him *drunk*? Great.

Suddenly, he started walking toward me, his head down. He
came up my steps and walked right up to me, gathering me in his
arms. He held on to me tightly and buried his nose in my neck, inhaling deeply.

I froze in his embrace. Oh God, he smelled like another
woman's perfume—reeked of it, actually. Some vanilla, dime-store
stink. My heart seemed to thud to a stop in my chest and then start
up again erratically. What in the hell had happened during guys'
night out?

"Archer," I said again, pushing him away from me gently. He
took a step back and made a movement that made me think he was
trying to shake his hair into his face. But he didn't have long hair
anymore. He ran a hand over his newly cropped style and looked
at me miserably.

He brought his hands up and signed, somewhat sloppily, *I didn't
like guys' night out. I don't like strip clubs.*

"Strip club?" I breathed out. And that's when I spotted the huge
hickey on his neck and the bright pink lipstick smudged on his collar. Oh God. My blood ran cold. "You were with another woman,
Archer?" I asked, my heart sinking. My hands seemed to be incapable of doing anything other than hang by my sides.

For several beats, he just stared at me, his tormented eyes telling
me everything going on in his head. He thought about lying to me
for a second, I *saw* it flash in those expressive golden-brown eyes, but
then a look of defeat came over his face, and he nodded his head yes.

I just stared at him for a good thirty seconds before speaking.
"Did they bring you up onstage or something?" I asked, hopeful
that this was all some sort of bachelor party shenanigans.

His brow furrowed, but then two dots of color appeared on his cheekbones, and he brought his hands up and signed, *No, in one of the back rooms.*

"The back rooms?" I whispered.

Archer nodded and we both just stared at each other for a few seconds.

"So you were *with her* with her?" I asked. I could feel the color drain from my face.

Torment washed over his features as he nodded yes. He looked down at his feet.

I closed my eyes for a couple of seconds trying to digest this, and then opened them. "Why?" I asked, tears filling my eyes now.

Archer stuck his hands in his pockets and just looked at me, stark misery washing over his features. But what was I supposed to do with that? He had to know I would be upset over the fact that he was with another woman. Did he know so little about the world? About relationships? About love? No, I couldn't believe that.

He took his hands out of his pockets and signed, *You kissed Travis.* His jaw twitched.

I paused, frowning. "I kissed Travis *once* when you and I were only friends," I said quietly. "But once we became more, I picked you, Archer..." My words faded and then I choked out, "I picked you." Hurt and anger and despair crashed through my body again as he swayed slightly in front of me, looking like a puppy dog who had just been kicked. But wasn't I the one who had just been kicked?

I cleared my throat so I wouldn't start crying. "You're drunk," I said. "I'll drive you home. You need to sleep it off." I felt numb now.

Archer grabbed my arm, and I looked down at his fingers on

my skin and then up into his defeated expression. He let go of me and signed, *I'm sorry.*

I nodded once, a twitchy movement of chin to chest, and then grabbed my light coat off of the hook by the door and walked through it. I heard Archer close the door and his footsteps following behind me.

I got in my car, and he let himself in on the passenger side, closing the door softly.

We drove in silence the short distance to Briar Road, and when I pulled up in front of his gate, he turned to me in the car, looking at me beseechingly.

"Just go, Archer," I said. I needed to go home and curl up in my bed. I didn't know how to sort through all my feelings right now.

Archer stared at me for a few seconds, turned, and got out of my car, closing the door behind him.

I did a three-point turn and started back to my cottage. When I looked in my rearview mirror, Archer was still standing at the end of his road, his hands stuffed in his pockets, watching me drive away.

When I got home a few minutes later, I took off my jacket numbly and walked back to my room, climbing back into bed and pulling the covers up over my head. It was only then that I let the tears flow, devastation gripping my heart. He had been with another woman—the man I was falling in love with had chosen to give his first time to some cheap stripper in the back room of a bar. And I knew I had played a part in making that happen.

* * *

I dragged myself out of bed the next morning after only two hours of sleep. I felt heavy with sadness as I went through my morning routine.

Once I got to the diner, I immersed myself in as much busy work as possible, trying fruitlessly to keep my mind off Archer. It was a worthless cause, though, and as I restocked the sugar containers at each table, I thought about how hard I had pushed Archer to step out of his comfort zone and be a little social. I wanted to laugh with the irony, and then I wanted to fall on the floor and cry under one of the tables. Instead, I took a deep breath and counted out Splenda packets.

Part of this was my fault. I shouldn't have persuaded him to do something he wasn't ready for. I had just thought that maybe he'd never be completely ready, and a little nudge from someone who cared about him was a good thing. He couldn't live on his little plot of land his whole life, never venturing out beyond the grocery and hardware stores. I didn't think he wanted that, either. But maybe I should have been the one to help him step out into the world, instead of taking Travis up on his offer. *Travis.* What was his role in this whole thing? I had the feeling it was less than innocent. I had a vague notion that I might have thrown Archer to the wolves instead of helping him break out of his safety cocoon. At the very least, Travis hadn't stopped what happened at the club. Archer was so withdrawn and so shy. Surely he wouldn't have sought out sex with another woman himself. A stab of hurt pierced my heart, and I wanted to cry again when I pictured him thrusting into some half-dressed woman. I closed my eyes and willed the tears away. I had been cheated on before—I would get over it.

Only…something about this didn't feel like he had cheated on me, exactly. It felt like…something else. I paused in my thoughts. No, I wasn't going to give him an excuse for a choice that was ultimately his. Oh God, I was so confused. And hurt.

That afternoon, after making a couple of batches of my side salads, I called goodbye to Norm and Maggie and headed home for the day.

I remembered I needed a few things at the grocery store, and so I made a quick stop there. As I was walking back to my car in the parking lot, my mind still turning over the situation with Archer until I thought I'd scream, I heard my name called softly.

I turned and a woman with short brown hair and glasses was walking toward me, pushing a cart.

I stopped my own cart and turned toward her, offering a small smile. "Hi," I said, tilting my head.

"Hi." She smiled warmly. "I know you don't know me. My name is Amanda Wright. Don't be weirded out about me knowing your name. I'm in a pinochle group with Anne." She smiled again, laughing softly.

"Oh, okay," I said. "I live right next door to Anne."

She nodded. "I know. She told us about you during our game last week. And when I saw you today, I figured you had to be the Bree that Anne had described."

I nodded. "Well, it's great to meet one of Anne's friends. She's been so nice to me."

"Yes, she's lovely." She paused for a minute. "I hope you don't think this is forward, but...she mentioned that you were visiting Archer." She looked at me curiously.

Things had changed just a bit from the last time I'd chatted with Anne, but there was no way I was getting into that, so I just answered, "Yes."

She smiled and let out a breath. "I was his mother Alyssa's best friend," she said.

I sucked in a surprised breath. "You knew his mother?"

She nodded. "Yes, and I've always felt...so bad that I didn't do more for Archer when Alyssa died." She shook her head sadly. "I tried to go out there a couple of times, but there were all these crazy signs up on that fence, warning about bombs and traps and...I just...I chickened out, I suppose." She looked thoughtful. "Then I heard around town that Archer had sustained some mental damage in that accident, and I just thought maybe his family was more capable of taking care of him and dealing with his situation." She pursed her lips. "Explaining it out loud makes me realize how weak I sound."

"Mrs. Wright—" I started.

"Please, call me Amanda."

I nodded. "Okay, Amanda, if you don't mind me being nosy, do you know what happened to cause the accident that day? Archer won't talk about it, and, well..." I wasn't sure how to finish that sentence, my words fading into nothing.

Amanda put her hand on my arm. "You care about him," she said, smiling. It looked like there were tears in her eyes.

I nodded. "I do." And in that moment, I realized that no matter what happened between Archer and me, I cared about him deeply, and I still wanted to help him live a life that included more than just him and some dogs and a slew of stonemasonry projects year after year.

Amanda stared off past my shoulder for a couple of seconds, thinking, and then she said, "All I know about the accident itself are the few details that were in the paper. Of course those came from an out-of-town reporter—we don't have a paper here in Pelion. Other than that, people just don't talk about it. If you ask me, it's because of Victoria Hale—*everyone* is intimidated by her. She holds the power to get rid of jobs, close businesses, and she's done it when someone's butted heads with her, so there's reason for all of us to be concerned. And I'll tell you what: to my mind, whatever *did* happen the day of the accident, it started with Victoria Hale.

She's never had any qualms about messing with people's lives to further her own agenda."

I sucked in a breath. "Victoria Hale?" I asked. "She came in the diner where I work last week to warn me away from him."

She nodded, looking as if she was deciding something. "I've never talked to anyone about this, but Tori Hale was always sick with jealousy of Alyssa. Always trying to manipulate people to get what she wanted. And in the case of Alyssa, she was successful more often than not." She shook her head sadly. "Alyssa always had a damn guilt complex about something—never felt worthy of anything or anyone. She grew up in an orphanage, didn't have a person on earth until she came here to Pelion…" Her voice faded away as she recalled the past. "Sweetest girl you'd ever meet, not a mean bone in her entire body, and those Hale boys fell hard for her." She smiled a sad smile.

"Anne told me she picked Marcus Hale." I smiled.

But Amanda frowned and shook her head. "No, not picked—was set up. We went to a party the night Alyssa got pregnant. Victoria was there—I'd never be able to prove it, but I know she spiked Alyssa's drink with something and that Marcus took advantage of her. His way of staking claim to her and one-upping his brother Connor, who it was becoming obvious was the one Alyssa loved. Of course, Marcus didn't anticipate her getting pregnant, but that's what happened. They got married three months later. Alyssa was heartbroken and so was Connor. And of course, Alyssa blamed herself and figured her punishment was being married to a man she didn't love. She made a lot of poor choices, but mainly because she just didn't think enough of herself."

She looked thoughtful again for a second. "I've always said that Tori Hale's special gift is being able to manipulate others to do her dirty work. Her hands are always clean somehow, and yet she's always the man behind the curtain, so to speak."

She shook her head sadly again, almost looking like she might tear up, but then seemed to snap back to the present, putting her hand on her chest and laughing softly. "Oh goodness, look at me gossiping about the past, standing here in the grocery store parking lot while your things are probably melting. Please forgive me. I really just wanted to introduce myself, and ask if maybe you'd say hi to Archer for me and let him know his mama was real special to me."

I nodded at Amanda, sadness sweeping through me at the information she'd given me about Archer's mom and dad.

Amanda went on. "I own a clothing boutique in town—Mandy's." She smiled. "Creative, right? You come in and visit me sometime and I'll give you a friend discount."

I smiled at her. "That's awfully nice of you, thank you. I will."

"Good. It was lovely meeting you, Bree."

"You, too," I said as she walked away.

I loaded the grocery bags and then got in my car, sitting there in the parking lot thinking about a sweet girl who came to a new town, and the brothers who loved her—and how the one she didn't love manipulated her into choosing him, and how it had all ended in tragedy. And I thought about the little boy that sweet girl had left behind, and how my heart ached for what we might never have again.

*　*　*

I spent the next couple of days working and then holed up in my cottage, reading mostly, trying to make time pass more quickly. *I hurt.* I missed him. And strangely, I wanted to comfort him. I didn't know exactly what had happened at that club, other than that Archer had gone to some back room with one of the strippers and had sex with her, which I didn't even realize was on the strip club menu, but what did I know? What *was* clear, was that Archer wasn't happy about it. So why had he done it? I tried to put myself in his shoes, tried to understand what it must have been like for him to be in a strip club of all places. But thinking about it too much just made it hurt more.

On Friday as I was getting off work, I saw Travis across the street in his civilian clothes. As I squinted into the sunshine, watching him chat casually with an older man, rage filled me. He had been there—he had taken Archer to a strip club. He had *planned* it.

Without thinking, I stormed across the street, a car horn blaring at me. Travis looked over and started to smile but saw the look on my face and went serious, turning to the older man and saying something before walking to meet me as I was heading toward him on the sidewalk.

As soon as I reached him, I slapped him hard across his face, the sound reverberating through the mild fall air. He closed his eyes and put his hand up to his cheek, rotating his jaw slowly.

"What in the hell was that for?" he hissed.

I got right up in his face. "You're a mean, selfish asshole, Travis Hale. What in the hell were you thinking, taking Archer to a strip club? I thought I could trust you to take care of him!"

"Take care of him?" he asked, laughing softly. "What is he, a damn child, Bree?"

"What?" I sputtered. "Of course he's not a *child*. But you *know* that he needed you to look out for him a little bit. He's never been out socially before! He needed you to—"

"Is that what you want? You want someone who has to be *looked out for* all the time? Is that the man you want?"

I was seeing red now, my hand itching to slap his face again.

"You're twisting this! You're making him sound like he's mentally incapable of getting the hang of things he's never done before. He just needed you to—"

"What? Hold his hand all night so he didn't fuck another woman?"

My mouth dropped open, and I gaped at him.

He breathed out, running his hand through his hair. "Jesus, Bree, I wasn't trying to create a situation where you got hurt. I was just trying to show the guy a good time—make him feel like a *guy*, give him some confidence so he didn't feel like he was so far out of your league. All right, it obviously wasn't the best plan—I figured that out, after he went in the back with a girl he liked when we were teenagers and fucked her, all right?"

"God, stop saying that!" I said, tears coming to my eyes. I swiped at them angrily, mad at myself for crying in the middle of the damn street in front of Travis Hale.

"He's not for you, Bree. He's…too different…too sheltered, too apt to make choices that will hurt you. I'm sorry you found out the hard way."

I shook my head back and forth. "You're twisting this," I repeated.

"I'm not," he said gently, pulling me toward him and putting his arms around me. "I'm sorry, Bree. Really, really sorry."

I pushed away from him and turned to walk back to my car. My head was swimming with hurt and anger—at Travis, at Archer, at myself. I just needed to get home.

"Bree," Travis called, and I stopped walking but didn't turn. "I'm here if you need me."

I kept walking, noting that people all around us had stopped and were staring. *Wow, subtle.* But we *had* just put on a show, or rather, I had.

I walked quickly to my car, got in, and drove numbly home, dragging myself into my cottage and collapsing on the couch.

Phoebe came up and happily jumped on my lap, wagging her tail and licking my face. I laughed, despite my rotten mood, and hugged her to me. "Hi, sweet girl," I cooed.

Phoebe jumped off of my lap and ran to the door, chuffing softly to go outside. She was so used to hopping in the bike basket and pedaling over to Archer's house every day, she had to be missing her friends, too, and that huge property where she ran around uninhibited, exploring.

"I miss him, too, girl," I said, not knowing what in the hell to do about that.

After a few minutes, I went to get in the shower. As I undressed in my bedroom, the first raindrops began to fall.

CHAPTER TWENTY-ONE

BREE

By eight o'clock that night, the rain was coming down hard and the thunder had started booming, lightning zigzagging across the sky.

I sat huddled in my room, Phoebe on my lap. The feeling of *that* night came flowing back over me as I sat there. I had a better handle on it now, but I knew the loud booming above me would always remind me of feeling alone and helpless.

I had several candles burning around my bedroom in case the power went out. Normally, candles provided a calming, romantic atmosphere, but tonight the shadows they cast on the walls surrounding me made the storm even scarier, more unnerving.

I heard a soft knock at my door and startled. Phoebe perked her ears up and barked softly. Who the hell was that?

I had already had *him* in the forefront of my mind because of the storm, and so my heart rate accelerated as I slowly got up off my bed and tiptoed down the hall, Phoebe at my heels.

I went to the front window and peeked out the curtain where I could just barely see my porch in front of the door. Archer leaned back, looking at me as I stared at him. My heart started pounding as I took in his drenched form: his jeans, white T-shirt, and unzipped sweatshirt plastered to his body. *Oh God, he must have walked here in the downpour.*

I hesitated for only a second before I hurried to the door and flung it open to the sound of the rain pounding the ground in front of my porch. A loud clap of thunder shook the cottage, and I jumped slightly, causing Archer to take a step toward me.

What are you doing here? I asked.

You don't like thunderstorms, he answered.

I tilted my head, confused. *You walked a mile in the rain because I don't like thunderstorms?*

He hesitated for a second, looking away, frowning slightly. Then he looked back at me and said simply, *Yes.* He paused, his expression pained. *I know I'm probably the last person you want to see right now, but I just thought if I sat on your porch, you wouldn't be scared. You wouldn't be alone.*

Oh God.

I couldn't help it; my face crumpled, and I started to cry.

Archer took a tentative step toward me and silently asked permission as he looked into my eyes. I nodded at him, acknowledging his unspoken question, and he took me in his arms and pressed me to him.

I brought my arms up around him and buried my face in his neck, breathing in his clean, rainy scent. I cried silently in his arms for several minutes as he held me, rubbing circles on my back, his warm breath on my ear, his drenched clothing soaking me, too. For those few minutes, I was oblivious to the thunder and rain coming down noisily all around us—for those few minutes, it was only him and me, and nothing else.

I wasn't sure what to think. I only knew that this felt right. He was still my best friend, my sweet, silent boy, and I had missed him so desperately. He had hurt me, and yet I clung to him as if my very life depended on it.

After a few minutes, I leaned back, looking up at his face. He looked down at me so sweetly and tenderly that my heart squeezed tightly in my chest.

You hurt me, I said, stepping back.

Sadness filled his expression and he nodded, acknowledging that he knew he had.

Let me fix it, he said, *please. I want to fix it. What can I do?*

I breathed out, dropping my shoulders. *You had sex with another woman, Archer.*

He shook his head. *I didn't have sex with her; I just…was with her.*

My brow furrowed and I jerked my head back. *What? I thought you were…wait, what does "you were with her" mean exactly?* I didn't know what he was going to tell me, but relief washed over me when I realized that he hadn't gone all the way with her.

He sighed, running a hand over his wet head, and then shaking his hand down at his side. *I…is this…* He sighed again. *She took me in the back room and kissed my neck and brought my hands to her breasts. My body…reacted.* He closed his eyes for a couple of beats and then opened them. *She told me Travis had paid for her to have sex with me, but it didn't feel right and so I left. That's what happened. I'm so sorry. I knew it wasn't right. I didn't want that. I mean…I…God.* Shame filled his face as he looked down again.

I released the breath I'd been holding and laughed softly, shaking my head. Archer took my chin in his freezing-cold fingers and tilted my head up. He looked at me with questioning eyes.

You got a lap dance, Archer, and it went too far. But you said no to her and left. I studied him for a second. *Why did you say no? Tell me.*

He didn't say anything for a few beats and then: *Because I don't want to be with anyone except you. I didn't want her. I only want you. I only want you, Bree.*

As we stood there in my doorway, looking into each other's eyes, I noticed that he was trembling, and his lips were turning blue, a pool of water forming on my dry porch beneath him.

I pulled him inside. "Oh my God, you're freezing," I said, my hands busy pulling him. "We have to get you warm."

I walked him into my bathroom and turned on the shower, warm steam immediately billowing out into the small room. I started pulling his clothes off, his sweatshirt and his T-shirt, and he let me, his eyes trained on my face, only helping out where I needed him to. He kicked his shoes off, and I kneeled before him and peeled his wet socks off his feet and then stood up again, my eyes moving up his abs to his chest as I came slowly upright. The room suddenly seemed even warmer. I bit my lip and looked up into his beautiful face.

You get in the shower, I said when he was standing in nothing but his jeans. *I need to change, too*, I said, looking down at my wet nightshirt.

He nodded, and I turned jerkily and left the bathroom. I shut the door behind me and leaned against it for a second, biting my lip again. I groaned softly. "Only you, Bree," I said quietly. "Only you would fall in love with the local mute loner." But then I grinned. Yes, local mute loner, but *my* local mute loner.

I changed out of my wet clothes and put on a new—cuter—nightshirt. Then I went to the kitchen and put on the kettle. I stood there looking out the window at the rain, waiting for the whistle.

A couple of minutes later I heard the shower turn off. A minute after that the door opened, and I called softly, "In the kitchen."

Archer came in with only a towel wrapped around his narrow

hips, rubbing a hand over his hair and looking at me a little self-consciously. I took in his drool-worthy naked chest and the way the towel left little to the imagination as far as his assets went, and swallowed.

"I'm just finishing up the tea," I said, opening a couple of tea bags. "If you want to gather your clothes and put them in the dryer—it's in the small closet in the hall."

He nodded and left the room as I finished up, and then rejoined me as I was taking the tea into the front room. He took one of the mugs from me and we sat down on the couch together, sipping our hot tea in silence for several comfortable minutes.

Finally, he put his mug down on the table next to the couch and turned to me. *Can I say something?*

I looked at him, tilted my head, and said, "Of course," and then took another sip of my tea.

He inhaled a long, slow breath and seemed to be gathering his thoughts. *I've been thinking a lot these past couple of days and…I was trying to be what you want me to be, but…it's a lot for me, Bree.* He shook his head slightly. *I hated that night—the noise, all the people, the fact that I can't talk.* He was silent for a beat before meeting my eyes. *I want to make you happy, more than anything, but…* He ran his hand over the top of his hair again.

I set my tea down on the coffee table in front of us and moved closer to him. *Archer, I made you feel like you were a project to me. I made you feel like you, just as you are…you weren't enough.* I looked down and then back up into his eyes. *I'm so sorry.*

He grabbed my hands, squeezed them, and then let go. *No, it's not your fault. I know you were trying to…expand my world. I just need to do that as I'm ready to, okay? And I don't know when I'll be ready. It might be a long time, Bree.*

I nodded, tears in my eyes. *Okay.* I laughed lightly and climbed onto his lap, straddling him and leaning forward, squeezing him tightly to me. "Just one thing, though," I whispered into his neck, not willing to let go of him just then.

He waited. I leaned back and said, "The only woman who gives you lap dances is me."

He grinned, his eyes dancing. I felt like that grin could easily cause me to fall over and die of heart failure brought on by an overdose of his beauty. I grinned back and leaned forward and kissed him deeply.

The thunder boomed, and a bolt of lightning made the room pulse with light for several seconds. I sighed contentedly and slid my tongue into Archer's warm mouth. He tasted like a mixture of cinnamon from his toothpaste and honey from the tea. His tongue met mine, sliding along it deliciously, eliciting a moan from deep in my chest. He took my face in his hands and tilted my head so that he could go deeper, taking charge of the kiss and exploring my mouth slowly and thoroughly until I was panting and rubbing myself on his thick, hard erection.

Archer was shy and unsure so much of the time, but when it came to something he had taken time to master, he was steady and confident about it. I wondered if he even noticed that about himself.

I broke the kiss, sucking in air and tilting my head back to give him access to my neck. He kissed and nibbled down it lightly as I ran my fingers through his hair.

His hands came up to my breasts and he rubbed my nipples lazily through the thin cotton of my nightshirt. I sighed with pleasure, grabbing handfuls of his hair.

I felt his erection grow even harder beneath me—nothing separating us except for the now-wet material of my underwear and the terry-cloth towel.

I reached down between us and trailed my fingers lightly down his tight abs. He inhaled a breath, his muscles clenching at my touch. I moved my hand down farther and stroked him over the towel as he looked at me with heavy-lidded eyes, his lips parted. Oh God, he was stunning to me. Wetness pooled between my thighs, and a furious pulse of need beat there, wanting to be filled.

"Archer…I want you," I whispered.

Without hesitating even a second, he scooped his arms underneath me and stood up, heading toward my bedroom. I brought my arms up around his neck. "I guess that's a yes," I said, laughing.

He smiled at me, looking slightly strained and just a little bit nervous.

When we got to my bedroom, he laid me gently on the bed and stood, looking down at me, gentleness and desire meeting in the expression on his face. My heart thundered in my ears.

Archer turned to the wall and flipped the overhead light off. The candles were still lit and they cast a dreamy glow on the room. What a difference half an hour made, I thought, remembering that I had been sitting in this very room just a little while ago, feeling alone and scared.

Archer turned and dropped the towel from around his waist, and I got a brief look at the full vision of his naked body before he put one knee on the bed and lowered himself down to me. Good lord. Building stone patios, chopping wood, and walking everywhere was a workout video he needed to put on the market. ASAP.

He brought his mouth to mine again and kissed me deeply for long minutes, bringing his mouth to my neck after we both broke the kiss to gulp in air. He sucked on my skin gently, and I leaned my head back even farther, giving him more access and pressing my hips upward into his hardness. He sucked in a breath and brought his head up, looking into my eyes.

He was leaning on his forearms, holding himself over me, so he couldn't use his hands to talk, and I chose not to speak, either. The look on his face told me everything I needed to know. There was nowhere else on earth he'd rather be than right here with me, doing what we were about to do. And as I gazed up at him, his eyes dark with lust and his expression tender with emotion, I knew there was nowhere else on this earth I'd rather be, either.

I reached my arms up, indicating that he should lift my nightshirt off. He leaned up and took hold of the hem and raised it slowly, sliding it up my arms, over my head, and tossing it on the floor next to the bed.

Then he stood again and watched my eyes as he hooked his pointer fingers in each side of my underwear and dragged them down my legs. I looked from his eyes down to his hard, straining cock, and the pulsing in my core picked up in intensity.

He stood staring down at me, and I began to squirm slightly as his eyes raked up and down my body. I had never simply stayed still as someone studied my nakedness, but when he met my eyes and said, *You're so beautiful*, I relaxed. I noted that his hands were shaking very slightly.

"So are you," I whispered as he came back down on top of me, the muscles of his forearms flexing again as he held his weight off of me and leaned his head in to meet my mouth again.

I ran my hands slowly up and down the hard ridges of his arms and then over his broad shoulders. Then I traveled down the smooth skin of his muscled back, ending at his ass, where I ran my hands over it, grabbing it lightly and pushing him down into me. I felt him smile against my mouth.

I broke free from his lips, smiling, too, as he kissed my neck again. "You like it when I grab your ass?" I asked, grinning. He smiled into my neck.

So I brought my hands back to his hard ass and kneaded it gently, pressing my hips upward into his erection, lying hard on my belly, the heat of it burning into my skin deliciously and making me tremble with my desire for him.

He moved his head down to my breasts, took one nipple into his warm mouth, and circled his tongue over it. "Oh, Archer," I gasped out, "please don't stop."

He brought his other hand up and played with one nipple while he sucked and teased the other one with his mouth and his tongue and then switched sides.

I moaned and pressed my hips up, seeking relief from the aching need between my legs, my clit so swollen, I thought I'd probably come the minute he touched it.

Archer brought one hand down between my legs and dipped his finger into my wetness, bringing some of it up and over my small bundle of nerves as he used his finger to make slow circles on it, just like I had shown him. I gasped and moaned, rolling my hips upward, pressing into his hand, begging for the release that was so close; I could feel the beginnings of it like little sparks of static electricity.

"Oh God, oh God, oh God," I chanted, moving my head back and forth. I felt Archer's cock jump against my belly, and that's all it took to send me over the edge, the orgasm hitting me hard and fast, rolling through my body with delicious slowness as I gasped and moaned through it.

When I opened my eyes, Archer was gazing down at me, that look of awe and tenderness on his face that I loved so much it hurt.

"I want you inside of me so badly," I whispered.

He kept looking into my eyes as he moved his hips between my legs and took himself in his hand, guiding his cock to my entrance. He swallowed heavily as I brought my knees up and opened my legs wider so that he had easier access.

Our eyes met again and something passed between us—that same indescribable something that I had noticed the first time we met—only now intensified tenfold.

I leaned up on my elbows, and we both watched as he entered me slowly, pushing inside me inch by inch, stretching and filling me. When he paused, I looked up at his face, and the look of pure pleasure there was so stark and raw I could only stare, spellbound. *I am putting that look on his face.* He throbbed inside me and then, with one thrust, pushed fully into me. I fell back, moaning softly, and he started to move in and out, slowly. I stared up at him, mesmerized by all the emotions flashing across his face as his thrusts increased in tempo—awe, hunger, an attempt to retain control, and then finally, surrender to the pleasure as his eyes drooped, and he thrust into me harder and deeper, his breath coming out in sharp pants.

I tilted my hips up and brought my legs around Archer's back. His eyes flared for a brief second before he buried his face in my neck. His thrusts grew jerky as he gave one final deep thrust and then pressed into me, rolling his hips slowly, drawing out his pleasure.

We lay together for long minutes, Archer breathing harshly into the side of my neck, me smiling up at the ceiling.

Finally, I brought both hands down and rubbed my fingernails over his ass, then squeezed it gently. I felt him smile against my skin, but he didn't raise his head and he didn't attempt to move, his body lying half on me, and half on the bed so I wasn't being crushed.

"Hey," I said softly, "you alive there?"

I felt another slow grin against my neck and then he shook his head no.

I laughed softly and his head came up, a sweet smile on his face.

He took my face in his hands and kissed my lips gently for several minutes before he sat up.

I sat up, too. I needed to go clean myself up.

I cupped my hand over his cheek, kissed him softly again, and then stood up to walk naked to the bathroom. I looked back at Archer and he was watching me, his eyes roaming over my naked backside. I scurried to the bathroom and cleaned up and then walked back to the bedroom, where Archer was still sitting on the side of my bed, looking a little unsure.

"This is the part where you cuddle me." I grinned at him. He smiled and breathed out and folded my covers back. We got in bed, and he pulled me against him as I brought the blankets up over us. We were turned toward the window, and the rain was still falling, although a little more gently now.

I had left the blinds open—there was only the lake beyond; no one could see inside. Thunder boomed in the distance, and a flash of lightning lit up the sky a few seconds later, but it was moving away from us now. I sighed contentedly as Archer pulled me even more tightly against him.

We lay like that for long minutes until I finally turned toward him and whispered, "I missed you so much these past few days."

He nodded at me and rolled to his back and signed, *Me, too. It made me feel crazy.*

I leaned over and kissed his chest and laid my head there, listening to his heartbeat for a few minutes as he played with my hair.

Wanna know the first thing I thought about you when we first met, other than how beautiful you were?

I watched his hands move next to me and then lifted my head, looking up at his face questioningly. He gazed down at me, warmth lighting those beautiful amber eyes.

You acted embarrassed in front of me, bashful—you even blushed—

about all those candy bars. He smiled and leaned down and kissed my forehead. My heart picked up speed.

He continued. *It was the first time in my life anyone had acted embarrassed in front of me. People had acted embarrassed for me, but never because of something they'd done in front of me. It made me feel like a real person, Bree. It made me feel like something about me mattered.*

I swallowed heavily. "You *are* a real person, Archer. You're the best person I know," I whispered, laying my head down on his chest.

He hugged me to him again, and we lay like that for what seemed like a long time, just enjoying holding each other, skin to skin, heartbeat to heartbeat.

After a little bit, I pressed my nose into his chest and inhaled, drawing in his clean, masculine smell. I smiled against him and kissed his skin again. He reached his hand down and grabbed my ass, and I startled and laughed. When I looked up at him, he was grinning. "Hey, that's *your* thing." I laughed.

What's your thing? he signed, and then he rolled me over and grinned down at me again, holding himself up on his elbows on either side of me so he could use his hands to talk. My own hands were trapped, so I responded, "I'm not really sure—I bet you'll figure it out, though." I smiled up at him, and he raised one eyebrow, accepting my challenge, apparently.

I reached down under the covers and stroked him gently, feeling him stiffen beneath my touch. "So, was it everything you hoped it would be?" I grinned up at him.

He smiled back down at me and then drew in a sharp breath when I ran one finger around the head of him. He nodded vigorously and then signed, *More.*

As I watched him, his brow furrowed slightly, and when I

asked, "What's wrong?" he answered, *I think I should go to the store and get some condoms.* He looked down at me a little nervously.

I stared up at him, wondering if his uncle had talked to him about birth control—thinking it was probably something I should have brought up.

They're ninety-eight percent effective in preventing pregnancy, he said, still looking in my eyes. *It says so right on the box at the pharmacy.*

I couldn't help it; I grinned up at him.

He raised an eyebrow and smiled. *Are you laughing at me?* he asked, but he didn't seem upset.

I put my hand on his cheek, going serious. "No, never." I shook my head. "I'm on the pill."

The pill?

I nodded. "It prevents me from getting pregnant."

When he just kept staring at me, I went on, "I've just refilled the prescription because it makes my periods lighter and…so…"

He nodded and leaned his face down and nuzzled his nose against mine, kissing my mouth, both eyelids, and then the tip of my nose. He smiled down at me, and my heart flipped in my chest.

He brought his hands up and pushed a few strands of my hair aside as I gazed up at him. He studied my face for long minutes as if he was memorizing everything about me.

"What are your dreams, Archer?" I whispered, wanting to know what was in his heart.

He looked at me for another couple of beats and then pushed himself back onto his knees and pulled me up so that I was straddling his lap. I smiled at him, wrapping my arms around his neck, but pulling back to let him speak.

He brought his hands up and said, *I didn't know enough to dream you, Bree, but somehow you came true anyway. How did that happen?* He rubbed his nose along mine, pausing and then pulling back again. *Who read my mind and knew exactly what I wanted, even when I didn't?*

I breathed out, smiling around the lump in my throat. "I feel the same way. You're my dream, too, Archer. Just as you are."

He looked into my eyes again, and then pulled me to him and kissed me deeply, his tongue swirling inside my mouth, tasting me everywhere.

I felt him swell and harden beneath me, and I sat up slightly and guided him to my entrance and then lowered myself down on him until he was buried inside me completely. He sucked in a breath and held me loosely around my waist as I started rocking slowly, moving up and down on his hard length.

Every time I came down, my clit hit his groin, sending delicious sparks of pleasure through me. I started gasping, throwing my head back and riding him faster and harder.

Archer leaned forward and sucked one nipple into his mouth, now right at the level of his face, and swirled his tongue around, adding to the pleasure shooting through my body. I could feel an orgasm right within reach, and I raced to claim it.

His breath was coming out in sharp pants against my chest as he moved between breasts, licking and sucking at the stiff peaks, making me crazy with lust.

My body tightened and pulsed around him as an orgasm washed through me, and I cried out Archer's name, shivering with bliss.

I opened my eyes and looked into his, half-closed and dark with desire. He took over and thrust up into me as I held on to him and moaned out at the small aftershocks he was inducing.

After a couple of thrusts, I felt him swell even more inside of me, and his lips parted and his eyes lowered further as he climaxed, his chest rising and falling in heavy pants.

He was so beautiful. I felt something catch in my chest and knew it was just him, taking my breath away.

I wrapped my arms around him and pulled him to me, and I stayed seated on him for several minutes as our breathing slowed.

Then I leaned up and pulled off of him, making a small noise of loss that made him smile up at me. I smiled, too, and collapsed back on the bed, sighing contentedly.

Archer lay down next to me and signed, *Is there any reason we need to leave this bed for the next…three months or so?*

I laughed, looking over at him and signed, *Nah, not really. I mean, other than that I'll get fired from my job and won't be able to pay my rent, and all my things will be out in the road at some point.*

He grinned, his chest rising and falling in a silent chuckle. For a single heartbeat, I wished desperately that I could hear that chuckle—I'd bet it was deep and throaty—a beautiful sound. But almost as quickly as the thought came, I dismissed it. I wanted him just as he was. I'd never hear his chuckle, but that was okay. I had his heart, and his thoughts, and *him.* And it was more than enough. In fact, it was everything.

I wrapped my arms around him and squeezed him and then pulled back and said, *Come take a shower with me.*

He smiled and followed behind me to the bathroom, where I quickly pinned my hair up, and then turned the water on to hot and climbed in.

Archer followed behind me, and we took turns washing each other's bodies. He touched me tenderly, almost reverently, as he rubbed body wash over my skin. He cleaned every part of me, even between my toes as I giggled and pulled them away, signing, *Too ticklish!*

He grinned and stood up and kissed me hard on the mouth, and I grabbed the body wash from him and washed him from shoulders to toes as well, spending an extra bit of time on his muscular ass—but that was purely selfish. He had an exceptional ass.

When the water started cooling, we rinsed off one final time and stepped out, drying each other off.

I blew the candles out and then we climbed under the covers together, naked. Archer pulled me into him as I rested my head on his chest, drawing lazy circles on his skin with my pointer finger.

Outside, the rain was falling down gently now, and the moonlight over the lake shined in, casting just enough light that I could see Archer's hands when he raised them and said, *You're my everything, Bree.*

I leaned up and looked at his face in the semidarkness. How was it that he looked happy and sad at the same time? "You're mine, too, Archer," I said. "Everything."

"And now," I said dreamily, drifting toward sleep, "when a thunderstorm comes, I'll think of you, not anything other than you."

CHAPTER TWENTY-TWO

BREE

Over the next week we fell into an easy routine, so wrapped up in each other that I could barely wait to get off work, practically racing home to shower and collect Phoebe before heading straight to Archer's house. The smile he greeted me with each day made me feel treasured as I ran into his arms, feeling in my head and my heart that I was finally home.

Not the place, but his arms. Archer's arms were my home—the only place I wanted to be, the place where I felt safe. The place where I felt loved.

We made love everywhere, spending long nights exploring each other's bodies and learning everything about what brought pleasure to the other. And just like Archer, he became a master in the fine art of lovemaking—leaving me languid and drugged with pleasure at the end of every interlude. Not only did he know how to make me wild with desire with his hands and his tongue and his impressive male parts, but he knew that when he scratched the backs of my knees with his short fingernails, I would purr like a cat, and that it relaxed me entirely when he ran his fingers through my hair. It was as if my body was his instrument and he learned to play it so perfectly that the melody vibrated within my very soul. Not only because of the pleasure he brought, but because he cared so much to know every little thing about me.

One day, he put a bowl of potato chips out while I was preparing lunch, and as I snacked on them, I noticed that they were all the folded ones that I loved but usually had to hunt for.

I looked down at the chips and then up at Archer, confused. "These chips...they're all folded," I said, thinking I sounded crazy.

Aren't those the ones you like?

I nodded slowly, realizing he had gone through several bags of chips to collect the ones I liked the best. And realizing that he had noticed that small fact about me at all, I didn't know whether to laugh or cry. But that was just Archer. He wanted to please me, and he'd do anything in that effort.

Sometimes we would be doing something on his property when I would look over and notice him looking at me with that lazy expression on his face that meant he was thinking about what he wanted to do to me in that moment, and I would become almost instantly wet and needy, my nipples pebbling beneath his silent stare.

And then he would either pick me up and carry me to his bed, or if we were so overcome, he would take me right where we were—on a blanket on the grass, the bright sunlight shining above us, or in the two-person hammock, or on the sandy shore of the lake.

After one such session, as my body was still quivering with the orgasm he had given me, I whispered breathlessly, "I dreamed this, Archer. I dreamed of you and me—just like this."

His eyes burned down into mine, and he leaned up and studied me for long minutes before kissing me so tenderly that I thought my heart would break.

I rolled him over in the wet sand, grinning against his mouth as he smiled, too. And then we both stopped laughing as I laid my head on his chest and lived right there in that moment, thankful for the air in my lungs and the sunshine on my back, and the beautiful man in my arms. And his hands made letters on my skin, and after a few minutes, I realized that he was spelling, *My Bree...My Bree...* again and again and again.

The weather was cool now, and after a little bit, we ran inside laughing and shivering and climbed in the shower to get all the sand off us.

We curled up on his couch, he lit a fire in the fireplace, and we snuggled for a little while before I leaned back and looked at him.

Archer had this way of doing things that were so sexy and supremely male, it made my heart skip a beat at how naturally and unknowingly he did them. He would lean a hip against the counter in a certain way, or stand in a doorway holding on to the molding above him as he watched me—things he had no idea affected me the way they did. It was just him being *him*, and somehow that made it even more appealing. There was no way I would tell him. I loved having that secret—I loved that those things were all mine, and I didn't want to affect his actions by making him aware of them. As for me, well, I was a total lost cause when it came to Archer Hale.

It made me wonder at the man he would have been if he hadn't been in that terrible accident, hadn't lost his voice...would he have been the quarterback of the football team? Gone to college? Run his own business? I had teased him once about being good at everything he did...and truly, he was. He just didn't see that. He didn't believe he had much of anything to offer.

He still hadn't opened up to me about the day he lost his parents, and I hadn't asked him again. I wanted to know desperately what had happened to him, but I wanted to wait until he felt safe enough to tell me.

What are you thinking about? he asked, cocking one eyebrow.

I smiled. *You*, I said. *I was thinking about how I thank my lucky stars every day that I ended up here...right here, with you.*

He smiled that sweet smile that made my stomach quiver and said, *Me, too.* Then he frowned and looked away.

What? I asked, taking his chin and turning his face back to me.

Will you stay, Bree? he asked. *Will you stay here with me?* He looked like a little boy in that moment, and I realized how much he needed me to tell him that I wouldn't go away like everyone else in his life had.

I nodded. *Yes*, I said. *Yes.* I meant it with my whole heart. My life was here now—my life was this man. Whatever that meant— I wasn't going anywhere.

He looked in my eyes as if trying to decide if I was being completely honest, and seemed to be satisfied with what he saw. He nodded and pulled me to him, holding me tight.

He hadn't told me he loved me, and I hadn't said it to him, either. But in that moment, I realized I was in love with him. So deeply in love that it almost bubbled to the surface of my lips, and I had to physically clamp my mouth shut not to shout it. But somehow, I thought I needed to wait for him to say it. If he was falling in love with me, too, I wanted him to come to that realization on his own. Archer had lived a life so devoid of human kindness, of touch and attention. It had to be overwhelming for him. We hadn't discussed it, but I had watched his eyes as we did simple things over the past week, like lie on the couch and read, or eat a meal together, or walk on the shore of the lake, and it was as if he was trying to organize all the thoughts and feelings in his head— playing sixteen years of emotional catch-up. Perhaps we should have talked about it, perhaps that would have helped him, but for some reason, we never did. Inside, it was my deepest hope that my love would be enough to heal his wounded heart.

After a minute he let go of me, and I sat up and looked at him. He had a small smile on his face. *I have a favor to ask you*, he said.

I furrowed my brow. *Okay*, I said, giving him a suspicious look. *Will you teach me how to drive?*

How to . . . yes! Of course! You want to drive?

He nodded his head. *My uncle had a pickup truck. I keep it in a garage in town. They start it up every once in a while and drive it around. I always meant to sell it, but I just never got around to it, never really . . . knew exactly how I'd do that. But now maybe that's a good thing.*

I was excited and practically bounced up and down on the couch. This was really the first time Archer had indicated on his own he wanted to do something that would take him away from his property—other than grocery shop.

Okay! When? I asked. *I don't have to work tomorrow.*

Okay then, tomorrow, he said, smiling and gathering me to him.

And so it came to be that Archer was behind the wheel of a big, piece-of-junk-looking pickup truck, while I sat in the passenger seat, trying to teach him the rules of the road and how to operate a stick shift. We had chosen a large open space a couple of miles down the highway, just off the lake.

"Smell that?" I asked. "That's the smell of burning clutch. Eeeeease off it."

After about an hour of practice, Archer pretty much had it, with the exception of a few lurches, which had me stomping on my imaginary brake and laughing out loud.

He grinned over at me, his eyes roaming down to my bare legs. I followed his gaze and crossed my legs, hiking my skirt up just a little bit in the process and then glancing back at him. His eyes were already dilating, making them darken and droop very slightly. Oh God, I loved that look. That look meant very, very good things for me.

"Driving is serious business, Archer," I said teasingly. "Letting your attention roam from the task at hand could be dangerous for everyone involved." I smiled prettily, tucking my hair behind my ear.

He raised his eyebrows, amusement filling his expression, and turned back to the front window. The truck moved forward, Archer speeding up and shifting into second gear easily. The dirt area we were in wasn't so large that Archer could practice fourth gear yet, but he moved to third gear and steered us in wide circles.

I crossed my legs in the other direction and ran a finger up my thigh, just stopping at the hem of my skirt. I glanced at Archer, and his eyes were riveted on my finger. He glanced out the front window briefly and kept driving in wide circles.

I was distracting him, but there was no danger here.

I let my finger continue to trail up my thigh, hiking my skirt up now so my pink polka-dot underwear was showing.

I glanced at Archer. His lips were parted slightly, and his eyes were hungry as they watched to see what I would do next. Truth be told, I had never done anything like this before. But Archer brought things out in me no one ever had—he made me feel sexy and experimental and *safe*. He made me feel more alive than I'd ever felt in all my life.

As I watched him, he swallowed heavily and glanced at the front window before looking back at me.

I reached my fingers down the front of my underwear and leaned my head back on the seat, closing my eyes and moaning softly. I heard Archer's breath hitch in his throat.

I arched my hips up as my fingers slid farther, finally reaching the slick wetness between my thighs. I brought some of it up to my small nub, waves of pleasure radiating out from my own touch. I moaned again and the truck lurched.

I used my finger to stroke myself, bursts of pure pleasure making me gasp and press upward into my own hand.

Suddenly, I was jerked forward as the truck came to a sudden stop, Archer not even downshifting, just taking his foot off the gas so it lurched and stalled. My eyes flew open in time to see Archer pull the emergency brake up and push me gently backward onto the seat as he crawled over me.

I gazed up at him as he moved me so my head was at the passenger-side door and he scooted back. The look on his face was tense and primal, and it made my insides clench. He leaned down and kissed my belly as I tangled my fingers in his soft hair and moaned.

He leaned up very briefly to bring my underwear down, and I arched my hips up so they slid over my ass and down my legs. My entire body was vibrating with need, an intense throb between my legs.

Archer leaned back and opened my thighs, gazing down at me for several seconds before leaning into my sex and just breathing. I gasped at the feel of his nose rubbing over my clit and his warm breath washing over my most sensitive parts. "Please," I moaned out, threading my fingers through his hair again.

Archer had pleasured me in so many ways over the past week, but this was something he hadn't done yet. I waited, holding my breath, and when the first stroke of his tongue touched my folds, I pressed upward, moaning softly again. The pulsing in my clit grew stronger, my excitement spiking as he began circling the small nub with his tongue as I'd taught him to do with his fingers. He moved faster and faster, the warm, slick wetness of his tongue gliding over me, and his warm breath coming out in pants against my folds as his hands gripped my thighs, holding me open to him. Oh God, it was exquisite. The beginnings of an orgasm shimmered around me in beautiful pulses of light right before I shattered completely, bucking upward into Archer's mouth and crying out his name. "Archer, Archer, Oh God, Yes."

I came back to myself as I felt his warm breath against my belly and felt him smiling against my skin.

I smiled, too, stroking his hair, still unable to form words.

All of a sudden, a loud knocking sounded on the window, and Archer and I both startled, panic washing through me. What the hell? I swung my legs down as Archer sat up, wiping his mouth on his shirt as I fumbled my underwear up my legs and smoothed my skirt down.

The windows were fogged up—thank God. Or maybe not. Oh no. Embarrassment washed over me as I looked at Archer, and he nodded and pointed to the hand window crank. I rolled it down, and Travis was standing there in his uniform, a tight look on his face as he bent down to the open window and peered in at us.

The smell of sex hung heavy in the air of the small cab. I closed my eyes very briefly, color filling my face. "Hi, Travis," I said, trying to smile, but grimacing instead.

Travis looked back and forth between Archer and me before his eyes landed on me, moved downward to my lap, and swung back up to my eyes. "Bree," he said.

Neither one of us spoke for a second as his expression got tighter. I looked forward, feeling like a little girl who was about to get expelled by the principal.

"I got a call about a stalled truck out here," he said. "I was right in the area, came to see if I could help."

I cleared my throat. "Oh, uh, well..." I glanced over at Archer and went silent for a second as I took him in—he was sitting casually, one hand resting on the steering wheel in front of him, looking like the cat that ate the canary. And in this case, I was definitely the canary.

A small, hysterical laugh bubbled up my throat, but I pulled it back and instead narrowed my eyes at him. His smug look only increased. "I was giving Archer a driving lesson," I said, turning back to Travis.

Travis was silent for a second. "Uh-huh. Does he have a learner's permit?" he asked, raising his eyebrows, knowing very well he didn't.

I let out a breath. "Travis, we're out here in an open, dirt space. I'm not taking him on the road or anything."

"Doesn't matter. He still needs a learner's permit."

"Come on, Travis," I said softly, "he just wants to learn how to drive."

Travis's eyes narrowed, and he spoke slowly. "He can do that, but he needs to follow the rules of society." He looked over at Archer. "Think you can do that, bro?" He raised one eyebrow.

I looked over at Archer, and the smug look had been replaced by an angry one, his jaw clenched. He raised his hands and signed, *You're an asshole, Travis.*

I laughed nervously and looked at Travis. "He said, sure, no problem," I said. I heard Archer shift in his seat.

"Anyway," I went on, raising my voice, "we'll just be on our way now. Thanks for being understanding, Travis. We'll see what we can do about that learner's permit before any more lessons. I'll drive home, okay?" I smiled what I hoped was sweetly. This was a totally embarrassing situation, despite the fact that I was still pretty mad at Travis for what he had done to Archer with the whole strip club scenario.

Travis stood back from the truck as I scooted over and climbed over Archer's big body. I felt Archer's hand on the back of my bare thigh as he moved under me and, when I looked down at him, saw he was looking toward Travis. I huffed out a breath and plopped down on the seat, turning the key in the ignition.

I looked out the window at Travis as I shifted into gear, and he had that same tense, slightly angry look on his face. Archer still had his head turned, looking at him, too. I smiled tightly and pulled away.

When we got on the road, I looked over at Archer. He looked at me and we looked away again. After a second, I looked back over at him, and his body was shaking in silent laughter. He grinned at me and said, *I like driving.*

I laughed and shook my head. "Yeah, I bet you do." Then I punched him lightly on the arm and said, "I like it when you drive. But maybe we should drive in a more private location next time." I raised my eyebrows.

He laughed silently, his teeth flashing and those sexy creases forming in his cheeks.

I regarded Archer's beautiful profile as he stared happily out the front window. He was happy with what had happened between us, but pleased about Travis catching us, too. I bit my lip, thinking about those two and how Archer probably hadn't had a lot of cause to gloat over anything in his life. After a minute, I said, "Archer, I hope you know you don't have to compete with Travis. I hope I made it clear that I chose you. *Only* you."

He looked over at me, his face going serious. He reached across the seat and grabbed my hand and squeezed it, looking out the window again.

I squeezed his hand back and held it, driving with one hand the whole way to his house.

* * *

The next day at work was one of the busiest I'd worked in a while. At about one thirty, when it was finally slowing down, Melanie and Liza came in, sitting down at the counter where they had been the first time I met them. I grinned when I spotted them. "Hey there!"

They greeted me back, smiling big. "What's up, girlfriend?" Melanie asked.

I sagged against the counter. "Ugh. Day from"—I brought my voice to a whisper—"hell. I've been running around like a chicken with my head cut off."

"Yeah, it gets busier this time of year because all the people who worked on the other side of the lake all summer now spend more time here. Norm talked about hiring someone to work dinner shift and keep the diner open after three, but I guess they decided not to do that. Of course with all the expansion plans, no one knows what's going on, so who can blame them." She shrugged.

"Hmmm, I didn't know that," I said, frowning.

Liza nodded and it snapped me back to reality. "So what can I get you girls?"

They both ordered burgers and iced tea, and I turned around to the iced tea machine behind me and started getting their drinks. A couple of seconds later, I heard the bell on the door, and a few more seconds after that, Melanie squeaked out, "Holy crap on a cracker," and Liza's voice behind me whispered, "Whoa."

I dropped a lemon in each glass. A hush seemed to fall over the place. *What the heck?*

My brows came down, and I turned around on a small, confused smile, wondering what was going on. And that's when I spotted him—*Archer*. I sucked in a breath, a grin immediately spreading over my face. His eyes were focused solely on me as he stood in the doorway, looking...oh God, he looked gorgeous. He had obviously bought himself some new clothes: jeans that fit him perfectly, showcasing his long muscular legs, and a simple, long-sleeved black pullover with a gray T-shirt just showing underneath the collar.

He was freshly shaven and his hair lay perfectly, even though he had gotten a kitchen-chair cut from a girl who was so turned on she could barely see straight. I grinned bigger. He was *here*.

"Who is *that*?" I heard Mrs. Kenfield say loudly from a table by the door. She was about a thousand years old, but still. Rude. Her grown granddaughter, Chrissy, shushed her and whispered loudly out of the side of her mouth, "That's Archer Hale, Grandma." And then more quietly, "Holy hell."

"The mute kid?" she asked, and Chrissy groaned and shot Archer an apologetic look before turning back to her grandma. But Archer wasn't looking at her anyway.

I put the iced teas I was holding down on the counter, my eyes never leaving Archer's, and wiped my hands down the sides of my hips, my smile growing even bigger.

I walked around the counter, and when I cleared the side of it, I increased speed, fast-walking the rest of the way to him and laughing out loud before I jumped into his arms. He picked me up, a relieved-looking grin spreading over his handsome face before he put his nose into the crook of my neck and squeezed me tightly.

If there was ever a time to let someone know they were wanted, this was it.

As I stood there holding on to him, it occurred to me that not all great acts of courage are obvious to those looking in from the outside. But I saw this moment for what it was—a boy who had never been made to feel that he was wanted anywhere, showing up and asking others to accept him. It made my heart soar with pride for the beautiful act of bravery that was Archer Hale stepping into this small-town diner.

You could have heard a pin drop around us. I didn't care. I laughed again and brought my head back, looking into his face. "You're here," I whispered.

He nodded, his eyes moving over my face, a gentle smile on his lips. He placed me down on the floor and said, *I'm here for you.*

I smiled. They were the same words he had said to me the day he met me outside the diner several weeks before.

"I'm here for you, too," I whispered, smiling again. I meant that in so many ways, I couldn't even begin to list them all.

We stared into each other's eyes for several long seconds as I realized that the diner was still quiet. I cleared my throat and looked around. People who had been staring at us, some with small smiles on their faces, others looking perplexed, returned to what they had been doing. Chatter in the diner slowly started up again, and I knew exactly what the chatter was about.

I took Archer's hand, led him to the counter, and went back around to the other side. Melanie and Liza looked over at him, replacing their still-slightly-shocked expressions with big smiles.

Melanie reached her hand out to him. "I'm Melanie. We've never properly met."

He took her hand and smiled just a little timidly at her.

"Archer," I said, "that's Liza, Melanie's sister." Liza leaned forward and reached across Melanie to shake Archer's hand as well.

He nodded and then looked back at me. "Can you give me just a minute? I need to take care of a few customers and I'll be right back."

I handed him a menu, and he nodded as I went to deliver the

food that had just come up at the window and refill a few drinks. When I got back, Liza and Melanie's food was up, so I grabbed it and set their burgers down in front of them, and then turned to Archer. *Hungry?* I signed.

No. I'm saving my appetite for dinner with a special girl. He grinned. *Just…* He looked around behind me at the soda machines.

Chocolate milk with a twisty straw? I asked, raising an eyebrow.

He chuckled silently. *Coffee*, he said, winking at me.

"God, that's sexy," Melanie said. "It's like you two are talking dirty right out in the open."

Archer smiled over at her and I laughed. I shook my head. "Maybe you two should learn sign so you can join us." I grinned.

Liza and Melanie laughed. I turned around and grabbed the coffeepot and poured Archer a cup, and then watched as he poured creamer in it.

Maggie came up next to me and put her hand out to Archer. "Hi there." She smiled, glancing over at me quickly. "I'm Maggie. Thanks for coming in."

Archer smiled shyly at her and shook her hand, signing to me, *Please tell her I said it's nice to meet her.*

I did and she smiled. "I met you many years ago, honey. Your mama used to bring you in here when you were a little guy." She looked off in the distance as if she was recalling. "That mama of yours was just the sweetest, prettiest thing. And, oh, did she love you." She sighed, coming back to the present and smiling. "Well, anyway, I'm so glad you're here."

Archer listened to her, a small smile on his face, seeming to drink in her words. He nodded and Maggie went on, looking at me. "So, Archer, this girl here has worked a lot of overtime recently. I think she's earned an early day. Think you can come up with something to do with her?"

"Geez, Maggie, that sounds dirty." Liza snorted.

Archer tried not to smile and looked away, picking up his coffee cup as Maggie put her hands on her hips and glared at Liza as we laughed.

"It's your dirty mind that makes that sound dirty," she said, but there was a twinkle in her eye.

Archer looked at me. *Think we can come up with something dirty to do this afternoon?* he asked, grinning at me. I laughed and then bit my lip to stop myself.

"See!" Melanie said. "I knew you two were talking dirty. I'm totally learning sign language."

I grinned. "He just asked me if I'd like to go on a nice picnic," I said, deadpan.

"Right!" Liza said, laughing. "A naked picnic!"

I laughed and Maggie snorted, causing Archer to grin bigger. "You people aren't right. Now get outta here, you," Maggie said, nudging me.

"Okay, okay, but what about my side work and the salads—?"

"I got it," she said. "You can make the salads on your next shift."

I looked at Archer. "Well, okay then. Let's go!"

He started taking some money out of his pocket for the coffee, but Maggie stopped him by putting her hand on his arm. "It's on the house."

Archer paused, looking at me, and then nodded okay.

"Okay," she said, smiling.

I came from around the counter, and we said goodbye to Melanie, Liza, and Maggie, and then walked out the front door together.

When we got outside, I looked across the street and saw a familiar figure. Victoria Hale was just coming out of a store with an older dark-haired woman. I knew the moment she saw Archer and me—the temperature on that street seemed to drop about fifty degrees, and a chill moved through me. I wrapped my arms around Archer's waist and he smiled down at me, pulled me to him, and kissed the side of my head, and as quickly as that, Victoria Hale ceased to exist.

* * *

Later that evening, Archer built a bonfire down on the lakeshore, and we sat on the old Adirondack chairs he told me his uncle had built years ago. We brought a bottle of red wine and blankets with us as the weather was getting colder, especially in the evenings. Archer had a small glass of wine, and I had a larger one; he nursed his like it was strong liquor. So many things I took for granted were so new to him.

We sat in silence for a little bit, sipping the wine and just watching the fire blaze and jump. I felt happy and content, the wine moving through my blood. I leaned my head on the back of the wooden chair and looked over at his handsome profile, all alight in the glow of the fire. For a second he looked like a god, maybe of the sun, all golden and beautiful, his own magnificence outdoing that of the dancing flames. I laughed slightly to myself—feeling drunk from half a glass of Merlot. Drunk on him, on this night, on fate, on bravery, on life. I stood up, the blanket on my lap falling to the chair, and I set my wine down on the sand. I walked to him and sat on his lap, and when he smiled, I took his face in my hands and simply gazed at him for a second before I brought my lips down on his, tasting red wine and Archer, a delicious ambrosia that made me moan and tilt my head so he would take over the kiss and give me more of himself. He did, leaning into me and teasing my tongue with his as I adjusted myself on his lap and sighed into his mouth. He responded to my sigh, his tongue plunging slowly into my mouth, mimicking the sex act, and making my core pulse to life, almost instantly slick and wet, ready for him to fill me and satiate the deep need that was making me ache and squirm on his lap.

He smiled against my mouth—he knew exactly what he did to me, and he liked it. It was so easy to get lost in him now, the way he paid attention, the way he looked at me as if he adored me, the way his intense sexiness was all natural and unabashed—he barely knew it existed. But he was learning, and in a way I felt the loss of the unsure man who looked to me to show him how to pleasure me, to tell him I wanted him at all. But the other part of me gloried in his newfound confidence, in the way he took charge of my body and made me weak with desire.

After a few minutes, I leaned back, both of us breathing harshly, catching our breath. I kissed him lightly one more time on his mouth. "You get me worked up, too quickly," I said.

His hands came up. *Is that a bad thing?* he asked. He eyed me—it was an actual question, not rhetorical.

I ran my thumb over his bottom lip. "No," I whispered, shaking my head.

I caught sight of his scar in the dancing flames, the raised skin red in the firelight, the shiny skin golden, stretched. I leaned in and kissed it and he shuddered slightly, going still. I ran my tongue over it, feeling his body tense even more.

I whispered against his throat, "You're beautiful everywhere, Archer."

He let out a breath and leaned his head back very, very slightly, giving me more access, baring his scar to me, a beautiful act of trust.

"Tell me what happened," I whispered, rubbing my lips up and down the puckered skin, drawing in his scent. "Tell me all of it. I want to know you," I said, leaning back and looking up at him.

His expression was a mixture of tense and thoughtful as he looked down into my face. He let out a breath and brought his hands up. *I felt...almost normal today. At the diner.* He paused. *I don't want to remember how I'm broken tonight, Bree. Please. I just want to hold you out here, and then I want to take you inside and make love to you. I know it's hard to understand, but please. Let me just enjoy you for now.*

I studied him. I did understand. I had been there. I had tried so hard to get back to a place of normalcy after my dad died. I had tried so hard to stop missing exits on the highway that I'd taken a thousand times; tried so hard to stop zoning out at the grocery store, standing in front of the oranges, just staring into space; tried hard to feel something—anything that wasn't pure pain. And no matter who had asked me, no matter how much they'd loved me, I couldn't have talked about it until I was one hundred percent ready. Archer had lived with his own pain for a long, long time, and asking him to revisit it on my time schedule would never be fair. I would wait. I would wait as long as he needed me to.

I smiled at him, smoothed his hair back from his forehead, and kissed him gently again. When I leaned back, I said, "Remember how you told me that I did fight the night my dad was killed and I was attacked?"

He nodded, his eyes dark orbs in the dim light just beyond the reach of the firelight.

"Well, so did you," I said quietly. "I don't know what happened, Archer, and I hope someday you'll tell me. But what I do know is this scar tells me you fought to live, too." I ran my fingertip lightly up the ruined skin of his throat and felt him swallow thickly. "My wounded healer, my beautiful Archer."

His eyes glittered at me, and after a few silent beats, he picked me up and placed me down for a few seconds as he dumped some sand on the fire. Then he picked me up again as I laughed and clung to him, and he carried me up the hill to his house and his bed.

CHAPTER TWENTY-THREE

BREE

The next day I left Archer tangled in the sheets of his bed. A blanket barely covered the muscular globes of his ass, and his arms were wrapped around the pillow under his head so that his beautiful back, all hard planes and ridges, was fully on display. I briefly considered waking him up so I could enjoy all those planes and ridges again, but I knew that Phoebe probably needed to do her business, and I had sadly neglected my cottage and my life—it was a mess and I didn't have any clean underwear left. So I tore myself away to do some necessary chores, leaving a small, light kiss on Archer's shoulder. He was tired—he had exerted a whole lot of energy the night before. I squeezed my thighs together at the memory and forced my feet to move me out of the small bedroom.

When I got home, I let Phoebe out quickly and took a long, hot shower.

After I got dressed, I powered up my phone and saw that I had a couple of messages—both from Natalie, both telling me that the detective who had worked on my dad's murder investigation had called her a couple of times, looking for me, and I should call him. I took a deep breath and sat down. I had called the detective many times in the months following my dad's murder, and there had never been a scrap of evidence. Once I took off, I hadn't checked back in. I hadn't figured it was necessary. But now there was suddenly something new? Why?

I dialed the number that I still knew by heart, and when Detective McIntyre picked up the line and I told him who it was, he greeted me warmly. "Bree, how have you been?"

"I've been good, actually, Detective. I know I haven't checked in for a while, and my phone number changed..."

"It's okay. I'm glad you'd given me your friend's number where you were staying after the crime." I noted that he didn't say *murder*.

"So is anything new?" I asked, getting right to the point.

"Actually, yes. We have a person of interest in the case. We want you to come in for a photo lineup," he said gently.

My heart started beating faster, and I breathed out, "Oh," and then sat there quietly.

The detective cleared his throat. "I know, it's surprising after so many months have passed, but we actually got this information from a low-level drug dealer trying to save himself some jail time."

"Okay," I said. "When do I need to come back?"

"As soon as possible. When can you get here?"

I bit my lip. "Uh..." I considered for a minute. "Three days?"

"If that's the quickest you can get here, then that will have to work."

I felt slightly numb. "Okay, Detective, I'll call you as soon as I get back into town."

We said our goodbyes and hung up, and I sat on my bed for a good long while just staring out the window, feeling in a way like some bubble had just burst. I wasn't sure exactly how to classify it, though, because I knew I was happy that there might possibly be a breakthrough in my dad's case. If there was an arrest made…I wouldn't have to wonder anymore…I could finally feel completely safe. And my dad would get the justice he deserved.

I picked up my phone and dialed Natalie and told her the news. When I was done, she let out a big breath and said, "God, Bree, I'm afraid to hope too hard, but…I'm hoping so hard," she finished quietly.

"I know," I said. "I know. Me, too."

She was quiet for a second before she said, "Listen, I have an idea. What if I fly there and drive back with you to keep you company?"

I let out a breath. "You'd do that?"

"Yes, of course I would. Plus, you know my mom has so many miles saved up from all the traveling she does. It won't even cost me a thing."

I smiled. "That would…I would love that. We'll have a good long car ride to catch up."

I heard the smile in her voice when she said, "Good. I'll arrange it. Are you gonna be able to get the time off at work?"

"Yes, I'm sure it will be fine. The people I work for are great, and when I tell them what it's for…"

"Bree, they know you're only there temporarily, right?"

I paused and lay back on my bed. "I didn't mention that to them, no." I put my hand on my forehead. "And the thing is, it's not temporary, Nat. I kind of…I've decided to stay." I closed my eyes waiting for her reaction.

"What? Staying? Are you being serious? Because of that guy you mentioned?" She sounded surprised and confused.

"Mostly, yes. I just…it's sort of complicated. I'll tell you all about it on the car ride, all right? Is that okay?"

"Okay…okay, yes. I can't wait to see you, honey. I'll text you with the details of my flight."

"Okay. Thank you so much. I love you."

"Love you, too, babe. I'll be in touch."

We hung up and I lay there for a few minutes, thankful that my best friend was coming to make the trip back with me. It would make the whole thing easier. And then I'd come back. I had told Natalie I was going to stay permanently. And in saying it out loud to someone other than Archer, I realized how right it felt. There was no way I was moving back to Ohio. My life was here now. My life was with Archer—whatever that meant, I knew it was true.

* * *

The next morning at work, I hesitantly told Maggie about the situation in Ohio and how I was needed back there. I hadn't shared the details of my dad's death with her, but she was just as understanding and sympathetic as I knew she would be. Her warm hug and comforting words soothed me—it had been a long time since I was mothered by anyone.

Although I was thankful there was a break in the case, as I knew it was a rare occurrence once a certain amount of time had passed, I worried that simply being back in Ohio would dredge up my feelings of hopelessness and grief. I felt safe in Pelion—I felt safe with Archer. I still needed to tell him about this development. I had done stuff around my cottage the day before and then was so tired, I'd fallen asleep at about seven o'clock. I hated that I had no way of communicating with him when we weren't together. But I knew it was good for us to spend a day apart here and there. We'd been practically inseparable lately, and a little distance was a healthy thing.

As the end of my shift was nearing, the bell jingled and I looked up to see Travis walking in, uniform and aviator sunglasses on. I almost rolled my eyes at how ridiculously good-looking he was, not because that in and of itself was cringe-worthy, but because it was so obvious he knew it.

"Travis," I said, continuing to wipe down the menus in front of me.

"Hey, Bree," he said, his lips curving up in what appeared to be a sincere smile.

"What can I get you?" I asked.

"Coffee."

I nodded at him and turned to get him a cup. I poured coffee and placed it in front of him and turned away.

"Still mad at me?" he asked.

"Not mad, Travis. Just not impressed with the way you treat your cousin."

He pursed his lips. "Listen, Bree, he's my family, and we didn't communicate for a lot of years—I can see that was mostly my fault, but me and Archer were always…competitive as kids. Maybe that carried forward a little more than I should have let it when it came to you. I'll admit that. But he's game, too, trust me there."

"Competitive?" I scoffed. "Jesus, Travis." I raised my voice slightly, and a few people looked over and then looked away when I gave them a tight smile before turning back to Travis. "Don't you think he deserves for someone to be on his side for once in his life? Don't you think he deserves for someone to root *for* him, rather than competing *against* him? Couldn't you have tried to be that person?"

"So that's what it is for you—some pity deal?"

I closed my eyes and took a deep breath so that I didn't throw a pot of hot coffee in his face. "No, he doesn't need anyone's pity.

He's…he's incredible, Travis." I pictured him in my mind, his gentle eyes and the way his smile lit up his face when he was truly happy. "He's incredible." I looked down, feeling slightly embarrassed all of a sudden.

Travis was silent for a second. He opened his mouth to say something, when the bell jingled again and I looked up. My eyes grew big.

Natalie was standing there, and our friend Jordan was standing slightly behind her, his hands in his pockets, looking embarrassed.

I dropped the menu in my hand and hurried around the counter. "Oh my God! What are you doing here?" I squealed. I was still waiting for a text telling me when her flight was getting in. Natalie walked quickly to meet me and we hugged, laughing.

"Surprise!" she said, hugging me one more time tightly. "I missed you."

"I missed you, too," I said, my smile fading as I looked over at Jordan, who still hadn't moved away from the door.

Natalie looked over and then looked back at me. "He practically begged me to bring him with me so he could apologize to you in person."

I let out a sigh and gestured for Jordan to come over to us. Relief filled his expression and he walked to me, hugging me to him. "I'm so sorry, Bree," he said, his voice gravelly. I hugged him back. I had missed him, too. Jordan was one of my best friends. Jordan, Natalie, our friend Avery, and I had been inseparable since we were in grade school. We had grown up together. But Jordan was also the figurative straw that had caused me to throw my stuff in a backpack and drive out of town.

At the height of my grief and emotional turmoil, I had gone to him as a friend and he had cornered me and kissed me, pushing it even though I resisted, telling me he was in love with me, begging me to let him take care of me. It had been too much and the very last thing I had needed at the time.

Natalie put her arms around us both and we all laughed softly, finally pulling apart. I glanced at the room around me—there were only a couple of people in the diner, and Maggie was in the back with Norm, closing the kitchen.

"Come sit at the counter while I finish up," I said, smiling.

Natalie sat down next to Travis, who looked over at her, taking a sip of his coffee.

"Well, hello there," Natalie said, flipping her long blond hair and crossing her legs as she swiveled the counter stool so she was half facing him. She smiled her best flirty smile. I snorted. She ignored me and so did Travis.

"Travis Hale," he said, smiling back and reaching for her hand.

I shook my head slightly and introduced Travis to Jordan.

They all said hi and then Travis stood up, placing a five on the counter.

"Bree," he said, glancing at me. "Natalie, Jordan, enjoy your stay in Pelion. Nice to meet you. Bree, tell Maggie I said hi." Then he turned and made his way out of the diner.

I turned to Natalie, who was still watching his ass as he walked outside to his police cruiser. She turned back to me. "Well, no wonder you want to stay here."

I laughed. "He's not the reason I want to stay here."

Natalie glanced over at Jordan, who was looking at a menu. I went serious and changed the subject. I'd had an idea for years that Jordan had a crush on me, but I hadn't known he thought he was in love with me. I loved him, too, but not like that, and I knew I never would. I just hoped we could somehow go back to the friendship we'd had before. I really did miss him.

"Have you eaten?" I asked. The kitchen was closing, but I could make them a sandwich or something.

"Yeah, fast food about an hour ago." Natalie looked at Jordan perusing the menu. "You're not hungry again already, are you?"

He looked up. "Nah, just looking." He set it down, obviously still a little uncomfortable.

I cleared my throat. "Okay, let me go tell Maggie I'm leaving, and I'll grab my stuff."

Fifteen minutes later we were in my little car headed to my cottage.

I got Jordan settled in the front room, and Natalie brought her stuff back to my bedroom. We all took turns showering and then sat in the front room chatting and laughing at Natalie's stories about dating her new boss. Jordan already looked more comfortable, and I was so happy to have them there.

"Do you want to go to dinner in town?" I asked. "I'll run over and ask Archer if he'd like to come with us while you get ready."

"Why don't you just call him?" Natalie asked.

"Well, he doesn't exactly speak," I said quietly.

"Huh?" she and Jordan both said at the same time.

I told them about Archer and how he had been raised, a little bit about his uncle and what I knew of his accident, even though he hadn't personally told me anything about it.

They both stared at me with wide eyes. "Holy shit, honey," Natalie said.

"I know, guys," I said. "It's a crazy story—and I don't even know all of it yet. But wait until you meet him. He's so sweet and just... amazing. I'll have to interpret for you, but he speaks sign fluently."

"Wow," Jordan said. "So if he never really even came off his property all those years, and he doesn't speak, what exactly is he planning on doing with his life?"

I looked down. "He's still figuring that out," I said, feeling suddenly defensive of him. "He will, though. He's just still working on a few of the basics."

They looked at me, and I felt suddenly embarrassed for some reason. "Anyway," I went on, "I'll go tell him our plans and hopefully he'll agree to come with us." I got up and went to put on my shoes and coat.

"Okay," Natalie said. "So is this a jeans and T-shirt type of place, or should I go dressier?"

I laughed. "Definitely jeans and T-shirt."

"Think Travis will be there?" she asked me.

I groaned. "Oh, guys, I have so much to catch you up on. This could take a while. I'll be back in a few, okay?"

"Okay," Natalie sang, getting up. Jordan was rooting through his small suitcase for something.

"Okay," he said, too, looking back.

I headed out, jumping in my car and turning toward Archer's road.

CHAPTER TWENTY-FOUR

ARCHER

I stood at my kitchen sink, drinking down a glass of water in big gulps. I had just gotten back from a run on the shore with the dogs. I wouldn't be able to do that for too much longer once the weather turned.

I stood there thinking about what I was going to do today, feeling a heaviness in my gut that I wasn't sure how to handle. I had felt the same way before my run, too, and thought that the exercise would clear my head. It hadn't.

I was restless, pure and simple. And it wasn't a physical restlessness, apparently. It was mental. I'd come half-awake that morning, the smell of Bree still clinging to the sheets, and for a moment I'd felt happy and content. But then I'd realized she wasn't there, got up, and tried to figure out what to do with the hours that stretched out before me. A repeat of the day before. There were any number of projects I could work on, but none of them interested me. I had a vague sense that it was a topic I needed to give some serious consideration. *What are you going to do with your life, Archer?* Bree had shaken things up for me—and at the moment, all I could feel was unease. I never expected anyone to come in and open up the world for me, but that's what she had done. And now I had possibilities I didn't think I'd had before. But they all revolved around her. And that scared me. That scared the living hell out of me.

I heard a knock on my gate and set the glass down. Was Bree off early?

I walked outside my house toward the gate and spotted Travis walking down my driveway toward me.

I stood waiting for him to approach, wondering what the hell he wanted.

He put his hands up in a *don't shoot me* mock pose, and I cocked my head to the side, waiting.

Travis took a folded paper out of his back pocket, and when he got to where I was standing, handed it to me. I took it, but didn't open it.

"Application for a learner's permit," he said. "You'll just need to bring your birth certificate and proof of address with you. A water bill or whatever."

I raised my eyebrows, glancing down at the paper. What did he have up his sleeve now?

"I owe you an apology for what I did with the strip club thing. It was…immature and uncool. And I'm actually glad to see that you and Bree worked it out. I think she really likes you, man."

I wanted to ask him how he knew that—I knew she liked me, maybe more, but I longed to hear what she had told Travis about me, if anything. Of course, even if I'd been able to, it wouldn't be a good idea to ask him—he'd just mess with me, most likely. But I didn't know how to talk about all my feelings with Bree. I knew sex didn't equal love, so how would I know if she loved me if she didn't tell me? And if she wasn't telling me, did that mean she didn't love me? I was all twisted up, and I had no one to talk to.

And the hell of it was, I knew I loved her—fiercely and with every part of my heart, even the broken parts, even the parts that felt unworthy and without value. And maybe those parts most of all.

"So," Travis went on, "can we call a truce? All's fair in love and war and all that? You win; you won the girl. Can't blame a guy for trying, though, right? No hard feelings?" He held his hand out to me.

I looked at it. I trusted Travis about as far as I could throw him, but what was the point in making this some kind of ongoing war between us? He was right—I'd won. Bree was mine. With the thought alone, a fierce possessiveness roared through me. I reached out and shook his hand, still eyeing him distrustfully.

Travis rested his thumbs on his gun belt. "So I guess you already know that Bree's friends are in town—her hometown friends."

I frowned and pulled my head back slightly and gave myself away. Travis got an *oh shit* look on his face. "Shit, she didn't tell you?" he asked. He looked away and then back at me. "Well, I'm sure it's gotta be hard for her; I mean, here she is, she likes you, and at some point, she's gotta go home, back to her real life. That's a tough position to be in."

Home? To her *real life*? What the hell was he talking about?

Travis studied me and sighed, running a hand through his hair. "Shit, man, you don't have some kind of delusion that she's going to stay here and work in a small-town diner all her life, do you? Maybe come live in this little clapboard shack you call a house and have lots of babies that you'll have no way to support?" He laughed, but when I didn't, his smile drained away and a pitying look replaced it. "Oh hell, that's exactly what you hope, isn't it?"

Blood was roaring in my ears. I hadn't exactly pictured any of that, but the thought of her leaving at all had icy fear racing through my veins.

"Fuck. Listen, Archer, when I said you won her, I just meant for the meantime, for a few warm nights, a couple of dalliances in your truck. I mean, good for you—you deserve that, man. But shit, don't start fantasizing about more than that. She might tell you she'll stay—she'll probably even mean it for a little while. But a girl like Bree, she went to college, she wants a *life* eventually. She's here to get away temporarily, to heal a wound—and then she'll leave. And why wouldn't she? What do you have to offer her? Bree's beautiful; there will always be a guy who wants her and can give her more." He shook his head. "What can you give her, Archer? Really?"

I was standing frozen in front of this asshole. I wasn't so stupid that I didn't see what he was doing. He was playing a card. But, unfortunately for me, the card he was playing was based in truth. He had a winning hand and he knew it. That's what he had come to do—destroy me with the truth. To remind me I was nothing. And maybe it was a good reminder.

I didn't even know if he wanted her anymore. He might not. But now it was about me not having her, either. He was going to win, one way or another. I saw it; I knew. I had seen that same look on another man's face once. I remembered what it meant.

He took another deep breath, looking slightly embarrassed, or maybe pretending to. He cleared his throat. "Anyway"—he pointed to the piece of paper in my hand—"good luck with the permit. You shouldn't have to walk everywhere you go." He nodded at me. "Take care, Archer."

Then he turned and walked back up my driveway and out through the gate. I stood there for a long time, feeling small, imagining her gone, and trying to remember how to keep breathing.

CHAPTER TWENTY-FIVE

BREE

I drove over to Archer's and called his name when I walked in the gate. No answer, so I walked down to his front door and knocked, calling his name again. Still no answer. The door was unlocked, and I went in and looked around. As always, it was neat and tidy, but there was no sign of him. He must be somewhere on his property, too far to hear me calling, or maybe he walked to town?

I grabbed a piece of paper and a pen and wrote him a quick note about how my friends were in town and I'd explain when I saw him. I told him where we were going to dinner and asked him to join us. I hoped he would. I hoped coming to the diner had made him feel comfortable enough to come out again. I wanted to introduce him to my friends. I wanted him to be a part of every aspect of my life.

I drove back home and finished getting ready, and then Natalie, Jordan, and I drove into town to the local pool hall/pizza place for a very casual dinner.

We ordered a large pizza, brought it over to a table next to one of the dartboards, and started a game.

We were half a pitcher of beer in when I looked up and Archer was at the door. The grin that spread over my face was instantaneous, and I dropped the dart in my hand and ran to him, throwing my arms around his neck and kissing him on his mouth.

He let out a breath that felt as if he'd been holding it all day. I leaned back, looking up into his face, seeing a tension there that I wasn't used to. "You okay?"

He nodded, his face relaxing. I stepped away from him so that he could talk. *You didn't tell me your friends were coming.*

I didn't know until yesterday after I left your house. Then they flew in early. Archer, there's a person of interest in my dad's case. I talked to the lead detective yesterday, and he wants me to come in and look at a photo lineup. There could be an arrest, I finished, looking up into his eyes, emotion suddenly coming over me as I talked about the possibility "out loud."

Bree, that's great, he said. *That's really great.*

I nodded. *I'll have to go home for a few days. Natalie and Jordan are driving home with me, but then I'll be back.* I frowned again, thinking about how it'd feel to be back in Ohio. When I looked up at Archer, he was watching me closely, that tense look on his face again.

You could come with us. I smiled up at him.

His eyes softened for a minute, but then he breathed out. *I don't think so, Bree. You...catch up with your friends.*

"Hey, Bree, stop making us wait here! It's your turn," Natalie called.

I tugged on Archer's hand. "Come meet my friends," I said, then more softly, "They're going to love you."

Archer looked slightly dubious, but he let me lead him to the table where our pizza was.

I introduced him to Natalie and Jordan, and the guys shook hands while Natalie tilted her head and said, "What the *hell* is in the water around here? Some sort of mineral that creates ridiculously hot guys? I'm moving."

I laughed and leaned into my hot guy, breathing him in and
smiling into his neck. Jordan's eyes darted away and his face
blanched. God, I hated that it made him uncomfortable to see
me with a guy now. Maybe we needed to talk a little more. I
looked up at Archer, and his eyes were narrowed on Jordan—
he hadn't missed his reaction, either. Of course not—Archer Hale
never missed anything. Since I met him, it had occurred to me that
it would probably be amazing what we could all see and hear if we
would just shut our mouths a little more, and stop trying to constantly hear our own voice.

We played darts, chatted, and ate pizza for a little bit. Archer
smiled when he should at Natalie's nonstop stories, but his silence
was more pronounced than usual. I tried to draw him out, but he
seemed to be having something internal going on that he wasn't
sharing with me.

Natalie asked him questions, and I interpreted for him. He was
sweet and answered everything she asked, but I could still tell he was
a little off, and I didn't know why. I'd have to ask him later, though.
At a bar in front of my friends wasn't the right time or place.

We ordered another pitcher of beer, and Archer had a glass and
then excused himself to go to the restroom. As soon as he did, Jordan came up to me. "Can I talk to you for a minute?" he asked.
I nodded, thinking we probably needed it. He had been shooting
Archer looks all night, and I was fed up with it.

He pulled me off to the side where we were away from Natalie
overhearing and took a deep breath. "Listen, Bree, I'm sorry for
what I did back in Ohio. It was an asshole move. I knew you
were...fragile and dealing with a hell of a lot, and I took advantage of that. I'm not even going to lie and say I didn't. You'd know

anyway." He raked his hand through his dark blond hair, leaving it sticking up, but in a charming way. "I know you don't think of me as anything more than a friend, and that's enough for me. Really, it is. That's what I came here to try to convey to you, and I've been acting like an ass again. It's not easy seeing you with another guy...it never was. But I'll work on that. Your friendship means more to me than anything, and so does your happiness. That's all I wanted to tell you. I want you to be happy, and anything I can do—as a friend—that's what I want to do. Will you forgive me? Will you be a bridesmaid in my wedding when I find someone even better than you?"

I laughed out a small sound, almost a cry, and nodded my head. "Yes, Jordan. I forgive you. And you will find someone better than me. I'm...kinda high maintenance, and really cranky when I don't get my way."

He grinned. "You lie. But thank you. Buds?" He held out his hand.

I nodded, taking his hand and pulling him to me for a hug. "Yes," I whispered in his ear, "and stop giving my boyfriend evil glares. If you were paying more attention to anything else, you'd see the hot blond girl eye-licking you from the table next to us." I leaned back and winked.

Jordan laughed and glanced over at the table where the girl was sitting and then looked back at me. He cleared his throat, and his expression sobered.

"What? You don't think she's hot?" I asked, pointedly not looking in her direction so she didn't know I was talking about her.

"Oh, she's hot," he said, "and your boyfriend is seriously pissed. He's looking at me like he wants to kill me right now."

I looked over at our table, where Archer had returned, and saw him draining another glass of beer.

"I'll go talk to him. Thanks, Jor." I smiled and started walking back to our table.

When I got there, I smiled at Archer and leaned into him, saying, "Hi," and kissing the side of his neck. I put my hands on his waist and squeezed. There was absolutely no extra anything there, all hard muscle and tight skin. I inhaled his scent—God, he smelled so good, soap and exquisite man. *My* man. He smiled that crooked, unsure smile, his eyes darting down to mine and then away.

"Hey," I whispered. "Have I told you yet that I'm glad you're here?" I smiled at him, trying to thaw his mood. I figured he was a little bit tense about Jordan's obvious discomfort with him, but it wasn't exactly the time for me to explain the whole situation. I'd just try to reassure Archer with my attention. He had nothing to worry about—Jordan was no threat to him.

Suddenly, Archer stood up and took my hand and led me toward the restrooms in the back. I followed behind him, his long legs making me have to fast-walk to keep up with his strides.

We turned into the hallway where the restrooms were, and he looked around, looking for what, I wasn't sure. "Where are you taking me, Archer?" I asked, laughing shortly. Apparently he was on a mission.

He didn't answer me, just led me to the far end of the dim hall where there was a doorway set back slightly from the wall. He pressed me into the alcove and leaned into me, taking my mouth in a kiss that was immediately deep and possessive. I moaned, pressing back into his hard form. This was a new side of Archer, and I wasn't sure what was happening here. His intensity was confusing me. But I was turned on by it nonetheless. I guess I was turned on by anything this man did.

He reached his hand down and cupped one breast and rubbed

the nipple through the thin fabric of my shirt. I gasped and brought my hands up into his hair and tugged gently at it. He tore his mouth from mine and simply breathed against my mouth for a second before I tipped my head back, leaning it against the door behind me. He bent his head to my throat and kissed and licked it gently.

"Archer, Archer," I moaned.

Suddenly, I jumped slightly as he sucked at the skin on my neck, scraping his teeth up the now-tender area. I brought my head forward, the lust fog clearing as I took in his challenging expression.

I brought my hand up to my neck. "Did you just…*mark* me on purpose?"

He looked at my neck then back to my face, his eyes glittering. He took a small step back and said, *How many men in your life want to be with you? I'm assuming me, and Travis, and that Jordan guy aren't the only ones? How many more?* His jaw tensed.

I stared at him for a second, at a loss for words. "I'm not…are you kidding?" I asked. "None. But…what does it matter how many men want to be with me? I already made it clear that I chose you. What does it even matter?" I finished, hurt evident in my voice.

A look of confusion skated over his features before they hardened again and he said, *Yes, it matters. Yes, it fucking matters*, his jaw clenching again. My eyes widened. He'd never sworn before and it startled me. He took a deep breath, vulnerability filling his eyes, whether he meant for it to or not. *I can't even tell them to stay away from you, Bree. I have to sit there and watch, and I can't do a damn thing.* He spun away from me, and despite the fact that he was angry and I didn't like it, I felt the loss of his heat as if someone had thrown a bucket of cold water over me. He ran his hand through his hair and looked at me, his whole heart sitting right there in his expression. *I'm not even a man. I can't fight for you.*

"Stop!" I said loudly. "You don't need to fight for me. There's nothing to fight anyone for. I'm yours. I'm already yours." I walked the few steps to him and wrapped my arms around his middle. He didn't resist me, but he didn't return the embrace, either. After a minute, I stepped back.

There's always going to be some guy, he said.

I looked up at him and then stepped away, taking a deep breath. Just then, Jordan appeared from around the corner, stopping and squinting down the dim hall and calling out, "You okay, Bree?"

I saw Archer's body tense, and I closed my eyes momentarily as he turned and walked away from me, down the hall, and past Jordan.

"Archer!" I called, but he didn't turn around.

"God!" I groaned and put my hand to my forehead and walked toward Jordan.

"Sorry, Bree, I didn't know I was interrupting anything. I just came to use the bathroom and saw you guys in what looked like a standoff."

I shook my head. "It wasn't a standoff. Just Archer being...I don't know. I need to go after him, though. Are you guys ready to leave?"

"Natalie is. I think I'm gonna get my own ride home." He smiled a sheepish smile.

Despite the fact that I was upset over Archer, I grinned at Jordan and punched him lightly on the arm. "That's the Jordan I know and love," I said. "You sure you're safe?"

He laughed. "Yeah, I think I can take her if she tries to attack me."

I laughed and shook my head. "Okay."

I hugged him and he said, "Sorry again. Nice hickey, by the way. I haven't seen you with one of those since we were fifteen."

I snorted. "I think that was a certain man's way of telling you and every other guy in here that I'm taken." I sighed.

Jordan smiled. "Well, go reassure him that's not necessary. Us men can act like real assholes when we're insecure and needy."

I raised an eyebrow. "You don't say?"

He laughed softly and squeezed my arm. "You'll work it out. I'll be home in the morning."

I nodded and gave his arm one more squeeze, and then I walked out to the bar, where Natalie was waiting for me.

"Hey," she said, "your boy toy just went stalking out the front door."

I sighed heavily. "He's not a toy, Nat. I don't know what's going on with him."

She raised her eyebrows. "Well. If you'd like my expert opinion, I'd say he's in love, and he doesn't know what to do with it."

"You do?" I asked quietly.

She nodded. "Yup. All the signs are there. Jaw clenched, glaring at other men who come into your proximity, broody, unpredictable behavior, branding..." She gestured to my hickey. "You gonna go put him out of his misery?"

I laughed softly, and it ended on a groan. I sat there for a few seconds considering the situation at hand and then said, "I hope so. Ready?"

We walked out to my car, and I handed Natalie my keys since she had agreed to be the DD. As she started the car, she said, "By the way, I know he's not a toy to you. I see the way you look at him, too. And I can see why you like him...and that scar"—she groaned out the last word—"it makes me want to rock him in my arms and then lick him."

I laughed. "Whoa! Careful there or my jaw is going to start clenching, and I'm going to brood the rest of the way home."

She laughed, but after a second I looked over to her and she was thoughtful. "What I'm wondering is, do you see something long-term with him? I mean, how will that work exactly?" Her voice was gentle.

I sighed heavily. "I don't know. This is all new. And, yes, his situation is so different—there are challenges. But I want to try. I know that. Whatever that means...It's like, the second I saw him, my life started. The second I started loving him, everything clicked into place for me. As confusing as our situation is, inside it feels like it all makes the most perfect sense."

Natalie was silent for a second. "Well, that's poetic, babe, and I believe every word you say, but life isn't always so poetic. And I know you know that better than anyone. I'm just encouraging you to be a realist about this situation, too, okay?"

She glanced at me, continuing, "He's damaged, honey, and I don't just mean his vocal cords—I mean, Jesus, from what you told me, he grew up in an abusive household, his uncle *shot* him, his parents both died *right in front of him*, and then he was kept alone and isolated until he was nineteen years old by a crazy uncle, not to mention the fact that he has an injury that keeps him locked away in his own mind for all intents and purposes—that's gotta leave a mark, babe. Is it any *wonder* he's damaged?"

I let out a big breath, letting my head hit the seat back. "I know," I whispered. "And when you put it like that, it sounds crazy to even believe in the possibility that we can work—that he could work with *anyone*, but somehow...I do. I don't even have any way of explaining it other than despite everything you just mentioned, he's still good and kind, and brave and smart, and even funny sometimes." I smiled. "I mean, think of the strength of spirit you have to have to come through what he did and not be as mad as a hatter, to still retain a gentle heart."

"True," she agreed. "Still, damaged people do things because they can't trust or believe in anything good. He's never had anything good. I'm worried that the more serious it gets with you, the more it's going to freak him out. Where he'll work, what he'll do with his life, that's almost the easy stuff compared to the emotional baggage."

I looked at her, biting my lip. "I have baggage, though, Nat. I'm damaged, too. Aren't all of us?"

"Not to that extent, honey. Not to that extent."

I nodded and laid my head back on the seat. "When'd you get so insightful into the human spirit anyway?" I asked, smiling over at her.

"I'm an old soul, babe—you already knew that." She winked at me and I grinned.

We pulled up in front of my cottage, and I hugged Natalie good night before she hopped out with my key, waving over her shoulder. I went around the car and got in the driver's seat. I'd be okay driving a mile to Archer's house. I already felt completely sober.

When I got there, I let myself in the gate and walked down to his house. I knocked lightly, and a few seconds later, he answered wearing only a pair of jeans and rubbing a towel through his hair.

I took him in as he stood there, looking so damn beautiful, and so damn insecure.

I laughed softly. "Hi." I sighed and walked in his house, turning to look at him when I heard his door close behind him.

Why are you laughing? he asked.

I shook my head and brought my hands up. *Because I wish you could see yourself through my eyes. I wish you could read my mind so that you would know how much I want you, no one else. There could be three hundred men after me right now, and it wouldn't matter. Because none of them are you, Archer Hale.* I dropped my hands for a second and then immediately brought them back up. *None of them are the man I love.* I shook my head slightly and then continued. *And I was going to try to wait until maybe you were ready to say it, too, but... I can't. Because it literally wants to burst out of me all the time. And so it's okay if you don't love me, or if you're not sure if you do. But I'm sure. And I can't stand letting another minute go by where I don't tell you I love you, because I do. I. Love. You. I love you so much.*

He stood frozen as I rambled, but at the start of my final five words, he moved across the space separating us so quickly that my breath caught in my throat and my hands fell. He grabbed me to him and pulled me against his body so tightly that I squeaked, a high-pitched sound somewhere between a laugh and a sob.

He picked me up and buried his face in my neck, and as I wrapped my arms around him, he pulled me even tighter. I rested my head on his shoulder and breathed in his singular scent. We just stood like that for several minutes.

Finally, I pulled back and took his hand as I led him to the couch, and we both sat down.

I'm sorry about what happened at the bar. Can I explain? He nodded, pursing his lips slightly, and I went on. *Jordan is just my friend, he always has been, never anything more. We grew up together—I met him when we were twelve. I've been aware that he had a crush on me for a while, but I made it clear to him that I only had friendly feelings for him.* I paused before continuing. *He pushed the issue after my dad died, and that was the straw that made me take off.* I smiled slightly. *So, I guess you could say you actually have Jordan to thank for sending me your way.*

Archer smiled, too, and looked down at his hands in his lap. When I began speaking again, he looked back up at my hands.

Anyway, that's what you saw tonight—him working through the fact that we'll never be more than friends, and then us coming to a good place as far as that goes. That's all.

Archer nodded, ran his hand through his hair, and said, *I'm sorry—sometimes I feel like everything is over my head. It makes me feel…weak and angry, and not worthy of you. Not worthy of anything.*

I grabbed his hands quickly and then let go. *No. Don't feel that way—please don't. God, give yourself a break. Look at everything you've accomplished already. Look at who you are despite everything you have going against you.* I brought my hand up to his cheek, and he shut his eyes and turned into it. "And did I mention that I love you?" I whispered. "And that I'm not in the habit of loving un-worthy people?" I smiled a small smile at him.

His eyes opened and they roamed my face for several beats, his expression almost reverent, before he said, *I'm in love with you, too.* He let out a breath. *I am so desperately in love with you.* His eyes widened as if the words that he had just "spoken" were almost a surprise. His lips parted and his hands asked me, *Is it enough, Bree?*

I let out a breath and smiled, allowing myself to take a minute to rejoice at the knowledge that the beautiful, sensitive, brave man in front of me loved me. After a second I said, *It's a really good start. The rest we'll figure out, okay?* I took his hands in mine.

Vulnerability washed over his expression as he nodded at me, his face conveying his doubts. My heart squeezed. *What's wrong, Archer?*

After a few seconds, he leaned forward and took my face in his hands and kissed me tenderly on my mouth, his lips lingering there as he rested his forehead on mine and closed his eyes. He leaned back and said, *I love you so much it hurts.* And truly, he looked pained.

I brought one hand to his cheek, and he closed his eyes for a beat before I brought my hand away. *It doesn't need to hurt.*

He breathed out. *It does, though. It does because I'm afraid to love you. I'm afraid that you'll leave and I'll go back to being alone again. Only it will be a hundred times worse because I'll know what I'm missing. I can't...* He sucked in a shaky breath. *I want to be able to love you more than I fear losing you, and I don't know how. Teach me, Bree. Please teach me. Don't let me destroy this.* He looked at me beseechingly, pain etched into every feature on his face.

Oh God, Archer, I thought, my heart constricting painfully in my chest. How do you teach a man who has lost everything not to fear it happening again? How do you teach a person to trust in something none of us can guarantee? This beautiful man that I loved looked so broken, sitting before me expressing his love for me. Expressing his devotion. I wished with all my heart that could be a happy thing for him—but I understood why it hurt.

Loving another person always means opening yourself up for hurt. I don't want to lose more than I already have, either, but isn't it worth it? Isn't it worth giving it a chance? I asked.

He searched my eyes and nodded his head, but his own eyes told me he wasn't convinced he meant it. I took a deep breath. I would make it my job to help him believe. *I* would believe strongly enough for the *both* of us if I had to. I took him in my arms and then scooted over so that I could climb up on his lap and nuzzle him more closely. "I love you, I love you, I love you," I whispered, smiling, trying to make this moment a happy one.

He smiled back and put his lips against mine, mouthing, *I love you, too,* as if he were breathing love into my body.

I kept breathing against him, and after a while, he started fidgeting, adjusting me on his lap. My heart rate quickened as my body reacted to his nearness, his smell, the feel of his big, hard body right up against mine, and specifically something hard and hot pressing into my hip.

I reached my hand down and rubbed the bulge at the front of his jeans and smiled against his neck. "Are you constantly hard?" I asked, my lips on his skin.

I felt him chuckle silently against my chest and smiled at the fact that the sadness and tension from a few minutes before seemed to dissolve as our bodies heated. I leaned back and looked at him, tenderness and desire shining in his eyes. He brought his hands up. *Yes, when you're around—it's why I'm always grimacing.* He faked a pained expression.

I tilted my head. "I thought that was just your natural personality."

That, too.

I laughed, and when I put more pressure on the grimace-causing bulge in question, he closed his eyes, his lips parting.

When he opened his eyes, he asked, *Do you miss hearing the sounds I might make during sex if I had a voice?* He watched my face as I thought about that.

I moved a piece of hair off his forehead and then shook my head slowly. *No, I don't think about that. I don't rely on the sounds you might make to read you. I watch your expression and your eyes.* I leaned in and brushed my lips against his mouth and then leaned back. *I listen to your breathing and the way you dig your fingers into my hips right before you're about to come. There are so many ways to read you, Archer Hale. And I love every single one of them.*

His eyes glittered at me before he moved forward suddenly, grabbing my face in his hands and laying me back down on the couch before covering me with his body. I had a feeling the time for talking had just ended. Heat blossomed across my skin, and my belly clenched. I moaned, a deep, breathy sound that came up my throat, and let him take over, arching up into him, my core beginning to throb insistently. How was it that this man had just started having sex, and only with me, a couple of weeks ago, and yet I trusted him with my body over anyone more experienced I'd been with before? Archer, overachiever that he was. I smiled onto his mouth and he smiled back onto mine, although he didn't lean back to ask me what exactly I was smiling about. I swept my tongue inside his mouth, the taste of him making me feel like I was going to combust—how could the inside of someone's mouth taste so delicious that it made you instantly dizzy with lust? It had been hours since I'd had a sip of beer, but I felt drunk on him—drunk with love, with lust, with something indescribable I couldn't even name, and yet it owned me, body and soul—some kind of primal connection that must have been there before I existed, before he existed, before he or I ever breathed the same air, something written in the very stars.

He ground his erection down on my core, making me gasp and tear my mouth from his, groaning as I threw my head back, intense pleasure vibrating through my veins.

"Archer, Archer," I breathed, "there will never be anyone else for me." My words seemed to ignite him, his breathing coming out in sharp pants as he pulled my T-shirt up and popped my bra open in one movement, releasing my breasts to the cool air.

He sucked one nipple into his warm mouth as I moaned and wove my fingers into his hair, sparks of electricity shooting from my nipple down to my engorged clit. My hips surged upward, bucking into his hardness, and he hissed in a breath and pulled back, looking down at me with his eyes at half-mast. More wetness trickled down to my core at the look on his face alone, and my mouth dropped open. Intensity and lust were stark in his expression, but so was his love for me. I'd never seen anything like it. The power in that expression was so jaw-dropping, I could only stare for several seconds as the blood continued to course south, making me desperate with want. I felt like my entire body was a live wire—and so was my heart. It was almost too much.

Suddenly, Archer stood up and gestured for me to bring my arms up over my head. I did, and he pulled my T-shirt off and then moved to my jeans, unbuttoning them and bringing them down my legs. He took off my shoes and then pulled my jeans and underwear fully off, tossing those on the floor, too. He stood over me for a few seconds, breathing hard, his jeans tented, his beautiful chest on display, and his eyes roaming my body. My own eyes widened, and blood pulsated in my clit at the look of him alone. I couldn't help it; I reached my own hand between my legs and dipped a finger into my wet, needy opening. I moaned at the sensation. Archer's eyes flared as he watched my hand, and then he was moving down over me, spinning me over so my belly was now on the couch as I sucked in a surprised breath. I looked over my shoulder as he stripped his jeans off and came down on top of me again, just hovering over me so that I could feel his heat, but not his skin.

I looked back over my shoulder again, and that intense look was still there. My brain was cloudy with lust, but I acknowledged that, although I loved sweet, gentle Archer, I loved take-charge Archer, too. Whatever had brought this side of him to life, I embraced it, and I wanted more. "Please," I said on a whispery breath, and his eyes flew to mine, clearing marginally, almost as if he was coming out of a trance.

He took himself in his hand and rubbed his stiff cock down the crack of my ass—up, down, up, down—until I was panting and pressing myself into the couch cushions.

He brought himself to my opening and pushed gently inside,

slowly, inch by inch, and I moaned out with relief. I couldn't open
my legs because of the way he was pressing down on me; the feel
of him entering me was almost too much, too tight, and his size
too much for me to accommodate from that angle. But he stilled
for a minute, letting my body adjust, and when I breathed out, he
started sliding in and out of me in slow, leisurely strokes.

I put my arms under the pillow my head was resting on and
turned my face to the side. He leaned down farther and took my
lips in a searing kiss, licking and sucking my tongue to the rhythm
that his cock was gliding in and out of my wetness. When he broke
the kiss and leaned back up, I saw our reflection in the big window
across from the couch—anyone could have seen in, but of course,
no one could on this fenced-in, remote property, and so I didn't
worry about that. I just watched our reflection, mesmerized by the
sight and the feelings.

Archer had one knee on the couch on the other side of my legs,
and one foot still on the floor, knee bent as he drove into me from
behind. The sight of it was primal and the feel of it delicious as his
big, hard cock pounded into me, and my clit ground against the
couch each time he moved down. It was as if he wanted to own
me, possess me, merge our bodies into one being. I couldn't move,
could only take what he was giving, trust him with my body and
my heart. And I did. I trusted him with everything in me.

I turned my face into the pillow and bit down on it, not wanting
to come yet, wanting this to go on and on and on. *He loves me*, my
heart sang. *And I love him, and he owns me, body and soul. I don't
care about all the other stuff. All of it will work itself out.* And in that
moment I believed it with every fiber of my being.

Archer started moving faster, pounding into me harder, almost
punishing, and I loved it, loved it so much that I couldn't stop the
orgasm that gripped me suddenly, moving through my internal

muscles with almost agonizingly sweet slowness, spreading outward through my core, up to my belly, and all the way down to my feet. I screamed into the pillow, burying my face into it as my body spasmed and convulsed in ecstasy.

Archer's thrusts sped up and grew jerky, his breathing growing louder, and I felt a small aftershock in my core at the knowledge that he was about to come.

He took three long strokes, exhaling loudly with each one as he pressed into me, his hands coming down on the couch on the side of my body as he held his own weight. I felt him grow even larger inside of me, stretching me, right before I felt the heat of his release and he collapsed on top of me, half-on, half-off so the majority of his weight was on the edge of the couch.

We both just breathed for long minutes, getting our heart rates under control. Archer nuzzled his face into the back of my neck, kissing down my spine as far as his mouth could travel without moving his body. I calmed under the feel of his warm mouth, closing my eyes and sighing contentedly. He ran his nose over my skin, and then I felt his lips again as his mouth formed the words, *I love you, I love you, I love you.*

* * *

A little while later, after we had gone to bed, I woke up alone. I sat up groggily and looked around, but Archer was nowhere in sight. I got up and wrapped the sheet around my naked body and went in search of him. I found him sitting in a chair in his front room, wearing just his jeans, his golden skin glowing in the moonlight that was coming in the window, looking beautiful and broken, his elbows on his knees and one hand massaging the back of his neck as he looked down.

I went to him and kneeled down in front of him. "What's wrong?" I asked.

He looked at me and smiled a sweet smile, one that reminded me of the man who had come out with a newly shaven face, looking at me so unsure. He brushed a piece of hair from my face and then said, *Do you want kids, Bree?*

My brow furrowed, and my head came back slightly as I let out a small laugh. "Eventually, yes. Why do you ask that?"

Just wondering. I figured you did.

I was confused. "Do you not want kids, Archer? I don't..."

He shook his head. *It's not a matter of that. It's just... how would I support a family? I couldn't. I can barely support myself out here. I have a little bit of money left from my parents' insurance policy, but most of it went to my medical bills. My uncle supported us out here on his disability money from the army and now, I have a small insurance policy that he left—it'll last me as long as I don't live to be a hundred and ten... but that's it.* His eyes moved away from me, back out the window.

I sighed, my shoulders drooping. "Archer, you'd get a job, do something you like. You don't think people with disabilities of one kind or another have careers all the time? They do—"

Do you want to hear about the first time I left this land on my own? he asked, cutting me off.

I studied his face and nodded my head yes, sadness suddenly gripping me and I wasn't even sure why.

My uncle passed away four years ago. He made all his own arrangements and was cremated. The medical examiner's crew came to take his body away, and they brought his ashes back a week later. I didn't see another person for the next six months.

My uncle had a food stockpile down in the cellar—part of his crazy paranoia—and it kept me alive for that long. I started growing my hair, my beard...I didn't know exactly why at the time, but now I think it was another way to hide from the people I knew I'd eventually have to face. Crazy, right? His eyes found mine again.

I shook my head vigorously. "No, not crazy at all," I said softly.

He paused, looking at me, and then went on. I held my breath. This was the first time he had really opened up to me on his own, without my probing.

The first time I left for the grocery store, it took me two hours to walk up that driveway, Bree, he said brokenly. *Two hours.*

"Oh, Archer," I breathed, tears coming to my eyes, my hands gripping his thighs, anchoring me to him. "You did it, though; it was hard, but you did it."

He nodded. *Yeah, I did it. People looked at me, whispered. I grabbed some bread and peanut butter and lived off it for a week until I worked up the courage to go back out again.* He huffed out a small breath, his face pained. *I hadn't been off this land since I was seven years old, Bree.*

He looked past me for a minute, obviously remembering. *After a while, though, it got better. I ignored people and they ignored me— I just started blending in, I guess. If someone spoke to me, I looked the other way. It was fine after that. I took up projects around here and stayed busy. I was lonely, so damn lonely.* He ran a hand through his hair, his expression tortured. *But I tired myself out most days...*

I felt the tears shimmering in my eyes, understanding even more deeply the bravery it had taken for Archer to even take one step off this land.

"Then you went out with Travis...and to see me at the diner," I said. "You did that, Archer. And it was incredibly courageous."

He sighed. *Yeah, I did it. But it had been* four years *by that point. It took me four years to take another step—and I didn't even like it.*

"You didn't like it with Travis because he was the wrong person, untrustworthy, but you liked it with me, right? It was okay then?"

He looked down at me, his eyes filled with tenderness when he put one hand on my cheek for a second. *Yes, it's always okay when I'm with you.*

I leaned into him. "I won't leave you, Archer," I whispered, blinking the tears out of my eyes.

His expression gentled even more as he gazed down at me. *That's a big burden for someone, Bree. To feel like if you leave a person, their whole life is going to crumble to dust. That's what I've been out here thinking about. What a burden I might end up being to you, the pressure you'll feel just loving me.*

I shook my head. "No," I said, but my heart hammered hollowly in my chest because I understood what he was saying, too. I didn't agree, and as far as I was concerned in that moment, there would be no reason on earth I would ever leave him, but his insecurity hit me square in the gut because it made sense.

Archer reached down and tilted my head slightly, his eyes moving to the side of my neck where the hickey he had given me was— still dark red and angry looking, I was sure. He cringed and let go of me and then brought his hands up. *I don't know how to do any of this. You deserve better than the nothing I have to offer you. But it hurts even more to think of letting you go.* He sighed, his eyes moving over my face. *There are so many things I feel like I still need to figure out and so many things working against us.* He brought one hand up and raked it through his hair, his face pained. *My brain hurts when I think about it all.*

"Then let's not think about it now," I said gently. "Let's take it one day at a time and just figure it out as it comes, okay? It feels overwhelming now because you're thinking about it all at once. Let's just take this slowly."

He gazed down at me for several seconds and then nodded his head. I stood up and sat on his lap and hugged him close, burying my head in his neck. We sat that way for several more minutes, and then he picked me up and carried me back to bed. As I drifted off to sleep in his arms, it occurred to me dreamily that I had thought saying we loved each other would make us stronger—but instead, for Archer, it just made the stakes higher.

CHAPTER TWENTY-SIX

BREE

The next morning I got up early for work and Archer got up with me, kissing me at the door. He looked sleepy and sexy, and I took a few more minutes than I should, lingering at his lips, just rubbing mine over his. I still needed to go home and shower and get my uniform. Hopefully Natalie had taken Phoebe out and fed her. When I leaned back away from Archer, I said, *Natalie and Jordan are picking me up right after work, so I'll see you as soon as I get back, okay?*

He nodded at me, his face going serious.

Hey, I joked, *take this time to get some actual sleep. Think of it as a weeklong break from having to service my insatiable sexual needs constantly.*

He grinned a sleepy grin and signed back, *I love your insatiable sexual needs. Hurry back to me.*

I laughed. *I will. I love you, Archer.*

I love you, Bree. He smiled a sweet smile and I lingered, not wanting to say goodbye. Finally, he smacked me playfully on the butt and said, *Go.* I laughed softly and waved at him as I walked up the driveway, blowing him kisses before I shut the gate behind me. He stood there in his jeans, no shirt on, his hands in his front pockets, a small smile on his face. God, I'd miss him.

* * *

It was a busy day at the diner, which was good since the day passed quickly, and I didn't have too long to linger in my thoughts over how much I was going to miss Archer—hell, how much I was going to miss the entire town. It had been such a short time, really, but already I felt like this was home. I missed my friends back in Ohio, but I knew my life was here now.

Natalie and Jordan picked me up right at three o'clock, and I changed into jeans and a T-shirt in the bathroom, and said quick goodbyes to Maggie and Norm. We hopped in my car, Jordan driving and Phoebe chuffing softly at me from her carrier, and got right on the road.

"What'd you guys do all day?" I asked, trying to distract myself from the ball of emotion that was already moving up my throat as we got on the highway and moved farther away from Pelion.

"We walked along the lake for a little bit," Natalie said. "But it was so cold we didn't stay long. We drove across the lake to the town on the other side for lunch and checked out some of the shops. It was really nice, Bree. I can see why you like it here."

I nodded. "The summer was beautiful, but the fall is—" My phone chimed, cutting me off. I frowned. Who could that be? Maybe Avery? The only other people who ever texted me were sitting in the car.

I picked my phone up and looked at the text from an unknown number. I frowned, clicking on it. It read:

Is it too soon to start missing you? Archer

My eyes widened and I pulled back from the phone, surprise taking over. I sucked in a breath. *Archer? How in the world?*

I looked up to the front passenger seat, where Natalie was sitting. "Archer's texting me!" I said. "How is Archer texting me?"

Natalie just smiled a knowing smile. I gaped. "Oh my God! Did you get him a cell phone?"

Natalie shook her head, smiling and pointing next to her to Jordan in the driver's seat. He sheepishly looked in the rearview mirror at me.

"You got Archer a cell phone?" I whispered, tears springing into my eyes.

"Whoa, whoa. Don't get all emotional. It's just a cell phone. How else are you guys gonna communicate while you're gone? I'm surprised you didn't think of it yourself."

Tears were sliding down my cheeks now, and I choked out a little laugh, shaking my head. "You're…I can't…," I sputtered, looking back over at Natalie, who was crying and laughing now, too, swiping the tears off of her cheeks.

"Isn't he?" she asked.

I nodded, a new flood of tears falling out of my eyes as I laughed and wiped them off my cheeks. We were a mess—both of us laughing and crying.

I looked back at Jordan in the rearview mirror, and he rubbed a fist into one eye, cringing slightly and saying, "Something in my eye there. Okay, stop all the blubbering. You two are embarrassing. And text him back already. He's waiting, I'm sure."

"What'd he say when you brought it to him?" I asked, my eyes wide.

Jordan shrugged and glanced in the rearview mirror at me. "He looked at me like he was wondering what my ulterior motives were. But I just showed him how to use it and left." He shrugged again like it was no big deal.

"I love you, Jordan Scott," I said, leaning forward and kissing him lightly on his cheek.

"I know you do," he said, grinning at me in the mirror again. "And getting laid by hot blondes puts me in a generous mood, so there you go."

I laughed, sniffling and bringing my phone up again.

Me: I hope not because I started missing you before I even left. We're about twenty minutes outside of town. What are you doing?

I waited about a minute before his next message came through.

Archer: Reading. It just started raining outside. Hopefully you're moving away from it.

Me: I think so. Skies look clear ahead. Wish I was cuddled up with you. What are you reading?

Archer: Wish you were too. But what you're doing is important. I'm reading Ethan Frome by Edith Wharton. Have you read it?

Me: No. Is it good?

Archer: Yeah. Well, no. It's well written, but it's probably one of the most depressing books of all time.

Me: Lol. So you've read it before? Why read it again if it's depressing? What's it about?

Archer: What's lol?

I paused and smiled, realizing this was Archer's very first time texting. Of course he didn't know what *lol* meant.

Me: Laugh out loud. Text lingo.

Archer: Oh, okay. I'm not sure why I picked this book up today. My uncle seemed to like it. It's about a miserable man in a loveless marriage who falls in love with his wife's cousin and they try to commit suicide to be together, but only end up broken and paralyzed and still miserable.

Me: Oh God! That's...that's awful! Put the depressing book down, Archer Hale!

Archer: Lol.

I laughed out loud for real when I saw his reply. "Keep it down back there," Natalie grumped, keeping her eyes closed but smiling slightly as she turned her head on her seat back. My phone dinged softly again, indicating another text from Archer.

Archer: No, really, it's about isolation and a girl who represents happiness for a man who's never had any. I guess I can relate to some of the themes.

I swallowed heavily, my heart squeezing for the man I loved.

Me: I love you, Archer.

Archer: I love you too, Bree.

Me: Pulling into a gas station. Text you in a bit.

Archer: Okay.

* * *

Me: What's on your happy list?

Archer: What's a happy list?

Me: Just a short list of a few simple things that make you happy.

My phone remained quiet for a few minutes before it finally dinged.

Archer: The smell of the earth after it rains, the feeling of falling asleep, the small freckle on the inside of your right thigh. What's on your happy list?

I smiled and leaned my head back on the seat.

Me: Summer evenings, when the clouds part and a ray of golden light suddenly breaks through, knowing you're mine.

Archer: Always.

I leaned back on the seat again, a small, dreamy smile on my face. After a minute or two, my phone dinged again.

Archer: When do you think you'll get to Ohio?

Me: Probably about 8 a.m. I'm up next to drive so I better try to get some rest. I'll text you constantly to let you know what's going on, okay?

Archer: Okay. Will you tell Jordan I said thanks for the phone? I'd like to pay him for it. I didn't think to offer when he came over.

Me: I doubt if he'd take it anyway. But I'll tell him. I love you.

Archer: I love you too.

* * *

Me: Slept for a couple of hours. Dreamed about you. Stopping for dinner and then I'm going to drive for the next five hrs or so.

Archer: Dream? What kind of dream?

I laughed.

Me: A really, really good dream. ;) Remember that time on the lakeshore?

Archer: I'll never forget. I was washing sand out of places sand should never be for a week.

Me: Lol. It was worth it though, right? I miss you.

Archer: Very worth it. I miss you too. Guess what? I went into town for a few things and now I'm walking down the street texting you. I think Mrs. Grady almost had a heart attack. I heard her refer to me as the Unabomber Jr. once when she passed me in the grocery store. I had to look up who that was at the library. I realized it hadn't been a compliment.

I groaned, not knowing whether to laugh or cry. Some people could be so ignorant. I pictured that isolated teenager bravely fighting his way up to the gate where he would walk out into the world for the first time since he was a small child, and then getting a reception like that. I cringed. Every cell in my body screamed out to protect him, but I couldn't. It had already happened. I didn't even know him then—but the fact that I hadn't been there shot through my body as guilt and grief anyway. It wasn't rational. It was love.

Me: I'd read your manifesto, Archer Hale. Every word. I bet it'd be beautiful.

Archer: Lol. Which, incidentally, in my case should actually be los (laugh out silently).

Me: :D You being funny? :D

Archer: Yes. What's on your funny list?

I grinned, thinking for a second before typing.

Me: Watching the puppies waddle because their tummies are so fat, hearing other people laugh (it's contagious), funny fail moments. What's on your funny list?

Archer: Mr. Bivens in his crooked hairpiece, the look on a dog's face as it rides by with its head out the window of a car, people who snort when they laugh.

Me: I'm laughing now (maybe snorting) as I'm walking into the restaurant. :D I'll text in the morning. Ilu.

Archer: Okay. Good night, Ilu too.

"Geez, Bree, you're not supposed to be writing novels on text. Both of your fingers are going to be too tired for anything good when you get back," Natalie joked.'

I laughed and sighed—it might have been slightly swoony. Natalie rolled her eyes. "I love it. I feel like I'm getting to know him even better this way."

Natalie wrapped her arm around my shoulder and pulled me into her, and we walked into the restaurant smiling.

* * *

Me: Morning. You up? We only have another hour on the road. Nat's driving now.

Archer: Yeah, I'm up. Walking on the shore with the dogs. Hawk just ate a dead fish. He won't be coming inside today.

I smiled, still sleepy. I sat up and moved my neck from side to side. Sleeping in the front seat of a car was not comfortable. Natalie was at the wheel, sipping a cup of McDonald's coffee, and Jordan was snoring softly in the backseat.

Me: Eww! Hawk! What's on your gross-out list?

Archer: Really long, curved fingernails, barnacles, mushrooms. What's on your gross-out list?

Me: Wait—you don't like mushrooms? I'm going to cook something that will change your mind when I get back.

Archer: No, thanks.

I laughed.

Me: Cigarette breath, maggots, gas station bathrooms.

Archer: I'll be right back. I need to go take a shower.

Me: Lol.

Then I paused before typing.

Me: Thank you, I needed that. I'm a little nervous about today.

Archer: You're going to be fine. I promise, it's going to be fine. You can do this.

I smiled.

Me: Do you think you could do me a favor? If I call you right before I go into the police station, and put the phone in my pocket, will you just . . . be with me?

Archer: Yes, yes. Of course I will. And I promise not to say any-thing.

I laughed.

Me: Funny. Ilu, Archer.

Archer: Ilu, Bree.

* * *

I sat in the police station and looked at the pictures in front of me as the detective sat across the table, his hands folded, watching me closely.

My eyes zeroed in on the face I'd never forget. *Lie down*, I heard him command in my mind. I closed my eyes and took a deep breath, feeling Archer on the line against my body, feeling his very being as if he were right there, holding me close, whispering in my ear, *You can do this, you're brave, you can do this.* And as I sat there, Archer's voice was stronger, louder. His voice was all I heard.

"This one," I said, pointing my finger at the man on the page in front of me. I didn't even shake.

"You're sure?" the detective asked.

"One hundred and ten percent sure," I said steadily. "That's the man who killed my father."

The detective nodded and took the pictures away. "Thank you, Ms. Prescott."

"Are you going to bring him in now?"

"Yes. We'll notify you as soon as we do."

I nodded. "Thank you so much, Detective. Thank you."

Twenty minutes later, after completing some paperwork, I
was walking down the police station steps. I took my phone out
of my pocket and said into the open line, "Did you hear all that?
I picked him out, Archer! I didn't even hesitate. I saw him in the
picture in front of me and I knew it was him the instant I looked
at him. Oh my God, I'm shaking like a leaf now." I laughed
softly. "Thank you for being there. You made all the difference.
I'm going to hang up now so you can text me. God, I love you.
Thank you."

A second later my phone dinged.

Archer: You did good, Bree. So, so good. This is really hard. I want
to hold you right now.

Me: I know, I know, Archer. I want that too. Whew. Deep breath. Oh
God, the tears are coming now. But I'm happy. I can't believe this.
My dad's going to get justice.

Archer: I'm so happy about that.

Me: Oh God, me too. What are you doing right now? I need to talk
about something else while I calm down.

Archer: I just started a run.

I laughed and sniffled.

Me: You're on a run and texting at the same time???

Archer: I've gotten good at texting.

Me: No kidding, overachiever. Why am I not surprised?

Archer: You shouldn't be. Technology loves me.

I laughed, and then cried a little more, emotion overcoming me.

Me: Thank you for being with me. It made all the difference. You made me brave.

Archer: No, you were brave long before you met me. What's on your calm list?

I took a deep breath, thinking of the things that calmed me, soothed me, comforted my heart.

Me: The sound of the lake hitting the shore, a cup of hot tea, you. What's on your calm list?

Archer: Flannel sheets, looking up at the stars, you.

Me: Hey, Natalie's pulling up at the curb. We're going to my dad's house to pack up a few more things. I'll text you later. Thank you, thank you. Ilu.

Archer: Ilu2.

* * *

Me: Guess what? I'm back on the road.

Archer: What? How?

Me: I miss you. I need to come home.

Archer: Is this your home, Bree?

Me: Yes, Archer, my home is where you are.

Archer: Did you sleep this morning? You shouldn't drive when you're tired.

Me: I'll be okay. I'll make lots of coffee stops.

Archer: Drive safely. Drive carefully. Come back to me, Bree. I miss you so much it feels like a part of myself is missing.

Me: Me too, Archer. My Archer. I'm coming back to you. I'll be there soon. I love you.

Archer: I love you too. Always.

* * *

Archer: Don't text me while you're driving, but next time you stop, let me know where you are.

* * *

Archer: Bree? It's been a couple of hours and I haven't heard from you . . .

* * *

Archer: Bree? You're scaring me. Please be okay.

* * *

Archer: Bree...please...I'm losing my mind. Please text me.
Please be okay. Please be okay. Please be okay.

CHAPTER TWENTY-SEVEN

Archer—Seven Years Old, May

Archer!" my mama called, her voice sounding just a little bit scared. "Baby, where are you?"

I was sitting under the dining room table, the heavy tablecloth hiding me as I kneeled on the floor with my action figures.

I hesitated, but when my mama called me again, sounding more worried this time, I crawled out from under the table and went to her. I didn't like to hear my mama scared, but I also knew something was going on, and I was scared, too.

My mama had been whispering into the phone all morning, and for the last half hour, she'd been upstairs stuffing clothes and other things into suitcases.

That's when I'd hidden under the table and waited to see what would happen next.

I knew that whatever was going on was happening because my daddy had come home last night, again smelling like some other lady's perfume, and had slapped my mama in the face when she said his dinner was already cold.

I had a feeling my mama had finally had enough. And if I had to guess about who she was on the phone with, I'd say it was Uncle Connor.

My mama turned the corner into the dining room just as I was crawling out from beneath the table, and let out a loud breath. "Archer, sweetheart," she said, putting her hands on my cheeks and bending down so her eyes were right in front of mine. "You worried me."

"Sorry, Mama."

Her face got soft, and she smiled at me and moved the hair back from my forehead. "It's okay, but I need you to do something for me, and it's really important. Do you think you can listen and do as I say and not ask questions right now?"

I nodded.

"Okay, that's good." She smiled, but then it disappeared and the worried look came back into her eyes again. "We're going to go away, Archer—me, you, and your...uncle Connor. I know that's probably confusing to you right now, and I'm sure you have questions about your daddy, but—"

"I want to go," I said, standing up taller. "I don't want to live with him anymore."

My mama just looked at my face for a couple of seconds, her lips pressed together. She breathed out and ran her hand over my hair again. Tears came into her eyes. "I haven't been a good mama," she said and shook her head back and forth.

"You are a good mama!" I said. "You're the best mama in the world. But I want to live with Uncle Connor. I don't want my daddy to hit you anymore or make you cry."

She sniffled and wiped a tear from her cheek and then nodded her head at me. "We're going to be happy, Archer, do you hear me? You and me, we're going to be happy."

"Okay," I said, keeping my eyes on her pretty face.

"Okay," she said, finally smiling.

That's when our front door opened and Uncle Connor walked quickly inside. His face looked tight.

"You ready?" he asked, looking at my mama.

She nodded. "The suitcases are right there." She tilted her head toward the four pieces of luggage sitting at the bottom of the stairs.

"You okay?" Uncle Connor asked, his eyes moving over my mama as if he was looking to make sure she was all there.

"I will be. Take us away from here," she whispered.

Uncle Connor's face looked like someone was hurting him for a couple of seconds, but then he smiled and looked at me. "Ready, sport?"

I nodded and followed him and my mama out the front door. They both looked around as Uncle Connor put our suitcases into the trunk of the car. There wasn't anyone outside, though, and when they both got in the car they seemed relieved.

As we drove away, heading out of Pelion, I watched as Uncle Connor grabbed my mama's hand in the front seat and she turned toward him, letting out a breath and smiling a small smile.

"Me, you, and our boy," Uncle Connor said softly. "Just us."

"Just us," my mama whispered, that same soft look moving across her face.

My mama looked back at me, and paused for a second before saying, "I packed your Legos and some of your books, baby." She smiled and leaned the side of her head on the headrest, still looking at me. Her shoulders seemed to be dropping lower by the mile.

I just nodded. I didn't ask where we were going. I didn't care. As long as it was away from here, anywhere was fine.

Uncle Connor looked over at my mama. "Put your seat belt on, Lys."

My mama smiled. "This is the first time in years I feel like I'm not strapped down against my will," she said and laughed softly. "But okay, safety first." She tilted her head and winked at him, and I grinned. This was the mama I loved seeing—when her eyes would shine, and she'd get that sweet, joking tone in her voice and say something that would make you laugh at yourself, but in a good way, a way that felt warm and nice.

My mama reached for her belt, and all of a sudden there was a large jolt and our car swerved crazily. My mama screamed and Uncle Connor yelled, "Oh shit!" as he tried to keep us on the road.

Our car spun all over, and then all I heard was the scream of metal on metal, glass shattering, and my own screams as our car flipped for what seemed like hours, finally coming to a stop with a loud creaking sound.

The terror hit me hard, and that's when I started to cry, squeaking out, "Help! Help me!"

I heard a loud groan from the front, and then Uncle Connor was saying my name, telling me it would be okay as I heard him moving himself out of his seat belt and then kicking the door open. I couldn't open my eyes. It seemed like they were glued shut.

I heard the back door being pulled open, and then Uncle Connor's warm hand was on my arm. "It's going to be okay, Archer. I got your belt undone. Crawl toward me. You can do it."

I finally made myself open my eyes and look up into my uncle's face, his hand reaching toward me. I grasped his arm and he pulled me out into the warm spring sunshine.

My Uncle Connor was talking again, and his voice sounded funny. "Archer, I need you to come with me, but I need you to turn your back when I tell you to, okay?"

"Okay." Terror and confusion made me cry more.

Uncle Connor took my hand and walked down the deserted highway with me just a little bit behind him. He kept looking backward at the car we'd gotten into a wreck with, but when I glanced back once very quickly, it didn't look like anyone was climbing out of that one. Were they dead? What had happened?

"Turn your back, Archer, and stay here, son," Uncle Connor said, and his voice sounded like he was choking.

I did as he said, letting my head fall back so that I was looking up at the clear blue sky. How was it that anything bad could happen under a sky that clear, that cloudless and blue?

I heard a strange wailing yell behind me and I turned around, even though I knew it wasn't following directions. I couldn't help it.

My Uncle Connor was on his knees on the side of the road, his head thrown back, sobbing up at the sky. My mama's limp body was in his arms.

I leaned over and threw up into the grass. I stood up a couple of minutes later, sucking in air and tripping backward over my own feet.

That's when I saw *him*, coming toward us. My daddy. With a gun in his hand. A look of pure hate on his face, and zigzagging. He was drunk. I tried to feel fear, but I didn't see that there was anything more he could do now. I felt numb as I moved toward Uncle Connor.

Uncle Connor laid my mama's body back down gently on the side of the road and stood up, seeing my daddy now, too. Uncle Connor moved toward me and pushed me behind his own body.

"Stay back, Marcus!" he yelled.

My daddy stopped a couple of feet away and glared at us, weaving, his eyes bloodshot. He looked like a monster. He *was* a monster. He waved the gun around crazily and Uncle Connor grabbed me tightly, making sure I was right behind him.

"Put the fucking gun down, Marcus," Uncle Connor spit out. "Haven't you done enough here today? Alyssa..." He let out a noise that sounded like a hurt animal, and I felt his knees give out just a little before he pulled himself back up.

"You think you're just going to ride out of town with my family?" the monster shouted.

"They were never your family, you sick son of a bitch. Alyssa…" He made that same choking sound again, and didn't finish that thought. "And Archer's *my* son. He's *my* boy. You know that as well as I do."

I felt a feeling like someone punched me in my belly, and squeaked out a small sound as Connor's hands held me tightly again. I was his son? I tried to understand, tried to make sense of that. I wasn't related to the monster? I wasn't any part of him? I was Connor's son. Connor was my daddy. And my daddy was one of the good guys.

I peeked out at the monster as he looked at us. "Alyssa always was a slut. I don't doubt it. And the boy does look just like you, can't deny that." All his words ran together, just like they always did when he had been out drinking.

Connor's fists balled by his side, and as I peeked up at him, I saw that his jaw wasn't moving as he talked. "If our mama could see you now, she'd cry her eyes out at the sick piece of shit you grew up to be."

"Fuck you," the monster said back, more anger filling his eyes, swaying some more. "You know who had to tell me you were trying to drive out of town with *my wife*? *Your* wife. Yup, she came and got me and told me you were on your way out and I better go collect what's mine. So here I am, collecting what's mine. Although I see I'm a bit late on one count." He pointed over to my mama, lying on the side of the road.

Hot anger filled my head. Connor was my daddy. He was taking me and my mama away from the monster—and the monster had messed it all up. Just like he always messed everything up. I moved fast around Connor's legs and ran at the monster as fast as

I could. A loud roar came out of Connor, and I heard him scream, "Archer!" like his own life depended on it. I heard his feet running after me as the monster raised his gun to fire, and I screamed. But my scream sounded like a gurgle as something sharp and hot sliced through the side of my neck like a knife, and I went down on the hard road. I brought my hands to my throat, and when I brought them down to look, they were full of blood.

I heard another deep roar and I faded out, feeling myself fall, but when I came to, Uncle Connor, *No, wait*, I thought dreamily, my daddy, *my real daddy*, was rocking me in his arms, tears running down his cheeks.

My eyes found the monster, kneeling now where he had been standing a few minutes before. Or had it been hours? Everything felt foggy, slow.

"My boy, my boy, my sweet boy," Connor was saying again and again. He was talking about me. *I was his boy.* Happiness filled my chest. I had a daddy who was happy I was his.

"This is all *his* fault," the monster screamed. "If it wasn't for him, Alyssa wouldn't have still been hanging on to your sorry ass. If it wasn't for *him*, Alyssa wouldn't be lying in the road with a broken neck right now!" He sounded crazy, but sadness filled me up, and I wanted someone to say it wasn't true. *Was* this all my fault? Connor, *my daddy* I had to remind myself, wasn't telling him it wasn't, he was just pressing something down on my neck, a wild look in his eyes.

I kept looking dreamily up at my real daddy, and I suddenly saw his face seem to blank, and I felt him reaching for something at his side. Wasn't that where he carried his gun? I thought maybe it was. He usually had it there, even when he was off duty. I had asked him to look at it a couple of times, but he had told me no, said he'd take me shooting someday when I was older, and he could teach me gun safety.

His hand came out from under me, and he pointed his gun at the monster. My eyes moved to him in slow motion and saw right when he realized what my real daddy was about to do. The monster raised his gun, too.

Both of their guns exploded, and I felt my real daddy jerk beneath me. I tried to cry out, but I was so tired, so cold, so numb. My eyes moved back to the monster, and he was lying on the ground, a pool of blood spreading out slowly around him.

My eyes wanted to close, and my real daddy's body felt so heavy on mine. But how could that be when he was standing over me, my mama right next to him? They looked so peaceful. *Take me with you!* I screamed in my head. But they just looked at each other and my mama smiled gently, but sadly, too, and said, *Not yet. Not just yet, my sweet boy.*

And then they were gone.

Somewhere far away I heard another car screech to a stop and footsteps running toward me. In the ten minutes it took for my life as I knew it to end, not another car had driven by.

A loud scream filled the air, and I felt my body jerk.

"You!" a female voice screamed. It was Aunt Tori. I recognized her voice. "Oh God! Oh God! This is all *your* fault!" I opened my eyes. She was pointing her finger straight at me, and her eyes were filled with hatred. *"Your fault!"* And then she screamed it again and again and again as the world faded out around me, and the blue sky above me turned black.

CHAPTER TWENTY-EIGHT

BREE

It was early, early morning—the sun wasn't even up yet as I opened Archer's gate quietly, let Phoebe out of her carrier, and walked down the driveway to his house.

I tried his door and it was open, and so I tiptoed in, not wanting to wake him. I sucked in a breath and froze. His living room was torn apart, every book on the floor, furniture and lamps turned over, pictures lying broken on the ground. Ice water hit my veins. *Oh God, oh God, oh God.* What had happened here?

The light from the bathroom was on and the door just cracked, illuminating his short hallway enough to see as I walked toward Archer's bedroom on legs that felt like jelly, vomit coming up my throat.

I turned into his room and immediately saw his form huddled on the bed, fully dressed. His eyes were open, staring at the wall.

I rushed to him. His skin was clammy, and he was trembling slightly. "Archer? Archer? Baby, what's wrong?"

His eyes moved to me, unseeing, looking right through me. I started to cry. "Archer, you're scaring me. What's wrong? Oh God, do you need a doctor? What happened here? Talk to me."

His eyes seemed to clear a little, moving over my face. Suddenly in one swift movement, he sat up and grabbed me, his hands moving over my face, my hair, my shoulders. His expression cleared completely for an instant before torment filled his face and he pulled me to him harshly, making me cry out. He held my body in a vise grip, his body trembling so severely that it almost felt like he was having a seizure in my arms.

Oh God, he thought something had happened to me. "Oh, Archer, I'm sorry, so sorry. My phone got ruined. I'm sorry. I dropped it in a puddle in front of McDonald's. I grabbed my old phone when I was in Ohio but it didn't have any charge. I'm sorry," I cried into his chest, gripping his shirt. "I'm so sorry, Archer, baby. I didn't have your number anyway...so stupid. I should have written it down. I'm so sorry. Archer, I'm okay. I'm okay. I'm so sorry."

We held each other that way for what seemed like hours, his breathing returning to normal. His body stilled and his grip loosened on me until he finally sat back and looked into my eyes, his own still filled with torment, with something that looked very close to grief.

"I'm here," I whispered, brushing the hair off of his forehead. "I'm here, Archer."

He brought his hands up. *I had almost forgotten what it feels like*, he said, suddenly looking lost, like a little boy. My heart beat hollowly in my chest, breaking for the man I loved, so petrified of loss that his mind had checked out so he could deal with his agonizing fear. Oh, Archer. I stifled a sob. The last thing he needed right now was for me to lose it.

"What *what* feels like?" I whispered.

To be completely alone.

"You're not, baby. I'm here. I'm not going anywhere. I'm here."

He looked at me then and, finally, smiled a sad smile. *This is that burden I was talking about, Bree. This is what the burden of loving me looks like.*

"Loving you isn't a burden. Loving you is an honor and a joy, Archer." I used my voice to talk to him so I could keep gripping his thighs with my hands. The contact felt important—not just for him, but for me. "You couldn't talk me out of loving you if you tried anyway. It's not a choice for me. It's just a truth."

He shook his head, looking lost again. *If you hadn't come back, I would have lain here until I died. I would have just willed myself to die.*

I shook my head. "No, you wouldn't have. It feels like that, but you wouldn't have. Somehow you would have had the strength to go on. I believe that about you. But you don't have to, because I'm here."

No. I would have just faded to dust, right here. How does that make you see me? Do I seem strong to you? Am I the kind of man you want? He looked into my eyes, begging me to tell him what he wanted to hear, but I didn't know what that was. Did he want me to tell him he was impossible to love? Did he want me to tell him I wasn't strong enough to love him? That the reassurance he needed from me was too much?

He pulled me to him, and after a few minutes we moved over and lay down on his bed. I kicked my shoes off and pulled his quilt over us.

I listened to Archer's quiet breathing right at my ear, and after a few minutes, I closed my eyes, too. We fell asleep facing each other, arms and legs entwined, our hearts beating a slow, steady rhythm.

Sometime later, when the midday sun was lighting the edges of the shade over Archer's bedroom window, I awoke as he pulled my jeans down my legs and my shirt over my head. He moved his hands over my skin as he closed his eyes and kissed me, almost as if he needed the constant contact to assure himself I was truly there with him. When I wrapped my legs around his hips and held him tightly, the look of relief that passed over his features was almost heart-wrenching. He moved inside me with deep, powerful thrusts, and I dropped my head back on the pillow, sighing with pleasure.

The pleasure rose higher and higher until I tipped over the edge, breathing out his name as my body shuddered in release. A few seconds later he followed behind me on two last jerky thrusts and then pressed deeply inside me as he stuck his face in my neck and just breathed there for several minutes.

I ran my hands up and down his back, whispering words of love in his ear over and over and over.

After a few minutes, he rolled to the side and gathered me in his arms again and was almost instantly asleep.

I lay there in the dim light of his room, listening to him breathe. I had to pee, and my thighs were sticky with his release, but I refused to move. I knew instinctively that he needed me right where I was. After a little while, I fell back to sleep, too, my face next to his smooth chest, my breath against his skin, my legs entwined with his.

* * *

I woke up later and was alone in bed, and the sun had moved in the sky. The light around the border of the shade was now muted and golden. Had we slept all day?

I sat up and stretched, my sore muscles protesting with my movement. I didn't think I had moved at all—wrapped in Archer's tight embrace.

I looked up as he walked in the bedroom wearing a towel around his waist and rubbing another one through his hair that had already grown a little longer, starting to curl up slightly in the back and flop over his forehead a little. I liked it.

"Hi," I croaked out, smiling and bringing the sheet up over my breasts. He smiled back, a shy smile, and sat down on the side of the bed. He kept rubbing the towel through his hair absently for another minute as he looked down, and then he put the towel next to him on the bed and looked up at me.

I'm sorry about last night. I lost it, Bree, I was so scared, and I didn't know what to do. I felt alone and helpless again. He paused, pursing his lips and obviously gathering his thoughts. *I…freaked out, I guess. I don't even remember doing what I did to the living room.*

I grabbed his hands and shook my head. *Archer, do you remember how I reacted when I got caught in that net out there?* I gestured my head to the window. *I get it. Sometimes fear gets the best of you. I understand. I'm the last person you have to apologize to about that. You picked up where I left off once, and now I get to do that for you. That's how it works, okay?*

He nodded, looking at me so solemnly. *The problem, Bree, is that I feel like it's getting better for you and worse for me.*

I'm up for the challenge, I said, raising my brows and smiling, trying to coax a smile from him, too.

It worked, and he let out a breath and nodded. *Are you hungry? Famished.*

He smiled, but it still looked a little sad. I looked at him for a minute and then leaned forward and threw my arms around him. "I love you," I whispered in his ear. His body tensed slightly, but he wrapped his arms around me and squeezed me back tightly.

We sat there like that for a few minutes, and then I said against his neck, "I need a shower—bad. Like, really bad."

He finally laughed just a little as he picked me up and sat me down on the floor and stood up, straightening his towel. *I like you all dirty with me all over you*, he said.

Oh, I know. I winked, trying to coax another smile from him as I walked toward his door, using my voice as I turned toward him. "You can dirty me up again later. Right now, I'm getting clean, and you're going to feed me."

Yes, ma'am, he said, giving me another small smile.

I smiled back at him, and then I turned out of the room and walked down the hall toward the shower. I closed the bathroom door behind me and just stood on the other side for a minute, trying to figure out why I was still so worried.

CHAPTER TWENTY-NINE

BREE

I went back to work the next day to Maggie, who gave me a giant bear hug, pressing me tightly into her ample bosom as I laughed and struggled to breathe, and Norm, who said simply, "Bree," but gave me a rare Norm smile and head nod before he moved his focus back to the griddle where he was flipping pancakes. For some reason, the bear hug and the head nod both filled me with equal amounts of warmth. I was home.

As I worked, I chatted with the locals I'd come to know, making my way easily around the diner, delivering the food, and checking on my customers.

I thought about Archer as I worked, too, considering how difficult it was for him to become attached to another person. I'd had an idea before I left for Ohio, but not to the extent that I now understood. I loved him—I would do whatever was necessary to reassure him that I wasn't going anywhere. But I understood his struggle, too. I saw that it made him feel weak that I knew how reliant he was on me.

He had acted almost shy with me the day before, his eyes moving away from mine when he saw me watching him as we cleaned up his living room together. I had picked up *Ethan Frome* from the floor when I'd recognized the title, and opened it to read a passage, putting my hand dramatically on my chest and feigning a breathy, pained whisper, "I want to put my hand out and touch you. I want to do for you and care for you. I want to be there when you're sick and when you're lonesome." I had paused, my hand falling from my chest. I placed the book down and brought my hands up. *That was beautiful, actually*, I said.

He had smiled at me and said simply, *I guess if it wasn't beautiful, the tragedy ultimately wouldn't be sad.*

But then he had lapsed into more silence, seeming almost embarrassed around me. I tried to bring him out of it by joking with him and acting completely normal, but he was still slightly withdrawn even when I'd kissed him goodbye that evening, gathered Phoebe, and gone home to unpack and get ready for the next day. It would take a day or two for him to feel better, I supposed.

Over the next several days, he did return to his more normal self; the only difference I could still see was a deep intensity to his lovemaking that hadn't been there before. It was almost as if he were trying to meld us into one person when we connected. He was almost rough in his passion. I didn't mind it; in fact, I found all sides of Archer's bedroom personality to my liking. But I couldn't explain the change exactly, and I longed for him to open up to me and tell me what he was feeling. When I asked him, though, he just shrugged and smiled and told me he'd missed me while I was gone and was trying to make up for lost time. I didn't buy it, but as always, Archer Hale came around when he was good and ready and not a moment before. I had learned quickly—push and get nowhere, wait and hope that he trusted me enough to open up sooner rather than later in his own quiet way. I thought it had something to do with the fact that he liked to understand his own emotions before he shared them with me, and he didn't know exactly where he was at the moment.

* * *

Four days after I'd returned home from Ohio, I knocked on Anne's door and she answered, still in her bathrobe. "Oh, Bree, dear!" she exclaimed, holding her door open. "You'll have to excuse me. I'm having a lazy day—I've been so tired for the last week." She shook her head. "Sucks getting old, I'll tell you."

I grinned and stepped inside her warm, inviting home. As always, the comforting smell of eucalyptus scented the air. "You? Old?" I shook my head. "Not hardly."

She laughed and winked at me. "You're a good fibber, but I feel as old as the hills today. Maybe I'm coming down with something." She shook her head and gestured to her couch for me to take a seat. I handed her the small boxed pie I had brought. "I made you an apple pie," I said. "I've been baking a little bit and really enjoying it."

"Oh! Lovely. And baking again—that's wonderful." She accepted the pie, smiling. "I'll have this later with my tea. Speaking of which, would you like a cup?"

I shook my head and took a few steps to the couch and sat down. "No, I can actually only stay a minute. I'm meeting Archer, and we're going to some caves he told me about."

Anne nodded and set the pie box on the coffee table and took a seat on the smaller love seat to the left of the couch. "Pelion Caverns. You'll like them. There are waterfalls—lovely. I went there a couple of times with Bill."

"They sound beautiful."

"They are, and the drive will be beautiful, too, now that the leaves are changing."

I smiled. "It should be a nice day. We need one," I said, breathing out.

Anne was quiet for a beat. "Did Archer mention that I visited him while you were in Ohio?"

"No," I said, surprised. "You did?"

She nodded. "That boy has been on my mind ever since you first asked about his father and his uncles. I should have visited him years ago." She sighed and shook her head. "I brought him some muffins—used the last of the blueberries I had frozen." She waved her hand, dismissing her own comment. "Anyway, he looked...leery at first and can't say I blame him, but I chattered a bit and he came around—even invited me into his house. I had no idea the land was that lovely. I told him so and he seemed to take pride in that."

I nodded, wanting to tear up for some reason. "He works hard."

"Yes, he does." She studied me for a minute. "I told him a few things I remembered about Alyssa, his mother, and he liked that, too."

I tilted my head, wanting her to go on.

"I talked about you and he liked that best of all—I could see it in his expression." Anne smiled gently. "The way Archer looked when I mentioned your name, oh, Bree, dear—I've never seen someone's heart so clearly right on their sleeve." Her eyes warmed. "It reminded me of the way Bill used to look at me sometimes." She smiled again and so did I, my heart rate picking up.

"He loves you, dear."

I nodded, looking down at my hands. "Yes, I love him, too." I bit my lip. "Unfortunately for Archer, I think love is pretty complicated."

She smiled a sad smile. "I figure, now that I know what I know about the life he's led, giving his love to you feels filled with risk."

I nodded, my eyes filling with tears now. I told her about what happened when I returned from Ohio, and she listened with heartbreak on her face. "What should I do, Anne?" I asked when I was done.

"I think the best thing you can do for Archer—" She stopped midsentence, her eyes taking on a startled expression and her hand coming to her chest.

"Anne!" I said, jumping up and going to her. She was gasping now and had fallen back on the couch. "Oh my God! Anne!" I grabbed my phone out of the pocket of my sweatshirt and hit 911, my hands shaking.

I told the operator the address and that I thought my neighbor was having a heart attack, and the girl on the line assured me the ambulance was on its way.

I returned to Anne's side, reassuring her again and again that help was on its way. She continued to clutch her chest, but her eyes were focused on me, and I thought she was understanding what I was telling her.

Oh God! I thought. *What if I hadn't been here?*

The ambulance shrieked down our small street ten long minutes later, and tears streamed down my face as I watched them work on Anne as she lay on her couch. I took long, shaky breaths, trying to get my own heart rate under control. "Is she going to be okay?" I asked the tech when they brought a stretcher in to transport her. She had an oxygen mask on and looked slightly better already, some color returning to her cheeks.

"It looks good," he said. "She's conscious, and we got to her in time."

"Okay." I nodded, wrapping my arms around my body. "She doesn't have any family. Should I meet her at the hospital?"

"You're welcome to ride in the ambulance with her."

"Oh! Okay. Yes, please, if I can," I said, following them outside and closing Anne's door behind us.

As I moved toward the ambulance, I glanced to my right and saw Archer running toward me, a look that I could only describe as wild on his face. My heart plummeted to my feet. Oh God, he had run here—he must have heard the ambulance sirens all the way from his house. I walked quickly toward him. He came to an immediate halt when he saw me, not moving closer, his eyes wide and staring, his fists clenched. I jogged the last couple of yards to him and said, "Archer! Anne had a heart attack. She's okay, I think, but I'm going to ride to the hospital with her. It's okay. Everything is okay. I'm okay."

He put his hands up on top of his head and gritted his teeth, looking like he was struggling mightily to rein something in. He walked in a slow circle and then turned toward me, nodding his head once, that wild look still in his eyes, but not his expression. His expression suddenly looked strangely blank.

"I'll come straight to you when I know she's going to be okay," I said. I glanced back, and the back wheels of the stretcher were just disappearing inside the ambulance. I walked backward. "I'll take a cab straight to you."

Archer nodded, still expressionless, and then turned without saying a word and walked away from me.

I hesitated only a second before jogging to the ambulance and hopping in just before they closed the doors.

* * *

I stayed at the hospital until I knew for sure that Anne was going to be okay. When the doctor finally came out to tell me she was stable, he said she was sleeping, but he'd told her I was there. They had also called a sister whose number Anne had given them when they first brought her in, and she'd be in Pelion in the morning. That made me feel a lot better, and when I finally called a taxi, I felt like a weight had lifted.

I was worried about Archer, though. I had texted him when I first got to the hospital and then again when the doctor came out to speak to me, but he had never responded. I was anxious to get to him.

I bit my lip as the taxi made the thirty-minute drive to my cottage. I had told Archer I'd come straight to him, but I wanted to pick Phoebe up before going to his house. Surely he had calmed down by now. He knew I was fine, even if the initial scare had done a number on him. Why he wasn't answering his phone, I wasn't sure, though, and it sat heavy in my gut.

I paid the driver and hopped out, rushing into my cottage and calling to Phoebe, who came running, her nails clicking on my hardwood floor.

I pulled up to Archer's gate a few minutes later and let Phoebe and myself in. We walked to Archer's door, and I knocked softly before opening it and putting Phoebe down. It had just started to drizzle outside, gray clouds darkening the sky.

Archer's house was dark except for a standing lamp that was on in the corner of the living room. Archer was sitting in a chair in the opposite corner. At first I didn't see him, and so when I did, I startled and brought my hand to my chest, sucking in a short breath. His expression was somber, hooded. I went to him immediately and kneeled down at his feet, putting my head on his lap and sighing.

After a few seconds when I realized he was going to remain still, I looked up at him questioningly.

How's Anne? he asked.

I brought my hands up. *She's going to be fine. Her sister will be* here in the morning. I sighed. *I'm so sorry that whole episode scared you. I didn't want to leave you there, but I didn't want to leave Anne alone, either.*

Archer brought his hands up. *I understand*, he said, his eyes still shuttered.

I nodded, biting my lip. *Are you okay? What are you sitting here thinking about?*

He was quiet for so long, I thought he wasn't going to answer me, when he finally brought his hands up and signed, *That day.*

I tilted my head. *That day?* I asked, confused.

The day I was shot, my uncle came to take my mom and me away from my dad.

My eyes widened, but I didn't say a word, just watched him and waited for him to continue.

My dad was at a bar…supposedly busy for a while. He paused, looking off behind me for a second before his eyes found me again. *He hadn't always been like he was at the end. He'd been fun, full of charm when he wanted to be. But then he started drinking, and things went downhill from there. He'd slap my mom, accuse her of things he was the one doing.*

Either way, though, my mom only loved one man, and that was my uncle Connor. I knew it, my dad knew it, the whole town knew it. And the truth of it was, I loved him more, too.

He was silent again for a minute, staring past me. Finally, he continued.

And so when he came for us that day and I learned that I was his son, not Marcus Hale's son, I was happy. I was elated.

He looked down at me, regarding me with little emotion, as if he was deep inside himself, hidden. *My uncle shot me, Bree. Marcus Hale shot me. I don't know if he meant to or if the gun just went off when I ran toward him in anger. But either way, he shot me and this is what it did.* He brought his hand up to his throat, running it over the scar.

Then he gestured his hand to indicate all of him. *This is what it did.*

My heart sank. "Oh, Archer," I breathed out. He continued to look down at me. He seemed almost numb.

"What happened to them? To your mom?" I asked, blinking up at him and swallowing the lump that was threatening to choke me.

He paused for only a second. *Marcus had hit our car from behind in his attempt to run us off the road. Our car flipped. My mom was killed in the accident.* He closed his eyes for a minute, pausing, before he continued. *After Marcus shot me, there was a standoff between him and Connor in the road.* He lapsed into silence again for a minute, his eyes looking like deep, amber pools of sorrow. *They shot each other, Bree. Right there on the highway, under a blue springtime sky, they shot each other.*

I felt weak with horror.

Archer went on. *Tori showed up and then I vaguely remember another car coming along a minute after that. The next thing I remember is waking up in the hospital.*

A sob moved up my throat, but I swallowed it. *All these years—* I shook my head, unable to grasp the torment he must have experienced—*you've lived with that all these years, all by yourself. Oh, Archer.* I sucked in a huge breath, attempting to keep hold of my own emotion.

He looked down at me, emotion finally flashing in his own eyes before it moved away again.

I scooted closer to him and gripped his T-shirt as I laid my head against his stomach, tears running silently down my face as I whispered again and again, "I'm so sorry." I didn't know what else to say in response to the weight of the horror a little boy had held.

But I finally understood the depth of his pain, of his trauma, of the burden he carried with him. And I understood why Victoria Hale hated him. She hadn't just sought to take his voice, she had sought to take his confidence, his self-worth, his identity. Because Archer was the embodiment of the fact that her husband loved another woman more deeply than he had ever loved her, and that he had given that woman not only his heart, but his firstborn son. And that son had the ability to take everything from her.

I continued to hold Archer.

After what seemed like a long time, I leaned back. *You own the land this town is on. You're Connor's oldest son.*

He nodded, not looking at me, not seeming to care in the least.

You don't want it, Archer? I asked, wiping the tears off my wet cheeks.

He looked down at me. *What in the hell would I do with it? I can't even communicate with anyone except you. Much less run a whole damn town. People would look at me like I was the funniest joke they'd ever heard.*

I shook my head. *That's not true. You're good at everything you do. You'd be great at it, actually.*

I don't want it, he said, anguish washing over his face. *Let Travis have it. I don't want anything to do with it. Not only am I incapable, but I don't deserve it. It was my fault. It was all because of me that they died that day.*

I reared back, sucking in a breath. *Your fault? You were just a little boy. How could any of it have been your fault?*

Archer regarded me, an unreadable expression on his face. *My very existence caused their deaths.*

Their own choices caused their deaths. Not a seven-year-old child. I'm sorry, but you'll never convince me that you have one scrap of re-

sponsibility for what happened between four adults that day. I shook my head vehemently, trying to physically put emphasis on the words I'd just "spoken."

He looked over my shoulder, staring at something only he could see for several minutes. I waited him out.

I used to think I was cursed, he said, a small, humorless smile tugging at the side of his mouth before it morphed into a grimace. He dragged one hand down the side of his face again before bringing both hands up. *It didn't seem possible that someone could be handed so much shittiness in one lifetime. But then I realized it probably wasn't that I was cursed, more that I was being punished.*

I shook my head again. *It doesn't work that way.*

His eyes met mine and I let out a gust of breath. *I considered that, too, once, Archer. But…I realized that if I truly believed that, I'd have to believe my dad deserved to be shot in his own deli, and I know that isn't true.* I paused, trying to remember what it felt like to think I was cursed once as well. *Bad things don't happen to people because they deserve for them to happen. It just doesn't work that way. It's just…life. And no matter who we are, we have to take the hand we're dealt, crappy though it may be, and try our very best to move forward* anyway, *to love* anyway, *to have hope* anyway…*to have faith that there's a purpose to the journey we're on.* I grabbed his hands in mine for a second and then let go so I could continue. *And try to believe that maybe more light shines out of those who have the most cracks.*

Archer kept studying me for several beats before he brought his hands up and said, *I don't know if I can. I'm trying really hard, but I don't know if I can.*

You can, I affirmed, my gestures sweeping to add emphasis. *You can.*

He paused for a minute before saying, *It all looks so messy.* He ran one hand over his short hair. *I can't make sense of it all—my past, my life, my love for you.*

I looked up at him for a minute, watching the emotions cross his face. After a second I brought my hands up. *I don't remember a lot about my mom.* I gave a small shake of my head. *She passed away from cancer and I was so young when she died.* I licked my lips, pausing. *But I remember her doing these cross-stitches—they're little thread embroidery pictures.*

Archer watched my hands, glancing up at my face between words.

Anyway, one time I picked up one of her pieces and it looked awful—all messy, with all these knots and uneven strings hanging everywhere. I could barely make out what the picture was supposed to be. I kept my eyes on Archer, squeezing his hand quickly before bringing my own back up.

But then, my mom came over and took the piece of fabric out of my hands and turned it over—and right there was this masterpiece. I breathed out and smiled. *She liked birds. I remember the picture— it was a nest full of babies, the mama bird just returning.* I paused, thinking. *Sometimes I think of those little pieces of fabric when life feels really messy and difficult to understand. I try to close my eyes and believe that even though I can't see the other side right then, and the side I'm looking at is ugly and muddled, there's a masterpiece that's being woven out of all the knots and loose strings. I try to believe that something beautiful can result from something ugly, and that there will come a time when I'll get to see what that is. You helped me see my own picture, Archer. Let me help you see yours.*

Archer gazed down at me, but he didn't say anything. He just tugged gently on my arms and dragged me up onto his lap and pulled me into his body, holding me tightly, his warm breath in the crook of my neck.

We sat that way for several minutes before I whispered in his ear, "I'm so tired. I know it's early, but take me to bed, Archer. Hold me. Let me hold you."

We both stood up and walked to his bedroom, where we undressed slowly and got under his sheets. He pulled me close and held me tightly, but didn't attempt to make love to me. He seemed better, but still distant, like he was somewhere lost inside of himself.

"Thank you for telling me your story," I whispered in the dark.

Archer just nodded his head and pulled me closer.

CHAPTER THIRTY

BREE

The next day was the Pelion Police Memorial Parade. I stood in the window of the diner, blearily watching the cars and trucks go by, the people lined up on the sidewalk, waving flags. I felt numb, heartsick, achy.

I hadn't slept very well. I'd felt Archer tossing and turning most of the night. When I had asked him in the morning if he couldn't sleep, he had just nodded, not offering more of an explanation.

He hadn't said much as we ate breakfast together, and I got ready to head home to get my uniform for work and drop Phoebe off. He seemed deep in thought, still lost inside his own head, and yet when I went to leave, he'd pulled me to him tightly.

"Archer, baby, talk to me," I'd said, not caring if it made me late for work.

He had just shaken his head, offering a smile that didn't reach his eyes, and told me he'd see me after work and we'd talk some more.

And now I stood at the window, worried. The diner was mostly empty since the whole town was at the parade, so I could lose myself in my thoughts uninterrupted for a few minutes.

I watched the old-fashioned police cruisers go by, the crowd cheering louder for the vintage cars, and a bitterness swept through me. Archer should be here. Archer should be at his father's memorial dinner. And he hadn't even been invited at all. What was wrong with this town? Victoria Hale, evil bitch extraordinaire, that's what was wrong with this town. How did someone like her live with herself? She had ruined so many lives—all for what? Money? Prestige? Power? Pride? Just to win?

And now the whole town bowed down to her out of fear of the repercussions.

As I stood there, thinking about everything that Archer had told me last night, my stomach turned, and I felt like I was going to vomit. The reality of what it must have been like for a seven-year-old boy to be there that day was revolting, horrifying. I wanted to go back in time and hold him in my arms, comfort him, make it all go away. But I couldn't, and it hurt.

I was snapped out of my thoughts by my phone vibrating in my uniform pocket. I pulled it out quickly and saw that it was a call coming in from Ohio. I walked back to the counter where a couple of customers sat, and stood off to the side near the break table as I took the call.

"Hello," I said softly.

"Bree, hi, this is Detective McIntyre. I was calling because I have some news."

I glanced back at the counter, noting that everyone looked like they had what they needed, and turned my back.

I distantly heard the bell over the door ring, but didn't turn. Maggie could take care of new customers until I was done.

"You have news, Detective?"

"Yes. We made an arrest."

I sucked in a breath. "You made an arrest?" I whispered.

"Yes. His name is Jeffrey Perkins. He's the man you identified. We brought him in for questioning and his prints matched ones we found at the scene. He lawyered up so he's not talking. His father owns a big Fortune Five Hundred company here in town."

I paused, biting my lip. "Jeffrey Perkins?" I asked. "His father is Louis Perkins, isn't he?" I asked, closing my eyes, recognizing the last name of the man that owned one of the biggest insurance companies in Cincinnati.

The detective paused. "Yes."

"Why would someone like Jeffrey Perkins come in to rob a small deli?" I asked, feeling numb.

"I wish I could answer that," he said. "My best guess is it was drug related."

"Hmm," I said, remembering Jeffrey's jitters and shiny, dilated eyes. He had to have been on something. Rich boy with a bad drug habit? I shivered, shaking my head in an attempt to bring myself back to the present.

"What happens now, Detective?"

"Well, he's out on bail. His arraignment is in a few months, so now we just wait for that."

I paused for a minute. "Out on bail. So, more waiting." I sighed.

"I know. It's difficult. But, Bree, we have some really good evidence against him. And with your ID, I'm hopeful here."

I took a deep breath. "Thank you so much, Detective. Please keep me updated on anything else you might get?"

"Absolutely, I will. Have a good day."

"You, too, Detective. Bye."

I hung up and stood with my back to the diner for another minute. This was good news, so why couldn't I feel the happiness, the relief, I should be feeling? I stood biting my thumbnail, trying to figure myself out. Finally, I took a deep breath and turned around. Victoria Hale and Travis Hale were sitting at the end of the counter, just to the right of where I was standing.

My eyes widened, and I took in Victoria's icy stare and then Travis's furrowed brow.

I spun on my feet and called, "Maggie! I'm taking a short break. I don't feel so good."

Maggie turned to me with a worried look. "Okay, honey," she called as I rushed to the back and stayed there until Travis and Tori left the diner.

They only stayed ten minutes or so—presumably for a warm drink—and right after they'd left, I was wiping down a table near the window when I caught sight of Archer on the other side of the street. My heart started racing. "Maggie!" I called, "I'll be right back!"

"Oh, okay," I heard Maggie call, confused, from the break table where she was sitting and reading a magazine. She had to be wondering what was going on with me today.

I went out the front door and called to Archer. He was stopped on the side of the street, watching the police cruisers go by, a tight expression on his face. Had he been thinking the same thing I had?

As I was about to step off the curb, a hand grabbed my arm, and I halted and turned slightly to see Travis. I looked to the left of him, and Victoria Hale was standing there, trying to pretend I didn't exist, her eyes focused solely on the parade in front of her, a phony smile on her face and her nose in the air.

I looked over my shoulder at Archer, who was now starting to walk across the street toward us.

"I have to go, Travis," I said, attempting to pull away.

"Whoa, wait," he said, not letting go. "I overheard your phone call. I'm concerned. I just wanted to—"

"Travis, let me go," I said, my heart beating faster. This was the very last thing Archer needed right now.

"Bree, I know I'm not your favorite person, but if there's something I can do to help—"

"Let me go, Travis!" I yelled, wrenching my arm away. The crowd around us suddenly seemed to quiet, eyes moving away from the parade, traveling slowly down the street in front of them, and toward us.

Before I could spin around, a fist was flying at Travis's face and he went down hard, a spray of blood seeming to move in slow motion through the air in front of me. I gasped and so did Tori Hale and several people standing close by.

I looked over my shoulder, and Archer was standing there, breathing hard, eyes wide in his face, opening and closing his fist by his side.

I gaped at him and then looked back at Travis, who was just standing, his eyes filled with rage as he took Archer in. "You motherfucker," Travis hissed, gritting his teeth.

"Travis!" Tori Hale exclaimed, her face not pulled quite tight enough to hide her alarm.

I brought my arms out between the two of them, but it was too late. Travis lurched around me and attacked Archer, and they both went down as people gasped and stumbled backward, some tripping over the curb as others steadied them.

Archer got one more punch in before Travis flipped him harshly, Archer's back slamming onto the pavement with a loud thud. I watched as the air went out of him and he gritted his teeth. Travis swung at his face, connecting with his jaw.

I sobbed out, fear sweeping through my body like a quick-spreading forest fire.

"Stop!" I screamed. "Stop!" Travis lifted his hand and was just about to bring it down in Archer's face again. Oh God, he was going to pulverize him into the ground, right here in front of everyone, in front of me. Everything inside my body seemed to speed up, my heart beating loudly in my own ears, and my pulse rate skyrocketing. "Stop!" I yelled, my voice hitching on a sob. "You're *brothers*! Stop this!"

Time seemed to freeze as Travis's fist stopped in midair and Archer's eyes flew to me. I heard Tori inhale sharply. "You're brothers," I said again, tears running down my face now. "Please don't do this. Today is about your father. He wouldn't want this. Please. Please stop."

Travis pushed on Archer's chest, but got off him and stood up. Archer stood up quickly, too, rubbing his jaw and looking around him at all the people gawking. The expression on his face was a pure mixture of confusion, rage, and fear, all three taking turns flashing in his golden-brown eyes.

Another pair of golden-brown eyes found mine as Travis pushed Archer out of his way, but not very hard. "We're not brothers. We're cousins," he said, looking at me like I was crazy.

I shook my head, my eyes trained on Archer, who wasn't looking at me. "I'm sorry, Archer," I said. "I didn't mean to blurt it out. I'm sorry," I whispered. "I wish I could take it back."

"What the fuck is this?" Travis asked.

"Let's go!" Tori Hale screeched to Travis. "He's an animal," she spit out, pointing at Archer. "They're crazy, both of them. I won't listen to a second more of this nonsense." She attempted to pull on Travis's arm, but he shook her off easily.

He looked at her closely; something seeming to register in his eyes, some understanding seeming to occur.

"Well, that kind of thing is easily enough proven with a simple blood test," Travis said evenly, his eyes looking into his mother's. Tori blanched and turned her head. Travis watched her.

"Oh, Jesus," he said. "It's true. You knew."

"I don't know any such thing," she said, but her voice sounded hysterical.

"I thought so." Another voice came from the crowd, and I swiveled my head to see Mandy Wright walking toward us. "The minute I saw your eyes looking up at me from your mama's arms, I thought so. Those are Connor Hale's eyes—your daddy's eyes," Mandy whispered, her gaze focused on Archer. I closed my eyes, more tears falling down my cheeks.

Oh God.

"That's it!" Tori shouted. "If you're not leaving, I am. That's my husband you're talking about! And of all days to tarnish his memory—you all should be ashamed of yourselves." She pointed a red-polished, bony finger at each of us individually, that same icy glare on her face. And with that, she turned and pushed her way through the crowd.

I looked at Travis briefly, but then my eyes moved back to Archer. Archer looked at me once, then at Travis and Mandy and finally at the crowd, all eyes trained on us. Panic swept his expression, and I realized that people were gaping at him, whispering. My heart lurched and I took a step toward him, but he took a step back, his eyes moving through the crowd again.

"Archer," I said, reaching for him. He turned and started pushing to get through the mostly still throng of people. I stopped, dropping my hand to my side and hanging my head.

"Bree?" Travis asked and I glared at him.

"Don't," I said through gritted teeth. Then I turned away from him and ran back to the diner. Maggie was standing at the door.

"Go after him, honey," she said gently, putting her hand on my shoulder. She'd obviously seen the whole thing. The whole town had.

I shook my head. "He needs time to himself," I said. I wasn't sure how I knew that. I just did.

"Okay," Maggie said, "well, go home at least. It's dead today anyway."

I nodded. "Thank you, Maggie."

"Of course, honey."

"I'm going to go out the back. My car's in the alley so I can get out without running into blocked-off streets."

Maggie nodded, sympathy shining from her kind eyes. "If you need anything at all, you call me," she said.

I conjured up a small smile. "I will."

I drove home like a homing pigeon, not even remembering the drive once I got there. I dragged myself into my cottage and collapsed on the couch, and when Phoebe jumped up on my lap and started licking my face, the tears began to fall. How had everything gotten so messed up in the course of a couple of days?

I felt like Archer was a ticking time bomb, ready to blow at any minute. I wanted to help him through it, but I wasn't sure how. I felt helpless, unequipped. I wiped the tears away and sat there for a while longer, trying to come up with a solution.

Maybe we needed to get away from this town—just throw our stuff in my car and drive away somewhere new. God, that sounded familiar. Wasn't that exactly the idea Connor Hale had had, too? And look how that turned out. Not well.

And anyway, how would that make Archer feel? He was already struggling with the fact that he didn't feel like a real man. How would it make him feel when I got a job somewhere new and he sat around in some apartment all day? At least here he had his land, his projects, his house, his lake…

Although now, I'd probably ruined it for him. My face crumbled as guilt washed over me. It'd taken him so long to feel comfortable enough to leave his house, and now he was going to feel like hiding on his property again—worried that people would be whispering and staring at him, judging his disability, making him feel less than.

After a few minutes, I got up wearily and took Phoebe out and then returned inside and took a shower, my mind still turning over what had happened at the parade. I needed to go to him and apologize. I hadn't meant to blurt out the secret he hadn't wanted told. But I had. And now he was the one who was going to have to live with the consequences if there were any.

I put on some warm clothes, unable to shake the chill that felt like it went down to my bones, and dried my hair slowly.

I lay down on my bed and let the sadness wash over me again. I was weak and I couldn't see any optimism in the situation, other than the fact that I loved Archer desperately. I thought maybe it was because I was so insanely tired. Maybe I just needed to rest for a few minutes...

I opened my eyes what I thought was a few minutes later and glanced at the clock. Oh God, I had slept for two hours. I bolted up and smoothed my hair back.

I needed to go to Archer. He would be wondering why I hadn't come directly to him. He had turned away from me...but I had given him a few hours' time. Hopefully, he was in a better place now. *God, please don't be angry with me*, I thought as I got in my car and started the engine.

A few minutes later, I was walking through his gate and down to his house. I knocked and turned the knob and utter silence greeted me, the lowering sun outside the window casting a dim light on the room in front of me.

"Archer?" I called, an ominous feeling rushing through my body. I shook it off and called again, "Archer?" Nothing.

It was then that I saw the letter with my name written on it propped up on the table behind the couch.

With shaking hands, I picked it up and unfolded it, fear enveloping my body.

Bree,

Don't blame yourself—what happened at the parade today wasn't your fault. It was mine, all mine.

I'm leaving, Bree. I'm taking my uncle's truck. I don't know where I'm going yet, but I need to go somewhere. I need to figure things out, and maybe even learn a little bit more about who I can be in the world—if I can be anyone at all. The very thought of it is filling me with fear, but staying here—feeling the things I'm feeling—seems like the more terrifying alternative. I know that's hard to understand. I don't even fully understand it myself.

I thought I lost you twice, and just the possibility destroyed me. Do you know what I did when you were just a few minutes late and I heard the ambulances going toward your house? I threw up on my lawn and then I took off running to you. It scared me to death. And the thing is, there's always going to be something—not just an ambulance, but the day you're late coming home from work, or the guy who flirts with you, or…a million different scenarios I can't even fathom right now. There's always going to be something that threatens to take you away from me, even if it's something small, and even if it's only in my own mind. And eventually, that's going to be the thing that destroys us. I'll start hurting you because you won't be able to fix me—you'll never be able to reassure me enough. You'll just end up resenting me because you'll constantly have to carry the weight for both of us. I can't let that happen. I asked you not to let me destroy what we have together, but I don't think I'm capable of doing anything else.

Last night, after you fell asleep, I couldn't stop thinking about the story you told me about the embroidery pictures your mom used to make. And I've been thinking about that today, too—and I want to believe so badly that what you said is true—that something beautiful can come from all the ugliness and mess—from all the pain, from all the things that have made me who I am. I want to see what's on the other side. But I think in order to do that I need to be the one to turn it around. I need to be the one to take those steps. I need to be the one to understand how it all comes together, how it all makes sense—what my own picture looks like.

I'm not asking you to wait for me—I'd never be that selfish. But please don't hate me. I never, ever want to hurt you, but I'm no good to you. I'm no good to anyone right now, and I need to learn if maybe I can be.

Please understand. Please know that I love you. Please forgive me.

Archer

My hands were shaking like leaves now, and tears were coursing down my cheeks. I let out a sob and dropped the letter, bringing my hand to my mouth.

Sitting under the letter was a set of keys, his phone, and a receipt for dog boarding for an open-ended amount of time. I let out another sob and fell down on the couch—the same couch where Archer had rocked me on his lap after saving me from his uncle's trap, the same couch where he had kissed me for the very first time. I sobbed into the pillow, wanting him back, wanting to hear his footsteps coming through the door behind me so desperately, I felt the longing in every cell of my body. But the house remained silent around me, broken only by the sounds of my choking sobs.

CHAPTER THIRTY-ONE

BREE

The days dragged by. My heart felt like it had cracked open and lay heavy in my chest, and the tears constantly threatened. I missed him so badly that most days I felt like I was underwater—looking at the world around me and wondering why I couldn't connect, why everyone and everything was cloudy and distant, inaccessible.

I worried, too—what was he doing? Where was he sleeping? How was he communicating with those he needed to communicate with? Was he scared? I tried to turn that off, as it was one of the reasons he'd left. He felt like less of a man because he depended on me for so much in the outside world. He hadn't said that exactly, but I knew it was true. He didn't want to feel like I was his mother, but rather that he was my equal, my protector, the one *I* depended on sometimes.

I understood. It still broke my heart that leaving me was his solution to that problem. Would he come back? *When?* And when and if he did, would he still love me?

I didn't know. But I'd wait. I'd wait forever if I had to. I had told him I'd never leave him, and I wouldn't. I'd be here when he got back.

I worked, I visited Anne, who was recovering quickly, I walked along the lake, I kept Archer's house clean and dusted, and I missed him. My days inched along, one rolling blankly into the next.

The town had gossiped fervently for a while, and from what I had caught wind of, once it was revealed, no one was too surprised that Archer was Connor's son, too. People speculated about whether Archer would come back and demand to take what was rightfully his, or whether he would come back at all. But I didn't care about any of that. I just wanted him.

Surprisingly, after the day of the parade, there had been radio silence from Victoria Hale. I thought distantly that maybe that should be worrisome—she didn't seem like the type of woman to lie down quietly and accept losing—but I was hurting too badly to do anything active about it. Perhaps she just believed that Archer was no threat to her. And maybe he wasn't. My heart ached.

Travis tried to talk to me several times after the day of the parade, but I was short with him, and thankfully, he didn't push it. I didn't hate him, but he had missed so many opportunities to be a better person when it came to Archer. Instead he'd chosen to belittle someone who was already struggling in so many ways. I'd never have any respect for him. He was Archer's brother in name only.

Fall turned to winter. The vibrantly colored leaves withered and fell off the trees, the temperature dropped dramatically, and the lake froze over.

One day in late November, several weeks after Archer had left, Maggie came up to me where I was restocking behind the counter and put her hand on my shoulder. "You planning on going home for Thanksgiving, Bree, honey?"

I stood up and shook my head. "No. I'm staying here."

Maggie looked at me sadly. "Honey, if he comes back while you're gone, I'll call you."

I shook my head more vehemently. "No, I need to be here if he comes back."

"Okay, honey, okay," she'd said. "Well, then you're coming to our house for Thanksgiving. Our daughter and her family will be in town. And Anne and her sister are coming over, too. We'll have a real nice time."

I smiled at Maggie. "Okay, Maggie. Thank you."

"Good." She'd smiled, but somehow she still looked sad.

Norm sat down with me at the break table later that day when we were closing up after all the customers had gone, a piece of my pumpkin pie in front of him, and took a big bite. "You make the best pumpkin pie I've ever had," he said, and I started crying right there at the break table because I knew that was Norm's way of telling me he loved me.

"I love you, too!" I sobbed out.

Norm stood up, scowling. "Aw, geez. Maggie!" he called, "Bree needs you."

Perhaps I was slightly overemotional.

* * *

November rolled into December, and Pelion got its first light snowfall. It blanketed everything, casting a magical feel to the town, making it seem even more old-fashioned, like one of those Thomas Kinkade paintings.

December second was Archer's birthday. I took that day off and spent it in front of the fire at his house, reading *Ethan Frome*. It wasn't the best choice—he was right, it was the most depressing book ever written. But it was his day, and I wanted to feel close to him. "Happy Birthday, Archer," I whispered that night, making my own wish. *Come back to me.*

One cold Saturday, a week or so later, I sat cuddled up on my couch with Phoebe, a blanket, and a book, when I heard a soft knock on my door. My heart jumped in my chest, and I got up quickly and peeked out the window, the flash of a boy standing soaked from the rain racing through my mind.

Melanie was standing on my porch wearing a big down jacket and a hot-pink scarf and hat. My heart sank. I loved Melanie, but for a brief second there, I had allowed myself to hope that it was Archer coming back to me. I went to let her in.

"Hi." Melanie smiled.

"Get in here," I said, shivering in the blast of icy cold that came in through the open door.

Melanie stepped inside and closed the door behind her. "I'm here to pick you up for the Pelion Christmas tree lighting. Go on. Get dressed," she bossed.

I let out a sigh. "Melanie…"

She shook her head. "Uh-uh. I'm not taking no for an answer. I refuse to let you become the cat lady of Pelion."

I laughed despite myself. "The cat lady of Pelion?"

"Hmm-hmm." A look of sadness swept her pretty features. "He's been gone for over two months now, Bree. And I know you miss him—I do. But I'm not going to let you sit in this cottage and pine for him around the clock. It isn't healthy." Her voice gentled even more. "He chose to go away, honey. And I know he had his reasons. But you still have a life. You still have friends. You get to miss him, but please don't stop living."

A tear ran silently down my cheek, and I swiped at it and sniffled. I nodded as another tear ran down my other cheek. Melanie took me in her arms and hugged me. After a minute she stepped back. "It's cold. You'll need to bundle up. Wear something without cat hair on it."

I breathed out a small laugh and wiped the last tear off my cheek. "Okay," I whispered, and went to get dressed.

As we drove downtown, Christmas lights twinkled everywhere. For the first time since he'd left, I felt something close to serenity as I looked around at the small town that I'd grown to love so much, full of so many people who were part of my heart now.

We met Liza in the crowd at the center of town, and I smiled more than I had in two months. Both girls regaled me with their most recent dating stories and linked arms with mine as the tree blinked on to cheers and whistles.

I inhaled the crisp December air and looked up at the sky, full of stars, and whispered in my mind, *Come back to me.* A feeling of peace washed over me, and I looked around, hugging my friends closer and smiling at nothing in particular.

* * *

Christmas came and went. Despite the fact that Natalie begged me to come home and spend it with her, I said no and instead spent another holiday with Maggie and Norm. I was doing better, making an attempt to live my life, but I needed to be in Pelion. I needed to be home where Archer knew how to find me.

Was he okay? I stood at my window looking out at the frozen lake, the snow gently falling, and I wondered if he was warm, whether he had enough money. Was that old truck still running all right? Was he missing me as much as I was missing him? "Come back to me," I whispered for the thousandth time since he'd left.

On New Year's Eve, the diner was only open until noon.

Melanie and Liza had asked me to go out with them to a big party on the other side of the lake at the home of some guy they knew who lived there year-round. I had said yes, but now, as I slipped into the little black dress I had bought at Mandy's boutique for the occasion, I considered calling the girls and begging off. I wasn't in a party mood. But I knew they'd just railroad me and not take no for an answer, and so I sighed and continued doing my hair and makeup.

I took some time pinning my hair into an updo that I thought looked nice, and applied my makeup carefully. I felt pretty for the first time since Archer had left and taken his look of lust and adoration with him, the one that made me feel like the most desirable woman on earth. I closed my eyes and took a deep breath, swallowing down the lump in my throat.

Liza and Melanie picked me up at eight o'clock and we arrived at the party half an hour later, a sprawling mansion just outside of town. I gasped as we drove up the long driveway. "You girls didn't tell me we were going to a movie star's home."

"Nice, isn't it? Gage Buchanan. His daddy owns the resort here. He's kind of a dick when he wants to be, but he throws epic parties, and we usually get an invite, because we're friends with his sister, Lexi."

I nodded, taking in the beautifully lit house and all the cars pulling up in front of it. A valet in a red coat opened our doors when we stopped, and Melanie handed him her keys.

We walked past the large fountain out front and up to the door, where we were welcomed by a butler who didn't smile but gestured us inside with a sweeping motion. Liza giggled as we walked to the coat check.

The inside of the house was even more jaw-dropping, a sweeping staircase right off the foyer, lots of marble and glittering chandeliers everywhere, the furniture classic and expensive looking, and large enough to fill the huge rooms. Everything seemed grand and oversize. It made me feel like Alice in Wonderland as I walked through the wide hallway with the large portraits and floor-to-ceiling windows, each leading to an individual balcony.

We wandered through the house, me taking it all in while half-heartedly listening to Liza and Melanie chat.

The house was beautifully decorated for the holiday with gold and black streamers and balloons everywhere and tables full of blow horns and confetti to toss when the clock struck midnight. People were laughing and talking, but I just couldn't buoy my mood. I felt anxious, hot, like there was somewhere I needed to be right that second, but I wasn't sure where, or why. I turned in a slow circle, looking at the people all around me, searching for something... but I didn't know what.

When we entered the ballroom, a woman with a tray came over and offered us a glass of champagne. We each took one and I looked around distractedly.

"Bree? Earth to Bree," Liza laughed. "Where are you?"

I smiled at her, coming back to the here and now. "Sorry, this place is just sort of overwhelming."

"Well, drink up! We have some dancing to do!"

"Okay." I laughed, trying to shake the strange feeling.

We finished our champagne and headed to the dance floor, and as we danced and laughed, and the champagne hit my system, I was able to come back to the moment.

We started to leave the dance floor when the fast song we were dancing to ended and a slow song came on.

"Oh, hey, there are Stephen and Chris," Melanie said, looking toward two guys standing to the side of the dance floor and chatting. They spotted Liza and Melanie and gestured them over.

I put my hand on Melanie's arm. "You go talk to them. I need some air anyway."

Melanie frowned. "Are you sure? We can come with you."

I shook my head. "No, no, really, I'm fine. Promise."

They hesitated but then said, "Okay, but we'll come find you if you're gone too long." She smiled and winked. "And if we do and find you in an empty room petting the family cat, there *will* be an intervention."

I laughed. "I promise I won't be long."

I walked out of the ballroom toward the larger balcony I'd seen on our way in, and when I stepped outside, I inhaled a deep breath. It was chilly but not frigid, and after all the dancing, I welcomed the cool air on my skin.

I walked along the balcony, trailing my hand on the stone railing. It felt magical out here—large, potted trees adorned in twinkle lights were placed along the outside of the house, and in between were small, intimate benches just big enough for two. I leaned over the side, looking down at all the guests talking and laughing on the balcony below and then straightened up and just stood there for a few minutes, inhaling deeply and looking up at the stars.

I had the strangest sensation that someone was watching me. I turned in a slow circle, that same feeling I'd felt inside the house coming over me again. I shook my head slightly and brought myself back to the present.

A couple burst out onto the balcony, laughing as the man groped at the woman and she teasingly pushed him away from her before pulling him in for a kiss.

I looked away, my chest tightening at the sight of the intimacy between them. *Please come back to me*, I said in my mind.

I walked toward the door, moving around the couple and leaving them to their privacy, and entered the house again. Once I was back in the hallway, I stood still and took another deep breath before moving toward the ballroom. I startled as I felt a hand on my arm. My breath caught, and I turned slowly. There was a tall, good-looking man with jet-black hair and beautiful, deep blue eyes standing just behind me. His gaze was trained on me. "Dance?" he said simply and then held out his hand as if my yes was a foregone conclusion.

"Um, okay," I said softly, releasing my breath and taking his hand.

The man led me onto the dance floor and stopped in the middle, pulling me into him. "What's your name?" he whispered into my ear, his deep voice like silk.

I leaned my head back, looking up into his blue eyes. "Bree Prescott."

"Nice to meet you, Bree Prescott. I'm Gage Buchanan."

"Oh, this is your house. Thank you for having me. I'm Liza and Melanie Scholl's friend. Your house is so beautiful."

Gage smiled and then turned me effortlessly, moving his body fluidly to the music. He was easy to follow, even though, admittedly, I wasn't a very good dancer.

"And why is it I haven't met you before tonight? I find it hard to believe a girl as beautiful as you hasn't been the talk of the town. I would have made it a point."

I laughed, leaning back slightly. "I live in Pelion," I said. "Perhaps—" I stopped talking abruptly as the loud chatter going on around us seemed to cease, the conversation now just a low murmur moving through the crowd, the music, "In My Veins," seeming to rise in volume as the voices around us died. Gage stopped moving and so did I as we looked around, confused.

And that's when I saw him. Standing on the edge of the dance floor, those gorgeous whiskey-colored eyes trained on me, his expression unreadable.

My heart flew into my throat, and I drew in a loud gasp and brought my hands to my mouth, pure happiness filling every cell in my body. He looked like a god standing there, somehow taller, bigger, seeming to have an authority he didn't have before, but still that beautiful gentleness in his eyes. I blinked, mesmerized. His dark hair was longer, curling up over his collar, and he was wearing a black suit and tie and a light-colored dress shirt. His shoulders seemed even broader, his frame larger, his beauty more intense. I drank him in, my heart beating triple time.

I vaguely noted that people were watching us as I took a step toward him and he moved toward me, like magnets being drawn together by the force of something neither one of us controlled. I heard an older woman in the crowd mutter, "He's the spitting image of Connor Hale, isn't he?" her voice soft, dreamy.

The people on the dance floor moved aside to make way for him, and I stood waiting now. The lights twinkled around me and the music swelled as Archer approached me on the dance floor and looked somewhere just to my right.

I felt a hand on my arm, and when I tore my eyes from Archer and looked up, Gage, whom I had forgotten was there, smiled and leaned in, whispering, "It's suddenly become obvious to me that you're already taken. Nice meeting you, Bree Prescott."

I let out a breath and smiled back at him. "Nice meeting you, too, Gage." It seemed Gage Buchanan was a nicer guy than Liza and Melanie gave him credit for. He nodded at Archer and moved off, disappearing into the crowd.

I looked back up at Archer and, for several moments, we did nothing but gaze at each other before I brought my hands up and signed, *You're here*, tears springing into my eyes, joy enveloping me.

He let out a breath, warmth filling his expression as he brought his own hands up. *I'm here for you*, he said. And that's when his face broke into the most beautiful smile I'd ever seen in my life and I launched myself into his arms, crying and gasping against the crook of his neck, holding on tight, holding on for dear life to the man I loved.

CHAPTER THIRTY-TWO

ARCHER

I held her close, inhaling the delicious, calming smell of her, my heart exalting at the sweet relief of the weight of her in my arms. My Bree. I'd missed her so desperately, I thought I'd die without her those first few weeks. But I hadn't died. I had so much to tell her, so much to share with her.

I leaned back, looking down into her emerald eyes, the golden flecks I loved so much even brighter under her shimmering tears. She was stunning. And I hoped to God she was still mine.

I don't really know how to dance, I said, unable to tear my eyes from her.

She breathed out on a small smile. *I'm not very good at it, either*.

I took her in my arms anyway and held her against my body as we started to sway to the music. We'd figure it out.

I ran my hand down the bare skin of her back, and she shivered in my arms. We both watched as I used my other hand to entwine my fingers with hers, my eyes moving quickly to her face. She swallowed and her lips parted as she met my gaze.

I pulled her closer and pressed her body against mine, feeling serenity wash over me.

When the song ended, Bree asked, *Is this real?*

I smiled at her. *I don't know. I think so. But it feels like a dream.*

She breathed out a small laugh. *How'd you know I was here?*

I went to your house, I signed. *Anne saw me and told me where you were.*

She reached up and put her hand on my cheek as if she was checking to make sure I was really there, and I closed my eyes and leaned into her touch. After a second, she brought her hand down and signed, *Where have you been, Archer? What have you been—?*

I put my hands around hers, stopping her words, and she blinked up at me in surprise. I let go of her and brought my hands up. *I have so much to tell you, so much we have to talk about.*

Do you still love me? she asked, and her vulnerable eyes blinked up at me again, fresh tears filling them. Her whole heart was right there in her expression, and I loved her so intensely, I felt it in the marrow of my bones.

I'll never stop loving you, Bree, I said, hoping she could see in my eyes that I meant it in my very soul, in the very fabric of who I was.

She studied my face for a few seconds, and then focused on my chest as she said, *You left me.*

I had to, I answered.

Her eyes ran over my face, studying me intently. *Take me home, Archer*, she said, and I didn't need to be asked twice. I took her by her hand and started moving through the crowd I had forgotten was there.

When we stepped out into the chilly night air, Bree said, "Wait, Melanie and Liza—"

They saw me, I signed; *they'll know you left with me.*

She nodded.

The valet brought my truck around, looking completely out of place among the BMWs and Audis. That was okay. I had Bree Prescott on my arm, and I intended to keep her there.

I grinned at her as I started up the truck. Just as I was pulling away, it backfired, making the people standing around us jump and scream, one woman in a mink stole hitting the ground. They must have thought someone opened fire. I grimaced and waved my hand at them in apology.

As we drove away, I glanced at Bree, who was biting her lip and obviously trying to hold back laughter. She glanced at me and I glanced at her, and then we both looked straight ahead. After a couple of seconds she glanced at me again and threw her head back and started laughing uproariously. My eyes widened and then I couldn't help it, I cracked up, too, grinning and laughing along with her, while simultaneously trying to keep my eyes on the road.

She laughed so hard, tears were rolling down her cheeks, and I was gripping my chest, trying to get control of the hilarity that seemed to have taken us over.

After several seconds, I glanced over and her face suddenly went from hilarity to crumbling into a bout of tears. My laughter died and I glanced at her nervously, wondering what the hell had just happened.

I put my hand on her leg and she swiped it away, crying harder, looking as if she was having trouble catching her breath. Panic coursed through me. What was happening here? I didn't know what to do.

"You were gone for three months, Archer. Three months!" she choked out, her voice fading on the last word. "You didn't write. You didn't bring your phone. I didn't know if you were even alive. I didn't know if you were warm. I didn't know how you were communicating with those you needed to communicate with." She let out another sob.

I pulled the car off the road, onto a small dirt patch next to the bank of a river. I turned to Bree just as she opened my truck door and jumped out, walking quickly along the side of the road in her little black dress. What the hell was she doing? I jumped out, too, and jogged to catch up, gravel crunching beneath my feet as Bree wobbled ahead of me on her high heels.

The moon, large and full above us, lit the night so that I could see her clearly in front of me.

When I finally made it to her, I grabbed her arm and she stopped and spun around, tears still coursing down her cheeks. *Don't run from me*, I said. *I can't call to you. Please don't run from me.*

"You ran from *me*!" she accused. "You ran from me, and I died a little more each day! You didn't even let me know that you were safe! Why?"

Her voice broke on the last word, and I felt my heart clench in my chest. *I couldn't, Bree. If I had written to you, or contacted you, I wouldn't have been able to stay away. And I had to stay away, Bree. I had to. You're my safety, and I had to do this without feeling safe. I had to.*

She stood there silently for several minutes, her eyes on my still hands, not looking up into my face. We were both shivering, our breath coming out in white puffs.

I suddenly understood. Bree had been holding in the emotion of my absence for three long months, and my return had opened the floodgates. I knew what it felt like when emotion, bubbling to the surface, made you feel sick, out of control—I knew better than anyone. It's why I had gone away. But now, I was back. And now it was my turn to be strong for Bree. Now, I was finally able.

Come back to the truck. Please. Let me get you warm and then we'll talk.

"Were there other women?"

I leaned in and spoke with my hands right against her body, looking into her eyes as she glanced between my face and my hands. *There has only ever been you. There. Will. Only. Ever. Be. You.*

She closed her eyes, and fresh tears rolled down her cheeks. She opened them and we both stood there silently, our breath dissipating as it rose into the sky.

"I thought"—she shook her head slowly—"I thought maybe you figured out that you were lonely." She heaved in a big breath. "And that you would have fallen in love with any girl who walked down your driveway that day—that maybe you needed to find out." She looked down.

I took her chin in my fingers and tilted her face back up to me. Once she was looking in my eyes, I brought my hand down and said, *There's nothing to find out. What I* know, *is that you walked through my gate that day, and I lost my heart. But not because it could have been any girl—because it was* you. *I lost my heart to* you. *And, Bree, in case you're wondering, I don't ever want it back.*

She closed her eyes again momentarily, and I saw her body relax.

"What were you doing?" she finally asked quietly, hugging herself with her bare arms.

Please let me get you warm, I repeated, holding out my hand to her.

She didn't say anything, but she took my hand and we walked back to my truck together. When we reached it, I helped her up and then walked around to my side and climbed in as well, turning to her.

I looked out the window behind her for a second, thinking of all the things I'd done in the last three months, answering the question she had asked me outside. *I went to restaurants, coffee shops...I went to the movies once.* I smiled, and her eyes flew to my face.

She blinked at me, her tears drying up. "You did?" she whispered. I nodded.

Her eyes searched my face for several seconds before she asked. "What'd you see?"

Thor, I spelled out.

She laughed softly, and the sound was like music to my ears. "Did you like it?"

I loved it. I sat through it twice. I even ordered popcorn and a drink, even though there was a line of people behind me.

"How'd you do it?" She looked at me with wide eyes.

I had to point and gesture a little, but the kid got it. He was nice. I paused for a minute. *I had this realization about a month after I'd been gone. Whenever I went somewhere and had to communicate with someone, and they'd see my scar and understand why I was gesturing, they each had a different reaction. Some people were awkward, uncomfortable, others were kind, helpful, and there were even some that were impatient and put out.* Bree's eyes softened and she was listening to me raptly.

I realized that people's reactions had more to do with them, more to do with who they were, than anything about me. It was like a bolt of lightning hit me, Bree.

Tears sprang to her eyes again, and she reached out and touched my leg, just laying her hand on me.

She nodded. "It was like that with my dad, too. What else?" she asked.

I got a job. I smiled and a look of surprise came over her face. I nodded. *Yeah, I stopped in this small town in New York state and I saw an ad about needing guys to unload delivery trucks at the airport. I wrote a letter about my situation, explaining that I could hear and understand directions and I was a hard worker, but that I couldn't speak. I handed it to the guy in person and he read it and hired me on the spot.* I grinned with the memory of the pride I had felt in that moment.

It was boring work, but I got to know another guy there, Luis, and he spoke incessantly, telling me his life story while we worked. How he had come over from Mexico without knowing the language at all, how he still struggled to support his family, but they were happy, they had each other. He talked a lot. I got the impression that no one had ever just listened to him. I smiled with the memory of my first real friend other than Bree.

He invited me to his home for Christmas dinner, and his little girl learned a few signs before I got there, and I taught her a few more. I smiled, thinking of little Claudia. *She asked me the sign for love and I spelled out your name.*

Bree let out small sound, somewhere between a laugh and a sob. "So now she's going to go around saying, 'I Bree you'?" she asked, smiling, her eyes soft.

I nodded. *Yeah.* I turned toward her more fully, focusing on her face. *I stand by my logic, though. I think love is a concept, and each person has an individual word for what sums it up for them. My word for love is "Bree."*

We stared at each other for several slow heartbeats, me drinking in her beauty, her sweet compassion. I had known that about her before, but not to the extent I did now.

Finally, she asked me, "What made you decide it was time to come home?"

I considered her question. *I was sitting in this small coffee shop a couple of days ago, and I saw this old man sitting at a table across from me. He looked so lonely, so sad. I was, too, but it suddenly occurred to me that some people go through their whole lives never being loved or loving as deeply as I love you. There's always going to be the chance that I could lose you in this lifetime. There's nothing any of us can do about the possibility of loss. But in that moment, I decided I was more interested in focusing on the great privilege I've been given in having you at all.*

Tears shimmered in her eyes again as she whispered, "And what if I hadn't been here when you got back?"

Then I would have come for you. I would have fought for you. But don't you see, I had to fight for myself first. I had to feel like I was someone worthy of winning you.

She stared at me for a second, more tears coming into her eyes. "How'd you get so brilliant?" she asked, letting out a breathy laugh and a small sniffle.

I was already brilliant. I just needed some world experience. I needed Thor.

She let out another small laugh and then grinned at me. *You being funny?*

I grinned back at her, noting that she was finally using her hands to speak. *No, I never joke about Thor.*

She laughed and then looked at me silently again, her face going serious.

Mine went serious, too, and I asked, *Why did you stay, Bree? Tell me.*

She breathed out, looking down at her hands in her lap for a second. Finally, she brought them up and said, *Because I love you. Because I'd wait for you forever.* She gazed into my eyes, her beauty taking my breath away again. *Take me home, Archer*, she said.

My heart soared as I started up the truck and pulled back onto the road. We drove the rest of the way in comfortable silence. When we were almost there, Bree reached her hand out for mine, and we held hands for the remainder of the ride.

I pulled up in front of my house, and we walked through the gate and to my front door, not saying a word.

When we got inside and she turned to me, I said, *You kept my house clean.*

She looked around as if she was just remembering, and then nodded.

Why? I asked.

She seemed to consider. *Because doing it made me feel like you were coming back, like you'd be home soon.*

My heart constricted. *I'm sorry, Bree.*

She shook her head and looked up at me with wide, vulnerable eyes. *Don't leave me again, please.*

I shook my head and moved closer to her. *Never again*, I said and then took her in my arms. She lifted her mouth to mine and I pressed my lips to hers, silently moaning at the taste of her as I slipped my tongue into her mouth. I couldn't help the shiver that ran through my body as the taste of peaches and Bree exploded on my tongue. My cock stiffened immediately and I pressed it into her. She sighed into my mouth and, impossibly, I got harder. It felt like a lifetime since I'd been inside of her.

She tore her mouth from mine and said, "I missed you so much, Archer. So much."

I let go of her for a second and signed, *I missed you, too, Bree. So much.*

I started lowering my mouth to hers again, when she brought her hand up to my hair and said, "It's longer. I'm going to have to give you another haircut." She grinned. "Maybe you won't throw me out of your house when I try to molest you this time."

I chuckled silently and then grinned and brought my hands up. *Chances are good that I won't. Also, Bree, I'm going to stop talking now and use my hands for other things, okay?*

Her eyes widened, her lips parting slightly as she whispered, "Okay."

I scooped her up, carried her down the short hallway to my bedroom, and stood her up right next to my bed.

I kicked off my shoes, unknotted my tie, and started unbuttoning my dress shirt as she kicked off her heels and turned around for me to unzip her dress.

I brought the zipper down slowly, exposing more and more of her skin. Her tan lines were gone now, and her skin was creamy and lighter than it was the last time I'd seen all of her. She was so beautiful. And mine, all mine. A deep satisfaction filled me, and the desperation I felt to be inside her ratcheted up another level.

She turned to me and let her small black dress fall and pool at her feet. My cock pulsated as she looked up at me through her lashes, her pink lips parting.

I bent down to remove my socks, then stood back up and undid my belt and my pants, letting them fall to the floor, where I kicked them off. Bree licked her lips and looked down at my straining erection and then back up into my face. Her eyes were shiny and dilated.

I reached for her and unhooked her strapless bra and let it fall to the floor. I felt a drop of precum bead on my tip as I took in her perfect breasts, the pink nipples already hardened and begging for my mouth.

I looked behind her and nodded toward the bed. Bree sat down and lay back as I came down on top of her, skin to skin. Her heat caressed me, sending bolts of pure arousal down my spine; her eyes told me I was loved. I was loved by the beautiful woman lying beneath me, ready to invite me into her body.

All the times I had made love to her before, my head had always screamed, *Mine!* desperately, but now it felt like a gentle acknowledgment, a comforting truth. Mine, mine, always mine.

I leaned my head down and took a nipple into my mouth, laving it with my tongue as Bree moaned and pressed her hips up into my hardness. Oh God, that felt good. The taste of her, the feel of her hot, silky skin beneath me, the knowledge that I was going to sink into her tight heat soon...but not too soon. I wanted this to last.

I sucked and licked her nipples for several minutes as she ran her fingers through my hair, tugging gently. My body pressed into her belly of its own accord, trying to ease the intense throbbing in my cock.

Bree arched her back and moaned deeply. "Archer, oh God, please," she breathed out.

Reaching a hand down between her legs I felt the slippery liquid that meant she was ready for me, more than ready for me. I brought some to her clit and massaged it gently in slow circles as Bree panted. "Oh God, Archer, please, I'll come and I don't want to. I want to come with you inside me. Please."

I leaned up and took her mouth again, her tongue dancing with mine, soft and wet and unbelievably delicious. I'd never get enough of her mouth, of her.

I took myself in my hand and lined the straining head of my cock up at her entrance and pushed inside, sinking in fully on one deep thrust. I closed my eyes at the exquisite feel of her surrounding me so tightly and just stayed still for several moments.

Bree pressed up into me, silently asking me to move, and so I did, her extreme wetness making it easy to glide in and out. The tight friction was bliss beyond words.

At first I went slowly, the relief at being inside of her so intense that I never wanted this moment to end. But after a minute, my own body demanded that I move, so I picked up the speed of my thrusts.

Bree moaned out and said breathily, "Yes," and closed her eyes, pressing her head back on the pillow. *Mine, mine, always mine,* my mind sang as I pumped into her and watched her beautiful, pleasure-filled expression, her hair splayed out all around her on the white pillowcase, like a goddess, an angel, her small white breasts bouncing with my movement.

I pumped into her, holding myself up with my arms as she panted and whimpered in pleasure. I brought one arm under the back of her right knee and pulled her leg up so I could go deeper, and she moaned again, opening her eyes and grabbing my ass with her fingernails. God, I liked that.

After a few minutes, Bree's cheeks flushed, the sign of her impending climax, I knew from experience.

Her hands moved to my straining biceps, and she ran her hands up and down them as her eyes clouded over and her lips formed a silent O, right before I felt her muscles clench even tighter on my shaft and begin to convulse. She gasped and arched up into me as that beautiful expression of satisfaction rolled over her face, and she moaned out softly as her body relaxed.

She looked up at me dreamily as I continued to thrust into her, and said softly, "I love you."

I love you, I mouthed, and then closed my eyes as I felt the first tingles along my spine. I came up on my knees, and reached under Bree, grabbing her ass and tilting her hips up so I could go even deeper than before. I was thrusting into her hard and fast now, the pleasure spiraling higher and higher.

"Oh God!" Bree gasped out, pressing up into me as I watched another orgasm roll through her. Her lids popped open, and she looked at me with round eyes. I would have smiled at her look of shock, but the pleasure that was circling through my abdomen, tightening my balls and making my cock strain and thicken with my impending orgasm, was so intense I was almost out of control.

I thrust into her, once, twice, and then my world exploded into a million points of light, the air itself seeming to shimmer around me as ecstasy, deep and intense, raced through my body, my cock jerking inside of her as I climaxed.

When I came back to myself, Bree was still gazing up at me with a look of wonder on her face. I could only imagine that I was wearing the exact same look. I pulled out of her, taking my semi-hard cock in my hand and using it to rub my cum, now running out of her, up and over her clit and around her folds.

I wasn't sure why I did that; it was almost instinct, nothing I actually thought about. But I was mesmerized by what we'd just shared, and the visual of her and me together and the proof of my pleasure all over her excited me, made me feel a peaceful possessiveness I loved.

I looked back at Bree—her face had softened and she looked sleepy and content, her eyes hooded, her expression still filled with love.

I took my hand off my cock and signed, *I love you.*

She smiled at me and reached her arms up and pulled me to her, stroking her fingers up and down my back until I felt like I was in danger of falling asleep right on top of her. I kissed her lips quickly and then stood up and pulled her with me to the bathroom, where we showered and washed each other, not sexual this time, just loving, tender.

When we were done, we dried off and returned to my bed and climbed under the sheets, naked. I pulled her to me and held her there, feeling content and happier than I'd ever felt in my entire life.

I turned her around to face me and brought my hands up. *Someday*, I said, *when we're old and gray, I'm going to look at you lying in bed beside me, just like this, and I'm going to look into your eyes and know that it's only ever been you. And that is going to be the great joy of my life, Bree Prescott.* She smiled as her eyes filled up with what I knew were happy tears, and I pulled her into my chest, holding her tight, breathing her in.

Just a little bit later, I came to for a brief second when I heard fireworks in the distance. I sleepily realized that it was midnight, a brand-new year, a brand-new start. I pulled my beautiful girl closer against me as she sighed out in her sleep, and I closed my eyes. I was home.

CHAPTER THIRTY-THREE

BREE

We left Archer's house only twice in the following two days—luckily for us, the two off days I had in a row that week. We went to the grocery store once the morning after he'd arrived home, and picked up Phoebe on the way back. And we went to dinner on the other side of the lake that night. The pride in Archer's eyes as he ordered a glass of wine for me and a Coke for himself made me grin and wink at him. Watching him come into himself was a thing of beauty, and I felt privileged to be a witness to it. I wanted to sigh and swoon at his easy charm and beautiful smile, and I could see that the waitress who served us felt the same way as she glanced at his scar and fawned over him all night. I didn't mind, though; in fact, I liked it. I loved it. How could I blame her? Like Natalie had said, he inspired women to want to cuddle him and then lick him. But he was mine. I was the luckiest girl on earth.

We talked a lot more about what he'd done the three months he'd been gone, the people he'd seen, the rooms he'd rented, how the loneliness he'd felt was no less than before, but that it was different this time. The difference, he'd concluded, was that he finally had *himself*, and he was more able than he'd known or believed.

I need to get my license, he said as we ate dinner.

I nodded. "Yeah, I know, illegal driver," I said, raising a brow.

He smiled around his food. *If Travis catches me, he'll lock me up and throw away the key.* He raised both eyebrows. *Speaking of Travis, have you seen him at all? Has he tried to talk to you?* He stilled as he waited for my answer.

I shook my head. "A few times, but I avoided him. I was short, and he didn't push it. And it's been radio silence from Victoria Hale."

He studied me for a second and then nodded. *I left you shouldering that whole mess, and I'm sorry about that. I'm the one Tori hates, though, not you. I guess I thought it might be easier on you in that respect as well if I was gone.* He looked away for a second and then back at me. *I'm going to go talk to Travis and Tori. I was wondering if you'd come and interpret for me?*

I blinked at him. "Of course I will, Archer, but what exactly are you going to say to them?"

I'm thinking of taking ownership of the land, Bree...the town. His eyes held mine steadily as he waited for my reaction.

I gaped at him for a few seconds and then closed my mouth. "Are you ready for that?" I whispered.

I don't know, he said, looking thoughtful again. *Maybe not...but I feel like I could be. I feel like maybe there might be a few in this town who will help make it a little easier...Maggie, Norm, Anne, Mandy...a few others. And that's what will make the difference. That's what's making me think I should at least try.*

He took a bite and then went on. *My parents, they made a lot of mistakes, right up to the very end. But they were good people. They were loving people. My uncle Marcus was not a good person—and Travis is mostly questionable, too. And Victoria is the worst of them all. They don't deserve to win, here. And maybe I don't, either, but maybe I do. And just that possibility makes me want to try.*

I reached out and grabbed his hand, pride racing through my blood. "Whatever you need, I'm with you. Whatever that is."

He smiled at me and then we ate in silence for a while, before I remembered the call I'd gotten from the detective the day of the parade and told Archer about it. He looked concerned. *Out on bail? Could you be in danger?*

I shook my head. "No, no, I don't think so. He has no idea where I am, and he's surrounded by lawyers. The police know who he is. It's just…disappointing that the whole process takes so long. I just want the whole thing to be over, and now there's probably going to be a big trial…I'll have to travel back to Ohio." I shook my head again.

Archer reached out and grabbed my hand. He squeezed it and then brought it back and signed, *Then I'll go with you. And they'll convict him. It will all be over. And in the meantime, you're safe here with me, right by my side.*

I smiled, warmth filling me. "Nowhere else I'd rather be," I whispered.

Me neither.

We finished our dinner and drove back to Archer's house, where we spent the rest of that night and most of the next day in bed, rediscovering each other's bodies and just soaking in each other's presence. Happiness surrounded us. The future looked bright and full of hope, and for just that moment, the world was perfect.

* * *

The next morning, I got up early, peeled myself off Archer, and kissed him softly goodbye as he slept. His arm snaked out and pulled me back into him as I laughed out loud, and he grinned a crooked, sleepy grin. My heart lurched at the ridiculous beauty of that early-morning smile, and I leaned back in and said, "Stay right here, just like this. I'll be back as soon as possible." He chuckled silently and opened one eye at me and nodded yes. I laughed again and stood up and headed out the door before I decided to blow off work entirely.

Just as I was leaving his room, I turned once more to gaze at him. He smiled at me again and brought his hands up and signed, *You make me so happy, Bree Prescott.*

I stopped in the doorway, tilted my head, and smiled back at him. Something about the moment seemed very, very important. Something told me to stay right there and soak it in, cherish it. I wasn't sure why that feeling washed over me, but I leaned my head against the doorframe and drank him in for a minute. "I'm going to keep making you happy, Archer Hale." Then I grinned and walked out the door.

We had plans for Archer to meet me at the diner for an early lunch right before the crowd started coming in, so I knew I'd see him soon. I didn't need to miss him too much.

The diner was extra busy that morning, and the hours flew by. At about ten forty-five, I served the last breakfast special and started cleaning up from the rush.

"Hey, Norm," I called. "How'd those red velvet cupcakes work out while I was gone?" I had baked a batch New Year's Eve day, before I'd left the diner. God, that seemed like a million years ago. I had left this place still longing for Archer, deep in my bones, and I had walked back in after leaving him in bed. My strong, beautiful, silent man. I was so deliriously proud of him.

"People seemed to like 'em," Norm said. "Maybe you should make another batch."

I grinned. That meant they were a hit and he'd appreciate it if I'd make more. I had learned recently that often, love was all about learning to speak a person's language.

"You gonna sit with me over here for a cup of coffee?" Maggie asked as I married two ketchup bottles. "I think you owe me about three hours of update. But I'll take the fifteen-minute version." She laughed.

I smiled. "Actually, Maggie, Archer's coming in in about fifteen minutes. How about the thirty-minute version right after lunch?"

She huffed out a breath. "Fine. I guess I'll take what I can get." She feigned a look of annoyance, but I laughed because the look on her face earlier that morning and the tears that had rolled down her cheeks told me all I'd needed to know. She was over the moon for me, and relieved that Archer was back, safe and sound.

The bell over the door rang a few minutes later, and the man in question stood in the doorway, smiling at me. I thought back to the day months earlier when he'd first gathered up the courage to walk through the doors of this diner, and I took him in now. That same sweet, gentle look was on his face when he caught my eye and smiled, but now he held himself in a way that told me he felt confident in the fact that he'd be welcomed.

I allowed myself to drink him in for a few moments before I rushed out from behind the counter and jumped into his arms. He spun me around as I laughed and then put me down, looking shyly over at Maggie.

Maggie waved her hand. "Don't stop on account of me. Nothing makes me happier than seeing you two together. Welcome home, Archer."

Archer tipped his head and smiled and then looked up as Norm came out of the back. "Why don't you two quit making a spectacle of yourselves and go sit at that table in the back there? Plenty of privacy." He looked at Archer, and his face softened ever so slightly. "Archer," he said, "you're looking well."

Archer smiled at him and reached out his hand and shook Norm's, and then smiled at me and I grinned back, my heart singing. "Shall we?" I asked.

We sat down at the table toward the back of the diner, and Maggie called over, "What can I get you?"

"It's okay, Maggie," I called. "I'm gonna put in a lunch order in a minute."

"Okay," she called back, taking a seat at the break table again.

I reached across the table and took Archer's hand just as the bell over the door rang again. I looked up; my blood froze in my veins, my skin prickling, and a strangled sound coming up my throat. It was *him*.

No. Oh God. No, no, no. Bells seemed to be clanging loudly in my ears, and I was frozen.

His wild eyes found mine almost immediately, and a look of pure hatred filled his face.

This isn't real. This isn't real, I chanted in my head as I felt the vomit coming up my throat. I swallowed it down and squeaked again.

Archer's head swiveled back in the direction my eyes were trained, and he stood up immediately when he saw the man behind him. I stood up, too, on legs that were shaking so badly, I didn't know if I'd stay upright, a huge surge of adrenaline rushing through my system.

The man didn't even seem to see Archer just in front of me and to my right, his eyes still focused only on me.

"You ruined my fucking life, you bitch," he gritted out. "Do you know who I am? My dad was going to hand the company over to *me* before you pointed your finger. Do you think I'm going to let you walk away while I lose everything?"

My mind was screaming, the loud sound of the blood rushing in my ears not allowing me to make any sense of his words.

His eyes looked bloodshot and overly bright, just like they had the last time. He was on something. Either that, or he was stone-cold crazy.

Please, please be calling the police, Maggie. Oh God, Oh God, how is this possible?

And then it all happened in an instant. Something flashed in the man's hand, and the room seemed to tilt on its axis as I saw that it was a gun. He brought it up and aimed it straight at me. I saw a brief flash of fire as Archer threw his body in front of mine, slamming back into me as we both went down, me falling on the floor just behind Archer.

And then I heard another gunshot and Travis's voice yelling, "I need assistance!" over the crackle of a radio.

I scuttled backward, noticing immediately that the man who had fired at me was lying still on the floor, blood already pooling under his head, and that Archer wasn't moving, either. I let out a strangled sob and lurched forward, reaching for him. He was lying on his side, his face turned toward the floor. I pulled him toward me so he was on his back, and let out an anguished cry when I saw the front of his shirt was already soaked in blood.

Oh no, Oh God, no, no, no. Please, no. Please no.

My own sobs mixed with all the noise starting up around me now, footsteps, what I thought were Maggie's soft cries, Norm's gravelly voice, and chairs scraping against the floor. But my eyes didn't move from Archer.

I pulled him into me, rocking him, smoothing my hands down

his face as I whispered to him over and over, "Hang on, baby, hang on. I love you, Archer, I love you, don't you dare leave me now."

"Bree," I heard Travis say quietly as the sound of an ambulance grew louder outside the diner. "Bree, let me help you up."

"No!" I screamed, pulling Archer closer to me. "No! No!" I rocked him some more, putting my face right next to his, feeling his rough cheek against my own, and whispering to him again, "Don't you leave me, I need you, don't you leave me."

But Archer didn't hear me; he was already gone.

CHAPTER THIRTY-FOUR

You brought the silence,
The most beautiful sound I'd ever heard,
Because it was where you were.
And now you've taken it away.
And all the noises, all the sounds in the world,
Aren't loud enough to pierce my broken heart.
I look up at the stars, endless and forever, and whisper,
Come back to me,
Come back to me,
Come back to me.

CHAPTER THIRTY-FIVE

BREE

The whole town gathered to honor Archer Hale.

The people of Pelion, young and old, came together to show their support for the man who had been a quiet part of their community since the day he was born. His silent wound, his unnoticed isolation, now understood by all, and finally, his gentle heart and act of bravery, inspired shops to close, and those who rarely came out of their homes to join with the other citizens in the largest show of support the town had ever seen. A small, silent star, always on the outskirts, hardly noticed before, had shined so brightly that the whole town stopped to gaze upon his brilliance, to finally open their eyes enough to welcome him as part of their small constellation.

I heard again and again that Archer's and my story made people want to be better, to reach out to those no one else saw, to be friends to the friendless, to look at others more closely, recognize pain when they came across it, and then to do something about it if they were able.

I walked in that cold day in February, Maggie on one arm and Norm on the other, and we took our seats as people smiled kindly at me and nodded their heads. I smiled and nodded back. This was my community now, too. I was part of the constellation as well.

Outside, the rain had just begun to fall, and I heard a boom of thunder in the distance. I wasn't afraid, though. *When a thunderstorm comes*, I had told him, *I'll think of you, not anything other than you.* And I always did. Always.

Archer had gone away once before—three long months where I missed him desperately every single day. This time he was gone from me for three solid weeks before he came back. He was in a deep coma, and the doctors couldn't tell me when they thought he might wake up, or if he would wake up at all. But I waited. I would always wait. And I prayed and I whispered to the heavens every night, *Come back to me, come back to me, come back to me.*

On another rainy day at the end of January, just as the thunder boomed and the lightning flashed in his hospital room, he opened his eyes and looked at me. My own heart thundered in my ears, louder than that outside the window, and I'd jumped up from the chair I'd been sitting in and rushed to his side, choking out, "You're back." I picked up his hands and brought them to my lips, kissing them again and again, my tears falling onto his fingers, his knuckles, those beautiful hands that held a whole language, that allowed me to know what was in his mind and his heart. I loved those hands. I loved him. My tears continued to fall.

He'd looked at me for several minutes before he brought his hands away from mine and signed slowly, his fingers moving stiffly, *I'm back for you.*

I laughed out a strangled cry, and put my head down on his chest and held on to him tightly as the nurses rushed into the room.

And now, the whole town waited as Archer walked toward the podium, still stiff from the bandages surrounding his torso and the surgeries he'd had to repair his internal organs.

I looked around once more. Travis stood in the back of the room, still in uniform from his shift. I caught his eye and nodded at him. He nodded back, and gave me a small smile. I still wasn't sure how I felt about Travis exactly, but he deserved my respect for his own act of heroism that awful day.

It had recently come to light that the man who had found me that day, Jeffrey Perkins, had gotten hooked on heroin and was cut off from his family. He'd shown up at our family deli that night in need of money and a fix.

His dealer had given over his name as part of a plea deal to save his own skin. Apparently, Jeffrey had shown up that night splattered in blood and babbling about shooting a guy in a deli.

He had started to get his act together and his father had begun to accept him back into the family fold, when I identified him in that photo lineup.

After his arrest, his father disinherited him again, and Jeffrey turned back to drugs.

Travis had confronted his mother. He was a good cop, with good instincts, and he recognized his mother for who she was—a vindictive woman so filled with hate and bitterness that she would do anything to keep what she saw as rightfully hers: the town, money, respect, social standing.

He had also been there when Victoria Hale overheard me talking about Jeffrey Perkins's arrest. He put the pieces together.

What other way would a strung-out heroin addict have to find me in the diner that terrible day? We had underestimated her hatred for me, the person who had, in essence, undone all that her manipulation had accomplished for her over the years.

When Travis came to me and told me about his confrontation and her denial, a denial he didn't believe, he said he'd told her to move away, or he would bring an investigation against her.

Now that Jeffrey was dead, he knew he didn't have enough evidence to prosecute; there was nothing left for her in Pelion except shame.

Now, with Victoria's departure and in the absence of an executor to the trust, Archer inherited the will and land of the Hale family a year before his twenty-fifth birthday.

Travis looked haggard, unshaven, and almost numb, like he wasn't sleeping. He had had his own career in trying to manipulate lives. But after all, he had learned from the best. Deep down, though, I didn't think Travis wanted anyone to come to any real harm. His mother was a different story. I got the impression that seeing her for who she really was, and what she was capable of doing, had changed him in some dramatic way. There was a deep sadness in his eyes, and he'd delivered the information to me in a monotone and then left me to my grief once again as I waited in the hospital for Archer to come back to me.

A hush fell over the auditorium as Archer walked toward the short set of stairs.

Norm, standing off to the side, signed, *Knock 'em dead*, and raised his chin at him, his expression serious. A look of surprise washed over Archer's face, and then he nodded at Norm. I bit down on my lip, holding back a sob.

Mrs. Aherne, the town librarian, who had checked out hundreds of books to Archer over the last four years on subjects from masonry to sign language but had never once asked him a single question or tried to engage him in any way, signed, *We're all behind you, Archer*. Tears were shimmering in her eyes, and the look on her face told me she wished she had done better. Archer smiled at her and nodded, signing back, *Thank you*.

As he took the stage and stood behind the podium, he nodded at the interpreter, standing to his right, a man he had hired to help him when he needed to address the town as a whole, on occasions such as this one.

Archer began to move his hands, and the interpreter began speaking. My eyes only held Archer, though, watching as his hands flew, so graceful and sure in their movements. My heart soared with pride.

Thank you all for coming, he said, pausing and looking around. *The land this town is on has been in my family for a long, long time, and I intend to run it as each Hale has run it before me—with the knowledge and belief that each person who lives here matters, that each of you gets a vote on what happens and doesn't happen in Pelion.* He looked around pointedly at all the faces in the crowd before continuing. *After all, Pelion is not the land it sits on, but the people who walk its streets and run its shops and live and love in its homes.* He paused again. *I think you'll find me an agreeable landlord, and I've been told I'm a good listener.* The crowd laughed softly, and Archer looked shy for a second, looking down before continuing. *There will be a vote tonight about the development slated for this town, and I know some of you are very passionate about getting to that. But I'd like everyone to know that if ever in the future any of you have concerns or suggestions, my door will always be open.*

The crowd kept watching him, smiling and nodding with approval, finding other eyes and nodding at them as well.

Finally, Archer looked out at the crowd, and the gentle, quiet murmurings ceased completely as his eyes found mine. I smiled at him encouragingly, but he just kept gazing at me for a few seconds before bringing his hands up again.

I'm here for you. I'm here because of you. I'm here because you saw me, not just with your eyes, but with your heart. I'm here because you wanted to know what I had to say and because you were right…everyone does need friends. I laughed softly, swiping a tear off my cheek. Archer kept gazing at me, his eyes filled with love.

I'm here because of you, he said, *and I'll always be here because of you.*

I heaved out a big breath, tears running unabashedly down my cheeks now. Archer smiled gently at me and then looked back around at the crowd.

Thank you again for being here, for your support. I look forward to getting to know you all a lot better, he finished.

A single clap started in the back of the room, and then several more joined in until the whole room was clapping and whistling, and Archer grinned and looked down shyly once more, and I shed a few more tears, laughing through them now. A couple of people stood up, and more followed until the entire audience was standing and clapping vigorously for him.

And as he smiled around at the crowd, his eyes landed on mine again, and he raised his hands and signed, *I Bree you*, and I laughed and signed, *I Archer you. God, I Archer you so much.*

And then he shook hands with the interpreter and stepped down off the podium and I moved out of my seat, Maggie squeezing my hand as I scooted by her. I walked toward him, single-minded, and when we reached each other, despite the bandages under his shirt, he swept me up in his arms and swung me around as he laughed silently against my lips, those golden-brown eyes filled with warmth, with love.

And I thought to myself, Archer Hale's voice was one of the most beautiful things in the whole wide world.

EPILOGUE

Five Years Later

I watched my wife swing lazily in our hammock, one foot dragging lightly on the grass as she moved back and forth under the summer sunshine. She twirled a lock of her golden-brown hair around one delicate finger, her other hand flipping the pages of the paperback that was propped up on her swollen belly.

Fierce male pride filled me as I gazed at my Bree, the woman who loved me, and our children, to the very edges of her heart.

Our three-year-old twin boys, Connor and Charlie, romped in the grass nearby, spinning themselves around until they got dizzy, their laughter spilling joyously out of their mouths as they fell on the grass in fits of giggles. Boys.

We had named them after our fathers, the men who had loved us so fiercely that, when faced with life-threatening danger, their only thought had been to save us. I understood that. After all, I was a father now, too.

I walked slowly to Bree, and when she saw me, she turned her book over on her belly and laid her head back and smiled dreamily at me. *You're home.*

I squatted down at the side of the hammock and signed, *The meeting wrapped up quickly.*

I had been at the bank negotiating the purchase of a piece of land that was just outside the town limits as of now. It'd gone well.

The town had voted down Victoria Hale's expansion plans five years ago when I took over the land. But as it turned out, the residents weren't against expansion or bringing in a little more business, they were just against the particular type that Tori Hale had in mind. So when I proposed opening up several bed-and-breakfasts, all with the quaint, historic feel the town had always loved, the residents overwhelmingly voted yes.

The fourth one would go up on the land I had just purchased this morning.

The town was thriving, business was booming, and as it turned out, I was a pretty good businessman. *Who knew?* I had asked Bree one night, smiling when the first vote had come back in support of my plan.

"I knew," she said quietly. "I knew." And she had. She had told me my voice mattered, and her love had made me believe it might be true. And sometimes, that's all it takes—one person who's willing to listen to your heart, to the sound no one else has ever tried to hear.

I plucked a dandelion full of fluff out of the grass beside me and smiled as I offered it to Bree. She tilted her head, and her eyes warmed as she took it from my fingers and whispered, "All my wishes have already come true." She glanced at our boys and said, "This one is for them." She blew softly, and the fluff danced into the air and was carried up to the summer sky.

My eyes met hers again and I put my hand on her belly, feeling our baby move beneath it.

It's a boy, you know, she said, smiling.

Probably. I grinned. *I think that's all we Hale men make. You okay with that?*

She smiled softly. *Yeah, perfectly okay*, she said, and then added, *As long as there's only one in there, I'm okay if it's a goat.* She laughed, looking over at the little duo still spinning on the grass, the ones who hadn't stopped moving since the day they came into the world. Little rabble-rousers.

I laughed silently and then clapped my hands three times, getting their attention. Their little heads sprang up and they started yelling, "Daddy, Daddy!" while simultaneously signing the word.

They ran to me, and I let them believe they knocked me over, going down on my back on the grass as they tackled me, laughing again, the beautiful sound ringing out through our property.

I sat up, bringing the boys with me. *Which one of you men is going to help me with the construction today?*

Me! Me! they both signed together.

Okay, good. We've got a lot of work to do if we're going to finish this addition by the time your little brother or sister comes. I put my hand out to them, and they put their little dimpled hands on top of mine, looking up seriously into my eyes.

I took my hand away and signed, *Brothers 'til the end*, and they signed along just after me, looking solemn, serious.

That's right, I said. *The most important pact there is.*

Perhaps someday I'd have more of a relationship with my own brother. It had gotten better since I'd taken over the town and he'd become the chief of police, and even I knew that Travis loved his nephews, but we still had a ways to go.

My boys nodded their little heads, their golden-brown eyes large in their faces—the two identical faces that looked just like my own. Even I couldn't deny it.

I smiled as we all stood, and then I whistled for the dogs who must be off playing and roaming the property.

Bree glanced in the direction of the distant answering barks and smiled. "Okay, Connor and Charlie, you boys run inside. I'll be in to make you lunch while your daddy feeds those doggies and gets his tools," Bree said, sitting up in the hammock, laughing at herself when she fell backward, unable to pull her weighted body up.

I grabbed her hand and pulled her into my arms, kissing her lips and falling in love with her, just like I still did a thousand times a day.

That evening four years ago in the Pelion church when Bree had walked down the candlelit aisle toward me on Norm's arm, taking my breath away, I had vowed that I'd love her forever, only her, and I meant it to the depths of my soul.

And even now, even with all of life's craziness and noise, even with my own job and Bree's thriving catering business, each night before I fall asleep, I make it a point to turn to my wife and silently say, *Only you, only ever you.* And her love slips quietly around me, holding me, anchoring me, reminding me that the loudest words are the ones we live.

**SEE THE NEXT PAGE TO READ AN
ALL-NEW EXTENDED EPILOGUE!**

I heard the soft, muffled crunch of snow and smiled as I wiped my hands dry and hung the kitchen towel over the stove handle. Scurrying to the back door—as fast as a woman who is nine months pregnant could scurry—I looked through the glass and saw my husband just arriving at the door, snow crystals glittering in his dark hair. A blast of frigid air made me shiver as he came inside, smelling like crisp snow and Archer, the singular scent of the man I loved.

"Hey," I greeted, happy he was back so quickly. "That was fast."

Norm came to the truck to get the boys and the dogs so I didn't have to track any extra snow inside their house, he signed before he ran a hand over his hair, brushing the snowflakes away.

Are you sure they were okay taking the dogs, too?

Archer shrugged. *They insisted that we have a completely quiet night. They have a big house. I think they secretly enjoy filling it with noise and chaos once in a while.* He smiled with affection.

I smiled back, gratitude filling my heart at the thought of all the love and support surrounding us here in Pelion. The family we'd created.

Archer hung up his jacket on one of the hooks he'd installed in the new mudroom that was part of the addition he'd completed just the month before. The addition included not only the mudroom/laundry room, but an extra bedroom that was now the boys' room, and a new bathroom. I'd always loved this cozy house—it was where I'd fallen in love with Archer, and I was so happy we'd been able to figure out a way to accommodate our growing family.

Kicking off his snowy boots, he placed his hand on my belly and leaned in and kissed me. *How is he?* he asked as we walked to the living room where I had a blazing fire going, warming the room and providing a glow to the dim interior.

I grinned. *Stop calling him a he.* It was our familiar joke, though we both believed it to be a boy, not just because I had a feeling, but because there hadn't been a Hale girl in Archer's family for four generations. The last girl had been a great-aunt born in 1912. I didn't think this baby would break that trend, but I was just as happy with a houseful of rambunctious boys.

We settled in on the couch, and I snuggled up to Archer as he put his arm around me, pulling me close. Outside the window, the snow was falling a little more steadily, fat, fluffy flakes drifting from the sky. "Hmm," I hummed. "The silence is…strange." I laughed softly and tilted my head to look up at him.

He smiled. *And nice*, he added.

"Yes, and nice," I agreed. It was Archer's birthday, and Norm and Maggie had taken the boys and the dogs so we could have some alone time, and because the hill behind their house was perfect for sledding and dog frolicking and it was supposed to snow through the night. The boys loved having sleepovers at Norm and Maggie's in general, but with the promise of sledding, they had been jumping out of their skin to get to their house. I smiled at the thought of my twin babies, my sweet, noisy boys.

"Happy birthday," I whispered, running my hand down Archer's chest, and sliding it under the hem of his T-shirt to rest on the warm skin of his ridged abdomen. I traced each muscle slowly with my index finger and felt them tighten as he sucked in a slow breath, releasing it on a whoosh of air. My blood heated in familiar response to his nearness, the way he smelled, the feel of his hard male body beneath my hand and how he reacted to my touch. Still, after all this time.

He turned his body and took my face in his hands, bringing his lips to mine and mouthing, *Thank you*, against my mouth. Archer pulled me to my feet, and we undressed slowly in front of the fire. And though I laughed self-consciously at my large, cumbersome belly, the light of pride in his eyes made me feel beautiful and desirable despite my advanced pregnancy.

"You do know what they say about inducing labor, right?"

He shook his head, raising a brow as my bra slid down my arms and dropped to the floor. His eyes flared at the sight of my naked breasts, larger than they normally were, the nipples dark and puckered.

"That the same thing that got the baby in there will help get him out?" I murmured teasingly.

His eyes met mine and he chuckled silently. *As long as I still get a night alone with you.*

I smiled, remembering the three days I was in labor with the boys, how slowly it'd built, how long it had taken. *I think we're good.* Still, I wouldn't mind if things at least got started. My due date was three days away, and I was ready to *not* be pregnant anymore. More than ready.

Archer kissed me again, and suddenly the lights flickered and went out. We both stilled before Archer grinned against my mouth, looking over his shoulder at the snow still falling steadily. *Good thing we have the fire for warmth*, he said as he grabbed a soft blanket off the recliner and spread it on the floor. I watched him for a moment as he collected a few pillows off the couch to make us more comfortable, watched the shifting muscles beneath his skin and the way he moved with such fluid grace. God, I admired everything about him, his uncomplicated sexiness, his huge heart, his bravery, and the intelligence I'd always seen shining behind his watchful gaze. I loved him so much I ached with it.

I went down on my knees on the blanket and lay back with an inelegance that made me laugh softly at myself. The heat of the fire warmed my skin, and I felt languid and happy. "Come here," I murmured, holding out my arms as Archer lowered his nude body to mine. "I love you," I said softly as he spooned me, reaching around my body and doing things to make me moan.

I love you, too, he wrote on the skin of my back, causing me to shiver.

The fire crackled and warmed. The wind kicked up outside, the snow swirling before the window, and my own gasps and cries of pleasure filled the room, my husband's breath coming out in pants against my neck. For a long while we were lost in each other, in the feel of warm, bare skin, shiver-inducing kisses, and tangled limbs. In the bliss of having this snow-hushed night—the last one we'd get to ourselves for a while. And the joy of knowing we also looked forward to the happy mayhem that would follow.

For a long while, there was only us, and the world melted away slowly like icicles under a warm winter sun.

As the last vestiges of daylight faded into darkness and firelight danced and flickered on the walls, our breathing calmed, and Archer wrapped the blanket around us as I snuggled into his chest. *This is what it must have been like hundreds of years ago as cavemen held their women in a dark, firelit cave*, he said.

I laughed softly, kissing his bare chest. "Hmm," I hummed, my hands trapped against his body so I used my voice to speak. "But if that were the case, you'd have to deliver this baby yourself when the time came."

I'm a caveman. I hunt beasts and kill them with my bare hands. I'm afraid of nothing.

I laughed again. "Oh, how quickly you forget how scary a woman is when she's in labor. Scarier than any—" My words snapped off as my belly tightened painfully. "Ooph."

Archer lifted his head, a concerned look on his face. *You okay?*

The pain diminished and I let out a breath slowly. "Yes, I'm fine. Just a little false labor. Or maybe you really did get things moving."

His expression took on more concern as he glanced at the window.

"Archer"—I reached up with one hand and ran it through his thick, silky hair—"it's okay. It took days last time. Even if things are—" I let out a sudden, loud moan as my belly tightened again, this time even more painfully. My God. I didn't remember feeling pains this strong until I was five or six centimeters.

Archer sat up and pulled me with him once my grimace softened. The hall was dimly lit by the fire, and he led me down it to the bedroom. The light from the fire barely reached inside, but I could see enough to make out the furniture, and I sat down gingerly on the bed.

A light came on behind me, and I looked over my shoulder to see that Archer had found a flashlight in his bedside table drawer. He handed it to me.

I'm going to go get the other flashlight in the kitchen. I think we need to start timing your contractions. Those two were less than five minutes apart.

I opened my mouth to agree, and just then another one came

on and I braced myself with a hand behind me on the bed as pain radiated through my abdomen. I moaned out a garbled sound of pain. When I opened my eyes, Archer was squatting in front of me, looking up at me with stunned fear.

All right. That's it. Three in a row and all less than five minutes apart. We need to text your doctor.

I nodded, agreeing. I'd only had three contractions, but I'd been in labor before and I recognized these for what they were. There was nothing false about them.

As Archer went to get his cell phone, I hauled myself up and went to the bathroom. As I was standing up, I had to lean against the sink and breathe through yet another sharp pain. Sweat broke out on my forehead, and my legs felt wobbly. I shuffled back to the bedroom and was just pulling on a shirt when Archer came back in the room, looking slightly pale, a flashlight held under his arm so he could use his hands. He'd pulled on his jeans but was still shirtless. *There's no cell service.*

What? Because of the snow?

It's not just snow. It's a raging storm out there. The weather forecasters must have missed the severity of what was coming.

I walked the few steps to the bedroom window and pulled up the shade, squinting through the whirling white and then gasping when I saw the depth of snow under the pale moonlight—snow that had been accumulating steadily since we'd been in our own private cave in front of the fire. I turned to Archer. *Will the truck make it in this?*

He let out a heavy breath, raking a hand through his hair. *If I put chains on, I think it'll be okay. I doubt any snowplows have been out, especially since this was unexpected.*

I nodded, feeling the first bunching of nerves. I doubted plows had been out yet, either, but in any case, they'd only be on the main roads. We lived on a dirt road near the lake with no close neighbors on either side. *How long will it take you to put on chains?*

Fifteen minutes.

As I turned from the window, another contraction hit, and I grabbed the wall to keep me steady, groaning loudly as the tight agony rolled through me, the pressure increasing so much that my knees shook. Oh God, this was serious. I felt Archer's hands on me and leaned into him just as a gush of water rolled down my leg and hit the floor. I gasped. "Oh God, my water just broke."

I felt Archer's whole body jerk, and then he picked me up in his arms, walked around the bed, and set me on my feet while he pulled the comforter back and then eased me down on the sheets, my back resting against the pillows so I was sitting slightly. I was uncovered, but the house was small enough that the warmth of the fire reached our bedroom, making it comfortable despite the storm outside.

With the flashlight still under his arm, Archer rushed into the bathroom and was back in a few seconds with several towels that he laid under me as I scooted right and left to help him. I cried out as another contraction rolled through me, more water gushing onto the towels. When it was over I relaxed limply against the pillows and looked up at Archer. His eyes were wide with fear. *I'm gonna have to leave you here and go get help. You can't travel like this.*

I reached for him. "No! Don't leave me here. This baby's coming. I can't do this alone. Even after you put on chains, it's fifteen minutes to the police station in *good* weather. You might get stuck…or ahhhh," I cried out as another contraction hit, and my arm dropped back to the bed.

I felt Archer's heat as he sat on the bed next to me, putting his cheek against mine as I breathed through the pain. As my muscles relaxed, I sagged back on the pillows, opening my eyes blearily.

This baby was coming. Fast. I told Archer as much on a gust of breath.

I can't deliver a baby, Bree. I've only ever seen puppies being born. What if something goes wrong? I can't lose you.

He looked around the room wildly, blinking, as if there might be some better answer in one of the corners or just outside the window. I grabbed his hand. "You saw our sons being born. You can do this, caveman. You're afraid of nothing." I was scared myself, but I knew we didn't have a choice. We were going to have to get through this. Just as we'd accomplished so many other scary, unexpected things, so we were going to manage *this*—together.

He let out a whoosh of breath on a small smile as he stared at me, his eyes filling with loving resolve as if he was having a similar thought. I watched him gather himself right before me and felt my chest expand with love and pride for all the ways he'd shown his bravery since I'd met him. I trusted him. I trusted him to my soul.

Finally, he nodded and squeezed my hand back and then let go of me, nodding again. *Bree, listen, I know you pushed two babies out last time, but if this is even remotely similar, you won't be able to focus on my hands. I won't be able to talk to you. I'm going to write my words on your skin and you have to try to listen, all right? It's going to be the only way we can communicate while you're bringing this baby into the world.*

I managed a small lift of my lips. I was going into my own zone—I had to, but I knew what Archer meant. He wasn't going to be able to jerk me out of it with a loud call of instructions or encouragement. I was going to have to rely on hearing him in the same way he spoke to me in intimate moments. God, I hoped I could.

I'm going to grab some supplies. You okay for a minute?

I nodded as another pain overcame me. Archer stayed with me

through it, and then his warmth left me as he went off to collect what he needed.

I closed my eyes and drifted in that strange plane between the internal and external worlds that all birthing women know. It was like floating on a placid, gently rolling sea, and suddenly a large wave would come and toss me under so that I was battered against the hard ocean floor, floundering, but always returning to surface again and float once more. I drifted…drifted…The waves came faster and faster, and the battering lasted longer and longer.

I opened my eyes after surviving one large wave and saw that there were candles lit around the room to provide more light. My eyes moved slowly to Archer, and though he looked slightly panicked, he smiled at me, so softly, so sweetly that my heart swelled with love. I felt like I was walking through mist, like galloping into battle—half dream walker, half warrior. The love that flowed through me felt both achingly gentle and powerfully fierce. He looked so beautiful in candlelight—a wavering god. "Remember the first night we made love?" I whispered. "There were candles then. I loved you so much. I didn't know it was possible but I love you even more now."

He released a breath, and mouthed, *I love you, too*, just as another wave crashed over me and I went back inside myself to face the assault. I felt his finger on my thigh and focused on the words he was writing on my skin: *I'm so proud of you. He's coming. He's almost here. You can do this.*

The waves crashed and the candles flickered and my husband coached me with loving words that felt etched not only onto my body, but onto my heart. Those words were mine for all time.

My body knew when it was time to push, and I screamed as I felt my baby's head crowning, that burning ring of fire that I remembered. *Slow, slow*, Archer wrote. I hung on, sweat dripping down my face, every muscle in my body straining until another contraction came and I curled into myself, bearing down for one final push.

I fell back, relief causing me to cry out as my eyes blinked open to see Archer holding our baby, tears streaming down his face as the beautiful wail of our newborn infant filled the room. He swallowed, staring at the baby with a look of alarm, and I sat up slightly, suddenly scared. "What's wrong?"

He shook his head, his face breaking into a beautiful grin as he laughed silently. He shook his head again as he held the baby to him and wrote on my leg, *Girl, girl.*

I laughed incredulously. "A girl? It's a girl?"

Snapped from the shock of having a daughter, Archer handed her to me, and I laid her against my chest and covered her with a blanket. I glanced at the clock. Eleven fifty-three, December second. She'd been born on her daddy's birthday.

Archer had spread out a plastic sheet between my legs from one of the boys' beds and had several towels and a first aid kit. I snuggled my daughter as he cut the cord and dealt with the aftermath of birth. *Being a caveman is not for the faint of heart,* he said as he covered me with a blanket and then used a warm, wet cloth to clean the baby.

I laughed softly. "Thank you," I whispered as he helped me dress her warmly and pull a tiny hat onto her head. She was already fast asleep. Tears welled as I put my hand on his cheek. "You did so good. You were my hero."

You did all the work. You were incredible. He leaned in and kissed me softly, a world of love in his eyes. He peeked at the baby, staring at her tiny features for several moments before he said, *She looks like my mother.*

I nodded. "I know. She's going to be a great beauty just like she was." He smiled again, his heart in his eyes—a heart filled with love and bravery and so much goodness it shined forth like a light.

What will we name her? he asked before moving one finger lightly over her velvety cheek. She rooted toward his finger in her sleep, but then stilled again. I smiled down at her perfect little face. She'd be hungry soon, but I was glad for a brief rest.

"I don't know," I whispered. We hadn't talked about girls' names, so sure we were having another boy.

With those words, Archer's phone, sitting on the dresser, beeped with the sound of several incoming texts—service had just been restored. I laughed. "Nice timing."

Archer grinned and kissed me once more, grabbing his phone and texting quickly. A ding came back immediately, and Archer replaced the phone where it'd been. *Travis is calling an ambulance.*

I nodded. *Travis.* Interesting that the first person Archer had called was his brother. He was obviously learning to put more faith in him if he trusted him with this. With us. I kissed my daughter on her head as I held her close, feeling love-struck and filled with unending joy.

The next day, as I rocked baby Ava in the rocking chair in the living room, both of us having been examined and deemed in perfect health, Charlie and Connor peered down at her with interest and a bit of suspicion. "We gots a sister," Charlie whispered to Connor, leaning his head close to his brother's. I pressed my lips together, suppressing a smile.

Connor nodded, his amber eyes serious as he glanced at his brother. "We's gonna have to teach her stuff."

I couldn't help laughing, though I held back the groan that wanted to follow. I could only imagine what those two would deem important life lessons once Ava was old enough to follow instruction. "Maybe *she's* going to teach you two a thing or two," I said on a grin. "Now you little 'we's' go on to your room and open those new Legos Daddy bought you."

They both grinned, bounding off to their room to check out their new toy. I sighed contentedly as I looked out the window at the winter white landscape, listening to the twins chatting happily as they played. I could hear Archer moving around in the kitchen as he heated up dinner—one of the casseroles Norm and Maggie had brought over earlier.

Ava whimpered softly in my arms, making the tiny sounds of an infant as she dreamed.

The snow glittered and sparkled outside, the landscape quiet and serene, and inside our small house on the lake, the moment felt full with the sounds of love.

WANT TO KNOW WHAT ARCHER WAS THINKING
WHEN HE FIRST STARTED FALLING FOR BREE?
TURN THE PAGE TO READ THE SCENE FROM
ARCHER'S POINT OF VIEW!

ALTERNATE POV

CHAPTER FIFTEEN

ARCHER

Can I come back later? she'd asked. And then she'd wrapped her arms around me. I hadn't known exactly how to respond. It'd been so long since I'd been touched, and her closeness brought a distant sense of panic, but mostly a wild yearning. I'd wanted so badly to return the gesture, to put my arms around her and know the feel of holding her while she was holding me back. I'd almost done it, but then she'd moved away and the moment had been lost.

But she'll be back. I caught sight of myself reflected in the window as I returned to my house and realized I was smiling. I'd woken up that morning far too early and hadn't been able to get back to sleep, so I'd taken the dogs down to the lake and thrown sticks for them for a while. The mindless activity had finally succeeded in tuning out all the thoughts—all the nerve-racking questions—circulating through my head in an endless loop, and for that I was grateful. Ever since I rescued Bree from the trap my uncle had set and carried her back to my house, where she'd confided in me about the pain of how she'd lost her dad, my mind had been whirling with questions, with doubts. The way her eyes had looked as I wiped her tears cut straight into my heart, and I knew then that my feelings for her were stronger than I'd allowed myself to admit. Every moment I spent with Bree felt both exciting and vaguely dangerous. I wondered what, if anything, she saw in me, why she kept returning, how and if I fit into her life at all. A million questions that didn't have answers unless I asked her, and I was too damn scared to do that.

I'd been returning to my house, where I thought Bree was still sleeping in my bed when she'd run outside, an exuberant smile on her beautiful face as she'd told me she hadn't had a flashback that morning. At the realization of what she was saying, my heart had squeezed harshly. I knew what it was to experience the same horrifying event again and again. I understood what it was like to never want to go to sleep for fear of the dreams that would come, the memories that would never fade no matter how hard you tried to forget. I looked up at the sky, the blue, blue sky, remembering a *different* blue sky and the horror that had happened beneath it.

It had been a long time afterward—years—before I'd trusted blue skies again.

A little while after she'd left, I went inside my bedroom and saw that Bree had made the bed. I stood staring at it for a moment, seeing in my mind the same thing I'd pictured last night: her, tangled in my sheets, that long, golden-brown hair splayed out on my pillow, lips parted, eyelashes dark crescents on her cheeks, her breasts rising and falling rhythmically with sleep. And I felt the same throbbing between my legs that I'd felt the night before as I'd lain on the couch in the living room, excited and aroused by the knowledge that the only thing between us was a wall. And yet, it wasn't *just* a wall. It was plaster and paint and a hundred fears.

Picking up the pillow where Bree had rested her head, I brought it to my nose and inhaled. I could smell the delicate scent of her shampoo, and I closed my eyes, allowing myself to enjoy what felt like a small intimacy before I put it back down.

The soft knock at my front door came moments after I'd stepped out of the shower and dressed. It had only been about an hour since she'd left, and so a short thrill ran down my spine that she'd returned so quickly.

When I pulled open the door, Bree smiled sweetly, a little bit shyly, and as always, her smile made my heart flip. So easily. Too easily.

Thanks for having me back here, Archer. I hope you don't mind...after last night...there was no other place in the world I wanted to be than here with you today. She tilted her head, and her ponytail fell over her shoulder. *Thank you.*

Ah, God, if she knew how much *I* wanted her here, how with her was the *only* place I wanted to be, would it scare her? My heart picked up speed. It scared *me*. Sometimes I felt as if the words I wasn't saying to Bree were so loud in my own head, she might be able to hear them from clear across the room, though I hadn't— *couldn't*—make a sound and hadn't lifted my hands.

Her gaze moved down to my feet, and her eyes widened as she took them in, but I quickly reassured her. I could pinpoint a whole list of aches that Bree elicited in my body just with her scent, her nearness. My feet were the very least of my physical frustrations.

And so when she nervously suggested a haircut, I was both slightly embarrassed that she'd obviously thought I could use some more improvement, and worried about what it would be like to have her in such close proximity, touching me in ways no woman had ever touched me before. But before I could fully think it through, my hands rose, seemingly of their own accord. *I'd like that.* Her answering grin helped dispel some of my uneasiness.

What do you want? she asked. *I'll do whatever you'd like.*

The way she'd looked at me last night when I'd come out of my room with a shaven face came back to me, bringing with it a sense of excited warmth. She'd looked at me with stunned approval—at least that's what I'd called it. Maybe it was even more, although I wasn't sure I dared hope it. The thought left me feeling as if I were holding my breath, though I was breathing just fine. *I want you to like it. Do whatever you want.*

Are you sure? Her hands moved hesitantly, her expression so full of care and compassion that I felt the words as if they'd brushed my skin.

Very. It was both the truth and a lie, but before I could talk myself out of it, I stepped into the kitchen, where I pulled a chair out and placed it in the middle of the room. After a minute, I felt a towel draped over my shoulders and the clatter of the cutting utensils being set on the counter. *Deep breath*, I reminded myself. I lay my hands flat on my thighs—my version of utter silence—and closed my eyes as I waited for her to begin.

Her hands rose tentatively to my hair, and her first touch was like a low hum of electricity against my scalp. She took a moment to run her fingers through the strands, seeming to be learning the feel of my hair, or perhaps just measuring it for the job she was about to do. She tugged lightly as she started snipping, and if I could have moaned, I would have. I closed my eyes as her fingers moved lightly over my scalp, causing me to shiver with pleasure. Oh God, to be touched like this...it was far too much and somehow not nearly enough at all.

As she moved around me, cutting my hair first on one side and then the other, I was able to watch her body move as her eyes were focused on what she was doing. I took the opportunity to drink in the swell of her breasts, the slim but feminine curve of her hips and her long, tanned legs. Up close like this, though, I was also able to see little details about her I hadn't seen before. I noticed the tiny blond hairs on her upper thighs, the silky smooth skin of the undersides of her arms, the delicate, blue veins that ran beneath her skin.

My body felt oversensitized by her closeness, her touch, the sweet smell of her surrounding me—the feminine scent that I'd only caught hints of before, something flowery and elusive. Something that was only Bree.

Everything about this felt intimate and personal, and I hardened, my whole body primed to experience more of her, to explore the contours of her body, to know the feel of her skin. *Jesus. Stop torturing yourself, Archer.* She was so beautiful that it hurt me just a little bit to be this close to her, knowing it might be all I ever got. A longing so strong it squeezed my soul made me feel suddenly weak, and I wondered if I should stop this, just tell her to go, to put me out of this blissful sort of misery. My breath hitched, and Bree stilled ever so slightly.

She smoothed the hair from my forehead, and our eyes met, shocking me with the desire I thought I saw in hers. My own eyes widened, moving over her face, trying to discern what I saw in her expression. But I wasn't sure. I didn't know. What if... what if I was wrong and... I clenched my eyes closed, breaking our connection, doubt in my own ability to read this woman—to read *any* woman—assaulting me.

My heart was beating so rapidly, I was having trouble catching my breath. She leaned forward and I noticed that her nipples were hard beneath the thin material of her shirt. A small whoosh of air escaped my throat. My skin felt prickly, my entire body inflamed with wanting her. It was pure and hot and like nothing I'd ever experienced.

Bree seemed to be breathing harder than she'd been before, too, and I wondered if she was feeling something even vaguely similar to what I was feeling. Was it even possible? How would I know? What was a man meant to do in a situation like this? Was I supposed to ask her or just follow my instincts? But my instincts scared and confused me. If I followed my *instincts*, I'd stand up and walk her backward until she was flush against the wall. I'd press myself into her in an attempt to get some relief from the hot ache in my groin. I'd taste her mouth first and then everywhere else. I'd run my hands down her body, under her clothes, know the feel of her naked flesh beneath my palms. I wanted to describe all the ways I desired her by using my fingers to write the thoughts on her skin. My hands clenched on my thighs, aching to say the words. I wanted to hear the sounds she might make when she was experiencing pleasure, and I yearned to be the one to elicit those sounds.

Oh Jesus, *Jesus*. I was trembling, and it all felt like too much. Images were punching into my mind more quickly than I could handle. Too many questions, too much doubt, too many emotions all at once. And I was so turned on, it was painful.

"There," she whispered. "You're done. It looks really good, Archer." She kneeled down in front of me and I took her in, her nipples still hardened points under her shirt, her eyes darker, her expression unsure. And the questions in her eyes made me feel even more afraid. I didn't have any answers. All I had were a million questions of my own.

She set the scissors on the counter and moved closer. Her gaze went quickly to my mouth and then away, and my heart jumped. I focused on her lips for a moment, full and pink, and I wanted to kiss her. I wanted to, but I was scared. I'd be clumsy. I'd be hesitant. I'd look as if I was afraid of her, which was mostly true. And if she pushed me away, if she didn't feel the way I did...

I swallowed, panic moving swiftly down my spine. This was too much. I needed to think, I needed…I stood quickly, needing distance, needing space. Needing to be alone. Bree came to her feet, looking stunned as well. For a moment we just stared at each other across the small expanse between us.

You need to go now. I wanted to grimace at the harsh words I'd chosen, but I didn't. I'd meant what I said, though I didn't want to offend her. I wanted her to understand, but I needed to understand first. I needed to get my body under control. My heart.

Go? she asked. Uncertainty skated across her face. *Why, Archer, I'm sorry, did I—?*

No, nothing, I just…have things to do. You should go.

"Okay," she whispered, color staining her cheeks. "Okay."

She moved self-consciously as she gathered her things. I recognized it—I'd moved that way seemingly all my life. But I didn't know what to do about it when I was struggling so badly with my own insecurity.

Are you sure? I didn't—

Yes, please, yes.

"Okay," she said again, moving toward the door. I thought I saw not only confusion but hurt in her expression, and it caused a sharp stab of guilt, making me wince. I knew she wouldn't belittle me if she knew how I was feeling. Bree was kind. She would be compassionate even in her rejection. And somehow that would make it hurt all the worse. My own overwhelming confusion felt like a living, breathing thing, filling the room, pressing against me.

I touched her arm as she moved toward the door, wanting to say so much, wanting to ask so many things. But all I could manage was, *I'm sorry. I really do appreciate the haircut.*

She stared at me a moment before she nodded, walking out the door and closing it softly behind her. I gripped my new short hair in my hands and yanked on it, clenching my eyes shut. *You id-*

iot, Archer Hale. The moan of sorrow and frustration that moved up my throat didn't have sound, but it existed nonetheless. I was angry at myself for being so afraid, so clumsy, so disconcerted by Bree's closeness. But, God, I didn't know if I could be anything else. I walked to my room and fell backward onto my bed, staring up at the ceiling for a moment, continuing to grip my hair. It felt strange in my hands. I felt strange in my skin.

My body still felt hot and painful, and I was desperate for release. I unbuttoned my jeans and took myself in my hand, pulsing with my desire for Bree. Several strokes and I shut my eyes, pressing my head back into the pillow as pleasure broke over me. *Relief.* My breath slowed, my mind clearing slightly.

I'd found a certain peace with the way I lived my life, an acceptance of who I was and who I'd *always* be. But Bree's presence had suddenly shifted everything I thought I knew, thought I *wanted*, and I had no idea how to manage the strange, unexpected… possibilities. Or if I should even allow myself to dwell on them at all. I was excited and frustrated and a thousand other things I couldn't even figure out.

I lay there for a while as my heart rate returned to normal. The sound of swaying trees outside the window lulled and calmed me, the soft lap of waves on the lakeshore calling. I stripped and put on an old pair of cutoffs and headed toward the water.

As I walked, I found myself unconsciously naming the things around me with my hands: pine tree, rock, warm sunshine. I'd taught myself sign and then I'd practiced by naming the items on my property as I worked or as I wandered. Sometimes I'd spoken to the dogs with my hands, feeling slightly ridiculous, but knowing I had no one else to practice with, no one else to talk to. Then Bree had walked through my gate…

Bree.

I stood staring out at the lake, sun glittering off the surface in a thousand pinpoints of light. And my heart felt calm.

The water was cool, but not cold, and it felt like silk gliding over my body when I waded out far enough and then dove in. I swam out to the point at which I could see the tops of the buildings of downtown Pelion, my muscles tight with fatigue and my lungs burning in a way that felt both pleasant and slightly painful. I floated for a minute or two, resting my body for the swim back. Here is where I felt sure and competent. Here is where I knew my strength and my skill, where I didn't dwell on all the ways in which I was lacking, and all the things I *couldn't* do. And as I gazed up at the fluffy, white clouds floating lazily above, I thought about how I'd learned to swim, how Uncle Nathan had taken me out in the small, rickety rowboat he'd owned and let me hang on to the side until I'd felt ready to let go. At first I'd sputtered and flailed, and I'd even cried, sure that I would start to drown and not be able to call out for help. But after a while I'd tried again, and then again, and I'd gotten stronger, better, until I was swimming laps *around* that rowboat as Uncle Nathan laughed and clapped for me.

And I thought that maybe I would try again with Bree, that maybe, *just maybe*, I could learn not to be so awkward with her. That I could learn how to be a man who could win a girl like Bree. And that not trying at all was a different sort of drowning.

And I didn't want to drown. I didn't. I wanted to *live*.

I turned over and started back, my arms cutting through the water as I pushed myself forward, heading to shore, heading toward home.

ACKNOWLEDGMENTS

Special, special thanks from the bottom of my heart, once *again*, to my Executive Editing Committee: Angela Smith and Larissa Kahle. I appreciate you both for making sure my grammar is clean and my words are spelled correctly; but more than anything, I appreciate the fact that two people who know my heart are editing my work. You understand better than anyone what I am trying to say and where I've inserted myself into the story. That is an immeasurable gift, and I'd like to think that my characters are stronger, my story clearer, and what I have to offer of myself is conveyed.

I am also lucky enough to have an amazing group of beta readers who were not only tough, but were thoughtful and connected to Bree and Archer's story, and gave invaluable advice, commentary, and cheerleading when I needed it most: Elena Eckmeyer, Cat Bracht, Kim Parr, and Nikki Larazo—huge gratitude!

Love, endless and forever, to my husband—my best friend, my muse, the man who has the biggest heart of anyone I know. Thank you for supporting me through this process and picking up all the slack around our home while I disappeared into my writing cave. You make everything possible.

An updated thank you to my editors at Forever who picked up the things that were missed during the first couple of rounds and who helped me perfect Archer and Bree's story. You teach me so much and I am grateful to be working with you.

ABOUT THE AUTHOR

Mia Sheridan is a *New York Times*, *USA Today*, and *Wall Street Journal* bestselling author. Her passion is weaving true love stories about people destined to be together. Mia lives in Cincinnati, Ohio, with her husband. They have four children here on earth and one in heaven.

Learn more at:
MiaSheridan.com
Twitter, @MSheridanAuthor
Instagram, @MiaSheridanAuthor
Facebook.com/MiaSheridanAuthor